Secrets of a Covert Lord

A LADIES COVERT ACADEMY NOVEL
BOOK TWO

BY JENNY HARTWELL

ARE YOU SIGNED UP FOR DRAGONBLADE'S BLOG?

You'll get the latest news and information on exclusive giveaways, exclusive excerpts, coming releases, sales, free books, cover reveals and more.

Check out our complete list of authors, too!

No spam, no junk. That's a promise!

Sign Up Here

www.dragonbladepublishing.com

Dearest Reader;

Thank you for your support of a small press. At Dragonblade Publishing, we strive to bring you the highest quality Historical Romance from some of the best authors in the business. Without your support, there is no 'us', so we sincerely hope you adore these stories and find some new favorite authors along the way.

Happy Reading!

CEO, Dragonblade Publishing

Dedication

To Fiona & Finn, who fill me with joy every day

ACKNOWLEDGEMENTS

I am so grateful to *you* for reading Jane and Dev's story. Thank you so much for supporting The Ladies Covert Academy series. I adore these books, where women find space to pursue their passions despite a society focused on molding ladies into conventional, tidy packages. I believe that women are still pressured to conform with messages about our bodies, our role as good girls, and our obligations to put other's comfort over our own safety. Let's all try to be more like Jane and do the things we love, even if others might disapprove.

Jane creating and sharing an early form of pepper spray reminds me of all the times that fear of harm out in the world dictated my actions. When I didn't go for a walk at night. When I held the whistle on my keychain at the ready in a dim parking garage. When I kept checking over my shoulder as I walked alone. We shouldn't have to live with this fear, and yet the fear is there, and I hope all of us find a way to keep ourselves safe—whether it's with pepper spray, a self-defense class, or some other method. Because we matter, our safety matters, and we deserve to live our lives fully without letting fear limit or stifle us.

I am very thankful to my family for supporting me during my deadline crunch. Steve, Fiona, and Finn, your encouragement, your willingness to let me disappear into the writing cave for endless hours, and your patience picking up the slack when I play chicken with my manuscripts are what allow me to create these stories. I love you.

When I was at the beach with my two sisters many years ago, we were laying on our backs in the sand, holding our books over our heads. One sister said, "This book is too heavy." The other asked, "Do you need something lighter? Maybe a romance novel?" First sister replied, as she peered at us over her hardcover of Anna Karenina, "No, this book is *literally* too heavy." Many thanks to my beloved sisters who make me laugh, who love reading as much as I do, and who have believed in my dreams from the very beginning. Let's all agree to bring paperbacks to the beach next time, ok?

I am grateful to my wonderful agent, Lesley Sabga, who is energetic, endlessly kind, and always enthusiastic. Thank you for being my partner in this, Lesley.

Cynthia Blackburn was the wonderful editor for this book, and her sharp eye and patience saved me from many errors.

I'm grateful to the whole team at Dragonblade, including Kathryn, Shawn, and Kim Killion who made this gorgeous cover.

Lastly (and most randomly), but I am very thankful to the Canadian Olympic ice curling team. I selected ice packs at the drug store based on their endorsement when my wrists rebelled at all the typing I did to make my writing deadline. Those were indeed the coldest icepacks I've ever encountered and doubtlessly saved both my aching wrists and this book.

Chapter One

London, 1818

WHEN MISS JANE Brickley imagined her future life of grand adventure, she did not picture herself accidentally poisoning an earl.

"What," wheezed Jack from his seat, "is in that tea?"

"I don't know," Jane cried, snatching up the porcelain teacup from which her cousin's husband had just sipped. "It's supposed to be mint."

She sniffed the concoction she'd brewed herself just a few minutes ago. Her nose wrinkled. Oh, merciful heavens. She *had* poisoned an earl!

"I think the mint must have cross-pollinated with another plant. Or perhaps I mixed up which leaves I used. I'm so sorry!"

Jane's cousin, married to Jack Dashwood, the Earl of Hartwick for only a few weeks, hopped up from her seat and grabbed a watering can from Jane's worktable beside their makeshift tea party.

"I'm sure it could happen to anyone." Pippa poured water into one of the empty teacups before handing it to her husband. "Why just the other day, I ended up knitting a glove with six fingers."

"Thank you, darling," Jack croaked before gulping down the

water.

Jane seized the watering can and doused a napkin, handing it to Pippa to dab at Jack's streaming eyes. His normally handsome face was red, and he continued to breathe like an elderly pug, but at least he wasn't incapacitated.

Or dead.

Jane had been so excited to invite her cousin Pippa and Jack into her lab to show off her latest botany success. Her creation of a new strain of mint that was more flavorful and heartier felt like the perfect opportunity to arrange a little tea party to thank them for their generosity. She'd thrown a tablecloth over a rickety worktable and borrowed three chairs from a nearby sitting room for this celebration. It wasn't fancy, but without Pippa and Jack's kindness in letting her relocate her botany lab to their home when the Ladies Covert Academy had shut down without warning, she would have no place to conduct her work.

She certainly couldn't do it at home.

After all, her parents, like everyone else in polite London society, believed the LCA was really the Ladies Charitable Association where young ladies sewed clothes for orphans and did other innocent good deeds.

And that didn't even take into account her parents' constant fear for her safety.

"Are you feeling any better?" Jane asked, refilling Jack's teacup with the watering can. If it was clean enough for her beloved plants, it was surely clean enough for people.

"I'm sure once the burning stops," he said between coughs, "I'll be right as rain."

"I'm so, so sorry." Jane wrung her hands before glancing around her laboratory.

She'd taken over a little-used art studio in Jack and Pippa's home. The corner room was small but flooded with sunlight from banks of windows along two walls. Her worktables were covered in plants. Empty pots on their sides spilled soil across pages scrawled with her notes. A bag of fertilizer lay next to several large cisterns of water. A jumble of academic books, journals, and more of her notes were scattered throughout. Herbs lay across drying racks awaiting transfer to glass jars currently laying in a pile in the corner.

In short, it was a mess.

Her old botany lab at the Ladies Covert Academy had been neat and tidy. But when the academy shut down following a burglary, she'd had nowhere to continue her research. Thank goodness for her cousin offering a place in her new home.

"It will be fine, Jane," Pippa murmured, smoothing back her husband's dark-blond hair from his forehead. "See, he's looking less like a newborn baby already."

Jack's face *was* less red and angry than it had been mere minutes ago.

"Are you feeling better?" Jane asked.

"I'll be back to my usual grumpy self in a few minutes," he said, voice less raspy than before.

Jane nodded, grateful for their understanding. The average person would not be so forgiving if he were invited to a special tea party and was instead served a hot beverage accidentally steeped with some mystery inflammatory herb. Thank goodness the effects weren't too severe.

Jack took the handkerchief from his wife and dipped it into his cup of water before dabbing at his eyes again.

"I feel wretched, I really do." Jane moved over to her worktable. "I used to be organized. I had a system." Jane tidied a pot here, a stack of notes there.

Pippa's dark eyebrows pulled together in sympathy. "Your lab *was* quite a bit bigger back at the LCA."

Jane nodded, needing a minute to swallow down the lump in her throat.

"I'm terribly grateful to the two of you, for letting me set up a temporary lab here in your home. But it's not the same as what I had before…"

Before. So much had changed in the last few weeks.

The Ladies Covert Academy, the center for young women pursuing studies and passions deemed improper by London society, had hidden in plain sight for years, posing as an innocuous charity group. In proper society, it was acceptable for women to gather to knit booties for orphans, but it wasn't acceptable for them to study topics that were interesting to them—outside the traditional feminine pursuits of needlepoint, watercolors, or pianoforte—or to pursue training that could actually benefit society.

Jane had belonged to the Ladies Covert Academy for over a year, conducting her botany studies in a spacious, light-filled room in the home of Lady Rowling, the LCA's benefactress. And she'd invited her cousin to join. Pippa had studied fencing, a skill she'd put to use only a few weeks ago, fighting and winning a duel, rescuing her then-future sister-in-law from the clutches of evildoers somehow trying to upset the House of Commons—Jane was still fuzzy on the details—and even saving her then-future husband from death's doorstep with a sword and pistol.

Truly, it was the stuff of legends.

Or perhaps a romance novel.

And Jane wanted that sort of excitement for herself. Well, not the kidnapped-by-ruffians part, or the having-to-stab-men-in-their-abdomen portion, but...*adventure*. Something grand and fun and legendary.

Because, truth be told, her life was rather dull. Her recent fencing lessons with Pippa and Lydia, Jack's younger sister who they'd rescued from kidnappers, had contributed to livening things up.

But...she wanted to make a difference in the world.

Like how the Ladies Covert Academy had made a huge difference in the lives of so many young women.

However, the academy's founder and benefactress, Lady Rowling, had closed the LCA. Swiftly and without explanation. Most of the ladies had been forced to give up their pursuits. Without a dedicated space or supplies, without funding, and most importantly, without the secrecy the LCA provided, they just couldn't continue their work.

Although what sort of work was it really, when Jane was aiming to improve a strain of mint and instead accidentally served a peer of the realm poisoned tea?

"I've gotten so sloppy," she murmured. "My focus is off. I wish I was back in my old lab."

"I wish the LCA was open again too." Pippa left her husband's side to lean her tall, lean frame against the plant-covered worktable near Jane. "Our fencing lessons are very satisfying here in the house, but I miss seeing the other ladies. I miss feeling like we're all part of something."

Jane nodded, unable to speak around the lump in her throat.

It wasn't right, that Lady Rowling had closed the LCA without explanation. Yes, there had been a burglary, but surely that didn't mean they had to shut down operations indefinitely.

If only Jane knew what had *really* happened, perhaps she could help fix it so that things could go back to normal.

Jane pictured Dev, one of Lady Rowling's servants, on that last day. He and the proprietress of the LCA had been huddled together in the hallway, their hushed words indecipherable but clearly heated. Jane's thoughts had often returned to him—just because of that inkling that he'd known more about the LCA's closure, not for any other reason. Certainly not because of his twinkling eyes. Or his warm smile. Or the way he and he alone could make Jane lose her words.

He was a servant, but somehow, he'd been so much more.

And...she suspected he knew much more about what had really happened. Dev always paid more attention than most people. His quick, knowing eyes missed nothing. So, what had he and Lady Rowling been arguing about that day?

If he knew the real cause of the LCA's closing, then he likely knew how to fix it.

She inhaled sharply and straightened up from the table as a plan took shape.

Dev was the key to this whole thing. She just had to talk to him, to convince him to help her. To help all the LCA members.

"What is it?" Pippa asked, brow furrowed.

"I have an idea," Jane announced. "I think I've figured out how to save the Ladies Covert Academy."

"I do believe," Jack drawled from his chair, his voice still hoarse from all his coughing, "that this is the most interesting thing to happen all week. Quite a feat, considering I was just poisoned."

Jane threw her soil-streaked apron onto the worktable, plucked up her pelisse from a nearby hook on the wall, and gave her cousin a hasty hug and Jack a quick pat on the shoulder.

"Take your guards," Pippa said. "Your parents will kill me if they find out you left here without them."

"I will," Jane lied, slipping into her pelisse. She'd long ago mastered the art of evading the armed guards her parents insisted follow her whenever she left the house and slipping out unnoticed. Freedom was unappreciated until a person no longer had it. And Jane hadn't been free since she'd been a child.

"Sorry again for poisoning you," she called over her shoulder as she reached the door. "I'm off to see if I can save the academy."

⇥⟫⟪⇤

DEV WIPED HIS tired eyes with the sleeve of his kurta before dropping a document onto the desk where it joined a sprawling pile. He'd been at it for hours, reading every word of estate accounts, legal documents, and letters in the current stack.

"Have you found anything?" asked his friend Parth from across the study.

"Yes," Dev drawled. "I found the evidence we need an hour ago but thought it would be fun not to tell you so we could both continue this numbing and pointless work."

Parth rolled his eyes. "You think you're so funny."

"Better to *be* funny than to *look* funny."

Parth ran a hand over his thick, dark hair. "You only wish you could look as handsome as me. You are almost as pasty as these sun-starved English."

Dev snorted. Although he was quite tan from a lifetime spent in India, he didn't have the same coloring as his friend who was born to Indian parents, unlike Dev.

Parth continued, adopting a forlorn expression. "Starved for sun, starved for a decent cup of tea, starved for all the pretty girls who used to liven up this place…"

Dev's smile faded.

It had been weeks since the Ladies Covert Academy had shut down. Lady Rowling's home had been strangely quiet ever since. He and Parth were members of Lady Rowling's retinue who'd accompanied her to London from Calcutta two years ago and worked as servants here in the household.

There used to be the sound of laughter in the hallways, as well as the noises of the ladies at their work and studies. The metallic clank of épée against épée during fencing training. The pounding of a chisel against marble as another member worked on her sculpture. Someone reciting lines from a play she was writing. Another memorizing tide charts for her shipping apprenticeship.

And the scent of green—rich soil, flowering plants, earthy fertilizer—coming from the corner room upstairs where one Miss Jane Brickley had worked. Dev's chest tightened at the thought of her.

Pretty—and very clever—girls who used to liven up the place, indeed.

"Dev?" A crisp voice from the doorway interrupted his musings.

"Lady Rowling." He stood, bowing to the mistress of the house.

Parth did the same, then murmured his excuses and left.

Roberta Stokes, Lady Rowling, pushed the door mostly

closed—one must maintain propriety even with servants in one's home, it seemed—and gestured toward the desk piled high with documents.

"Anything?" she asked.

Dev shook his head and moved toward the sofa. "No luck today either."

Lady Rowling sat before smoothing out invisible wrinkles in her silk gown of lavender—the color of half-mourning. She tilted her sharp chin to the side, her icy blue eyes regarding him steadily.

"If we do not find evidence of the marriage soon," she said, "Rowling's idiot cousin Sir Albert Skevington will press forward with his claim for the entailed portion of the estate."

Dev sighed. "I know."

"Time is of the essence."

Dev raised an eyebrow. "I know."

Lady Rowling pressed her lips together. "It would be an abomination if all this suffering ended with the wrong person being declared Rowling's heir."

"I *know*." Dev drew a calming breath. It wouldn't do to take out his frustrations on this woman, who *had* suffered much. She'd been married to the much older Lord Rowling when she was but seventeen, basically sold to the man by her family so they could pay off debts. She'd lived out years of unhappy marriage in a land far from her home and friends before being widowed and left to fend for herself when her husband died while on a trip doing East India Company business back in England. It was not the stuff of fairy tales, that was for certain. His chest tightened at the memories.

Dev drew a deep breath before continuing in a calmer voice. "I'm doing all I can. I searched through every scrap of paper back in Calcutta before the move to England. I'm doing the same here. But with the burglary, we don't know if they took—"

"They didn't." Lady Rowling's pale-blue eyes were shards of ice. "Otherwise, why would they ransack Rowling's solicitor's office the very night after they broke in here?"

"You're right." Dev shook his head. "I know you're right, but I can't sort out where the marriage certificate or some other proof could possibly be, if not in the hands of the burglars. Thank goodness everything had already been cleared out of the solicitor's office."

"Dev." Her voice wobbled.

Dev was struck anew by how very young she was. How vulnerable. Despite her icy exterior, he knew she was scared.

"If Rowling's cousin Sir Albert inherits the marquessate, everything I've built here will be for naught." Lady Rowling paused, her neck moving as she swallowed. "Giving young women opportunities and choices—choices I never had—is the only thing that can make all that happened worthwhile. If I can never reopen the LCA because the wrong heir inherits…"

"We'll find it." Dev took her hand and gave it a reassuring squeeze. Thank goodness she didn't stand on ceremony with him. "We'll make sure we have the evidence of Rowling's rightful heir before the courts meet in a couple of weeks to settle the estate. I promise."

Lady Rowling squeezed his hand in return. "All right." She exhaled slowly before gathering up her exterior of calm imperviousness. "Thank you for…everything. Keep me updated if you find anything." With a nod, she left the study.

Dev slumped down on the sofa, shut his eyes, and groaned.

How in the hell was he going to keep his promise to her? They'd been searching for the missing documents for what felt like forever and were no closer to the proof they needed. He couldn't let Lady Rowling down. He couldn't let that dimwitted cousin, Sir Albert Skevington, inherit the estate.

Things seemed hopeless.

What he wouldn't give for a distraction right now.

"Dev?"

His eyes flew open. Dev sat forward, hardly daring to breathe. He knew that voice. He knew who he'd find when he turned to face the door. Somehow, after weeks of not seeing her, she was here. And so, he paused for just a fraction of a moment before turning, letting the knowledge that she was here under the same roof as him warm his blood and send sparks through his chest. He could savor this. He could give himself this moment of anticipation.

To see her, to talk to her again… He hadn't thought it would happen.

After a prolonged moment, he turned to face the study doorway. He didn't have to fake the warmth in his voice when he said, "Hello, Miss Jane Brickley."

Chapter Two

J ANE BLINKED AND blinked again as if clearing her vision would somehow slow her pulse and calm the thoughts racing through her mind. She'd known what to expect, and yet somehow she was still surprised to find herself here in the LCA, looking at Dev.

Although he was one of Lady Rowling's servants, Jane had felt a certain…*closeness* to Dev when she'd been at the LCA every day, conducting her botany research. He'd carried heavy jugs of water up to her workroom. He'd undertaken the onerous job of mixing fertilizer to her specific instructions, grinning as he joked about the smell. He'd gently teased her, causing her to blush and stammer, something she never did.

Unless she was around him.

Dev rose from the sofa but made no move to approach where she stood in the doorway. "What are you doing here, Miss Jane? You know the LCA is closed."

She nodded, and for once was grateful for her history of getting tongue-tied around Dev. She couldn't have said a single word right now, not even if she'd received a lifetime of rich cow manure to fertilize her plants as payment.

"Is anything amiss?" he asked, his brow furrowing.

Jane shook her head. Ah, she was messing this all up. But how could a lady think when the man who made her cheeks warm— despite being a most inappropriate man for a lady to consider—

was standing right in front of her, looking even more handsome than she'd remembered?

Plus, she *had* overheard a scandalous secret while hiding in the shadows of the hallway just now.

Truly, any person would be tongue-tied.

Dev's deep-blue eyes twinkled at her despite the look of worry on his face. Jane had always assumed Dev was of European background with his blue eyes and pale gold skin. His English was tinged with a faint accent that Jane wanted to listen to all day long.

He wore the traditional clothing of India, a long-sleeved tunic that reached his knees with slashes up the sides to the hips. Beneath were linen pants. She knew from past conversations that he'd lived in India his entire life before traveling to England with the rest of Lady Rowling's household. Lady Rowling's retinue was a mix of Indian and European servants, secretaries, and estate managers; some wore the clothing of India while others donned English outfits. It had been a rich mix of culture at the LCA.

Stepping closer, Dev asked, "Do you wish to speak to Lady Rowling? I could fetch her for you."

He moved as if to leave the room, finally breaking the strange spell Jane was under.

"No!" She held her hands up.

His eyebrows rose in apparent surprise.

Jane's cheeks warmed. She lowered her voice. "That is, I'm not here to see Lady Rowling." Jane squeezed her hands at her sides. It was now or never. "I'm here to see you."

Dev's entire body stilled. "I'm afraid I don't understand."

Drawing a deep breath for courage, Jane offered him a smile. "May I?" She gestured toward the sofa and before he could respond, she took a seat.

After a moment's hesitation, he followed but remained standing beside the furniture.

"Have you been cleaning in here?" she asked, adopting an innocent expression—no hard task for her—before glancing around. The study was clean but there were papers scattered all over the desk and several side tables. Two plates, covered in crumbs and used cutlery, sat on the coffee table in front of the sofa.

"Ah, yes, cleaning." Dev snatched up what Jane assumed was a napkin from the table and began dusting a vase. "Because that's what servants do."

Jane bit back a smile as he flicked the cloth over the vase. Even though she was the daughter of a baron and did very little in the way of cleaning, even she knew that his strange swish and flick with the cloth wasn't the proper way to dust.

What was his job, aside from searching through papers for Lady Rowling?

Dev *had* been quite skilled at hauling water, fertilizer, and soil up to her office when the LCA had been open, so perhaps his usual duties had been altered with the academy closing. How stressful to be in service, especially in a household that conducted itself in a covert manner, when a person's job kept changing. One never knew what might be required.

Hunting for evidence to prove who was the legitimate heir to a marquessate, for example.

Given the conversation she'd just overheard, it was clear that Dev's current duties ran more toward clandestine than cleaning.

"Well, I'm sure you wish to know why I'm here," Jane said, all these thoughts of dusting, job insecurity, and espionage reanimating the practical portion of her brain.

Dev dropped the faux dust rag with apparent gratitude. "Yes. How may I assist you?"

Deploying her greatest weapon, Jane widened her already-wide eyes and blinked slowly. "I need your help to reopen the LCA."

He stared, seemingly stupefied.

Jane stopped herself from sighing. It wasn't her fault she had the face of a guileless innocent. Pippa had once told her that Jane could say the most obnoxious, inappropriate thing, but because she looked like a naive angel with her wide eyes and innocent stare, every single person would assume she didn't know the meaning of her words and it was all some sort of silly mix up.

And it seemed even Dev wasn't immune.

"H-help you reopen the LCA?"

Jane nodded. "I'm glad we are in accord. I knew I could count on you."

She must have shocked him because Dev sunk onto the sofa beside her, something a servant would never dare do under normal circumstances.

He shook his head as if to clear out the fog between his ears. "Miss Jane, I cannot. I'm terribly sorry, but that is impossible."

"Oh?" She gave him the wide-eyed stare again, but he seemed to have braced himself for it. Instead, Dev swallowed and looked at some point over her shoulder instead.

"The LCA is closed, Miss Jane."

"But you could help me change that."

His forehead furrowed. "Why would you say such a thing? I'm just a servant. I fetched the water for your plants. I dust the study." He gestured to the sad little napkin.

Jane laid out the first crumb leading to her trap. "I know that you know more than you're pretending to know."

He blinked at her. Well, perhaps that hadn't been her clearest sentence.

"What I mean is, I know that you and Lady Rowling were arguing the day she closed the LCA, the day after the break-in. I'm quite certain you have information about the real reason the LCA was shuttered."

"It was because of the burglary. It was no longer safe—"

She cut him off. "It wasn't a random burglary, was it?"

He stared at her hard for a moment, his blue eyes, usually so cheery, now assessing. "I don't know what you mean."

Pressing on, Jane said, "They were looking for something. A document."

Dev's eyes widened.

She laid out another handful of crumbs leading toward her snare. "Proof of Rowling's real heir, perhaps?"

A muffled, strangled sound seemed to escape from his mouth.

Jane leaned forward. "I know everything."

He blanched.

With a sigh, Jane continued. "You see, I'm quite adept at sneaking around. I've had to do it most of my life or my parents would have smothered me. So, I was hiding in the hallway and overheard your entire conversation with Lady Rowling just now."

"No."

"Yes." She smiled her real smile, the one that didn't rely on faux-innocent eyes. "I know everything. I was originally going to demand that you help me solve the mystery of the LCA closing so that we can get it reopened. Every member deserves a space to carry on their work. These women will be slowly smothered if they aren't allowed to pursue their passions. Believe me, I know."

His mouth pinched at that.

Jane wondered for a moment if the hint that her life had held difficulties pained him. But that couldn't be the case. He hardly knew her, after all.

"But it seems," Jane continued, "that your mystery—or Lady Rowling's mystery, I should say—and *my* mystery are one and the same. Whoever broke into the LCA was looking for the documents you need. I need to get the LCA reopened, and that can only happen if we sort out who the burglars were, and what they have, and also ensure that the threat is gone. So...we'll be partners."

Dev looked a bit green. She almost felt sorry for him.

Almost.

But her need to reopen the LCA for all its members outweighed her concern over the sensibilities of one Mr. Dev... Well, she didn't even know his last name. Or perhaps Dev was his last name?

Before she could ponder the particulars of his name any further, he replied. "And if I say no?"

Jane took a moment to study him. His deep-blue eyes, which usually twinkled with shared mirth, were instead full of worry. His brown hair, thick and wavy, was mussed from what she guessed had been hours of running his hands through it as he'd worked on his search here in the library. And his broad shoulders, likely honed from carting water for her plants up the stairs and other household tasks, were slumped. He was both handsome and worried, yes, but there was something more to him. Something compelling. Something that had drawn her, from her very first day as a member of the LCA when he'd shown her to the large corner room that was to be her botany laboratory.

And she was about to trample upon it, that special quality inside him. Her stomach turned, but she pressed on.

It was time to spring the trap.

"If you say no," Jane said, voice low, "I'll tell every single person I speak to at the many balls, soirees, teas, musicales, and garden parties I attend that the deceased Lord Rowling has a mysterious, missing heir. Lady Rowling's secret will be revealed."

There. She'd done it.

But she didn't feel gleeful or righteous or any of the things a person might expect to feel when they have their adversary at their mercy.

As she watched his face change from worry to shock to some hard, bitter expression, all she felt was sorrow at what she'd just ruined.

She gulped before powering through. "So?"

Dev's jaw pulsed.

"There are reasons why this will help you, you know," she said, rushing her words. He had to accept her offer. If he didn't, she'd never get the LCA reopened. And she needed it. Her plants needed it. Her research needed it. Today's fiasco with the tea proved that.

And all the other ladies needed to resume their work and studies as well. It didn't sit right with Jane, that she had a sympathetic countess cousin who could give her space to work but the other ladies were left high and dry.

"What other reasons?" he asked, his voice hard.

"As a daughter of a baron, I have access to people and places you don't. Because you're a servant."

Dev flinched.

Jane sucked in a breath. "I'm sorry. I didn't mean—"

He held up a hand. "No. You are correct. I *am* a servant. There's nothing shameful about being in service or working for a living."

Jane nodded, absorbing his words.

He was absolutely right. There was nothing shameful about honest labor, although *she* now felt ashamed for the words she'd just said, delineating the difference in their social status in such a stark way.

But if he wasn't ashamed, why had he flinched? Was it the reminder of the chasm between their stations? Did he perhaps think of her, in the way she sometimes thought of him? Not as Miss Jane the lady and Dev the servant, but as simply Jane and Dev? Two people who enjoyed one another's company and perhaps felt a deep current of attraction?

No, no. That wasn't it. It was time to set aside these wild thoughts.

He met her gaze, his eyes stony. "Miss Jane, it seems you have me at a disadvantage."

She held her breath.

Dev spoke again. "I agree to your demands."

DEV TORE HIS gaze away from Jane, his shock that sweet, kind Miss Jane Brickley, who could coax even the most stunted of plants to grow, was a blackmailer currently doing battle against his intrinsic desire to look at her lovely, guileless face.

Well, he'd assumed it was guileless. Apparently, she was...guile-full. Was that even a word? He'd grown up speaking Bengali, Hindi, *and* English, but on occasion, words in this language still confounded him.

She was full of guile and manipulation and sneakiness and...and all sort of other unsavory traits.

She probably picked at her teeth after eating. Pinched babies to make them cry. Tripped elderly people as they hobbled past.

He wanted to glare at her. He wanted to howl at how he'd been deceived. He wanted to throw all the papers littering the desk onto the floor and then spread her across the wooden surface and lean over her and touch his mouth to hers and—

Dev shook his head. Such thoughts were unhelpful before, and they were certainly wrong now. One didn't *lust* after one's enemy.

Jane spoke, pulling Dev's thoughts away from their wild wanderings.

"Should we shake on our...partnership?"

Dev stared at her hand. It looked strong and capable, unlike so many English aristocrats' soft hands, unused to any real labor. He'd seen Jane at work when the LCA had been open. He'd seen her potting plants, hunching over her notes as she wrote her scientific work, pruning, and mixing the foul-smelling fertilizer into the dirt.

She'd never complained.

She'd worked long hours, happy to be there in her laboratory.

And her hands were the hands of a worker.

Like his.

Without Dev's conscious thought, his hand, so large and calloused, reached out and engulfed hers. Her hand was warm and dry. It was both soft and strong. And it fit in his perfectly.

Dev said, voice low, "There is no partnership."

He heard her quick inhalation.

"There's you coercing me, and there's me going along with it because I do not wish for an innocent woman to be harmed." He looked into her wide, startled eyes. "I am speaking of Lady Rowling, of course—" he paused a beat before continuing—"as I now discover that there is nothing innocent about you."

Her hand spasmed in his.

"I didn't want it to be this way," she whispered fiercely. "I wanted us to help one another of our own volition. But you would not help me get the LCA reopened."

He bit down hard on his molars.

"And I'm not the one hiding a child away," Jane continued. "Why doesn't Lady Rowling just bring her son forward and present him to the courts? Surely no one doubts she was Rowling's wife?"

Dev stilled. *Lady Rowling's* son? Jane had heard all the pieces of the puzzle but had put them together in the wrong order.

He released her hand.

"I will share this with you, not because I trust you or want to confide in you, but because it seems we *are* to be partners of a sort." Dev shifted further away from her on the sofa. "If you have the full story, you can better help me with my search."

Jane nodded even as her jaw set at a mulish angle.

"When word reached us that Lord Rowling had died, Lady Rowling left Calcutta as soon as she could. Most of us in her household stayed behind as it took some time to close his business with the East India Trading Company and shut down the house."

Despite their frustration with one another, Jane was listening intently. She said, "I'm sure it was a shock for Lady Rowling, to learn of her husband's passing through a letter."

Dev nodded. It *had* been shocking to learn of his death. Although the old man wasn't kind or warm, losing one's family was still a blow.

"After a few months had passed," Dev continued, "there were several suspicious incidents that occurred to Rowling's son. A venomous snake was found in the bedroom. Stones fell off a worksite right as he walked by. So, it was decided that he would remain in hiding, at least until the courts ruled on Rowling's estate."

Jane's hazel eyes were round as coins. "Someone was trying to kill him?"

Dev exhaled. "That's what we assume."

"Who inherits if Rowling's son is dead?"

Despite his current ill temper at Jane, he felt a flash of admiration at her quickness. "Rowling's cousin and a baronet, Sir Albert Skevington."

"And Lady Rowling believes he would challenge the boy's claim to be Rowling's heir in court? That's why you're searching for the marriage certificate, to prove the child's legitimacy?"

Dev nodded. Jane was close enough.

She popped up from the couch and circled the study. Her hand trailed over the desk, across the windowsill, and along the fireplace mantle. "The burglary," she murmured. "The snake. The cousin." She continued to mutter quietly under her breath as she circled the room, again and again, her hands always in motion.

Dev stared, entranced. How fascinating, to see how another person's brain operated. When he was deep in thought, he simply grew still while he ruminated. But it seemed Jane needed to move, to touch things with those strong, capable hands of hers. And, it seemed, she needed to say her thoughts aloud, even though they were mostly incomprehensible mumbles.

She stopped in front of the window and faced him. The sunshine from the windows rimmed her in a golden glow. "You've been searching for a needle in a haystack with all these papers. Lord Rowling's work in the East India Company must have generated an astounding quantity of documents. Plus, there's his paperwork for the running of the estate, as well as his personal correspondence and financials. Instead of searching through all these endless papers, we need to go directly to the source."

Dev raised his eyebrows in question.

"We need to investigate Cousin Albert."

Chapter Three

J ANE STEPPED DOWN from the carriage in front of her home and was immediately flanked by the two footmen who'd ridden up front.

Two guards, more like.

Each was heavily armed and instructed to accompany her any time she left home.

"Your parents are waiting in the green parlor for you, miss," the family's butler greeted, after taking her pelisse and bonnet.

Jane sighed. "Thank you so much, Thompson."

The butler blinked owlishly at her but quickly nodded before taking her pelisse away.

Jane frowned as she walked down the hallway toward the parlor. Had she not thanked Thompson in the past? It was the general view of polite society that the whole point of a servant was to serve, so thanks weren't merited. She could practically hear what the matrons of society would say about the topic—*didn't their wages provide thanks enough?*

But her interaction with Dev today had her rethinking how she'd interacted with servants in the past.

And how she'd interact with them in the future would be different, she decided as she entered the parlor.

"Ah, here you are Jane." Her mother, Lady Prescott, set aside her needlepoint and rose from the settee. The low slant of sunlight coming through the windows turned her strawberry blond hair, the same color as Jane's, into a golden halo. "We were beginning to worry, dear."

Jane placed a kiss on her mother's cheek, then bent down to kiss her father as well. He glanced up from the newspaper, his eyes going to the ormolu clock on the fireplace mantle.

"You've been gone all day, Jane." His hazel eyes, the same color as her own, were crinkled in worry.

Jane sank down onto the chair at his side. "I must have lost time when I was visiting Pippa. We had tea." She nearly winced as she recalled the botched tea she'd served to her cousin's husband. Thank goodness Pippa and Jane hadn't sipped theirs as well or they wouldn't have been able to attend to Jack.

"Your guards were with you the entire time?" her mother asked, her hands pressed together in her lap.

"Yes, Mama. They accompanied me to Pippa's front door, then went into the kitchen to doubtlessly eat all of the pastries in the entire household. I fetched them when it was time to come home."

No need to tell her parents how she'd snuck out a side door and walked alone to the LCA. Jane was quite adept at keeping her guards in the dark about her true activities—they still believed, along with all of polite society, that the LCA was the Ladies Charitable Association, after all—but she'd never actually given them the slip and then ventured out completely on her own before. Pippa or another LCA member had always been with her. It chafed, having them always following her. Never allowing her to feel free.

Despite her frustration with the constant protection, her stomach still swooped with guilt when she saw her parents exchange a worried glance.

"We just want to be sure you're safe, dear, that's all," her mother said.

"I know," Jane replied, voice gentle. "I'm always safe."

Except for when she was sneaking about town and speaking to men alone.

"The world is a dangerous place," her father said, starting a very familiar topic of conversation. "You never know where criminals might lurk. It could happen to anyone, anywhere. When your uncle—"

"I know."

Jane rarely interrupted, but she couldn't bear to hear the tragic story of her uncle today, not right after she'd betrayed her parent's trust. "I—I have the beginnings of a headache. I'm just going to head upstairs, if you don't mind."

Jane's mother jumped to her feet. "I'll just call for a tincture. Or would you prefer a warm compress? Oh, I hope it doesn't develop into a megrim!"

Jane crossed to her mother and wrapped her in a hug. "I'm sure I'll feel better after I just lay down for a bit. No need to worry."

Her mother's mouth quirked. "Now you're asking the impossible, Jane dear. It's the job of parents to worry about their children, you know."

"I'll be fine," Jane insisted, heading toward the door. "I'll see you at dinner."

And with that, she made her escape, a cloud of guilt following in her wake as she headed upstairs.

First, she ditched her guards, leaving them in Pippa and Jack's kitchen while she visited the LCA alone before returning to Pippa and Jack's, pretending to her entourage as if she'd merely been upstairs the entire time. Then she spied on Lady Rowling and Dev. And then she *blackmailed* Dev. And now the final piece of her treachery was faking a headache to get away from her parents, causing them to worry even more than usual over her safety.

Was it possible that she wasn't actually a good person?

But truly, if she had to listen to the tragic story of highwaymen murdering her uncle, Pippa's father, one more time when she was already feeling full to the brim with guilt, she wouldn't have been able to pretend with her parents for another moment.

And most of her life was spent pretending to her parents.

Jane entered her chamber and flopped back onto her bed. She stared up at the plasterwork on the ceiling and heaved a sigh.

Her mother's brother had been traveling by coach with his wife and daughter. Jane's cousin Pippa had only been ten years old at the time. The family had been accosted by highwaymen, and the thieves had shot and killed Jane's uncle before they'd taken off, never to be apprehended.

The murder had been traumatic for young Pippa and her mother. It had also been traumatic for Jane's mother. She still remembered how, when the messenger had arrived with the news of her mother's beloved brother's death, her mother had collapsed to the floor and sobbed. How her father had held her, his face a portrait of sorrow.

And fear.

So much fear and all of it transferred to Jane.

If a strapping man like Viscount Everleigh could be gunned down in the prime of his life, it could happen to anyone. Anywhere. Even to his young niece Jane in the safe, quiet streets of Mayfair.

And so, from that day forth, Jane had not been allowed to set foot outside her home without armed escort. Her parents fretted from the moment she left the house until she returned to its safety. They let her join the LCA with the greatest of reluctance, only acquiescing once Lady Rowling herself had petitioned them for Jane's membership after they'd met at a garden party and the marchioness had been impressed with Jane's knowledge of the flora in the garden. Lady Rowling had assured Jane's parents that the guards would remain on the premises whenever their daughter was on site and that she had her own bruiser of a butler, a former boxing champion, guarding the front door as well.

But then even that freedom had been taken from Jane when the LCA had been mysteriously burgled and then promptly closed.

At least now, Jane knew the cause of the break-in. It wasn't a threat to the LCA's secrets at all. Instead, someone—likely the deceased Lord Rowling's own cousin—had broken in, searching for evidence of the missing heir's legitimacy so he could destroy it and inherit the title himself.

If she was to have any freedom in her life, Jane needed to get the LCA reopened. According to the conversation between Lady Rowling and Dev, that could only happen if the threat against the true heir to the Rowling title was neutralized.

Jane had hoped Dev would share a bit of information about the burglary, something worrisome enough to merit the LCA's closure but innocuous enough that Jane could address the problem. What that would have looked like, Jane couldn't say, but in her imagination, it had been a simple task, one she could solve with a minor bit of sleuthing.

Instead, she was now partnered with Dev in a *massive* bit of sleuthing.

Find the evidence that Rowling's mysterious heir was legitimate, most likely the marriage certificate for Lady Rowling and her deceased husband.

Investigate Lord Rowling's cousin and find evidence that he'd committed or orchestrated the break-in.

Get Lady Rowling's son declared the legitimate heir by the court who would decide on the estate in just a few weeks' time.

And somehow—more blackmail? Jane's stomach turned at the thought—ensure that the cousin gave up his desire to inherit so the new heir would be safe.

These were Herculean tasks. Jane glared at the plaster on the ceiling above her wide, comfortable bed as if the answers were written there, waiting to be viewed if she just squinted enough.

But alas, it seemed the answer was going to have to come from her.

Jane turned her mind toward planning her and Dev's first step in this ambitious scheme of theirs.

JANE KNOCKED ON the back door, shifting her weight from foot to foot as she waited. She'd never come to the back before. She was a lady, and ladies entered homes through the front door. But yesterday, Dev had been most emphatic. She was to come around the back of Lady Rowling's home through the alley and knock on the back door.

A middle-aged woman with round, rosy cheeks and wearing an apron liberally streaked with flour opened the door, her eyebrows flying up to meet her cap when she saw Jane.

"May I help you, miss?"

Jane adjusted her wicker basket from one arm to the other. "Good morning. I'm here to see Dev."

The woman's face cleared, and she stepped back. "Ah, he mentioned someone would be coming by to speak to him. Come have a seat at the kitchen table, miss."

Jane followed her into the kitchen of Lady Rowling's home. Jane had never been to this part of the LCA headquarters before. The kitchen was warmed by a massive stove with several simmering pots emitting a savory aroma. The woman murmured to another servant who was mixing something in a large bowl at a tidy counter, and the servant nodded before scurrying out of the kitchen.

"She's just off to fetch the lad now," the woman said, nodding at a long wooden table with benches on either side.

Jane bit back a smile at the thought of Dev as *the lad*. "Thank you," she replied, sinking onto the bench and setting the basket at her side.

The woman returned to her work, which appeared to be making bread. Jane watched in fascination as the cook seemed to do battle with the dough, repeatedly folding and mashing it with her fists. Jane ate bread every day of her life but had never considered the making of it. It seemed that there was much more to it than mixing flour and other ingredients and then throwing it into the oven. When she had toast at breakfast tomorrow, she'd be sure to send her compliments to the family's cook for her labor in making the tasty bread.

The door to the kitchen swooshed open, and Dev walked in.

Jane's breath caught.

His dark hair fell in a silky wave across his brow. His bright blue eyes gleamed from the sunlight filtering through a kitchen window. And there was a certain energy about him that Jane couldn't seem to look away from.

He hadn't said a single word to her, and she was already tongue-tied. What was it about him that made her feel like she was standing in the ocean with the current surging around her legs, keeping her off balance?

"Good morning, Miss Jane."

She rose from the bench. "Good morning, Dev." She smiled.

His lips pulled tight. Ah, he was still upset with her for the bit of blackmail yesterday. Well, that was to be understood. She would have been surprised if he'd given her his usual jaunty smile and eye twinkle as he had in the days before the break-in.

The cook banged a spoon against a metal bowl, and Jane startled. This was neither the time nor place for moon-eyed stares or wool-gathering.

"Come," he said, gesturing further into the house. "I have a place for us to speak."

Jane followed him through the kitchen and down a hall. He led her into a room with a scarred work table covered with a stack of silver cutlery, half of which gleamed and the other half still in need of polishing. A pile of clothing sat beside an open sewing kit, indicating that someone was working their way through the household's mending. *This must be a general workroom for the servants.*

"May I close the door so we can speak freely, or would you feel more comfortable if I left it open?" Dev asked, hand on the doorknob.

Jane paused. Yesterday, they'd been alone in the study, but she'd been the one to pull the door closed behind her when she confronted Dev. She'd assumed he would do the same, but instead, he asked about her comfort. That, in itself, was comforting.

"You may close the door."

He nodded and pulled it shut.

Jane sat in a wooden chair beside the neatly stacked pieces of polished silver. Dev remained standing, hands folded in front of him. Perhaps it was hard to switch from the dynamic of servant and lady to co-conspirators unearthing a wicked plot.

"Please, sit down." She gestured at a chair.

He frowned.

"You're giving me a crick in my neck."

Dev relented, sitting across the table from her beside the neat stack of clothing. "You said yesterday that you would come up with a plan for us?"

Jane picked up a gleaming silver ladle and fiddled with its intricate handle. "I can only be out when my parents think I'm at my cousin's house, so our forays need to be purposeful and quick."

Dev cocked his head. "Your parents do not know your whereabouts?"

Jane huffed. "I can hardly announce I'm off to my former charity group which was actually a secret school for ladies who wish to partake in scandalous areas of study, and that I'm now there in order to help the benefactress's servant hunt down evidence of her marriage so that the benefactress's secret child who was hidden away can inherit instead of some doltish relative, now can I?"

Dev's mouth quivered, and Jane worried for a moment that he was angry with her for spelling out their situation in such bald terms. But then she spied the old twinkle in his eyes and her shoulders relaxed. He was trying not to laugh, she realized.

Ah, her bluntness had charmed him. Perhaps he would no

longer glower at her as he had when he'd first spied her in the kitchen. Perhaps he'd forgive her for the blackmail. *Perhaps*, when she unveiled her genius plan, he'd even be pleased to be working with such a clever partner.

"It seems I did not think through what this investigation would mean for you, as a proper lady of the ton," Dev said, after gaining control of his mirth.

Jane sniffed before making a show of examining the intricate scrollwork on the ladle she held. "Well, I've had a bit of practice with keeping secrets from my mother and father, but I'd rather we didn't invite questions about me being gone for so long each day."

Dev nodded his head in assent. "So, what is the plan for to-day?"

She set the ladle back onto the table and leaned forward, all attempts to appear nonchalant abandoned. "I thought we could interview the neighbors."

He frowned. "I don't understand. What questions would we pose to the neighbors?"

"About the night of the break-in. We must find out if anyone saw anything."

"I believe Lady Rowling already had tea with the neighboring ladies, and they had no information to share."

Jane cocked an eyebrow. "Why, Dev, I'm surprised you didn't think of this yourself."

He cocked an eyebrow in return, waiting for her to finish, but Jane's cheeks heated at how readily his name had emerged from her mouth. It assumed a level of intimacy that didn't exist between them.

She cleared her throat. "What I mean is, has anyone ques-tioned the neighboring *servants*?"

She was petty enough to derive pleasure at the sight of his mouth falling open just a bit.

"I assume it's the same in all households," she continued. "Servants are quite observant. Kitchen staff pop out to the back garden for a bit of produce. Maids return from the market or the shops. Footmen stand beside the doors. Stable boys bring the horses around from the mews. They see all, don't they?"

Dev pursed his lips. "You are absolutely correct. I can't believe I didn't think to ask them. The entire household had traveled with Lady Rowling overnight to her estate in the countryside on the night of the burglary, so none of us were here when it happened. It completely slipped my mind that the servants in the adjacent homes were still here going about their usual routines."

Jane nodded. "I am hopeful one of them might have seen something that can be of use to us. If it was Rowling's cousin, then perhaps they saw him or one of his servants. And if it was someone else, then that's helpful to know as well. We need to find out as much as we can about whoever is after proof of the rightful heir. Especially if we are going to confront the cousin."

Dev rose from his seat. "If *we* are going to confront him?" He shook his head. "No, Miss Jane. That is much too dangerous for you."

Jane picked a bit of imaginary lint off her sleeve. "You'd be surprised. I'm more dangerous than I seem."

Dev's expression turned speculative.

"It's true! I've been training in fencing with Pippa, and she even gave me a knife of my own." She seized the silver ladle off the table and brandished it like a dagger.

Dev gripped the back of the chair, his mouth pulled open in horror. "A *knife*? What sort of task do you imagine in front of us? Fighting off marauders in dark alleys? Torturing a confession out of the cousin, who is a peer of the realm? This is, as the English say, beyond the pale."

Jane stood as well, dropping the ladle-dagger on the table. Her heart raced. "Well, you don't have to get so huffy about it. I didn't mean to imply that we'd be out looking for bloodshed. I only meant that I can take care of myself. And...and you never know," she continued, her voice growing higher, "there *could* be marauders in dark alleys. It happens, you know. People get held up by pickpockets. Brigands attack, or armed highwaymen… and…and…"

Jane hadn't even realized she was shaking until Dev's warm hands engulfed hers, stroking her trembling hand.

"Hush. Hush now, Miss Jane. You are right. I'm sorry. I'm sorry I upset you. It's all right now. You are safe here."

Dev inhaled slowly, holding his breath before releasing it in a steady stream. He met her eyes and gave a little nod. Despite the whirl of panic inside her mind, Jane understood his message that she should mimic him. Slowly she breathed in, filling her lungs as he did, then she pushed the air out through pursed lips. For a minute they did this, breathing in and out together, until Jane was herself once more, the trembling gone.

She retreated, eyes down, conscious of the slide of his large, warm hand against hers as she pulled away. "I…I apologize."

"There's no need," he murmured.

Jane swallowed. "I…I get into a bit of a state on occasion. A relative was killed by highwaymen, and every now and again when I think on it too much…"

"I'm so sorry." Dev's voice was warm and close even though she'd stepped back. "To lose a family member in such a way, it must have been terrible."

Jane looked up, and their gazes met and held. Her breath caught in her chest once more at the warmth in his eyes, the compassion, directed at her.

"Thank you," she breathed.

He nodded, saying nothing. They continued to stare into each other's eyes, and Jane's hand tingled where he'd held it.

She turned away, making a show of examining a silver urn awaiting polishing on the table. "So," she cleared her throat, "I was thinking we'd take some fresh herbs I've been growing in my temporary lab to the neighboring servants and ask them if they saw anything the night of the burglary."

"Herbs?"

Jane nodded. "I experiment with plants, as you know. And I've been growing several strains of herbs and spices that are rather expensive, actually. I think this little gift might help smooth things over for us, with the kitchen servants at least."

"You want to bribe them for information? With herbs?"

Jane scowled. "You make it sound both tawdry and ridiculous at the same time. What a talent."

Dev shrugged. "Well, you've already committed blackmail, so what's a bit of bribery in the grand scheme of things?"

Jane grabbed the handle of her wicker basket, plunking it on the table beside the silverware. "I'll have you know," she said, flinging open the lid, "that the contents of this basket are grown with the finest fertilizer in all of England. I water them to a very specific level of soil moisture that I've perfected over the last year. They are fresher and tastier than anything the cooks and housekeepers could hope to find in the market. So, yes, if you want to call this a bribe, then call it a bribe, but *I* shall call it a present!"

Dev's eyes danced, and Jane realized she'd ended her monologue shouting.

"Well, Miss Jane of the finest fertilized herbs in all of England, shall we take your present next door now, or once you've changed?"

Jane eyed him warily. "Changed?"

"Yes. We can't have you showing up at the back door with kitchen presents while dressed like a fine lady." He smiled. "No servant will speak with you candidly when they fear you have the power to see them sacked from their position." Dev shook his head and circled back to the other side of the table. After sifting through the pile of mending, he held up a simple black frock, clearly made of very durable, very plain fabric with no ornamentation whatsoever.

"If you want to get information from servants," he said, looking quite pleased with himself, "then you're going to have to look like a servant."

Chapter Four

DEV STIFLED A laugh at the look of dismay on Jane's face. Yes, he was angry at her for forcing him to work with her.

Although he was forced to admit, her help was already proving useful.

And yes, he didn't know how to interact with her anymore, given the wide gulf in their status. Before, he'd felt safe to flirt just a bit, to smile and sparkle at her, in order to see a lovely blush sweep across her fair skin. Then, their roles had been clearly defined. She was an aristocratic lady doing scientific work in a secret academy. He was a loyal servant, benignly enjoying the presence of lovely, clever women in the house. Nothing could ever come of his wide smiles and her delightfully demure blushes.

But now…

Now they were partners in this endeavor, and the lack of clear boundaries left him feeling unsettled.

Despite all these complicated thoughts and emotions, Jane's reaction to the practical, dowdy maid's dress filled him with delight. There was just something so sweet and charming about the way her nose crinkled in consternation.

Jane looked down at her current gown. "This won't do?"

Her dress, made of some fine, shimmering material in a sage green color that complemented her golden-red hair, was clearly tailored by an expensive modiste. Dev didn't know the details of

English women's garb, but the dress had fine lace at the hem, embroidery at the edge of the sleeves, and a tiny bow where the material gathered under her...ahem, breasts.

Now it was Dev's turn to blush.

"You'll need to change into this," he said, holding the gown up for an examination. "It should fit you just fine, and it's clean. I see a tear on the cuff of the sleeve that needs mending, but it's small and unlikely to be noticed."

"I'm to change *here?*"

Dev frowned. "I'll stand outside the door and make sure you aren't disturbed."

Ah, there went that lovely wave of pink across her cheeks again. "At home, I am assisted by my lady's maid. My gown..." She gestured over her shoulder. "I can't undo all the buttons by myself."

Dev froze.

He cleared his throat. He considered one unlikely option and then another before shaking his head. "I fear that if I fetch one of Lady Rowling's servants, they'll ask questions we'd rather not answer."

Jane nodded slowly.

"I suppose...you could put the dress on over your gown?"

They both eyed the black dress with speculation. It didn't look large enough to fit over Jane's dress.

"Well." Jane opened and closed her mouth several times. "Well, I suppose you could...unbutton me?"

Dev inhaled sharply.

"Ah, yes," he finally responded, his throat tight. "Yes, I could do that."

He didn't move.

Jane stared at him expectantly.

He stared back.

She slowly turned around, presenting him with her back and its row of a million tiny buttons that went from her neck to the center of her back.

Think of the burglars. Think of the doltish cousin Sir Albert. The marriage certificate. Boiled potatoes. Bad tea.

Basically, think of anything—other than undressing Miss Jane Brickley.

Dev moved slowly across the workroom until he stood a foot away from Jane. "I'm going to unbutton you now."

Was that gravelly voice his?

She nodded.

Dev reached up, his fingers brushing against the first button. It looked so small and delicate next to his work-worn hands. *Much like Jane.*

He slid the button through the hole. Then the next and the one after. The green fabric of her gown parted, revealing a sliver of smooth skin. He gulped, the sound audible in the stillness of the workroom. The shuddery sound of Jane's breath followed.

Dev's fingers stilled. What was he doing? This was madness, unbuttoning her dress slowly like this was their wedding night.

He would never undress her for real. To pretend otherwise, to devour her skin with his eyes while trembling and sighing like some besotted swain, was only asking for trouble.

Dev gritted his teeth. He made quick work of the rest of the buttons, pretending he was assisting some elderly invalid. "There," he said, voice impersonal. "I'll stand outside while you change."

Jane spun around, a hand holding the dress tightly to her chest. That tempting slice of her back was now hidden from view. She nodded, her eyes wide and uncertain before he turned away. Dev walked out of the room, his footsteps muffled by the loud whooshing in his ears. Closing the wooden door gently behind him, he felt the cool metal of the handle against his heated palm. In the safety of the hallway, he leaned back against the door and exhaled in a hard gust.

Devil take it all, as the English said. That had been a mistake.

He drowned out the rustle of fabric while she changed, by humming a tune his mother had sung to him when he'd been small. He scarcely remembered her as she'd died when he'd been quite young, but the ditty, an Italian song, remained lodged in his memory.

The thought of his mother and all that she'd endured centered him.

He could do this. He could find the evidence of who should rightfully inherit as Rowling's heir. He could work with Jane. He could keep his head on his shoulders.

Suddenly, Dev lost his footing as the door behind him opened, and he banged his head against the hard wood as he scrambled for balance.

"Oh, I'm so sorry," Jane gasped.

Dev righted himself. "My apologies. I shouldn't have leaned against a door you were about to open."

He turned and then gaped.

In the plain black gown, Jane looked just like a maid. She must have grabbed a mob cap from the pile of mending, for her shining crown of hair was tucked away. Her wide, hazel eyes peered up at him as if needing his approval.

She looked like a servant.

Like his equal.

Dev banished the thought before nodding. "You look ready to take a feather duster to some craggy old family heirlooms on a shelf."

She smiled. "So, it will work? The servants will talk to us?"

"I believe so." *I hope so.* He needed new information to help solve this mystery so he could get on with his life and leave Miss Jane Brickley and her bewitching blushes behind him.

THEY'D STARTED WITH the neighbors to the north, as Jane commented that she'd often noticed their garden looking rather sparse and assumed her fresh herbs and spices would be more appreciated there.

However, when Dev had knocked on the back door, the rather harried-looking kitchen maid eyed their offerings with suspicion until the head cook popped her head out. Despite her delight at fresh herbs for the kitchen, she reported, after sending the maid to ask the other servants to no avail, that no one had seen anything the night of the robbery.

"It did make the lord and lady quite nervous, I do admit," she had said. "Who would have thought such tomfoolery would go on here in quiet Mayfair?"

Dev had made the mistake of glancing at Jane, a high-born lady who belonged to a now-defunct covert academy and who was currently dressed as a maid, right under the very noses of these folks who declared Mayfair to be a staid bastion of respectability. Mirth had danced in her hazel eyes, and he'd fought to keep his expression serious.

"Thank you for your time," he'd told the cook with a nod, and he and Jane had made their way to the neighbors to the south of Lady Rowling's home.

A bright-eyed servant answered the door, and Dev introduced himself and Jane as servants from Lady Rowling's household next door.

"I'm Franny," the servant said, her wide mouth curving up in what looked like appreciation as she scanned him head to toe.

"I'd heard tale about the foreign chaps the lady had as servants next door, but I haven't met a single one of you yet," Franny cooed.

Dev blinked.

Jane stepped forward, holding her wicker basket in between him and the rather bold servant.

"We have extra herbs and spices fresh from our gardens and thought we'd share with the neighbors." Jane's voice was frosty.

"Awfully kind of you." Franny batted her lashes before peering into the basket once Jane had lifted the lid. "Cor, Cook will adore these. Let me grab her right quick."

While they waited in the open doorway, Jane glanced at Dev. "There's no need to make eyes at Franny. I'm sure the herbs will be enough."

Dev's mouth parted in surprise. "*Me* make eyes at *her*? Are you sure you don't have things turned around?"

Before she could reply, Franny came to the door with another woman, presumably the cook, given the streak of flour across her sleeve.

"Pleased to make your acquaintance," the cook said, sizing up the basket. "Franny says you've brought some fresh herbs around?"

Jane lifted bunches of greens from her basket. "I've been growing basil, thyme, sage, and others in…er, the greenhouse."

Dev assumed she realized referencing her laboratory wouldn't quite fit with the character Jane was playing.

The cook took a bunch from Jane's hand with care, inspecting the herbs before giving them a sniff. "Heavens, these are so much better than what we can buy at the market. You must have quite the green thumb."

Dev could feel Jane's small wiggle of pleasure at the compliment.

"And these are extra?" the cook asked. "For us to have, no charge?"

Jane nodded. "We didn't want any to go to waste. They're so much better fresh than dried, so we thought we'd share them with the neighbors."

The cook beamed. "Well, that's quite kind of you. Anytime you have extras, feel free to drop them by. Thank you kindly."

She made to step back, likely putting an end to the visit, so Dev hopped into the conversation.

"Actually, we were hoping we could ask you a quick question."

The cook sighed as if discovering that no-string-attached herbs were indeed too good to be true. Franny leaned forward, perhaps fearing those five inches of distance would have prevented her from hearing the latest neighborhood gossip.

"A couple of weeks ago, there was a robbery at Lady Rowling's home," Dev said.

The cook and Franny both nodded. It seemed the news had made its way around the square.

"The authorities were unable to find the criminals, and Lady Rowling is quite upset about it. We were wondering if anyone here saw anything strange that night."

The cook shook her head, but Franny clapped her hands together.

"I did," she exclaimed.

Dev's heart thudded.

"What did you see?" Jane asked.

"There was a carriage in the mews late that night. It was unmarked, but looked rather grand, if you know what I mean."

"And what were you doing, up and about in the wee hours?" the cook asked, shooting Franny a glare.

Franny cast her gaze to the ground demurely, but there was no disguising her self-satisfied smirk. "I couldn't sleep, so I wandered the back garden for a bit."

"No doubt meeting up with one of the stable boys," the cook grumbled.

Dev didn't care two hoots who Franny met or didn't meet in the wee hours as long as she had information to share, but before he could get the conversation back on track, Jane had interjected.

"What else did you notice, aside from the carriage? Did you see anyone? Did you recognize them?"

"Well…" Franny said, adjusting her own mob cap. "I saw a few men go in. Maybe three of them? I wouldn't have taken any notice, as people come and go at all hours through the mews. You know how the lords and ladies are, out at their grand balls practically until dawn."

She raised her eyebrows at Jane and Dev, clearly expecting some reaction.

"Ah, yes," Dev said after a moment's hesitation. "Putting on airs, with their fancy ways."

Franny touched her nose as if they were sharing a moment of deep insight. "I knew you were a clever one the moment I clapped eyes on you. So, like I was saying, I wouldn't have thought anything of it, but I did happen to notice one of the men looked an awful lot like a footman I used to know."

Dev couldn't believe it. Could it really be this easy? He was going to beg Lady Rowling to reopen the LCA immediately. He owed Jane so much for her insight into unraveling this mystery with her idea to question the neighboring servants. And if he felt a tiny pang at the thought of their partnership being over, well, surely that was normal. He just missed seeing the LCA ladies regularly. That was all.

"Who was it?" he asked.

Franny tilted her head to the side. "Like I said, he *looked* like someone I knew, but I couldn't be sure, on account of how dark it was. But Johnny had bright red hair and a particularly wide set of shoulders. I do like a man with broad shoulders."

She paused to examine Dev's shoulders.

Dev tried not to hunch. And laugh. Truly, this had taken an odd turn.

Once again, Jane interjected herself, stepping in between him and Franny.

"So, was it him?" Jane asked, getting the conversation back on track.

Franny frowned. "It was strange. Johnny and I had been...*friendly*. A while back. I thought he'd be glad to see me, so I called out his name. I'd been so certain it was him, with those shoulders and that bright hair. The chap glanced over, and I waved, but then he hurried into the carriage. It was like he didn't want me to see him, which would make sense if he was part of some criminal dealings and whatnot." Franny shrugged. "Or maybe it wasn't even him."

"Who is his employer?" Jane asked, her shoulders stiff with tension.

Franny shook her head. "He used to work for Lord and Lady Turnbull across the square. That's how we got acquainted you know, seeing as we were practically neighbors."

She batted her lashes at Dev again, and he pretended to be engrossed in examining his fingernails.

"But then he left that job and went to work for Lord Dunlop, or so I heard." Franny scowled. "He owes me two quid, he does. If you do track Johnny down, tell him Franny says to go sod himself, will you?"

"We shall be certain to deliver your message, exactly as you said it," Jane answered, and despite the seriousness of their investigation, he could detect a faint trace of laughter in her voice.

Truly, this interaction with Franny was both a godsend and the most entertaining encounter he'd had in weeks.

Dev slid his hand into his pocket and pulled out a few coins. "For your troubles," he murmured, passing them to Franny. Her mouth momentarily fell open, but she plucked up the coins without hesitation. He also gave a few to the cook, whose arms Jane had filled with herbs, and they both bid them a cheerful farewell once they stepped away from the door.

On the walk back through Lady Rowling's garden, Jane said, "I thought you looked down on bribing people? Or is that only when the bribe is comprised of vegetation?"

Dev laughed. "I thought we'd best reward Franny, especially since the fiendish footman owed her two quid, and we didn't want the cook to feel left out."

"Ah, making sure the fair damsel is compensated for her time *and* heartache?" Jane smiled at him as they passed under the dappled light of a tree. The wavy pattern of light and shadow kissed the smooth curves of her face, and Dev felt something tighten in his chest.

He murmured his assent, but his attention was consumed by the brightness of her eyes, the sweet curve of her lips, and a disobedient lock of her rose-gold hair that had escaped the confines of the borrowed cap. That silky tendril teased her seashell ear, and Dev fought his instinct to reach out and stroke the lock of hair before tucking it out of sight.

Instead, he motioned to a bench in the garden, tucked out of view from the house by a large bush. "Shall we plot our next step?"

Jane sat on the bench, smoothing out the sensible fabric of her black maid's skirt as if it were a fine gown. When Dev remained standing, she gestured to the other half of the bench.

"Won't you sit?"

"I prefer to stand."

She worried her lip with her teeth. "Is it because you prefer it, or because servants aren't used to sitting in the presence of a lady?"

Dev rocked back on his heels. "I'm not used to sitting with ladies," he admitted. It had been too long. In fact, when he thought back on his life in India, he realized that aside from Lady Rowling, he'd never sat about with those who weren't servants.

"Well, since we're partners in this endeavor, let us be equals. Take a seat." Jane patted the bench.

Dev sat beside her. They'd sat on the sofa in the study yesterday when she'd made her demand, but that had felt different. They'd been engaged in a power struggle of sorts. And this...

This was something else entirely.

Let us be equals.

Such small words, and yet they held so much meaning.

He exhaled. "We have a clue to follow now. We must investigate this Lord Dunlop and find out what we can about his red-haired, broad-shouldered footman."

Jane nodded, her gaze on the middle distance. "We want a chance to learn about the footman, as well as the lord he works for. For all we know Lord Dunlop himself could be behind the robbery. But we shouldn't neglect our investigation into Cousin Albert."

Dev leaned back against the bench back, watching as Jane's

fingers tapped against her leg. He'd never noticed until they'd begun this partnership how she was always in motion. At a casual glance, she seemed so serene and graceful, but there was a lively energy to her. She was always mobile somehow, her body moving even as her mind churned away.

"I have the feeling you're already halfway to a plan," he said.

Jane turned, her usually innocent eyes gleaming. "More than halfway. Here's what we're going to do…"

Chapter Five

J ANE ARRIVED AT Pippa and Jack's home accompanied by both her parents and a small battalion of armed footmen. As usual.

Her mother, Elinor Brickley, Lady Prescott, was petite and plump, and the originator of Jane's strawberry blond hair, although Jane's mother's hair color had faded a bit with the years.

Her father, Thomas, a baron, looked quite regal with his dark hair streaked with shots of silver. He escorted his wife up the stairs while gazing at her in adoration.

Jane felt a surge of love for her parents. Yes, they were outrageously overprotective, and she felt like a wretch for deceiving them, but that didn't blunt her affection.

"Thanks so much to you and Jack for throwing this musicale," Jane murmured to her cousin once she and her parents made their way inside.

Pippa greeted her aunt and uncle before pulling Jane to the side. "You're just lucky that no balls or other events were happening tonight, or no one would have shown up with such last-minute invitations. And I know there's more to this than a sudden desire to hear Agnes perform Mozart," she whispered.

Truly, the women of the LCA—well, the *former* women of the LCA—were a talented group, and Jane had been so relieved when Agnes, a singer with a beautiful voice who also wrote her own concertos and operas, had agreed to the last-minute performance request.

"I want to hear all the details when you come by tomorrow," Pippa continued "Don't leave a single thing out. Oh, and Lydia should be back from her visit to her friend's estate in the countryside, so we'll all have a chance to catch up."

Lydia, Jack's younger sister, had also belonged to the LCA. She'd written scathing articles for the newspaper criticizing the corruption in the House of Commons. An unscrupulous schemer had arranged for Lydia to be kidnapped. In their quest to find Lydia, Pippa and Jack had fallen in love.

According to Pippa, it had been most terrifying. And romantic.

Truly, the world was a mysterious place.

Jane nodded. "I look forward to seeing her, and I promise to fill you in on why this musicale was needed."

"Ah, I shall wait with bated breath. My life is rather dull now that I'm not deciphering clues hidden in newspaper articles or stabbing kidnappers with a decorative sword," Pippa said, voice mock-plaintive.

Jane lightly elbowed her in the side. "I know you're blissfully happy with your new husband, and I won't hear otherwise."

Pippa rolled her blue eyes. "Fine, fine. I'm completely besotted with Jack and my days are spent training with swords, knitting terrible-looking booties for orphans, and kissing my husband. But"—she held up a finger—"that doesn't mean I don't want to live vicariously through *your* adventures. This mysterious partnership with a certain handsome servant is most intriguing."

Jane's cheeks warmed, but before she could deny noticing Dev's handsomeness—or even playing that she had no clue who her cousin was speaking of—her mother approached.

"Jane dear, your father has gone off to chat with his friends. Shall we find some refreshments before it's time for the music?"

"Aunt Elinor, refreshments are right through that door," Pippa said, pointing across the room, "but there are also footmen circling with drinks if you'd rather not deal with the crowd."

Pippa had shot Jane a particular look when she'd mentioned footmen.

The back of Jane's neck tingled.

Even though she and Dev had come up with this plan together—Jane asking her cousin to throw a last-minute musicale and invite particular guests for Jane to subtly question while Dev listened to both the servants' chatter below stairs and the quiet conversations held in the corners of rooms—the idea of Dev circling the room just out of sight gave her a particular feeling.

It was just excitement about their plan, she told herself.

Or perhaps hunger. Her stomach had been too jangly to eat earlier.

"Let's see what delicacies have been laid out." Jane gestured to the door on the other side of the room.

She followed her mother, weaving their way through the large room with rows of chairs facing the front where the musicians would perform in a bit. The adjacent room had several tables laden with finger foods, a punch bowl, and ratafia.

"Oh, I just adore these little sandwiches," Jane's mother crooned, piling a few on her plate.

Jane selected a sandwich, cheese tart, and cookie. She was eyeing the punch bowl when a familiar voice said, "Care for a glass of champagne, miss?"

Jane's skin flashed hot.

She turned, and there he was.

"Dev," she breathed.

He smiled, eyes twinkling.

"Champagne, miss?" he asked again.

Jane realized with a start that she should not call him by name. She shouldn't stare at him, looking so tall and fine in the precise lines of Hartwick's livery. And she most certainly shouldn't wish he'd tell her she looked pretty tonight, or some other compliment, so meaningless when murmured by the bored bucks of the ton to every woman they encountered at these events, but that she was certain would somehow ring true if *he* were to tell her.

"Oh, champagne would be lovely." Jane's mother plucked a glass off the tray. "Would you like some, dear? It's much more refreshing than that cloying punch."

Jane watched her mother, worried she had noticed her interaction with Dev. But she didn't even look at him. She merely glanced from Jane to the champagne tray, her eyebrows lifted in polite question.

Jane's mother didn't *see* Dev. It was as if he didn't exist, as if his very personhood had been erased. Jane's stomach knotted. Was this what it was like for him—for all servants—every single day of their lives? Ignored, overlooked, treated as pieces of furniture?

"Jane? Are you feeling quite well?"

Her mother's voice pierced her thoughts. Jane swallowed before reaching for a glass from the tray Dev carried.

"Thank you," she said, making eye contact with him.

The edges of his lips twitched as if he held himself back from speaking. Instead, he merely nodded before drifting off across the room.

"Don't thank the servants, dear," her mother said. "It's unseemly."

Jane frowned at her champagne. "I think it's unseemly *not* to thank them."

Her mother blinked at her. "You're in a mood. Is aught amiss?"

Jane sighed. She couldn't blame her mother for dismissing her thoughts about servants. Hadn't she herself held ignorant beliefs about servants—or to be more accurate, not thought about them at all—until Dev had come into her life?

Offering her mother a placating smile, Jane said, "Doubtlessly being hungry is making me grumpy. My apologies, Mother."

She bit into the cookie—"dessert first" was a lifestyle she aspired to—and scanned the room. Her eyes automatically sought out Dev, like the unfurling sprout of a plant always making its way up toward the fresh air and sunshine.

How annoying.

Dev, nearly empty tray in hand, subtly jerked his head toward a group of three conversing near him. A middle-aged man with a receding pale-blond hairline and large, limpid eyes spoke to a woman of similar age, short with mousy brown hair styled in a cacophony of tight ringlets more suitable for a debutante. The third member of their party was much younger with the same pale-blond hair as the older man, indicating he was perhaps the son, although he was taller and had broader shoulders.

"Mother, who are those three, standing in front of that painting over there?" Jane discreetly nodded toward the group Dev had pointed out to her.

Her mother glanced over. "Oh, that's Sir Albert Skevington and his wife, Lady Skevington."

Jane's pulse sped up.

"And their son, I believe," her mother continued, "although I do not know his name. Sir Albert is a baronet. He and his wife were introduced to me by Lady Frampton at the Pump Room in Bath when I went with your father last year. Sir Albert is rather mutton-headed, but his wife seems a decent sort, although quiet as a church mouse."

Jane pushed back her shoulders. "Would you mind introducing me, Mother?"

Her mother looked from the Skevingtons to Jane then back again, her eyes widening. "Do you fancy the son?" she whispered. "He appears to be a bit younger than what I imagined for a suitor for you, Jane, although he is rather tall. I believe he is still up at Oxford or Cambridge—"

"No," Jane hissed. "I don't fancy the son." She looked around to make sure no one was listening to this mortifying exchange. Heavens. Her own mother, thinking Jane was out on the prowl for a man who'd most likely only started shaving within the past year or two.

"I just thought..." Jane's mind whirled. "I thought it would be nice to socialize more, since you know I am a bit shy. And they seem like a nice family. So, if you don't mind making the introductions…" Jane took a step toward the man who stood to inherit Lord Rowling's title and unentailed estate if she and Dev didn't find proof of the secret heir.

Thankfully, her mother followed suit. "No need to get in a tiff, Jane dear," her mother murmured before donning a wide smile. "Sir Albert, Lady Skevington, it's been too long since we met one another in Bath last year," Jane's mother said once they'd stepped forward.

"Lady Brickley, such a pleasure, such a pleasure!" Sir Albert chortled. "I hope those waters from the pump room last year did you well, wot?"

Jane's mother indicated that, indeed, the waters had been most healthful and invigorating. Meanwhile, Jane's stomach knotted with nerves. Was she standing right next to a criminal? But somehow, knowing Dev was close at hand calmed her. She glanced up and found his eyes on her, his gaze steady. She let one eyebrow twitch the slightest bit, a little message as if to say, *I see you keeping a watch out for me during this stressful time and I appreciate you.* Or…something. Maybe she just had a twitchy eye for all he knew. But his gaze seemed to warm in return, and Jane was glad they were here together, united in their shared goal despite the wide gulf that society erected between them.

"…and if I might introduce you to my daughter, Jane?" Her mother's words pulled Jane away from her silent communication with Dev.

"A pleasure to make your acquaintance, miss," Sir Albert said before clapping his hand on his son's back. "This is my boy, Nigel. He just finished up at Cambridge. Smart as a whip, this one is. Lady Skevington and I are proud as peacocks."

Nigel rolled his eyes at his father's words. Although his fair hair and light blue eyes paired with an appealing arrangement of features should have made him into a handsome young man, there was something hard about him.

"Did you enjoy your studies, Mr. Skevington?" Jane asked.

"I'm just glad to be back in London," he muttered, glancing about as if a more stimulating conversational opportunity were lurking behind Jane and her mother, promising rescue from the dullness of this moment.

"Oh, don't be modest, lad," his father crowed. "Studied history and literature and mathematics and all those sciences. So much to learn. Why, I was just reading about that German fellow, Copernicus—"

"Copernicus was Polish," Nigel interrupted, his upper lip curling in apparent disgust at his father's mistake.

"Right, Polish," Sir Albert continued. "And I just read that he was the one that discovered the earth went around the sun and not the other way around. Astounding, isn't it?"

Jane blinked. Her mother stared.

Lady Skevington remained silent as a plant and moved as much as one as well.

Nigel rolled his eyes so hard, Jane wondered if it was possible for them to complete a circumnavigation of his eye socket.

"Ah, yes," Jane finally responded, stepping into the silence that was growing exponentially awkward with each second that ticked by. "I believe that was quite a grand discovery." She cleared her throat. "Back in the Renaissance."

A choking sound came from the corner. Jane peeked to where Dev was covering his mouth as if he'd coughed, his eyes trained on the floor. There was no disguising the slight trembling of his shoulders as he silently laughed, though.

"Ah, yes, the Renaissance," Sir Albert cried. "Such a time for discovery. And painting. And…erm…cooking."

Jane nodded to show her appreciation for Sir Albert's insight into the Renaissance's greatest achievement—meal preparation.

Nigel watched her through narrow eyes. Jane blinked up at him, keeping her eyes as wide and innocent as a sweet, tiny kitten.

He shrugged, apparently deciding she hadn't been mocking

his father after all. "Well, I shall bid you all farewell," Nigel said after a few more pleasantries were exchanged.

"You're not staying for the music?" Jane's mother inquired.

Nigel shook his head. "The pater wanted me to accompany him and Mother tonight, but my mates are expecting me at the card tables soon."

Lady Skevington's head jerked up, but before Jane could get a good look at her expression, she tilted her face down once more.

"A pleasure," Nigel murmured, offering a truncated bow in their general direction before striding away.

Before any further conversation could ensue, the sound of musicians warming up signaled the imminent start of the night's entertainment.

"We'd best join your father and take our seats," Jane's mother announced.

Jane tried to catch Dev's eye, but her mother tugged her along into the other room where chairs were filling up with guests.

"Ah, hello Jane." Miss Lucy Moreton approached with a smile. She was another member of the Ladies Covert Academy, but Jane had heard from Pippa that she'd been able to continue her work despite the LCA shutting down. As far as Jane knew, she, Pippa, Lydia, and Lucy were the only members still able to continue their studies and passions in some capacity.

"How have you been?" Jane wanted to inquire about her training down at the docks, but with her mother right there, she didn't dare say more.

"Such a pleasure to see you, Miss Moreton," Jane's mother said before casting an anxious glance at the seats that were rapidly filling up. "Jane dear, I see your father waving us over. Why don't you finish a quick chat with Miss Moreton and then come sit down?"

Jane thanked her mother, then promptly turned to Lucy. "How has your work been without the LCA?" she asked, leaning in close.

Lucy pitched her voice low. "I've been so fortunate. Lady Rowling had connected me to a very open-minded man in charge of a shipping company before the LCA shut down. Thankfully, he agreed to allow my apprenticeship to continue. It's been so exciting. I get to help create the ships' manifests, choose the best routes and cargo, make sure all the duties are being paid, and I even met some of the old shipping boat captains." Lucy's eyes glowed.

"That sounds incredible." Jane reached out and squeezed Lucy's hand.

Lucy nodded. "It really is. Of course, I have to be introduced as the blue-stocking niece who just likes to follow her uncle around because she's an odd, quirky girl..."

They rolled their eyes in unison.

"...but I've learned so much already, and once I have control of my inheritance, I can start my own shipping company."

"Lucy, I'm so happy for you."

The sounds of musicians tuning their instruments interrupted whatever Lucy was going to say in reply. They bid farewell with promises to meet up for tea soon.

Jane found her mother and took her seat. Shortly thereafter, the musicians began to play the first piece, and Agnes broke out into a lovely aria. Despite the fine music, Jane barely heard it over her musings.

Hearing about Lucy's shipping work and seeing Agnes perform for an audience only furthered her resolve to save the LCA. This investigation she and Dev were undertaking was of the utmost importance.

And Sir Albert certainly did not strike her as a criminal mastermind...or even a master of his own mind. Surely the man wasn't clever enough to pull off an elaborate scheme such as robbing a family of its inheritance. But could his stupidity be an act?

Or could his own son and heir be the menace, setting himself up for a title grander than baronet down the road? There'd been a hard glint in Nigel's eye that had left Jane feeling uneasy.

At intermission, Jane turned to her mother, intending to ask if she could introduce Jane to Lord Dunlop, the newest employer of one broad-shouldered footman with bright red hair who may have been spotted in the mews the night of the robbery.

"Oh," her mother said, rubbing her temple, "that music— lovely though it was—gave me such a headache. Thomas," she said to her husband, "I fear we must miss the rest of the musicale, as I simply must return home to lay down."

Jane's father murmured words of concern before hurrying to the door to arrange for the carriage.

Jane bit her lip. What a disaster. How was she going to question Lord Dunlop?

"I'm sorry you're feeling so poorly, Mother." She attempted a casual tone. "Perhaps I can stay for the second half, and you can send the carriage back for me?"

"Absolutely not!"

When several people rising from their seats to get refreshments glanced their way, Jane's mother shifted uncomfortably on her chair. "What I mean is," she whispered, "that it just isn't safe. Your father and I refuse to let you out of our sights unless we have guards accompanying you, and there aren't enough to split them between the carriage and here. You know that, darling. How silly of you to even ask."

Jane sighed.

How silly of her to ever ask for anything different. How silly for her to want a bit of freedom.

As they were headed toward the door to retrieve their cloaks, Pippa approached. "Leaving already?"

"I'm sorry, Pippa dear, but I have the worst megrim and must be getting home. Thomas is out arranging the carriage." Jane's mother fastened her cloak around her neck. Her eyes were pinched with pain.

"Oh, Aunt Elinor, I'm so sorry you've taken ill." Pippa nibbled on her lip for a moment before she caught Jane's eye and gave a minuscule wink. "You know, it would be a great favor to me if you allowed Jane to stay behind. I'm in need of an extra pair of hands to make sure everything goes well with the second half of the musicale. In fact," Pippa clasped her hands together as if she'd just been struck by the most amazing idea, "she could spend the night. We haven't had a proper cousin sleep-over in ages."

Jane's mother frowned. "I don't know if—"

"Oh, it would be no problem," Pippa said, taking her aunt by the arm and steering her toward the door. She shooed Jane back with her other hand.

Jane bit back a smile as she watched her cousin so expertly handle her mother.

"Jack will post guards at both the front and back door all night so that we'll be as safe as the royal jewels in the Tower of London. Truly, you'd be doing me a great favor."

"Well, I suppose if there are guards…" Jane's mother said, being carried toward the door on a river of innocuous chatter by her niece.

A minute later, Pippa was at Jane's side.

"Impressive," Jane said, smiling.

"I know I am." Pippa grinned. "Now, let's get back before the second half starts, and then I'm sure you have some secret act of espionage to pull off with one of my guests before the night ends."

JANE DID NOT, in fact, pull off her intended second secret act of espionage that evening. Lord Dunlop left before the musicale concluded, and Jane had missed her opportunity to gently pump him for information on his footman.

Although how that conversation would go, Jane wasn't sure. It wasn't as if one could casually slip "So, do you have a broad, ginger footman in your employ who may or may not have participated in a robbery some weeks ago?" into casual conversation.

Sometimes speaking without any premeditation yielded better results. She'd just let her mind do the work in a flurry of in-the-moment brilliance. If she was lucky.

After all, people would only tolerate her speaking solemnly about a plant's swollen stamen so many times before she found herself running out of goodwilled assumptions about her naivete.

Once the music ended, Jack and Pippa's house was emptied of guests within the hour. Servants made quick work of returning the room set up for the musicale to its former state and putting away the food and drinks.

"I believe a few cups of hot chocolate while in our robes in front of a cozy fire would be just the thing," Pippa said to Jane after giving her final instructions to the servants.

"Hot chocolate sounds heavenly," came a familiar voice behind them.

Jane turned around to find Lydia, Jack's younger sister, grinning at them. Lydia had become a good friend to both her and Pippa, and the three often practiced fencing, Pippa's particular talent, together. She wore a rumpled traveling gown and had that look of someone who'd spent many hours in a bumpy carriage, but she was still lovely with her bright blond hair and elfin features.

Pippa gave her sister-in-law a hug. "I thought you weren't coming home until tomorrow."

"I didn't want to spend a night in an inn when we were so close to town," Lydia said. "Now, about that hot chocolate…"

Shortly, the three women were in front of a cheery fire with not only the promised hot chocolate, but also leftover delicacies from the musicale on a tray in front of them in the bedroom that would be Jane's.

Jane nestled into her borrowed robe, glad to be out of her silk gown from earlier.

After a quick recap of her stay at a friend's home out in the countryside for a fortnight, Lydia was succinctly filled in on the latest by an all-too-enthusiastic Pippa.

"So, if I'm understanding this correctly," Lydia said, after swallowing the last bite of a tart, "you're hoping to convince Lady Rowling to reopen the LCA by...proving that the break-in was related to someone trying to steal away evidence of the existence of Rowling's true heir, who is actually her secret son?"

Jane nodded.

"And she's kept the son in hiding—likely back home in India—because she worries these mysterious burglars, who may or may not be led by Rowling's cousin Sir Albert or his weaselly son, are trying to do him in?"

Jane grimaced and nodded again.

"And when you and the handsome servant Dev, who we've learned is also Lady Rowling's occasional covert operative in addition to being a regular servant, prove to Lady Rowling that the break-in has nothing to do with anyone snooping for information on the LCA, you believe she'll open it back up?"

Jane nodded once more, suddenly miserable.

"It sounds far-fetched when you say it," she mumbled, staring down at her cup of now-lukewarm chocolate.

"No," Lydia said gently, laying her hand on Jane's arm. "It sounds completely crazed."

Jane's head jerked up.

"And that," announced Lydia with a sly grin, "is why it's bound to work."

Pippa laughed.

"But...but..." Jane sputtered, "I thought you were implying that this whole scheme is ludicrous. You were pointing out how hairbrained it all is."

Lydia slurped on her hot chocolate. "Listen, I wrote anonymous articles published in the newspaper calling for radical reform in the House of Commons that resulted in my kidnapping and almost getting me, my big oaf of a brother, and Pippa here murdered." She shrugged. "Who am I to say that anyone else's schemes are hairbrained?"

Pippa set her mug down and stretched her feet closer to the fire. "I fought a duel against a man while disguised as my future husband. And I won! Life can take a person on most unexpected adventures." She smiled at Jane. "We support you. We are here for you, whatever you need."

Her throat swelling with emotion, Jane could only nod. She was a very lucky woman to have such supportive friends.

That was the whole reason for the Ladies Covert Academy. It was one woman—the rather mysterious Lady Rowling—supplying the opportunity for all these other women to pursue their passions. And the women supported one another. In between sculpting and pouring over mathematical equations and radical political writings and fencing lessons and botany experiments and studying shipping routes, they gathered in the parlor or breakfast room. They shared the details of their latest work, both the accomplishments and the setbacks. They cheered for one another. And they also did actual work on charity projects together, sewing or knitting clothes for orphans—although honestly, Pippa was dreadful at it—and preparing food for unwed mothers living in a group home.

We are here for you, whatever you need.

Truly, Jane was most fortunate.

"Thank you, both of you." She reached over and gave each of their hands a squeeze.

The thought of what she'd failed to accomplish tonight still weighed on her, however. Jane sighed. "If only I could speak to Dev and let him know I was unable to make the acquaintance of Lord Dunlop at the musicale. Then, perhaps, we could choose our next steps."

Pippa sat up straight. "I do believe," she said, her eyes alight with mischief, "that I can assist you with that."

Chapter Six

D EV SHIFTED HIS weight from foot to foot, hand hesitating in a fist before the thick wooden door.

Lady Hartwick had told him it was fine to go up to the third bedroom on the left. In fact, she had basically forced him to leave the kitchen where he'd lingered with the other liveried footmen and kitchen servants after the musicale. The lowly workers who'd served champagne and refilled the food table for the fine guests had been able to take a break at last, grazing on leftover food, enjoying a few sips from the untouched glasses, and comparing notes on the often odd behaviors of the rich and powerful.

Dev had enjoyed the delicacies, but even more, he'd enjoyed the sense of camaraderie among the below-stairs servants. It was so similar to his life in Calcutta when he'd been a boy, put to some small task at the table in the warm kitchen where the scent of tandoori meats, just pulled out of the clay oven, filled the room. The room was also filled with faces lined with the sun, with years, and with worries but that still offered a smile for one of their own—the young boy at the table, soaking in the feeling of belonging.

Although he hadn't belonged. Not entirely.

Not then, and not today either.

"Jane is waiting for you," Lady Hartwick had said as she'd led him from the kitchen to her home's main staircase. "She wants to compare notes on the evening's spying."

Dev had tried not to react, but Lady Hartwick must have seen the surprise on his face.

"Oh, she told me everything," she had said. To her credit, she hadn't appeared shocked. "And"—she leaned forward—"if you believe you have a real chance to convince Lady Rowling to reopen the LCA, then I am completely in support of your and Jane's schemes."

So apparently he and Jane had the blessing of a countess.

Dev reconsidered the door in front of him.

Stop being such a coward. He took a deep breath and knocked.

"Come," called a familiar voice.

Dev entered the room, pushing the door shut behind him. As she'd already established, Jane valued privacy for their planning over society's ideas of propriety for young ladies.

The room was spacious with a desk under a window, a large four-poster bed, and a fire with a cluster of pillows arranged in front of its cheery warmth.

And one beautiful woman, perched on a pillow.

"Ahmgh…" The noise that emerged from his mouth was more a gurgle than any sound resembling human words.

"Dev!" Jane sprung to her feet. She had taken down her hair, and the red-gold locks cascading down to her shoulders and chest were limned by the glow of the fire behind her. Her hands clasped the edges of her robe together until not even the skin of her neck was showing.

Because she was dressed in night clothes.

Dev gulped.

"Why did you come up?" Jane moved behind a chair set near the fire. "Pippa said she'd let me know if you were still below stairs."

Dev forced his gaze away from the hints of soft curves under her robe.

"I apologize," he managed to say without stammering. "Lady Hartwick told me to come up now, but perhaps I misunderstood her."

Jane snorted, and Dev's gaze jumped to her in surprise before he returned to staring most intently at one of the carved bedposts.

"It seems my cousin is not averse to a bit of mischief," Jane said.

Lady Hartwick had sent him up here without Jane's consent? Perhaps she hadn't been aware of her cousin's state of dress? Or more correctly, undress? But that word was far too provocative for the current state of his brain.

Jane was uncomfortable, as shown by her current position behind the chair clutching at her robe.

And so, Dev wished to be in any place other than this room if his presence upset her.

But—and some small, logical corner of his brain realized this made absolutely no sense—there was also no place he'd rather be in this moment than in this warm, cozy room with the woman who was rapidly worming her way into his affections.

He must stop this, immediately. She was Miss Jane Brickley, daughter of a baron. He was…well, it was unclear who he was at the moment, but it didn't matter. She was not for him, and he'd do well to remember it.

Plus, she'd blackmailed him. He couldn't let himself forget that he was still angry with her for that.

And most important of all, she did not wish him there.

"I beg your pardon." Dev turned toward the door, keeping his face averted. "I shall leave you to your privacy."

His feet were heavy as he walked away from her.

"Wait."

Dev's feet grew roots into the plush carpet at the sound of her voice.

Jane cleared her throat behind him. "Ah, since you *are* here…perhaps we ought to check in. Compare what we discovered, and all that. Time is of the essence, after all. If…if you feel comfortable?"

Dev considered. "I am only concerned about your comfort."

He heard light footsteps followed by a rustling sound. After a moment, she said, "It's fine, Dev. Will you come to sit by the fire?"

He turned slowly. Jane sat in the chair she'd been hiding behind before, a blanket from the bed wrapped around her.

"See?" She offered a smile. "It's all quite proper, now that I'm wearing a counterpane."

"Yes." Dev's mouth twitched in reply. "I'm sure your parents would not mind at all to see you here with me like this."

The smile vanished from her face, and Dev wanted to kick himself. "I apologize. I do not know your parents and should not have said that, even in jest."

A strained look passed over her face. Dev wanted to sit beside her and take her hand in his. He wanted to ask her what troubled her. And he'd sit there and listen for as long as she wished to speak while the fire gently crackled and popped in the background, keeping them both warm as they shared. Well, as she shared.

He had secrets that weren't his alone to give away.

Jane shook her head. "It's quite all right. I just…my parents are rather overprotective of me. It's…difficult."

Dev gestured to the other armchair with a questioning tilt of his head, and she nodded for him to take a seat.

"I'm sorry there are difficulties with your parents." Dev hoped he struck the right note of showing interest in her life without pressuring her to reveal details she wished to keep private. "I hadn't quite thought about how you managed so much time away from your home and family."

Jane shifted in her chair. "When I went to the LCA, they assumed I was doing charity work all day. That's what all the members' parents or wards believed, as I'm sure you know. But now, I tell them I'm paying a call on Pippa. They know we're close, so it all seems above board to them. But I have to sneak out once I'm here at Pippa and Jack's place, so my guards don't know I've left."

Dev sat forward. "Your guards?"

Jane's mouth twisted. "Any time I leave the house, I'm accompanied by at least two armed guards." She sighed. "Ostensibly, they're footmen, but they are retired soldiers and carry weapons at all times. I feel like a fat sum of gold being transferred from one bank vault to another. And...I am never really free."

Her usually sweet, open face looked worn as she relayed this. It was as if the weight of her parents' concern pulled at her very skin.

"I know aristocratic parents are protective of their daughters," Dev said, "but surely this is not the norm?"

Jane shook her head. "Most ladies are accompanied by a companion or maid when they go out, not an armed battalion." She hesitated before asking, "Have you heard the story of how Pippa's father died?"

"No."

"I had mentioned to you that a relative of mine was killed by highwaymen." She took a deep breath before continuing. "It was my uncle, Pippa's father, of whom I spoke. This happened many years ago when my cousin and I were both very young. Pippa and her mother were with him in the carriage when...when it happened. They were waylaid by highwaymen who shot him, and he bled out on the Great North Road."

She must have loosened her grip on the blanket and robe at some point because Dev noticed her neck move as she swallowed.

"Pippa's mother was wrecked. She and Pippa watched him die. It was...horrifying."

Dev was glad for the warmth of the fire because the room felt chillier than it had a few minutes ago. It was as if the tale's tragedy had cast a pall upon everything, like a thick, dark cloud passing in front of the sun.

He had never seen anyone die, but he could imagine to some small degree the horror of seeing a loved one perish from violence.

"When my mother heard what had happened to her brother," Jane continued, "she was beside herself. They had been very close. She and my father both became very fearful after that. The idea that at any time, some evil bandits could jump out into the street and leave murder and mayhem in their wake left a mark on them. They became afraid for their safety." Jane inhaled. "And very afraid for me."

"All their worry, they transferred to you?"

Jane nodded, her eyes showing some relief, perhaps because he understood and because she didn't have to spell it out.

"And so, they never let me go anywhere without an armed escort. It became normal to me for a while, but now..." Jane stared into the fire. "Now I just want..."

Dev waited for her to finish, but the seconds ticked by.

"You want what anyone wants," he finally spoke. "To live freely."

"Yes," she whispered.

They stared at one another, and something in Dev's chest shifted. The play of the fire's warm light on her face and hair only added to the light that already shone from Miss Jane Brickley. She was full of light, despite the occasional coldness of the world around them. Her kindness, her wit, and her steely determination disguised beneath her polite shyness all gleamed with it.

Jane looked away and seemed to give herself a little shake. "What about you?" she asked, her voice even once more. "What are your parents like? Are they living in India still?"

Dev sat back in his seat. "My parents are both dead."

His words seemed to hang in the air between them, and he felt like a cad for not saying it with more gentleness.

"Oh." Her voice was sad. Sad for him. "I'm so sorry."

Dev shook his head. "It's been a long time since my mother passed. She died when I was very young. As you say here in England, I was just in leading strings. And my father...he and I were not close."

"I imagine a distant father is even harder than one who is overprotective."

"Let us agree that they are both hard."

This was the longest he and Jane had ever spoken about something that didn't involve her needs in her laboratory or their partnership to solve the mystery, he realized. Perhaps it was the longest conversation he'd ever had with anyone who hadn't traveled with Lady Rowling from India since he'd left home.

They sat in companionable silence for a few minutes. The fire danced in its grate, the wood occasionally popping. The upholstered chair was wide and comfortable. The blue tones of the bedroom were soothing. And Jane was very pleasant company.

Dev enjoyed his life in Lady Rowling's house. He got along well with the other servants, many whom he'd known most of his life. His friend Parth was fine company, and they often explored London together on their day off. He didn't need much to be content, but he did need to feel he belonged. He had wanted to belong in Calcutta, but there had always been a bit of distance between him and the others that could not be breached despite a lifetime of familiarity and affection. And he did not entirely fit here, in this strange, cold land where he looked like one of them, but not enough to avoid strange glances. Despite his European coloring, he was too bronzed from a life under a bright sun and too foreign in the clothing and accent of the land of his birth.

A land that didn't accept him.

The land of his father didn't accept him either.

All he wanted was a place to fully, wholly belong. A home.

And for this quiet moment, he felt the possibility of it here before the fire, as he and Jane gently shared their stories with one another.

Could this sort of connection and comfort that came from feeling understood by someone who cared be his at some point?

Could this ever be his future?

Jane interrupted the quiet. "I fear I failed this evening."

"Oh?"

"I spoke to Sir Albert and his family at the musicale as you saw, but Lord Dunlop had left before I was able to track him down." She shook her head, her frustration with herself evident.

Dev sat up in his seat. "Let's come back to Lord Dunlop in a minute. What did you learn about Sir Albert? I overheard some, but I had to circulate with the champagne."

Jane relayed her interaction with the man, describing the conversation and demeanor of him, his wife, and their son.

"He just doesn't strike me as a schemer," she concluded. "Unless he is a very talented actor, he didn't seem nearly intelligent enough to pull off a complicated plan involving attempted murder on the other side of the globe, a successful burglary of a large aristocratic household, and the ability to track down and recognize important legal documents."

Dev frowned. Sir Albert had been their top suspect.

"However…" Jane's eyes narrowed. "There was something unsettling about the son, Nigel. He had a certain cunning look about him. Since he is Sir Albert's only son, he will inherit when his father dies. Would he be willing to commit crimes in order to set his father up with a grand title that he would inherit some-day?"

Dev exhaled.

So much plotting and scheming. Such willingness to harm others, and to what end? Greed, power, status…

In the end, those things meant nothing. He'd seen it himself, back at home. The rich and powerful men of the East India Company pillaged the beauty of India and tightened their grip on its people. They had so much already, and yet they wanted more. They wanted to take all they could from a land that wasn't theirs. Simply because they wanted. They wanted and wanted and wanted, and it was never enough.

They would never be satisfied. Dev knew this, in the very center of his being.

And if he ever had the means and the power, he would do

something about it. He would fight against the East India Company. He would fight for the people of India. Even though he wasn't one of them by blood, it was his homeland and he loved it.

So perhaps Nigel Skevington was not satisfied with being the son of a baronet. Perhaps he wanted more, including Rowling's title and unentailed land and wealth.

Perhaps he and Jane should turn their attention to the son.

But there was also the other matter for him and Jane to discuss.

"About Lord Dunlop—" he began.

"I'm so sorry I missed my chance to speak to him. He apparently left early in the second half of the musicale. Now we don't know about the footman—"

"I know."

She sighed. "I know you know, and you are very forgiving, but I just feel wretched."

Dev bit back a smile. "No, I mean *I* know about the footman."

It was very gratifying to see Jane's eyes widen.

"When I was below stairs with the other servants, I had a chance to speak to another of Lord Dunlop's footmen who'd accompanied the carriage. Many of the servants come in from the coaches to warm up a bit, get a bite to eat, and use the necessary."

Jane frowned.

"What is it?"

"I never even thought about the servants needing to use the facilities before." She shook her head, setting off a sunset of golden red as her swaying hair glinted in the reflection of the fire. "They would come with me to wherever I wanted to go, and then they'd be out of sight. I never thought about if they were hungry or needed anything..." Jane's voice trailed off and she stared at the fire, a look of almost anger on her face. "I feel..." she began haltingly. "I feel as if my eyes have finally been opened, just a fraction, from knowing you." She glanced at him, and their gaze held.

Dev's chest felt tight.

"And I feel ashamed," she whispered. "I feel so wretched for not considering the humanity of servants before I knew you. Before I…before you and I…"

Even in the dim light, he could see the color staining her cheeks. And he felt a touch warm too, truth be told.

What was it she wanted to say but couldn't? Or that she struggled to find the words for?

That they'd become friends, of a sort? That there was some sort of connection between the two of them, her a fine lady and him doing the work of both a servant and a detective?

"Well," he finally replied, striving for a gently teasing tone, "I am glad that my presence has been so instructive. I do consider myself to be a worldly man, having been to two whole countries in my life."

His words were received as he'd intended them, and she offered a soft smile.

"So," she said, bringing them back to the matter at hand, "what did you learn about the footman?"

Dev nodded. It was right and proper that they focus on their investigation, not on the softness of smiles and other tender matters.

"The footman from Lord Dunlop's household that I spoke to was quite hungry for a bit of attention," Dev shared. "It seems he is not fully appreciated among the household's servants. They do not respect his natural gifts as a leader, you see."

Jane's mouth quirked.

"And so, it was quite easy for me to get him talking. He told me about his master's predilection for eating in bed, resulting in terribly-stained sheets. He told me the scullery maid chose the valet over him for her affections. And, he told me that he might apply for a new position." Dev paused. "At Boodle's."

Jane frowned. "Boodle's?"

"Yes. It seems that this footman's one and only friend in the household, who had not been there all that long after leaving the employ of another grand house in Mayfair"—Dev raised his eyebrows when Jane leaned forward—"switched jobs yet again only recently to take on a position at London's second-most famous gentlemen's club."

Jane tapped a finger against her lips. "Johnny the broad-shouldered footman who was seen at the burglary is now working at Boodle's."

Dev nodded.

"We need to get in there," Jane announced.

Dev's eyebrows shot up in alarm. "You and me? In a gentlemen's club?"

In the glow of the firelight, Jane's eyes twinkled. "I have an idea."

Chapter Seven

JANE ROSE FROM her seat by the fire once she and Dev ironed out their plan to infiltrate Boodle's gentlemen's club the next day.

"Thank you," she said, feeling rather shy once he rose from his seat as well. "I'm glad we were both able to play a role in our intelligence-gathering tonight."

Dev dipped his chin in acknowledgment. They stood only feet apart. He looked so formal in his borrowed livery. The deep blue of his outfit looked almost like the sky just before it settled into night when hints of moody purple and navy slowly faded into darkness. His shoulders were wide beneath the precise cut of the jacket. His stomach was flat. His legs…

Jane forced her eyes back up, her cheeks blazing.

The fire's gentle crackle underscored the silence between them.

"Jane." His voice was low and deep.

She sucked in a breath and met his stare. He'd called her Jane, not Miss Jane as he usually did.

His eyes glowed in the reflection from the fire. His gaze roamed over her face, seeming to drink in the sight of her. Jane went breathless at the sensation, the feeling of not only being seen and admired, but being *known* by this man.

"Dev," she whispered, taking a half-step toward him.

In the quiet of the room, she heard him swallow. She studied his mouth, the fullness of his bottom lip. How did a man come to have such a soft, beautiful mouth? She wanted to know that mouth, all of a sudden. She wanted to feel it against hers.

She took another half-step forward.

Her eyelids dropped to half-mast.

She tipped her face up.

She waited.

Dev's exhalation seemed loud in the quiet space between them. He was suddenly there, right in front of her but not quite touching. She could feel his warmth and smell his scent, a heady mixture of soap and fresh bread and good, clean sweat.

His breath fanned against her face. She edged her chin up another degree, hoping, waiting…

And lightly, gently, something brushed her cheek. It was his fingers, she realized. He stroked the side of her face, his work-worn hands so tender and soft on her skin. He was touching her. He was touching her like she was special, precious. Like she was…fragile.

Jane exhaled.

She was *not* fragile. She was strong, so much stronger than anyone knew, especially her parents. And she did not wish to be touched as if she were a delicate flower bud.

She reached up, pressing his hand more firmly to her cheek. His hand was warm and textured with the callouses of his labor. She shivered, her skin tingling at the slight abrasion against her face. Reaching out, she seized his second hand. Dev's eyes flared with surprise, and then with something hotter, something darker, when she pressed it to her collarbone. Four of his fingers were on the fabric of the blanket she'd draped over her shoulders.

But one finger—his thumb—was pressed to Jane's bare skin.

She held her breath at the feel of that thumb. No one had ever touched her like this. The clandestine touch of a…a lover, she supposed. Someone a person wished to kiss, in the safe cocoon of a bedroom lit only by the coals of the dying fire. Someone a person wished to touch. Someone a person wished to care for.

She pushed the last thought away.

Breathing deeply, she pressed her chest against that one digit. Dev gave a muffled groan. His thumb moved the barest degree, sweeping across her skin. Jane wanted that thumb to move, to touch, to explore.

And she wanted to touch him as well.

She reached out, her hand pressing against the center of his chest. He was firm beneath her palm, under the borrowed livery. Firm and warm. And his heart was beating at a rapid pace. He was as affected by this as she was.

Dev inhaled sharply at her touch, and Jane looked up. His eyes gleamed in the dim glow of the fire, and he held her stare as his thumb swiped across her chest again and moved up to settle in the hollow of her throat. She could feel her pulse fluttering against his finger there. How fast her heart must beat to create a pulse like hummingbird wings.

"Jane," he said, his voice a velvet rasp, "do you wish for me to kiss you?"

She nodded, and his eyes dropped to her mouth. She imagined the heat of his stare on her lips and licked them. He gave a muffled curse, but she didn't know the word. Perhaps it was in the language he'd grown up speaking in India.

Jane leaned in, tilting her mouth up once more.

This was it. The moment of pure connection between them. The long-simmering tension that had existed from the very beginning when she'd first joined the LCA would finally be unbottled.

She wanted it.

She wanted his kiss.

Footsteps in the hallway sounded. The sudden noise was an intrusion in the cozy space surrounding them as if the reminder of the outside world and all its complications were a pistol shot in a peaceful meadow.

Dev jumped back. Jane missed the intimate press of his

thumb on her skin the instant his touch was gone.

Her lips missed his kiss even though she had yet to feel him there.

She watched in dismay as his face shuttered and the heat in his eyes extinguished. Jane reached toward him, but the absence of warmth in his expression had her dropping her hands back to her side before she'd fully extended them.

He backed away toward the door. "I need to return home." His voice was stiff and formal as if they were back to their old roles. Miss Jane, the baron's daughter. Dev, the humble servant.

Jane hated those roles.

But what else could she do except nod her understanding?

"I'll see you tomorrow, as we discussed," he added.

Jane swallowed past a thick lump in her throat and nodded again.

"Well…" He paused, his hand on the doorknob. "Goodnight, Miss Jane."

The door clicked shut behind him. Jane sat before the fire, keeping her eyes open wide to prevent a single tear from dropping.

THE NEXT MORNING, Jane shook out her hands. Her fingers had grown sore after a long session writing her latest observations on her plants. The early sunshine slanted into her cramped laboratory. She was relieved that her plants were getting such good sunshine here in the room she'd borrowed from Jack and Pippa.

She'd awoken early after a restless night. Thoughts of Dev's hand on her cheek, his thumb resting in the hollow of her throat, and the burning look in his eyes had kept her tossing and turning through the night. And then she'd replayed the cool formality that had engulfed him once he'd pulled back. The utter lack of warmth or connection in his voice had cut her. And so, when dawn finally made an appearance, she'd crawled out of bed, grateful for official authorization from the sky to leave her bed of rumpled blankets and an oft-turned pillow.

While Jane had completed her morning ablutions, she'd decided she needed a plan.

Today's mission was already plotted. She and Dev had their strategy to gain access to Boodle's so they could inquire—discreetly, of course—about the footman, currently their only lead in this investigation.

But she needed another plan, a plan just for her.

And it was how to survive the embarrassment of seeing Dev again. She'd basically begged him to kiss her, and he had left.

Had he been completely unaffected by the soft touches they'd shared in front of the fire?

Their interlude had been more profound than she could have imagined, but apparently, it had meant nothing to him. Perhaps he'd kissed many women. Perhaps he had a sweetheart, someone here in London, or perhaps back home in India.

What did she really know about him anyway?

Jane muttered a few choice words as she set her notes aside and began to water her plants.

He wouldn't arrive for another hour or so. They'd decided to show up at Boodle's in the late morning so that Jane could return home afterward and her parents would assume she'd simply had a lazy sleep-in after staying up late with Pippa.

Jane sorted through the jars of dried plants stacked on shelves along the side of the room. She not only cross-bred plants, but she also studied their properties once they were dried. Who knew what potential medicinal purposes or helpful usages she might uncover?

"Not mint." She glared at the jar that had nearly turned her into a poisoner.

This dried plant had been the start of all her troubles. She'd likely mixed up the real mint with this other, mystery herb, leading to her accidental poisoning of her cousin's husband with his tea.

So, what was actually in this jar?

She opened the lid and sniffed. Her eyes watered and she sneezed. Whatever it was, it was much more potent in dried form, as none of the plants she'd grown or cross-bred had caused her to have a physical reaction when they'd been in their natural state.

This stuff was potent.

Jane studied the jar. Had the original label come off when her laboratory had been roughed up during the break-in? Or perhaps the label had gone missing while she'd packed up, throwing things willy-nilly into crates as she'd rushed to leave the LCA after Lady Rowling's edict that the academy was to be shut down immediately.

Aside from the plants she collected herself when she traveled to the countryside, she obtained most of her seeds and starters from a plant seller in the market. The owner had become a friend of sorts, often suggesting new plants from foreign lands for Jane to try. He seemed to have connections to travelers from all over the world. He was the only seller she'd found who could provide seeds from far-flung and remote locations. On a recent trip before the break-in, he'd given her some seeds from South America.

"Don't quite know what they's do," he'd said, "but I figures you're the lady to find out."

Had these seeds grown into the plant with the poisonous properties? She could hardly remember even planting them.

Jane huffed in frustration.

Everything had been disrupted by the break-in that closed the LCA. Everything.

Her work was in chaos. Her plants were a hodge-podge of mixed-up pots. Her notes were out of order.

None of the other LCA members were able to continue their work unless they'd somehow managed to find an accommodating countess relative like she had, relatives who allowed them to break societal norms for proper young women who enjoyed doing improper things.

As if studying botany or training in fencing or writing compositions or testing mathematical formulas or mapping shipping routes or learning animal husbandry were actually improper in any way.

Only for ladies.

Proper society was maddening.

Jane drummed her fingers on her worktable. She needed to sort out what this herb was. Perhaps after her and Dev's trip to Boodle's, there would be time to swing by the plant seller's booth in the market and inquire.

Jane transferred a bit of the dried herb from the jar into a small glass vial and closed it with a cork stopper before nestling it in the corner of a wicker basket.

And then she clipped several bunches of fresh herbs, bundling them together with twine and adding them to the basket as well.

Jane glanced at the clock. She had just enough time to grab a bite of breakfast before she needed to sneak out a side door and meet Dev around the corner.

As Shakespeare had written in *Henry V*, the game was afoot.

The only problem for Jane was, she had more than one game at play now.

Chapter Eight

DEV SNUCK A glance at Jane as the hack rolled along the London streets toward Boodle's. Aside from an initial greeting when she'd arrived at the corner, she'd been uncharacteristically quiet this morning. Not that he could find fault.

He'd hardly spoken either.

What was a person supposed to say after asking a lovely lady if she'd like a kiss, and then disappearing when she said yes?

Dev had wished for the ability to give himself a swift kick in the pants last night. Their time in the bedroom had been like the fire in the hearth—starting out with cheerful, cozy warmth before burning into intense embers. He'd felt scorched by the simple act of touching the pad of his thumb to the smooth skin of her chest. The subtle pounding of her pulse at the base of her neck. The feel of her hand singeing his chest through his clothing.

And then, when the flames had been about to erupt, the sound of footsteps outside had reminded him of where he was— in the home of an earl and countess. And *who* he was—a humble servant in borrowed livery, yearning to press his mouth against an aristocratic woman's.

Never mind the fact that this was Jane. Intelligent. Curious. Kind. And wanting a kiss from him, despite who he was, or who she thought him to be.

He'd overstepped, and today they both paid the price if the

stilted conversation and awkward tension were any indication.

Should he say anything?

"Before we get to Boodle's—" he began.

"I am so very grateful for your assistance," she interrupted.

Dev watched her, curious as to her aim. She went from saying nothing at all to expressing her gratitude?

"Without you, there would be no hope of reopening the LCA. The truth is, I find I can think of little else these past few days." She laughed, but it sounded brittle to his ears.

"I am glad we are making progress," he said, uncertain how to proceed.

Was she not upset with him after all?

"In fact, I find myself quite appreciative of your friendship, Dev." She folded her hands together on her lap, nestled amongst the plain fabric of a dress he suspected she'd borrowed from a maid in Pippa's household.

"Friendship," he repeated.

"Why, yes." She offered a polite smile, the sort of smile one would give to their in-law's neighbor's cousin. "We are friends of a sort, aren't we?"

Dev nodded woodenly, understanding everything she chose *not* to say. The lines between them were redrawn. The status quo was re-established. They were partners solving a crime. They were friends…or at least, *friendly*.

But they weren't intimate.

They weren't close.

And they certainly didn't kiss.

"I understand," he said.

She met his gaze, and something flashed in her eyes before she whipped her head around to look out the window.

"We're here," Jane announced, gathering up her wicker basket as the carriage rolled to a stop.

Dev smoothed out his overcoat while she paid the hack driver. He'd considered wearing his usual kurta, but Parth had convinced him that wearing his normal Indian clothing to a place as stuffy as Boodle's would not do Dev and his mission any favors. Parth had loaned him some of his garments, telling Dev that he looked like a merchant.

So far, it seemed Jane hadn't noticed his change in garb. Or perhaps she simply didn't care.

That was a rather depressing thought. He shook his head. It shouldn't matter whether or not Jane cared. It *couldn't* matter.

"Shall we head to the back?" she asked, once the hack left.

Dev nodded and followed her past the ornate front of the gentlemen's club. The bottom floor was white stone with carved columns and ornamental plasterwork. The upper floors were a stately red brick with an arched window in the center flanked by more columns.

"Did they rob a temple in Greece?" he muttered as they passed.

Jane's snort ahead of him brought a smile to his face.

Despite this strange tension between them, it was good to know that they both retained their senses of humor.

"So," Jane said as they entered the alley behind the building. "I'll do most of the talking, and you can display the herbs."

Dev nodded. The plan she'd come up with last night was solid.

Hopefully, it would work.

He knocked on the back door, and they waited in silence until it was opened by a gangly boy of indeterminate age with dark, curly hair and a smattering of freckles.

"Hello," Jane said, smiling at the boy who blinked owlishly back. "We are herb merchants, and we'd like to speak to your cook."

"Chef's already got a seller for 'erbs." The boy swiped his sleeve across his nose.

"Ah, but these are the freshest herbs your chef will have ever seen. I'm sure he'll want to see our wares." Jane opened her basket and held out a bunch of fresh plants tied together with twine.

"Looks like all th'other green stuff what comes into the kitchen." The boy wrinkled his nose, apparently displeased with the presence of further *green stuff*, before taking hold of the door as if to shut it.

Dev reached into his pocket and pulled out a coin. He held it up for the boy to see, and thankfully it was bright enough outside that the coin gleamed a bit in the weak morning sunlight.

The boy halted the door's movement.

Dev flicked his eyes between Jane and the coin.

She stared back.

He cleared his throat and jerked his head to the money. Surely she recalled their agreement that she'd be the one to speak? He usually didn't worry that English people would judge him based on his accent, but Parth had been quite adamant that Boodle's was stuffy and old-fashioned and not the place to be different.

How frustrating.

And how wrong, really.

"Ah," Jane exclaimed, seeming to understand her role in this unplanned portion. "If you bring someone from the kitchen to talk to us—an adult, you understand—then we'd love to thank you for your work."

The boy stared at her.

"With this coin."

He blinked.

"We're paying you to help us," she said, eyes turning a little desperate as the boy continued to ignore the bribe.

Was the child lacking in intelligence? Surely in a place such as Boodle's where wealthy men gathered, coins were passed around freely in exchange for special errands or information.

The boy continued to watch them with a blank face, and Dev had a sudden rush of clarity.

He fished all the coins he had out of his pocket. "How about now?"

The boy's hand darted out to snatch up the money from Dev's palm. He flashed Dev a wink before saying, "Be back in a minute."

"Well," Jane huffed. "I do believe we've been hoodwinked."

Dev chuckled.

"The boy reminded me of someone," he said.

"Who?"

He gave Jane a pointed look. "You."

"Me?" Her face was a picture of astonishment.

"You are quite adept at feigning ignorance or pretending to be completely innocent of what's going on around you. I figured the boy was playing a similar game."

Jane narrowed her eyes. "I don't feign ignorance."

Dev raised an eyebrow.

"I don't." She sniffed and resettled the basket over her arm. "Well…perhaps I do on occasion. But that's only because people assume I'm a ninny." She chewed on her lip for a minute as she seemed to consider her words.

Dev stared at that plump, pink lip. What did it feel like, under her teeth? He wanted to bite down on it himself, test the give of her flesh beneath his teeth. Nibble it a bit, before licking the sting away and consuming her with a kiss.

He shook away the thought.

Herbs.

Bribes.

The footman.

He needed to stay focused. Much was a stake here, and lusty thoughts of his co-conspirator's mouth would not help their odds.

"A ninny?" he finally said, realizing he'd let her comment go unanswered.

She shook her head. "In addition to being a woman, who men assume are only interested in fashion and gossip and gothic novels—not that there's anything wrong with those things! I enjoy all of those!—I myself seem to be perpetually underestimated as to what's between my ears. I have this sort of…" She waved her hand in front of her face. "…this look of youthful innocence, and everyone assumes I have clouds for brains. It's most vexing."

Dev stared into her eyes. Their hazel shade created a beguiling mix of brown and gold and green. They glowed with intelligence. Anyone who took even a moment to know her would see that she was incredibly smart. She was curious. She loved botany, of course, but he'd noticed she always listened intently, wanting to know more and truly enjoying learning.

"They're fools," he murmured, "not to see how clever you are."

Jane's cheeks grew rosy, and he felt glad at having put that blush on her face. Hopefully, it was a blush stemming from pride.

She should be proud.

She was the smartest woman he knew.

No. The smartest *person* he knew. No qualifiers were needed.

The door opened once more, and a beanpole-thin man wearing a gleaming white apron glowered at them.

"I hear," he snapped, "that you wish to offer your services as herb providers for Boodle's. However, we already have—"

"Sir," Jane interrupted, "I'm sure you already have deliveries in place for all your ingredients, but we grow our herbs with only the richest soil, the most scientifically-balanced fertilizer, and the most meticulously measured purified water in England."

The man sniffed. "Bold claims, miss."

Jane drew herself up to her full height before pulling out a bundle of herbs. "My thyme speaks for itself."

She thrust the herbs at the man who eyed it doubtfully for a moment before taking hold with hesitant fingers.

He examined the bundle with a critical eye. Lifting it to his nose, he drew a deep breath. His eyes fluttered shut, and he sighed.

"Oh, that is quite lovely." He inhaled again. "Reminds me of my mother's roasted chicken."

His entire demeanor transformed as his rigid posture relaxed and a wisp of a smile crossed his face. "Come in, come in," he said, gesturing them into the building. "I'm Smith, assistant chef here at Boodle's."

Shortly, Dev and Jane were seated at a gleaming table in the massive kitchen. A score of servants prepared food, scrubbing vegetables, kneading dough, and basting several roasts. The savory scents soon had Dev's stomach growling. Perhaps he should have eaten more this morning for breakfast, but he'd been in a rush after rising later than usual. He hadn't slept well last night following his interaction with Jane.

"What a lovely kitchen," Jane said, glancing about with obvious admiration.

"We run a tight ship here at Boodle's." Smith beamed. "Now, tell me about your pricing—"

"Before we get into the details," Jane said, leaning forward in her chair with an innocent smile, "I was wondering if you could send a message to my cousin."

Smith frowned. "Your cousin?"

"Oh yes, he recently began working here as a footman, but his mother, my Aunt Tillie, is monstrously worried about him. She asked me to keep an eye on him once he moved to London from the countryside, you see." Jane blinked her wide eyes, all naivete.

"Ah." Smith nodded. "And your cousin works here at Boodle's?"

Jane widened her eyes even more. "I believe so. I lost track of him after he left Lord Dunlop's employ as a footman. Is Johnny here? He has very red hair. He's a good boy, my cousin."

Dev couldn't help but admire the manner in which Jane used her innocent expression to convince Smith that she was simply a kindly cousin looking after her relative.

"Ah, Johnny Brown." The assistant chef's face hardened. "Yes, he's been a footman here for a few weeks."

Dev frowned. Something was off. Had their mysterious footman with the broad shoulders and propensity to filch two quid from unsuspecting scullery maids made a bad impression here already? Perhaps it wasn't so mysterious why he had to keep finding new positions if he was burning bridges at every new post he took.

Or perhaps this assistant cook, Smith—or even the establishment of Boodle's itself—was involved in the theft at Lady Rowling's somehow?

How far did this scheme to steal the Rowling title go?

"Would it be possible to see if he's free to speak to me for just a few minutes?" Jane asked, clasping her hands together imploringly. "I'd be ever so grateful."

Smith sighed before calling over his shoulder for one of the other kitchen servants to let Johnny Brown know that his cousin was here to see him.

Beside him, Jane fidgeted in her seat. They hadn't accounted for this possibility. Smith was supposed to simply send for him, not announce his cousin was here. What if the man didn't have any cousins?

While they waited, Smith examined the rest of the herbs in Jane's basket. "May I keep these to show our head chef when he's free?"

"Certainly," Jane agreed.

"I'm curious who else you supply. And what do you charge?"

Jane shot a glance at Dev, a look of panic in her eyes.

Dev leaned forward, speaking for the first time. "We supply many fine households, including that of Lady Rowling, a marchioness, and we are certain she could provide a referral if you wish."

Smith nodded.

"We are ready to grow our business," Dev continued, "and can offer very competitive prices."

Beside him, Jane's taut shoulders loosened. Dev kept the conversation going with the assistant chef, inquiring about the quantity and type of herbs and spices Boodle's used in a typical week.

Thankfully, the servant returned right when Dev had exhausted his ability to fake insight into the business of herb selling.

"I couldn't find Johnny anywhere, sir," the servant reported to Smith.

Smith frowned. "I thought he was dusting the chandeliers this morning."

The other servant shrugged.

Smith turned to them and opened his mouth, but Jane cut him off.

"Well, we shall just pay another call tomorrow." She stood, and Dev followed suit.

"But…what of the herbs?" Smith asked as Jane began to make her way toward the back door.

Dev followed in her wake.

"Shall I tell him you came by, Miss…?" Smith called.

"Ah, we shall discuss it all tomorrow." Jane waved her hand over her shoulder at the assistant chef as she left the building.

Dev nodded his head at the obviously bewildered Smith before exiting behind her. They rushed down the alley and around the corner, and Jane leaned back against the side of the building.

"Oh my," she gasped. "That was quite a bit of lying all at once."

Her fair skin was tinged with pink.

Dev leaned against the building beside her. "Are you all right?"

She rolled her head to look at him. "I've been lying to my parents and sneaking out on my guards, but I suppose in general I am not so well-versed in the art of deception." She exhaled slowly. "I hadn't thought through all the details ahead of time—a fake name, how much to charge, or where the people at Boodle's should send a message."

"You did quite well, considering."

Jane smiled wryly. "It's the *considering* that caused us to run into problems, I'm afraid."

Dev's chest lurched at that smile. The slight crinkle at the corners of her eyes, the curve of her pink lips, and the way the light smattering of freckles across her nose seemed to shift as her face moved.

"At least we know for sure that he works there now," Dev said. "And we have a last name as well."

"Johnny Brown." Jane stared out at the traffic moving along the street. "Doesn't sound like a criminal's name."

"What would a criminal's name sound like?"

"Oh, I don't know. Maybe *One-Eyed Jack* or *Dagger Dan*."

Dev snorted. "Dagger Dan?"

Jane grinned up at him, and Dev found it the most natural thing in the world to brush his hand against hers where they dangled between them. He trailed his pinky along the side of her hand. His skin tingled at the contact.

Jane stilled, her eyelids drooping, before she cleared her throat and pulled away from the building. Away from his hand.

"I don't know about you," she said, "but that kitchen had the most delicious-smelling food I've ever encountered."

Dev drew away from the brick wall slowly. Had he just ruined a perfectly lovely moment by touching her hand? It had seemed so easy, so right, in that moment of shared mirth between them.

But apparently, she hadn't felt the same.

He straightened his shoulders, determined to be normal. They were partners solving a mystery, that was all.

"It did make my stomach growl," he admitted, finally answering her comment about the scents in the kitchen.

"I hate to lose a day in our search." Jane glanced up and down the street as if looking for something. "What if we found a nearby place to dine? We could get our lies prepared ahead of time like proper criminals—"

"—unlike Dagger Dan," he interrupted.

The corner of her mouth hitched. "Unlike Dagger Dan who blunders all his covert missions, and then we can return to Boodle's in an hour to see if our footman has been found."

Dev glanced around at their surroundings. This block was

more upscale than the places he and Parth visited when they went out to explore the town, but he recalled a public house just a handful of streets over that was welcoming to women and families, not just men.

And, it had an item on the menu very close to his heart.

"If a meat pasty and a pint of ale are acceptable to you, I know a place nearby." Dev held his breath. If she found this suggestion to be too far beneath her station, he wasn't sure what to offer next.

Jane's hazel eyes crinkled up at the corners. "That sounds delicious."

JANE FOLLOWED DEV to the corner. As he was about to step into the stream of pedestrians strolling by, she grabbed his arm and yanked him back.

He glanced around. "What?"

"Don't look," she whispered.

Jane turned away from the main thoroughfare and lowered her head, pretending to search through her basket. Bundles of thyme. Sprigs of rosemary. A little vial of mystery dried poison.

"What's wrong?" Dev whispered after a moment. He had followed her lead, turning his face away from the main street as well.

"Sir Albert and his son Nigel just walked by," she murmured.

"Perhaps they are members at Boodle's."

She nodded. The savory scent of her herbs filled her nose, and Jane felt the tension in her shoulder ease.

"That was a close call," she said after a long exhale.

If she had been seen by members of her social circle out with a man and no escort while dressed in a gown she'd borrowed from her maid, there was no chance her parents would not hear of it. And then they'd truly never let her out of their sights. She wouldn't be able to finish this investigation with Dev. They wouldn't solve the mystery of the burglary and ensure the rightful heir inherited Lord Rowling's title and properties. She'd never convince Lady Rowling to reopen the Ladies Covert Academy.

And…she'd never spend time with Dev again.

She swallowed.

"Can you check to make sure they're gone?" she asked. "They're not likely to remember a servant from Pippa and Jack's musicale."

His jaw tightened, and she regretted her words.

He *was* a servant, but he was Dev too. Kind. Humorous. Honorable. And so many other things that she could barely find words for. He'd become important to her these last few days. Important in a way that was hard for her to wrap her mind around.

She squeezed her hands together. "Dev, I'm sor—"

"I'll check," he interrupted, and before she could say more, he was poking his head around the corner. After a moment, he said, "No sign of them."

He gestured to the sidewalk and led the way to the eatery he'd mentioned, just a handful of blocks away from Boodle's.

Jane hesitated outside the eatery and Dev paused beside her. A cheerful sign proclaimed the establishment to be The Three Crowns public house.

Jane had never been to a public house before.

A trio of men passed by them, entering the establishment. They had a look of quills and ledger books about them, perhaps clerks at some nearby business. An older couple left, the woman's hand resting on the crook of her companion's arm as they smiled at one another.

"I've eaten here with Parth before," Dev murmured near her ear.

Jane shivered at the caress of his breath against her sensitive skin.

"It seemed like a proper sort of place with families and merchants and such," he continued. "But if you'd rather not—"

Jane straightened her spine. "I'm sure it's fine."

And in they went.

The public house was well-lit from the row of windows along the front. Dark wooden tables were mostly full, and a fire crackled in the massive hearth across the room from a gleaming bar.

A man in a tidy apron nodded them toward an empty table near the fire. Jane followed Dev and settled into her seat.

"What can I get you?" The server smiled with practiced ease.

"Is Arjun still the cook here?" Dev asked, leaning forward.

The man nodded. "Best curry pasty in town."

Dev raised an eyebrow in question. Jane hesitated for just a moment. Not only had she never had a pasty, which she'd heard was a hand-held pastry stuffed with meat and vegetables that was a staple of the middle and working classes, but she'd never had Indian curry before.

Still, she was on an adventure.

Jane nodded.

"Two curry pasties, please, and two pints of the pale ale as well," Dev told the man.

"A curry pasty?" she asked once the server had left them.

Dev's mouth curled up on one side. "Parth had heard about this place and its cook, Arjun, from a friend. We came here on our day off a while ago, and I've been hoping to return soon. The curry pasty combines flavors from both England and India."

The half-smile vanished, and his expression darkened. "Because of the East India Company, there is a large population of people from India who have moved here."

"You disapprove of the East India Company?" Jane asked. She knew only the basics—it was a joint stock company held by wealthy Englishmen who traded with India. It brought cotton and tea to England. Beyond that, she didn't know much else.

Dev thanked the server when the man placed their tankards

of ale on the table. He took a long swallow before speaking.

"The East India Company has brought famine, war, and poverty to India." His expression was hard. "It's a leech, sucking away India's strength and resources."

Jane touched the side of her tankard. It was cool beneath her fingers and condensation was already forming. "Tell me more."

"The company forces people to grow the crops it needs—cotton, or sometimes opium which it later smuggles into China—so the people of India don't have enough food crops for themselves. It took power away from the Mughals, the local rulers, and created its own government and army."

He shifted in his seat, and Jane had the sense he was frustrated by his inability to explain it as he wished. "Imagine… think about if France invaded here. If France stripped the Prince Regent of his crown, forced all the farmers to grow grapes for wine instead of wheat and potatoes, and replaced all the redcoat soldiers with French troops."

Jane clutched her pint of ale. "That's…" She breathed. Dev's analogy made it so clear. "That's just wrong."

Dev nodded. "My…my former employer, Lord Rowling, worked for the East India Company for a long time. Since before I was even born. He'd been a second son, so after his education and a bit of oat sowing, as the English say, he was shipped off to a position in India. He had a knack for bureaucracy."

Jane wrinkled her nose. "What a strange talent."

Dev sighed. "There are hundreds and hundreds of very skilled paper pushers in the Company." He took another drink of ale before continuing. "Lord Rowling rose through the ranks, I've been told, and when his older brother died and he inherited the title, he didn't want to leave. I suppose he'd grown used to his power and status as a leader in the Company."

"Lady Rowling never speaks of him."

Dev snorted. "I believe that. Her family married her off to him when she was seventeen and he was in his fifties. The instant we heard he'd died, she started packing her bags to return to

England."

Jane imagined that Dev had not been so eager to pack. How strange it must have been, to leave the home he'd known his entire life and move to this faraway land. Even though he was at least part English, England itself must have felt completely foreign to him.

And so, he looked for reminders of home.

A curry pasty.

Wearing the clothing he was used to.

Jane hadn't considered it before, but he was in English clothing today. Aside from last night with his borrowed livery, she didn't think she'd ever seen him wearing clothing that wasn't from his home.

"Rowling was partly responsible for the cruelty that England has forced on India," Dev said. "Even though he was my…my employer, a part of me loathed him." His neck moved as he swallowed.

Jane frowned. Something niggled at the back of her mind. Was he not telling the truth? Or only giving her part of the story?

"Why did you stay?" she asked.

Dev's head jerked up. "Pardon?"

"If you hated Lord Rowling so much, why didn't you leave his household? Find another job?"

Dev's eyes, usually so bright and hinting at some shared mirth, had grown as dull and hard as a boulder.

"And here you are, two curry pasties." The server set their plates down with a thud.

Dev thanked their server. Jane stared down at the steaming half-circle of golden pastry. For some reason, she felt ashamed, as if she'd torn off Dev's clothing and left him exposed.

She cleared her throat. "This looks delicious."

"Yes." His voice was flat.

Jane looked for a fork, but there was none.

"You pick it up with your hands. A pasty is a food for workers, so there is no need to fuss with cutlery," Dev explained.

She watched him lift the pasty to his mouth and take a bite. His eyes slid shut. Despite the awkwardness of their conversation, she felt inordinately glad that he'd shared this with her, this little taste of his home.

Jane followed suit, picking up her pasty and taking a bite from the corner. A rich, savory aroma emerged, along with a warm mouthful of deliciousness. Chunks of tender meat and vegetables combined with a rich sauce that was both earthy and bright. The crunch of the pastry contrasted beautifully with the decadent sauce.

"These flavors..." She spoke even though her mouth was full. What were manners in the face of such a delicious bite?

"I know." Dev's expression was open and relaxed once more. "I'm glad you like it too."

Jane took another bite and grinned at him as she chewed.

They ate in companionable silence until both the pasties were gone.

Chapter Nine

AFTER FINISHING THEIR meal—as well as coming up with the missing details of the fictitious herb company they'd need to give to Boodle's—Dev settled up the tab and they were out on the street once more.

"You could have let me pay, you know," Jane grumbled as they retraced their steps toward Boodle's.

"I could have." Dev smirked. "But I didn't want to."

Jane rolled her eyes, and Dev walked with a bounce in his step. Talking about the Company laying waste to India had been difficult for him, but their easy comradery had returned as soon as they'd taken their first bite of curry pasty.

It had been a risk, taking Jane to a public house. It was clear by her hesitation to enter that she'd never been to such an establishment before. Most of her meals were likely served on fine porcelain plates under a gleaming chandelier in a fine home. And he doubted she'd ever forgone utensils for an entire meal.

But she'd enjoyed it.

The look of pleasure on her face as she'd devoured her pasty had left Dev squirming in his seat. He could imagine her face looking like that in bed, her flame-colored hair spread out around her as he leaned down—

He cleared his throat. "I hope they've found Johnny Brown."

They rounded the corner to the alley behind Boodle's.

What would it be like to look this man in the eye, knowing he was likely one of the people to break in and steal the documents? "Do you think he'll confess to—"

Jane's eyes widened, and Dev jerked his head up.

A man leaped out from behind a stack of crates in the alley. His collar was turned up, his hat pulled low, and a kerchief covered the bottom half of his face.

And in his hand was a knife.

Dev's blood turned to ice.

"Run," he barked to Jane.

He could sense her stepping away, but she wasn't running out of the alley. What a stubborn woman.

The man ran at Dev, swiping toward his middle with the blade. Dev twisted to the side. He swung with his fist, but the blow glanced off the man's shoulder.

The man pivoted and came at Dev again. Dev's heart thundered in his chest. He dodged to the side, but the blade came down across his upper arm, slicing through his shirt and into his flesh.

Dev hissed at the white-hot pain.

The world had narrowed. There was no city, no plot, no heir. Only this alley, this man, this blade.

And Jane.

He risked a glance in her direction, hoping to see her running away from danger. Instead, she was rummaging through her wicker basket. What was she going to do, bludgeon the man with a sprig of thyme?

"Jane," he shouted, but the man was upon him again.

Dev jumped back as the blade swiped toward his middle. He swung out at the man's face with his right fist, but the hit lacked power because of the burning cut on his arm. The man's kerchief was knocked askew though.

A quick flash of nose and cheeks were visible, and then the man was circling, crouched low with the knife held loosely in his hand.

Dev's back was cold with sweat. If the man succeeded in killing him, what would happen to Jane? He prayed she would run to the street. Surely the attacker had enough sense not to follow a woman onto a major thoroughfare in the broad light of day.

"Hey!" Jane shouted.

The man turned his head a fraction to the side to see. Dev watched, horrified as Jane ran up to the attacker. She held her hand in front of her, fingers curled shut as if she carried something small in her palm.

The man raised his knife.

Dev's stomach plummeted. "No!"

Jane opened her hand and blew.

A small cloud blew into the man's face. He howled, dropping the knife and rubbing at his eyes.

What had Jane done?

The man coughed and gasped, stumbling back further.

Jane darted forward and picked up the knife. She clasped the hilt and drew her arm back. It almost looked as if she were prepared to fling it at the man.

Dev darted to her side, ready to step between her and the attacker if he changed course.

But the man rushed away down the alley, accompanied by the ugly sounds of his wheezes and choking gasps.

Dev and Jane stood in silence once he vanished around the corner.

He felt as if he'd run across a desert or swum the length of the ocean. He feared for a moment that his legs might give out beneath him, and he would collapse to the ground at Jane's feet.

But he couldn't do that to her. Dealing with a large, unconscious man in an alley outside the exclusive gentlemen's club they wished to infiltrate would be most onerous.

He drew a steadying breath. "Are you—"

Before he could finish his question, she'd spun to face him. Her hazel eyes were huge in her pale face. "You're bleeding."

She reached out toward his arm, but before she touched him, she glanced at her hand and blanched. Jane stooped down and reached under her dress. She…she was grabbing her petticoat.

Despite the steady loss of his blood from the knife wound, Dev still had enough of his facilities to know he was not supposed to witness a fine lady's undergarments. But he could no more look away than he could bid his skin to heal itself.

Jane wiped her hand on the white, frothy fabric, taking great care to rub thoroughly between each finger.

"What was that?" he asked, clutching at his arm.

She straightened up, her underlayers disappearing from view. "I'm not really sure, but I accidentally poisoned Jane's husband with one of my dried plants and it made my eyes water when I sniffed it, so I figured it wouldn't be pleasant for Dagger Dan."

Dev's mouth parted. "Dagger Dan."

Jane lifted one shoulder as if to show her helplessness to the power of the irreverent comment.

"Let's see what Dagger Dan did to you."

Dev tried not to wince as she nudged his hand aside and parted the sliced fabric on his arm.

It hurt. A lot.

Jane's expression turned grim. "We should get you to a doctor."

"We can't go to Lady Rowling's." Dev knew that while in theory Lady Rowling would be glad to hear of their progress thus far in tracking down the stolen wedding certificate, she would not approve of his partnering with Jane.

And she most certainly would not approve of them getting attacked by a masked man wielding a knife in the alley behind Boodle's.

What a mess.

Almost as messy as his arm.

"What about Lord and Lady Hartwick?" he asked. "Would they mind if a doctor treated me there?"

Jane's furrowed eyebrows relaxed a small degree. "That's the perfect place. Let's grab a hack."

"BLAST IT, WHERE is that confounded doctor?" Jane asked Lydia from the doorway of the same room she'd slept in last night.

From the hallway, Lydia answered, "I'm sure he'll be here soon." She handed over a stack of clean bandages. "My brother offered a hefty sum in the note he sent with the footman."

After taking the bandages and draping them over her arm, Jane accepted a pitcher of warm water Lydia had also carried up.

She was thankful that Lydia had been home to receive them. Jack and Pippa had been out visiting Pippa's mother, and although Jane spent countless hours visiting and working in her laboratory in their home, she wasn't confident the servants would have followed her orders to fetch a physician or even allowed a bleeding Dev inside.

Although, given their mistress's penchant for swordplay, perhaps they weren't completely shocked by the sight of a bleeding person in need of stitches.

"I imagine you'll tell me the full story later," Lydia said, her golden eyebrows pulled together in concern, "but can you at least let me know if you are in danger?"

Jane glanced over her shoulder to where Dev sat on the bed. She pitched her voice low. "Someone attacked us in broad daylight and didn't even ask for a purse." She let out a shaky breath. "It felt intentional. Someone is willing to kill to stop us from finding the evidence we need."

Lydia grabbed her arm.

"Don't tell me to stop," Jane warned.

Lydia's mouth tugged up on one side. "I would never give you such rubbish advice. I kept poking at a dangerous topic until I got myself kidnapped, remember." She paused for a moment. "But Jane, you *must* be careful. Those who have power will often go to extreme lengths to keep it when someone seems to threaten their status. Whatever you and Dev are investigating is clearly frightening someone with resources. Don't take that lightly. Believe me."

Jane swallowed back a lump in her throat. "I'll be careful," she whispered.

Lydia gave her arm a squeeze. "I'll send the doctor up the moment he arrives." Her friend and fellow LCA member headed back downstairs.

Staring into the empty hallway, Jane clenched the bandages tightly. The truth was, she *hadn't* been careful.

She'd always assumed her parents' fear that murderous bandits could appear at any moment and harm her had been nothing more than them allowing fear to rule their lives.

They'd taken a singular incident—a tragic, horrifying incident to be sure—and turned it into their entire worldview.

Jane hadn't wanted to live that way. She hadn't wanted to believe the world was so dangerous, capricious, and violent. That whether she lived or died could be left to something so out of her own control.

But perhaps her parents were right. Perhaps the world *was* a dangerous place.

It was a frightening thought.

And one she'd have to sort out before their next expedition to unravel this mystery.

Before turning into the room where Dev patiently waited, she drew a deep breath and squared her shoulders.

"Any word?" Dev asked when she shut the bedroom door behind her. His voice was steady, but Jane could tell he was in pain.

He was sitting on the edge of the bed on top of an old blanket.

"We don't want to get blood on the counterpane," Lydia had said when they'd first arrived. Thank goodness for levelheaded people. Jane felt like she was fighting a losing battle with panic ever since the man with the knife had popped out from behind the crates in the alley.

"Still waiting on the doctor." She crossed the room to his side and set the bandages and pitcher of water on the table next to the bed. "How are you feeling?"

Dev shifted and grimaced in pain. "To be honest, being sliced open is not an enjoyable sensation."

Surveying him, Jane took in his pale face and the pinched look at the corners of his eyes. He held his arm stiffly at his side. And even with all that, he was still absurdly handsome.

"Perhaps the fabric is pressing on the wound?" she said. "I'm sure you'd be more comfortable if we took off your jacket and shirt, and the doctor will need to see your bare arm anyway."

Had she sounded breathless on the word *bare*? What a time for her to turn into a panting ninny.

Dev hesitated.

"I just think you'd be more comfortable," Jane murmured, leaning close.

"And what about you?" he asked. "Will you be comfortable?" His eyes sparkled a bit despite the sheen of pain.

Jane bit back a smile. "If you can wiggle out of that jacket on your own, you're free to do so. But I imagine it will be rather difficult with only one functioning arm. And since I'm used to seeing a plant's bare stamen"—she added, arching an eyebrow—"I'm sure your bare arm will be quite tame in comparison."

Dev's lips twitched, and he nodded.

Jane stepped closer. "All right, let's get you naked." She made a show of clasping her hand over her mouth. "I mean…"

Dev's eyes gleamed. "If you are trying to distract me with your faux innocence, it's working."

Jane didn't confirm his guess, but she didn't need to. How strange to realize at this moment that they'd come to know one another quite well during their brief partnership. In some ways, he knew her even better than Pippa, who was not only her cousin but her best friend.

"I'll go slowly." Jane took hold of the sleeve of his uninjured left arm, helping to ease the jacket down.

Dev's entire body tensed, his shifting movements likely hurting his arm.

"I'm so sorry." Jane wished she could take some of his pain away from him.

"It's fine," Dev answered, teeth clenched tightly.

Working together, they slowly removed his jacket. Jane blinked back tears when Dev hissed in pain as the fitted sleeve eased past the slice in his arm.

"Now the shirt?" She tried to keep her voice light.

He nodded.

Jane reached for the top button, and she slid it loose with ease. A sliver of Dev's chest appeared. The skin was dusted with a bit of dark hair. Jane stared. And she stared some more. She reached for the second button, but it didn't slide through as easily. It seemed all her fingers had turned clumsy. After a bit more fumbling, she slid the button through.

The shirt gaped open more.

Jane stared more.

Dev's chest—

She shook her head. *He was bleeding, and she was ogling his chest.*

Jane glanced up to find Dev watching her. There was a strange mix of pain and humor and something else, something hotter, in his eyes. She couldn't hold his gaze and returned her attention to the next buttons.

"Here we go," she murmured and pulled the shirt off, moving slowly.

Dev inhaled sharply as the shirt moved past his arm. Jane dropped the sliced, bloody garment to the floor and got her first good look at his arm.

Jane narrowed her eyes. A fiery, ugly sensation churned in her belly. She could not recall being more furious in her life than she was at this moment, seeing the angry red gash on Dev's upper arm. It was a desecration, the slice across his flesh. She wanted to fling a score of knives at the man who'd done this. She wanted to poison his tea, smash in his face with a heavy terra cotta pot and leave him bruised and battered on the ground in a dirty alleyway.

"I'll kill him."

Dev started at her words. "I mean it," Jane said vehemently. "When we sort out who that…that *bastard* was in the alley, I'm going to end him for hurting you."

"Jane." Dev's voice was calm, soothing.

She met his steady gaze.

"Jane, I'll be fine. Yes, it hurts, but once the doctor stitches and bandages me up, I'll be all right. I'll heal."

Some of her red fury receded.

"I'll heal," he repeated, and then he took her hand in his.

She closed her eyes, the warm press of his fingers against her hand tethering her to the earth, to this room, to this moment. The vision of the broken corpse of her enemy disappeared.

She squeezed his hand and opened her eyes to meet his gaze. "Thank you."

He nodded. "Any time you need someone to pull you back from the brink of a murderous frenzy, I'm your man."

I'm your man.

Jane drew a deep, steadying breath. She would not think of his last few words, of their potential to most certainly un-steady her breath. Her heart. Her entire life.

"Let's get this wound cleaned up," she said, pouring some of the water into a smaller basin. After dipping one of the bandages into the warm water, she moved to Dev's side. Her hand hovered over the cut.

"Go ahead," Dev urged. "I trust you."

Jane swallowed. Keeping her touch light, she dabbed at the area around the cut. There was so much dried blood. It took several of the cloths, but she eventually removed it. The problem was that the wound continued to seep. He clearly needed stitches.

As Jane contemplated whether she should attempt to clean

the wound itself, the sound of heavy footsteps sounded in the hall.

"The doctor." She set the cloth down.

"Will you stay?" Dev asked. He looked vulnerable in some way that he hadn't before, despite his shirtless state and wounded arm.

The thought of an actual needle poking through his flesh, literally sewing him up like he was the seam on an article of clothing, made Jane's stomach feel like it was full of caterpillars.

But she couldn't say no.

She wouldn't.

"I'll stay," she promised.

After a courtesy knock on the door, Lydia entered, the doctor in tow. He was a middle-aged man with a round face and kind eyes.

He introduced himself, examined the wound, and declared that indeed it would need stitches. Lydia excused herself, and although a part of Jane wished she could follow her out of the room, instead she pulled a chair over.

It was one of the chairs by the fireplace where she'd sat with Dev only last night. It felt like forever ago somehow, their quiet conversation in front of the glowing fire. What a contrast between that sweet, almost magical, memory and what was happening right now. Dev hissed in pain as the doctor pinched together the slice in his arm. Jane caught Dev's eye, holding his gaze steady with her own while the doctor pulled the thread through his skin. Dev flinched. Without thought, she reached for his hand. He clasped hers, squeezing tightly at each poke until the last stitch was complete. She could scarcely decipher the emotions in his eyes, but it pulled at her, nonetheless.

"All done," the doctor finally said. The man rocked back on his heels and seemed to be admiring the row of even stitches along Dev's arm. "I'll show you how to apply a healing salve and wrap the wound so you can rebandage him tomorrow."

Jane realized with a start that the doctor had addressed that last comment to her. He must think they were related.

Or married.

Jane shifted in her seat. "Ah, I'm not sure—"

"Thank you, darling, for tending to me," Dev interrupted. He winked when the doctor turned to rummage through his medical bag.

Jane scowled at him but didn't voice a contradiction.

She supposed they could meet here at Pippa and Jack's every day. She was already coming here to work on her plants. After changing his bandage tomorrow, they could plan the next part of their strategy to find proof of Rowling's true heir and get the LCA reopened.

Assuming Dev was still up for it.

Jane thought back to Lydia's warning about the danger they now faced and added an addendum.

Assuming *she* was still up to it.

The game had changed now that someone was trying to murder them. Jane thought of her guards, left behind when she'd needed them most. In the end, she'd managed to save Dev and herself. And Dev had bravely fought against the attacker. Although the guards her parents insisted accompanying her would help keep them safe as they continued their investigation, there was no way she'd be able to search for the evidence with them in tow. The price for complete safety was a complete lack of freedom. Oh, what a mess.

And they'd have to sort out their next move as their lead at Boodle's had come to a dead end with it being far too dangerous to return there now.

Once the wound care instructions and supplies were dispensed and Jane had the doctor shown out, she leaned against the door and looked at Dev. The bright white of the bandage contrasted with the smooth gold of his skin. He still sat on the old blanket on the bed, the bed where Jane had slept just last night, as if he were afraid to move about the room. Perhaps he still worried about bleeding all over the place even though his wound was covered.

The fact that he'd had to bleed at all made Jane want to pound her fists against the heavy wooden door behind her. Or howl like some feral creature.

"You could have been killed today." She pulled away from the door.

"You, too." He watched as she walked toward him. "You should have run."

"I wouldn't have left you." She stood only inches away now, her dress nearly brushing against his knees.

"I wish you had." He reached out for her hand.

Jane's breath caught in her throat.

"Although if you'd run, I'd likely be dead."

Jane's heart stuttered.

Dev gently tugged on her hand, and Jane stepped forward between his spread thighs. He looked down where his hand held hers, and slowly, deliberately, he brought her hand up. Jane watched, transfixed, as he brushed the lightest of kisses against her knuckles. Her skin tingled.

"You saved me." His breath was warm against her skin.

Jane could only nod.

"You saved my life. What a brave woman you are." Dev kissed her hand again.

"Dev," she whispered.

Her skin was hot and sensitive. She wanted him to touch more than her hand. She wanted him to kiss more than her knuckles.

"Jane." His voice sounded like gravel, like need.

He tugged her again, and she moved willingly to sit on his thigh, tucked in against his left side. Despite the feeling of wanting pulsing through her, she was aware enough to be grateful that she was on his uninjured side.

"I want to kiss you," he whispered. "Do you want that too?"

Jane stared into his deep-blue eyes. There was no twinkle of shared mirth lurking in their depths now. Only intent. Only heat.

"Yes."

Her word hung in the air between them for a moment, and then his mouth was on hers.

Jane gasped, surprised by the warmth, the press, and the immediacy of his lips moving. Timidly at first, she returned Dev's kiss, but soon she understood the rhythm. The give and take. The sweet parting. The flick of tongue against tongue and lip and teeth.

My God.

It was incredible.

And she wanted more.

Jane's arms wound around Dev's neck, pulling him closer to her. Her back arched, and she pressed her breasts against him. Against his bare chest.

One hand untangled from the hair at his nape and trailed down his neck, along his shoulder, and across his chest.

Dev moaned.

Jane sighed into the kiss. His flesh was firm and warm beneath her fingers. The smoothness of his skin, the hardness of his muscles beneath, and the very maleness of him…she felt like she was going to combust.

He pulled away from her mouth and trailed hot, open-mouthed kisses along her jaw and neck.

"Jane," he murmured between kisses, "you are so beautiful. So brave. So very clever."

Her body hummed in response to his words. She raised her chin, granting him better access to her neck.

"Dev," she moaned. "It feels so good."

He kissed down her neck and along her collarbone as he made a low rumble of satisfaction. She traced the ridges of his stomach, where his muscles flexed and jumped in response to her touch.

She hadn't known it was like this.

With plants, they mated almost accidentally when bees, wind, or perhaps a determined botanist moved pollen from one plant to another. There was no wanting. No heat.

It was science. Nature. The practical way to continue life.

This was anything but practical.

Her skin was aflame wherever he touched. Her lips felt tender from their kisses. Her blood whooshed through her veins with the speed of a runaway carriage.

And then there was a knock at the door.

Chapter Ten

DEV JERKED AT the sound of knocking, the rushing awareness of their surroundings like a bucket of cold water poured over his head.

Pulling his mouth away from the sweet skin of Jane's neck felt almost as painful as getting his arm sewn shut.

He drew a deep breath. Part of him wanted to pretend he hadn't heard the knock. Pretend there was no one else in the house. There was no one and nothing else in the universe but him and Jane and their electrifying kisses.

But that wasn't true.

There was an entire world that would be scandalized by what they'd just done. In the eyes of proper English society, Jane was a proper lady who should not be touched until her wedding night and Dev was a lowly servant, worthy of the same amount of attention or kindness as they'd bestow upon a carpet.

Less, most likely, if the carpet was an Aubusson.

He gently eased Jane from his lap.

She stared, unblinking with her hazel eyes like two wide circles of autumn. Her lips were red and kiss-stung, her face flushed, and her chest heaving as she gasped for breath. She looked, in summary, like a woman who'd just been thoroughly kissed.

"Jane?" Lydia called from the hallway. "I've brought some

clothes for Dev."

Dev shifted on the bed, uncomfortably aware of the bulge in the front of his trousers and his own likely state of disarray after what had been a truly exceptional kiss.

It felt like a falsehood to think of it as a mere meeting of lips.

It had been perhaps the most erotic moment of his life, and aside from his sliced clothing, neither of them had even undressed.

"Jane?" Lydia's voice was louder.

The situation would not be improved if she barged in. If she found her sister-in-law's cousin—did that make them cousins-in-law?—staring at him with glazed eyes and kiss-swollen lips, things could get very unpleasant for them.

"Jane," he murmured, taking her hand.

She blinked a few times before finally focusing on him.

"Can you answer the door? Lydia's brought fresh clothes for me."

Jane seemed to consider his words for a few moments before finally nodding. He wanted to pull her back onto his lap so that he might brush tendrils of red-gold hair back behind her ear and hold her tenderly while they both waited for their racing hearts to return to their normal paces. He wanted to spend hours locked up with her in this room, kissing and touching and gasping together. He wanted to hear her thoughts on this newness between them, her thoughts on *everything*, really. Her nimble mind fascinated him.

But he did none of those things. He sat on the bed as he'd sat since they had arrived. As if it were his body sewn to the blanket and holding him immobile instead of his arm that had been stitched.

Jane opened the door.

Silence.

Then whispers from Lydia, quiet mumbled words he could not make out, but he could imagine.

The door shut with a quiet click.

Jane turned, clothing draped across one arm. "I have a shirt and jacket for you."

Dev rose from the bed, breaking the invisible bond that had held him there with a strange sort of inertia. "Thank you."

They stood, feet apart, staring at one another.

"I…" She licked her lips. "That was…"

Dev nodded. "I know."

Her eyes roamed over his bare chest, and he felt her gaze as if her fingers were exploring him once more. His temperature shot up a few degrees.

No.

They couldn't do that again.

Too much was at stake. He listed the reasons in his mind, reminders of why kissing Jane was a reckless decision. Someone wanted him dead. Their quest for the marriage certificate. The looming deadline with the courts to determine who was the rightful heir. And getting the Ladies Covert Academy reopened.

It mattered.

All these reasons mattered.

It would be the height of selfishness if he allowed his own feelings, his own desires, to come first.

He knew what a selfish man looked like. He'd lived with one his entire life. And he would not be that. He couldn't. It would crush his very soul.

He finally spoke. "We shouldn't have kissed."

Jane flinched.

His fingers flexed as he fought the desire to reach for her, to pull her close for comforting.

"I'm sorry," she whispered, looking down.

"Don't apologize." His voice was harsher than he'd intended. He tried again. "We were two consenting adults. It hurt no one. But…it puts our work in jeopardy. And our work matters to both of us."

Jane nodded. Her chest rose and fell in several deep breaths, and then her shoulders went back, and she stood straight. She stared him right in the eye, and despite the agony of watching her hide away, or perhaps even smother, the feelings that had just erupted between them, part of him was so very proud of her strength and determination.

"We are partners," she said. "We'll continue the work."

"Yes."

It was an oath of sorts.

And if part of him wanted to howl in protest and gather her in his arms and kiss every inch of her soft, warm skin, well…

That was just too bad.

⇛✦⇚

AFTER DEV LEFT—DRESSED in clothing borrowed from Jack, much to his horror—Jane went to work in her laboratory. She penned a quick letter to her parents informing them that she was enjoying her time with her cousin and would be home a few hours later than she'd originally thought.

Since she was here, she might as well spend some time with her plants. Hopefully, her work would take her mind off the kiss.

The kiss with Dev.

Her first kiss, truth be told.

But most certainly not her last.

Jane watered and repotted and measured and jotted down notes while she replayed the kiss over and over. The feel of their tongues caressing—that had been a shocking experience. She'd had no idea that was part of kissing. And while it seemed bizarre in theory, in practice it was wonderful. And the pleasure she'd felt pinging through her body when she'd touched his bare chest— that had been a surprise as well. She hadn't known the feel of her fingers on his skin would elicit such a thrill.

But she reminded herself, dropping a container of potting soil onto her work table, they were not to repeat the experience.

The expression on Lydia's face, once she had taken in Jane's disheveled appearance, was enough to drive that point home. And then Dev's declaration that it had been a mistake… Well, there was no use dwelling on that.

What she *should* dwell on, she decided as she set about organizing her many bottles of dried plants, was the efficacy of her mystery herb as a tool of defense.

Less thoughts on passion and more on plants.

Less smooches and more soil.

Yes, that was the spirit.

Jane studied the jar she'd taken her sample from that morning. This mystery herb—and she was certain she could sort out which plant it was with more time and a visit to the plant vendor in the market—had a most powerful effect.

Jack had become quite incapacitated after just a few sips.

When she'd sniffed it herself, she'd had an immediate reaction, sneezing and experiencing stinging eyes.

And when she'd blown it into the face of the man in the alley?

Well, she'd basically saved Dev's life. He was strong and quick and clever, but he'd been unarmed against a man with a knife.

When he'd shouted that she should run away, she hadn't even considered it. In what world had he thought she'd leave him alone with a masked criminal intent on murder?

She'd been training with Pippa and Lydia under the tutelage of Pippa's fencing master. Jane knew the basics of swordplay and could throw a dagger with relative accuracy. But she'd had neither sword nor dagger there in that alley, and unlike Pippa—who only left the house when armed—Jane wasn't yet skilled enough with a blade to ensure her parents would not see their worst fear come to fruition. In truth, she could not put herself in such danger again. It would destroy her parents if anything were to happen to her.

Whether she lived or died shouldn't be left to something out of her own control, such as the presence or skill of the guards her parents assigned to her. There should be a different way.

What if... Jane rolled the capped jar of herbs in her hand as thoughts swirled in her mind. What if women didn't have to be defenseless as they went about their lives?

What if this herb could act as a deterrent? As a weapon of defense?

From her limited understanding of fencing and knife throwing after several weeks of lessons with Pippa and her fencing master, Jane knew that most women were woefully unprotected if someone wished to do them violence. The typical woman didn't have access to the same training as men—pugilism, shooting practice, and fencing lessons. Men even carried a sword at their side for ornamentation. Meanwhile, women weren't even allowed pockets in their gowns to carry a handkerchief, let alone a weapon for self-protection.

But what if this nasty little herb could level the playing field?

What if Jane could find a way to package it so that a woman could deploy the herb if she ever needed to fight off an attacker?

She imagined her uncle at the moment the highwaymen had shot him. Her parents had spoken of it enough that she had a clear picture in her mind—him lying on the hard-packed dirt of the road, the ground around him slowly growing red as the blood seeped from his body. His wife and young daughter weeping over his still form.

Jane always viewed her parents' unceasing worry for her safety as smothering, but if she was armed with a defensive herb, they wouldn't need to worry. She wouldn't need to worry.

Women wouldn't need to worry.

Jane shook her head in wonder. This could change everything.

But her trip to the market to find out the herb's name and origin would have to wait. Right now, she had to return home, let her parents see that all was well, and then formulate the next part of her and Dev's plans.

But before she left her lab, she refilled the small vial with the herb and tucked it into her bodice.

If the man from the alley came for them again, she'd be ready.

Chapter Eleven

"YOU KNOW," LYDIA gasped two days later, leaning forward with her hands on her knees, "there might be easier ways to get rid of men than stabbing them."

"But none are quite as fun as running them through with an épée," Pippa replied. She was hardly out of breath after their lesson with *Señor* Martín, the fencing instructor.

As Jane wiped the sweat from her forehead, she decided she hated her cousin. Just a little bit.

Ah well, it wasn't Pippa's fault that she'd been at this a full year longer than Jane or Lydia. It turned out, studying botany and writing fiery political essays were not quite as physically strenuous as what Pippa had been up to during her time at the LCA.

"Is there any particular man you're interested in stabbing?" Jane asked between her own gasps for breath.

Señor Martín tutted from the far side of the sparring room that Pippa had set up in her new home once she and Jack had married. "Now, now," he called in a cheery Spanish accent. "Remember, fencing is about honor above all else. There is no honor in stabbing people simply because one doesn't like them."

"Thank you for the sound advice, *Señor*," Lydia called. She turned back to Pippa and Jane, and her expression turned almost sinister. "There is, in fact, a certain man I'd enjoy running through."

Jane bit back a smile. Lydia was an absolute chameleon—sweet, kind, and loyal one minute and practically Machiavellian the next. She supposed being kidnapped and nearly murdered by supposedly upstanding members of society because of her political writings could sour a person.

"Who?" Jane asked, wiping her brow again with the sleeve of her men's shirt. Pippa had recommended they wear breeches and lawn shirts for the fencing lessons, and although Jane had felt awkward at first, now she enjoyed the freedom of movement. Plus, it would be best to avoid awkward conversations with her lady's maid about why her gowns were sweat-stained.

Jane and Pippa both leaned forward when Lydia began to speak. "If you must know, I am currently quite vexed at Lord Lovell."

Pippa pulled back and frowned. "Benedict? What has the scamp done now?"

Jane visited Pippa and Jack's home often enough to have spent a fair bit of time with Jack's best friend, Benedict Southcott, Lord Lovell. He *was* a scamp, but in a loveable way. The ton's gossips declared him an irascible flirt, a bit of a rake, and perhaps even a ne'er do-well. Jane always found him to be great fun, although not someone a person could take seriously or rely on.

Lydia rolled her eyes. "What hasn't he done? He's always about, he constantly asks me how I'm doing or if I've read anything interesting lately, and the other day he even inquired about my *health*!"

Jane blinked.

Pippa opened her mouth and then shut it again.

"It sounds like he's...being a polite gentleman?" Pippa ventured.

"Exactly!" Lydia pointed a finger at her. "What's his game? He's never before asked me if I needed him to ring for a shawl because there was a bit of a draft in the air. It's complete madness."

Jane caught Pippa's eye and found her cousin biting back a smile. They likely sported similar expressions as they each attempted to contain their mirth. Unfortunately for Lydia, this was far too amusing to leave alone.

"You're absolutely right," Jane declared, shaking her head in mock horror. "The man is a monster. We should have him murdered."

Lydia rolled her eyes, but the corner of her lips twitched.

Pippa began to snicker, Jane joined in, and soon the three friends were all laughing together.

Ah, it felt good to laugh and let the tension that had been her constant friend the last couple of days fade a bit. Jane hadn't seen or heard from Dev since the day before last. He was supposed to come by Pippa and Jack's house each day so she could change his wrapping and reapply the salve, but he hadn't stopped by. He resided in a wealthy household where they likely had medical supplies of their own, but she had still been worried.

And although she understood his need to convalesce following the knife attack, she was itching to get back to their investigation. He needed to find evidence of Rowling's heir for his mistress, Lady Rowling, and Jane needed to convince the lady that the threat to the LCA was behind them so they could reopen the academy for all its members.

Why, just the feeling of companionship she had here with Pippa and Lydia was argument enough that the LCA needed to be reopened. Most of the women didn't have this sort of connection outside the walls of the LCA. They couldn't meet openly with fellow members for fencing lessons or uncensored conversations about political dissent and botany experiments.

Thoughts of all the moments of laughter those other members were missing out on dampened Jane's mood.

"I haven't laughed so much since I left the Smythe's house party," Lydia declared once they'd relocated to the sitting room.

"Was it a nice mix of people there?" Pippa asked as she poured them tea. Proper tea and not any of Jane's mixes, Pippa had been certain to check.

Jane had only rolled her eyes at her cousin's teasing. Was she forever to be remembered as the tea poisoner?

"There were several of my friends from finishing school," Lydia replied. "Some had husbands in tow and others came with a mother or a companion like I did."

Lydia and Jack had lost their parents and didn't have any other close relatives, so whenever Lydia needed a matronly presence in her life, Jack would pay a handsome sum to their old housekeeper from their childhood who lived most of the year in happy retirement at a countryside cottage. According to Lydia, she was wonderful company and made the perfect companion at events such as the occasional house party she attended.

"I was invited to another house party," Lydia continued, "but I decided to decline. I saw the guest list, and it contained quite a few gentlemen who are known to be more interested in a lady's dowry than her personality." She grimaced.

Pippa set down her teacup. "Who are these so-called gentlemen? I can't believe anyone would disrespect you so. Shall I challenge them to swords at dawn?"

Jane sipped her tea. Her cousin was joking, she was *mostly* certain.

Lydia waved her hand through the air as if it hardly mattered. "Oh, just the usual assortment of second sons, heirs to titles with empty coffers, and lowly sons of baronets. They see me in the parlor at these gatherings and instead of noticing my keen mind or even my face, they just see a big bag of money. It's rather…dispiriting."

Something niggled at the back of Jane's mind.

"Who are these men?" she asked. "Specifically? You said second sons…and"—it came to her in a flash—"sons of baronets? Who, exactly? Which sons of baronets will be there?"

Lydia pursed her lips. "Why? Is aught amiss?"

Jane set her teacup down. "Is Nigel Skevington on the invite list? Is he going to be at the house party?"

"Why, I do believe he is, along with his parents. His mother is the mousiest little thing, and the father is not the sharpest tool in the shed, if you know what I mean. Why, I once heard the man wax on for at least twenty minutes about how the French Revolution was caused by a game of tennis—"

"When is this house party?" Jane interrupted. "And is it out in the countryside?"

"It started today. And yes, it's out in Surrey at the estate of Lord and Lady Brambleton. But what does this have to do with anything?" Lydia frowned. "Jane, is there something we should know?"

Jane was on her feet and striding to the door. "I have an idea. Thank you so much for the fencing and the tea," she called over her shoulder. "And for the helpful information!"

AN HOUR LATER, Jane was creeping through a garden, frequently halting behind bushes and tree trunks. She'd had very little personal experience with espionage until quite recently. Was she even doing this correctly? What *was* the proper way to sneak up on a house where one had recently been a frequent guest but was no longer welcome?

Well, she *had* longed for a life of adventure.

Perhaps this was what it looked like—getting pricked by rose thorns while evading a maid beating out a small area rug by the back door.

Once the maid was gone and the garden was quiet once more, Jane crept closer to Lady Rowling's home.

She was almost as familiar with the LCA as she was with her own house. And she needed to locate one suddenly recalcitrant man with deep-blue eyes, a recently sewn-together arm, and a kiss that could—

No. She was not going to dwell on that. *No sir.*

Besides, she had a plan. Or at least, the beginnings of a plan.

After the attack on Dev, they couldn't return to Boodle's. Even though broad-shouldered Johnny might not be the attacker, it was too much of a risk. Dev could have *died*. So that avenue of investigation was closed to them.

But when one door closed, there was always a window to go through.

Sometimes literally.

Knowing that the Skevingtons were away at a house party in the countryside had gotten her brain churning, and before she'd known it, she'd developed a scheme worthy of a criminal mastermind.

Well, she *hoped* it would be worthy of a criminal mastermind. If it was, in fact, worthy of a Dagger Dan sort of crook, then she and Dev just might find themselves being shipped off to the penal colony in Australia.

Australia was lovely this time of year, wasn't it? Or was it too hot? Or...too cold? When she had a bit of spare time, she'd be certain to investigate that continent's weather patterns.

She scanned the back of the building. The window up ahead likely belonged to the study where she'd found Dev pouring through stacks of paper at the start of all of this. Or, as he'd wished her to believe, where he'd been diligently dusting with a napkin.

Men were such silly creatures.

Perhaps he was there again, looking through more papers in his quest to find proof of Rowling's true heir. A study was as good a place as any to recuperate after sustaining a knife wound, she supposed.

Crouching low as she hurried from bush to bush, she made her way to the window. She slowly raised her head, peering inside.

There on the couch sat Dev. He was in his usual Indian garb, and she briefly wondered if he'd had any trouble fitting his bandage under the sleeve.

And next to him on the couch sat Lady Rowling. She looked icy and regal, as usual. Her pale blond hair was pulled tight, and although Jane couldn't make out the color of her eyes from here, she knew they were a glacier blue. The woman somehow managed to both fund and guide a secret academy whose sole purpose was giving more freedom to women, and also arm herself in an invisible cloak of disdainful aloofness.

It was quite a feat to appear simultaneously heroic and haughty.

Right now, it looked as if Dev and Lady Rowling were in the midst of an intense conversation. Dev gestured with one hand—his left, as his right likely still pained him—while he spoke. Lady Rowling shook her head and gave a reply.

And then, Lady Rowling leaned forward and put her hand on Dev's arm.

She put her *hand* on Dev's *arm.*

Jane's fingers tightened around the windowpane.

What was going on? Why was the mistress of the household touching a servant? Why was she touching *Dev*? This wasn't right at all.

Inside the study, they both stood up. Lady Rowling wiped at her eyes.

Oh heavens, was she…was she *crying*? Jane could hardly imagine Lady Rowling possessing emotions, let alone functioning tear ducts. Perhaps she was distraught over the distance between her and her secret son who'd been left behind in India for safekeeping.

Lady Rowling leaned forward, resting her head against Dev's shoulder.

And Dev allowed it!

He allowed Lady Rowling to lean against him. No, they were hugging now. Her arms were wrapped around Dev's back.

Jane wanted to shout. She wanted to bang on the glass window until it rattled under her fists. She wanted to tear Lady Rowling's hair out and scream in Dev's face and…and…

The hug was over.

Lady Rowling left the study, and Dev sank back onto the sofa.

Jane could only stare at him through the window. She felt as if a hailstorm had blown in without warning, destroying a crop of tender plants growing in a field under the lethal rain of ice bombs. *She* was a little plant. She'd just started reaching out toward the sun after a lifetime buried in the safe, dark earth. She'd just started to unfurl, to seek adventure, to feel something deep and hot and yearning for another person, and then down came the hail.

It wasn't fair.

Lady Rowling had everything. She had a fortune. She had a child. She had the means to reopen the LCA.

And now it seemed she had Dev as well.

Jane pounded on the glass.

She jolted back in shock when Dev looked up, when she realized what she'd done.

Before she could decide on a course of action, he was there at the window, pulling it open.

"What's going on?" he said through the opening, eyes scanning over her. "Are you hurt?"

Jane laughed, but the sound wasn't humorous. "Why don't you tell me? What's going on, Dev? What's going on with Lady Rowling?"

His eyebrows shot up.

"Well?" She put her hands on her hips. "I saw you two embracing."

He said nothing.

"Are you having an affair with her?"

His mouth fell open.

"Because if you are, then it was quite unfair of you to kiss me."

"I am *not* having an affair with her!"

Jane glared at Dev. Dev glared right back.

"Well, it seems we are at an impasse," he said, "and I don't wish to have this sort of conversation through a windowsill.

Come on up." Dev reached his arms through.

Jane took a step back, but a rather poky bush that she'd be certain to identify later brought her up short. "I beg your pardon?"

"Come on. I'll pull you in. We can't risk someone spotting you out there in the yard, and now isn't a good time for you to come traipsing through Lady Rowling's home. So come on." He wiggled his hands at her in emphasis.

Jane considered. Would she rather have this conversation when they were face-to-face rather than arguing through a window like a pair of maniacs? Yes. Was she looking forward to being hauled through said window like a bag of laundry? No.

Well, she didn't actually know if laundry was hauled through windows, but Dev likely did.

Jane sighed. There was such a wide gulf between them. Perhaps the physical distance created by this window did not need to widen it even more.

"All right." She reached out and clasped his hands.

He pulled, and before she could shriek, she was through the window. Dev helped her get on her feet inside the study.

"Well," she huffed, smoothing down her skirt, "that was quite an entrance."

Dev's eyes crinkled at the corners, and for a moment she thought—she hoped, really—that he might twinkle at her. Instead, he rubbed his right arm in apparent discomfort.

"Your injury." She stepped close to inspect the area. "Did you tear your stitches?"

"No." He let his hand drop. "It was just a twinge. It's been healing nicely, actually."

"Oh."

Jane looked at Dev. The silence sat awkwardly between them.

"Would you care to sit?" He gestured to the sofa.

"Why yes, thank you kindly," she replied.

My goodness, had they ever been so stilted and polite to one another? This was torture.

"Listen," she said once they were both seated. "I know you and I are...well, there's nothing between us other than our investigation and one little kiss."

Dev's brows snapped together, and his expression turned stormy.

Jane held up her hand to forestall whatever grumpy sentiment he was about to express. "No, I completely understand how things stand. No need to explain. I'm a lady full grown, and you didn't hurt my feelings when you swept another woman up in an embrace, mere days after our passionate kisses. No hurt feelings at all. None whatsoever."

Jane stopped herself from further protests. She had perhaps said enough.

Dev shifted on the sofa. "Jane." His voice was soft. Placating.

She hated it.

"What you saw between me and Lady Rowling...it wasn't what you thought."

Jane crossed her arms over her chest.

"Lady Rowling came to India as Lord Rowling's new bride ten years ago. She was only seventeen. She didn't know anyone in India, and she was homesick and...and scared, although she'd gut me before allowing me to say that to anyone." His lip quirked.

Jane scowled.

Dev cleared his throat. "Well, her parents had basically sold her to Lord Rowling, a man in his fifties. He paid off the family's debt in exchange for a lovely, young bride. He'd been a widower for many years, you see"—he paused to swallow, the gulp sounding loud in the study—"and apparently he thought he'd go further in his career if he was perceived by the company as being a family man."

Dev's voice had gone bitter, a strange bleakness crossing his face. Jane fought the urge to reach out and take his hand. But no, he had Lady Rowling to comfort him. Lady Rowling, who had been a child bride, was basically friendless and alone when she arrived in a new place far from her home and family. Most likely in need of a friend…She recalibrated, adjusting what she'd seen through the window given this new information.

"So…you and Lady Rowling…" Jane watched Dev carefully. "How old were you when she arrived?"

"I was fourteen."

"And she was in need of a friend…"

Dev nodded.

"So, what you're telling me is…" Jane wondered how often a person could trail off after half a sentence before people assumed they were incapable of conversation.

"Lady Rowling and I became friends," Dev said, his voice clear. His eyes were clear too. "And we still are. I trust her and she trusts me. And when there's been a robbery, missing evidence, and an attempt on someone's life, you hold tight to those you trust."

Jane slowly filled her lungs before exhaling a cleansing breath.

She believed him.

"I believe you." She hadn't meant to say it, but there it was.

Dev nodded, and his shoulders relaxed in what was likely relief. Perhaps it wasn't restful to have someone pounding on the windows, interrupting a perfectly nice sit-and-think after a stressful conversation.

Speaking of…

"What were you and Lady Rowling speaking of before the, er, embrace?" Jane asked.

Dev grimaced. "She's concerned that the hunt has become too dangerous. She doesn't know of your involvement at all. I wasn't even going to tell her about the knife attack, but she heard through the servant gossip that I was using bandages and salve from the household's supply, and she confronted me about it."

Jane shook her head. "If you'd come to Pippa and Jack's as we'd agreed, this wouldn't have happened."

Dev wrinkled his nose at her. "You like to be right, don't you?"

"Doesn't everyone?"

Dev shrugged. "I suppose I'd rather be doing right than have others think I'm right."

Jane had never wanted to roll her eyes so badly in her life. "Did you know that you can be rather annoying? Does Lady Rowling know about this sanctimonious side of yours? Because if she did, I'm sure she'd reconsider the whole friendship thing."

Dev laughed.

Jane grinned at him, and it was like all the pressure, the awkwardness, and the tension between them had fled. All that remained was the very easy companionship they'd developed once they'd settled into this unorthodox partnership of theirs.

Well, one more thing remained.

The kiss.

Jane now knew the taste of passion, and the tug of it was still there between them, despite their own friendship, their own connection.

But this was not the time to get into that. She had to redirect them to the very reason she'd come here in the first place, sneaking about like the little criminal she soon hoped to be.

"So, despite our promising lead with Johnny the broad-shouldered footman, I don't think we should return to Boodle's," Jane said.

Dev touched his fingers to his right arm. "I agree. It's too dangerous now." He shook his head. "I'm not sure what our next steps should be though. I've continued to comb through the documents I have here from Rowling's own files and the barrister's as well, but so far, I haven't found the certificate or anything else that proves the marriage or the son's legitimacy. I even have both Parth and Meera helping me search."

Meera was Lady Rowling's secretary, a very no-nonsense woman who had capably handled many of the LCA's projects in the past, including when the whole academy had taken a last-minute trip to an orphanage in the countryside to hand out the clothing they'd sewn and knitted.

"I'm glad you have help," Jane replied. "I imagine decades of documents, both for the title and his position in the East India

Company, add up to quite a lot of reading."

Dev rubbed his eyes. "At this rate, I'll need spectacles before the year is out."

Jane's stomach flipped. The image of Dev in spectacles was just too much. Those expressive, twinkling eyes framed by carefully-wrought metal would be more handsomeness than should be permitted in any one place.

"Well, Parth and Meera can keep up the work on the documents," Jane said, "but you and I are undertaking a different challenge."

"Oh?"

Jane leaned forward. "I just learned that Sir Albert, his wife, and their weaselly son Nigel just left town today for a house party in the Surrey countryside. Aside from a few servants, their house is empty."

Dev watched her warily. "And?"

"And," Jane said, clasping her hands together, "that means tonight would be a perfect time for us to break in."

"Break in?"

Jane nodded. "We search the place. Carefully, of course. It wouldn't do to wake the servants."

"Servants need their sleep," he agreed, but he was clearly just humoring her.

"It's our best option right now," Jane argued. "If Sir Albert or perhaps Nigel were behind the break-in, then it stands to reason that whatever they stole would be in their house, right?"

Dev rubbed his hand through his hair. "This just seems so dangerous. What if we're caught?"

"We won't be. We'll be careful. Quiet. We'll use a minimum of light. And," she added, knowing this was her ace card, "we don't have any other leads to follow."

Dev sighed and closed his eyes. "Fine."

Jane did a little dance in her seat.

"But," he added, cracking one eye open, "if there's any sign of trouble, we leave immediately."

"Agreed. But there won't be any trouble. I'm certain of it."

Chapter Twelve

DEV RUBBED HIS hands together against the late-night chill, eyes straining for a glimpse of Jane in the darkness. They'd decided to meet at one in the morning around the corner from her house. He'd wanted to meet her in the back garden, but she'd successfully argued that with the strong guard presence maintained by her parents, it was too risky.

He heard a rustle, and there she was.

Dev tried to ignore the sudden pounding in his chest at the sight of her. The dark shadows of night accentuated the curves of her cheekbones and the fullness of her lips. The strap of a satchel draped across her chest over a simple, dark-colored gown, likely borrowed from a maid again.

"Ready?" she asked.

Dev nodded, and they walked a few blocks in silence until they reached a hackney stand. Jane gave the sleepy driver the address, and they climbed into the hired carriage.

Dev spied something suspicious—most likely a bit of greasy food left behind—on one of the seats. "We'll have to sit on this side together."

Jane wrinkled her nose at the abandoned food and took a seat beside him.

"Did you have any trouble sneaking out?" Dev asked. He tried to keep his leg from touching hers, but with them on the same side and with the jostling of the carriage, it was an impossible task.

"I've gotten a lot of practice lately, so I had no trouble."

In the close confines of the carriage, he could smell her scent. Soap and something floral. Had she dabbed a bit of perfume at her wrists and neck at some point today? The image of her rubbing the cool tip of a glass bottle against her skin had him shifting in his seat. Their sides pressed even more closely together. Dev's pulse kicked up, and he cursed himself for his foolish fantasies.

"Do you, ah, leave out the back door?"

Perhaps focusing on the details of her frequent escapes from her guards would help him to focus on what mattered—their quest to find evidence of Rowling's heir. And to get the LCA reopened.

Somehow, the two had become equally important in his mind. Jane's needs and wishes mattered as much as his own.

"Oh, I crawled out the window," Jane answered as if it were nothing.

Dev jerked to face her. "What?"

She shrugged. "There's a very sturdy tree right outside my bedroom. A lovely ash. I just crawled out and shimmied on down."

Dev pictured her falling from a great height, lying bruised and broken on the ground.

"I was very careful," Jane said as if reading his mind. "Look at me." She gestured to her body. "Not a single scratch."

Dev didn't wish to be rude, so he gave her body a look over. Even in the darkness, her sweet curves and graceful limbs were visible. His skin grew hot, so he blurted out, "How do you manage it in a dress?"

Jane's mouth quirked. "I pull the back of my dress up between my legs and tuck it into my bodice. One must keep their hands free when climbing a tree, you know."

Dev made some strangling sound in reply. Was it warm in

here? Perhaps they needed to lower the window.

The hack slowed to a stop.

Jane peeked out the window. "This is the place."

Dev hopped out and held out his hand to assist Jane. Despite her gloves, he could feel the warmth of her hand in his. And then she was upfront, paying the driver, and the hack pulled away, leaving them alone in the street.

"How did you manage to get Sir Albert's address?" Dev asked, keeping his voice quiet. He hadn't considered all that she'd done to make this happen until now.

"My mother's address book," Jane murmured. "She was introduced to him and his wife in Bath on a recent trip. She's very polite like that, sending correspondence to everyone she meets, even if she doesn't consider them friends. She feels it would be rude not to."

"She writes letters to people she doesn't care about because…otherwise it would be rude?" Truly, English society was most strange. What would it be like for an outsider to be plunged into the midst of such people?

Dev's stomach tightened.

"Forget about the letters," Jane whispered. "Let's sneak around to the back."

Dev followed Jane past the row of tidy brick homes. The Skevingtons didn't live in a grand house like Lady Rowling or Jane's family, but their neighborhood was considered respectable, and the houses were well-maintained and tidy.

In the back was a small garden separated from the neighbors by a brick wall. All the windows were dark, the house and its inhabitants asleep.

Dev led the way to the back door. He had little hope but gave the handle a try anyway. It was locked.

"Let me try," Jane said, moving forward.

She knelt down so she was at eye level with the doorknob and reached into her hair, pulling out a couple of pins.

Dev blinked. "You can pick locks?"

She grew her own poison, capably evaded armed guards, and even snuck out of upper-story windows, in the dark, to climb down trees, while wearing a dress. Why he continued to be surprised by Jane, he didn't know.

"Lydia taught me," she murmured as she wiggled the hairpins in the lock. "She was locked up for a while when she was kidnapped, and so she decided to study lockpicking once she was back home."

Dev contemplated this astounding bit of news in silence. Apparently, Jane wasn't the only woman who could surprise him. But then, the LCA had housed a variety of women adept at different and surprising skills, so he shouldn't be surprised at all. Lydia learned lock picking and taught her friend Jane. It made perfect sense if one knew the true nature of the LCA.

"Who taught her?" he finally whispered.

"I believe," Jane replied back absently, "that she paid a well-regarded thief to give her a tutorial. She probably could have asked Lady Rowling to arrange it back in the old days of the LCA, but now…" She shrugged.

Dev knew of Lydia Dashwood's kidnapping. Lady Rowling had been frantic with worry, not only for the potential exposure to the LCA but also genuine worry about the young lady's safety. That Miss Dashwood returned home and hired a dangerous criminal to instruct her in the art of lock picking so she'd never again worry about being locked up against her will was astounding.

All the women of the Ladies Covert Academy were astounding. And here Dev was, witnessing the powerful results of women being allowed to study and train in the areas of their interest, as Jane picked this lock for them. So that they could break into a baronet's home. And hopefully, find stolen documents.

Right and wrong had grown fuzzy for Dev a long time ago. But this moment, perhaps more than any other, crystalized why it was so essential that the Ladies Covert Academy be reopened.

All women should have the opportunity to learn lock picking.

Or study whatever it was that interested them. The world would be a sorrier, sadder place indeed if women were forced to stick to the so-called feminine arts instead of pursuing their own passions and interests, whatever they might be.

"Got it." Jane turned the knob and the door opened with a satisfying click.

"Well done," Dev murmured, reaching out a hand to help Jane to her feet.

He pushed the door open, grateful for well-oiled hinges when there was no squeak. They entered a kitchen, and the banked coals in the fireplace gave off enough light for them to see that the room was deserted. Dev closed the door behind them but left it unlocked. They might need to leave with speed.

Jane pointed to the door across the kitchen, but Dev held up a finger to forestall her. He pulled two small candles from his pocket and lit them from the coals in the fireplace. After Dev handed one to Jane, they moved through the door into the hallway.

Their candles provided just enough light to illuminate the hallway. It was narrow with wood paneling. They passed a dining room, and farther along the hallway were a study and a sitting room.

"Let's start with the study," Dev whispered.

"If we split up, we'll be quicker." Jane nodded her head to the front sitting room. "I'll search in there."

Dev nodded, watching Jane disappear in a swirl of shadow and flickering light.

The study was small and overstuffed with furniture. The bookshelves held several rows of titles, although it appeared from the stiff spines that the books had never been opened.

That seemed to match what he'd seen and heard about Sir Albert. He couldn't picture the man reading a book unless perhaps it came with an abundance of pictures and very short sentences.

Dev lit a few candles on the desk before blowing out his own and propping it against the candlestick to cool before pocketing it later. Then he sat in Sir Albert's chair.

This was the chair of the man who wished to be the next Lord Rowling.

Dev shivered.

Perhaps Sir Albert wasn't behind all this though. They still didn't know if the son Nigel might be to blame. Dev recalled how they'd seen both Sir Albert and Nigel heading into Boodle's when he and Jane had been leaving.

Was it possible that one of them was the attacker from the alley? He'd assumed it had been the footman Johnny, come to do away with those who'd been asking questions about him, but it just as easily could have been Nigel. The attacker had moved with the athleticism of a younger man, so it likely hadn't been Sir Albert. The man in the alley had also been broad-shouldered, which could apply to either Nigel or Johnny.

Dev ground his teeth together in frustration.

He and Jane could talk through this new theory later. Right now, he had a job to do.

Dev pulled the top desk drawer open, using slow and steady motions to avoid making noise. Hopefully, the servants were all sleeping soundly, content in the knowledge that they didn't have to wake up at the crack of dawn to serve the Skevingtons since they were out of town.

He pulled out a stack of files.

Bank statements. Correspondence. Bills from the milliner and grocer and boot maker. Nothing looked suspicious.

He put it all back and tried the next drawer. It was locked. He rose to find Jane, but just then she appeared in the doorway. Her face looked flushed.

"All is well," she whispered, perhaps seeing the quick look of alarm on his face. She rested her hand on her satchel strap. "But I did—"

"Can you pick this lock?" He gestured to the desk drawer. He couldn't wait to get this open and find whatever Sir Albert deemed valuable enough to lock away.

Jane came around and knelt beside him. She blew out her own candle and handed it to him before pulling out her pins again. Dev held the candelabra from the desk aloft to provide ample light. After a few minutes and a bit of mild cursing—which Dev found quite endearing—there was a click.

Would this be the evidence they needed? Would tonight bring this long quest to an end? Dev's heart pounded.

They were both silent as Jane slid the drawer open and Dev held the candle closer. They peered inside.

"What—" Jane gasped.

Dev blinked.

Jane reached into the drawer and pulled out a large glass jar. Inside, little round discs were striped with red and white. She unscrewed the lid, and the distinct scent of peppermint filled the air.

"Sir Albert's most secret item that he has locked up in the room that only he uses is... candy?" Dev's voice came out sounding a bit strangled.

Jane made a choking sound. "This is..."

"This is *ridiculous*." Dev shook his head, and the candlelight flicked around the room as the candelabra moved with him. "How could a man who would hide candies from his family possibly be a criminal mastermind plotting to steal a title?"

Was this some sort of trick? Had Sir Albert suspected they'd come and search his office, so he'd locked up this jar of candies to toy with them? Dev had no idea what to think.

Jane continued to stare at the mints. "It doesn't make any sense."

"Should we search another room?" Dev's mind spun. The evidence must be here. It had to be somewhere in this house. "Maybe upstairs? Perhaps it's in his bedroom?"

"Actually, when I was in the sitting room—" She froze at the sound of movement from elsewhere in the house.

Dev looked at Jane. Her eyes were huge in her face. She set

the candy back in the drawer and pushed it shut. They weren't being as quiet now because if someone was up, speed was more critical than silence.

Dev blew out the candelabra. They'd have to move in the dark from here on out. Thankfully, it was a straight shot down the hallway to the kitchen and through the back door.

As Dev rounded the desk, his hand found Jane's in the dark. He wasn't sure who reached out first, but he did know that as his heart raced and his ears strained to discover the source of the noise, he drew comfort from holding on to her.

They crept down the hallway.

Another noise came this time, a sort of shuffle sound followed by a moan. Dev froze. Jane was right behind him, her heat a welcome presence at his back. They were in this together, whatever this was. He didn't wish for her to be caught, but he was glad to have his partner with him.

They stood that way for what felt like forever but was likely only a minute. When no more sounds came, Dev continued down the hall. They passed the dining room. It remained as dark and quiet as it had been when they'd entered the house. Then they were at the door to the kitchen.

Dev put his hand out, ready to gently nudge it open.

"Get ready to run," he whispered. He would bolt through to the back door with Jane in tow if need be, pushing past anyone there who might raise the alarm or report them to the authorities.

Jane squeezed his hand. She was ready. He was ready. It was time.

He nudged the door to the kitchen open and peeked through the narrow crack. He didn't see anyone in his narrow view and the room seemed quiet.

He opened the door more and stepped into the room. He came to an abrupt halt when he took in the fire now dancing in the grill. A woman with a mob cap askew on her head leaned haphazardly against a counter, a bottle dangling from her fingers.

Jane had walked right into Dev's back.

"Who's there?" the woman slurred, her voice painfully loud in the quiet of the house. "T'is medicinal, it is." She took a swig directly from the bottle, glaring at them all the while.

Dev took a tentative step forward. Jane pressed a hand against his side, trying to push him out of her way so she could see, no doubt.

"Oh," Jane breathed, taking in the sight of the drunk woman, still in her servant's uniform.

Could it really be this easy?

"Of course, it's medicinal," Dev said, holding his hands up to show he meant no harm. "We aren't here to take it from you." He took a step toward the door.

"Am I dreamin'?" the woman asked, listing dangerously to the side. She didn't wait for them to answer before taking another healthy swig.

Dev didn't know how to answer.

"Yes," Jane replied, slipping around Dev. "This *is* a dream. We came here to tell you that it's absolutely fine to drink for medicinal purposes. Isn't that right?" She elbowed Dev in the ribs.

"Yes," he agreed, edging closer to the back door. "A bit of medicine now and then never hurt anyone."

"What 'bout the mis'ress?" The woman pulled herself to an upright position. "She'll flay me alive iffen she finds out I've taken the brandy." The woman shuddered, and Dev realized with some surprise that this servant was actually afraid of meek and mild Lady Skevington.

"You know," Jane said, taking a step toward the inebriated woman, "if it were me enjoying a nice medicinal drink and someone else noticed a missing bottle—"

"Two bottles," the woman interrupted, holding up a rather incongruous three fingers.

"Well," Jane continued, "if anyone notices two or three bottles missing, I think the rest of the household wouldn't find it hard to believe that Nigel was getting into his parents' liquor supply."

"You know young master Nigel?" the woman asked, plunking the bottle down on the counter. "Now there's a sneaky, shifty-eyed one, as I live and breathe."

The woman demonstrated by exhaling a deep breath. Dev blinked as brandy fumes engulfed him. Jane must have gotten blasted as well, because she turned her head to the side and coughed.

He and Jane hadn't found the evidence they were looking for, but perhaps the night wasn't a total loss. They could discover more about Nigel Skevington by gently questioning this woman.

She burped and swayed on her feet.

Perhaps the gentle part wouldn't be needed.

"Nigel's sneaky, you say?" Dev asked.

"Ah, my dream," the woman slurred, putting her finger to her nose before pointing at Dev. "I knew th' minute you came in here tha' you were a right smart one. Yes indeed. Only smart dreams, I be havin'."

"Smart dreams for a smart woman," Dev agreed.

"And smart insights into that sneaky Nigel," Jane prompted.

"Ah," the woman sighed before tipping back her head for another pull from the brandy bottle. "Nigel's one what's always into mischief. That one slipped outta th' nest, 'spite his mother what keeps an eye likes a hawk on 'im."

"He sneaks out a lot?" Dev repeated.

The woman nodded, her mob cap threatening to abandon ship.

Dev leaned forward. "Where does he go?"

"Out to sow 'is wild oats, I 'spose," the woman slurred. "Gamblin' and whorin' and gettin' into what have you…" She trailed off, staring morosely at the brandy bottle which was now close to empty.

"Do you know anything about a title?" Jane asked.

Dev turned sharply. It seemed a risky line of questioning.

Jane shrugged. "She's so drunk," she whispered, "that she thinks we're figments of her dream. She's not going to remember any of this tomorrow, so why not ask?"

Dev stared into her eyes, a kaleidoscope of colors in the flickering firelight. She looked so hopeful. What else could he do but nod?

"A title?" Jane prompted the woman.

The drunken servant weaved on her feet, scrunching her face up in a comical pose of contemplation. "Well, I heard someone what's talking about the Rowlands title. Was that what's your thinking of?"

"The *Rowling* title?" Dev corrected, heart thumping.

"Ah, tha's the one." The woman pointed her bottle at Dev. "Someone was saying as how the Rowboat title would be theirs, iffen they just…"

The woman trailed off, her eyes going distant.

"If they just what?" Dev demanded. "Who said this?" He stepped forward, touching the woman's arm. Was this the moment he learned everything? When the mystery was untangled and he had the answers?

The woman's eyes shut.

"If they what?" Dev repeated, taking hold of her arm.

The woman's head slumped forward.

"Tell me," Dev growled.

The woman's only reply was a gusty snore.

"Dev." Jane's hand was gentle at his back. "She's out." Jane pried the brandy out of the woman's hand, setting it on the counter. "Let's set her down."

There was a small pallet near the fire, perhaps the place where a kitchen boy would sleep at night when there was meat that needed turning over the fire. The woman had quickly turned into a dead weight. Dev hitched his hands under her arms, Jane took her legs, and together they carried her to the pallet.

"I want to search upstairs," Dev said once they had the woman settled. "There could be something in one of the bedrooms."

Jane shook her head. "It's too dangerous. Another servant might have heard the ruckus made by this one." She nodded toward the woman who had begun a session of very impressive snores. "We should go."

Dev's gaze moved between the door to the garden and the door that led to the rest of the house. What if this was their only opportunity?

"Dev." Jane's voice was firm. "We need to go."

Dev exhaled, then nodded. Within a minute, they were back on the street, picking their way through the darkness in search of another hackney.

"Well, that was a waste," Dev murmured once they'd put a few blocks between them and the Skevington's house.

"Not entirely."

Even in the dim light, Dev could make out Jane's mischievous smile.

"What do you mean?"

Jane patted her bag. "I found something in the sitting room."

Chapter Thirteen

D EV CLUNG TO the branch of the ash tree, which was part of the Oleaceae family, Jane unhelpfully informed him as she scurried along its thin branch to her window.

Although Dev didn't care to know about the Olea…whatever family, he very much *did* care to know whether this branch would hold his weight. Although the trunk of the tree was stout, the branch closest to Jane's window was not. And Dev imagined he weighed quite a bit more than Jane.

The branch creaked, and Dev shut his eyes.

"It's fine," Jane hissed from inside her bedroom.

Easy for her to say. She knew the blasted ash tree wasn't going to drop her to her death on the ground below. Well, most likely not death, but definitely an impressive scratch or two and some very colorful bruises. Probably a broken bone.

Dev clutched the branch tighter.

"The longer you stay out there, the longer it takes for us to figure out what's in this diary," Jane whispered.

Dev opened one eye to find Jane waving her find from the Skevington's house in the air.

He glared at her.

He had wanted to immediately examine the diary, which she'd discovered under a stack of newspapers in the sitting room. Jane had argued that there wasn't enough light in the hackney and no place for them to go other than her house at three in the morning.

And so here he was, stuck on a wiry tree branch like a literal scaredy cat.

"I suppose," she called in a quiet, sing-song voice, "that I can just start reading without you…"

Dev gritted his teeth and inched forward. The branch creaked ominously. After rushing the last few feet, he dropped onto the windowsill before the tree could drop him.

"See, that wasn't too hard, was it?"

He could see her batting her eyelashes at him playfully in the light of the candles she must have lit when she'd first come in through the window.

Dev felt an inappropriate urge to laugh. Even in the midst of all this madness—fighting off a knife-wielding attacker, breaking into a baronet's home, and risking discovery in the bedroom of an aristocratic lady in the wee hours of the morning—he felt such an easy joy in Jane's presence.

And she was so lovely in her kindness and her braveness. Those lips that could purse with such determination also distracted him with their soft, pink lushness.

"You're quite marvelous, you know," he murmured, smiling at her.

Dev wondered what Jane saw in his expression because her eyes grew smoky and dropped to his mouth.

"You…" She paused to clear the huskiness from her voice. "You're rather marvelous yourself."

Dev took a step closer to her.

"We did an impressive thing tonight," he murmured. "A brave thing."

"We are quite clever," she agreed.

And then Jane took a step closer to him.

"We work so well together," Dev whispered as he reached out to push a tendril of her strawberry-blond hair back behind her ear. The lock felt like silk, and he trailed his fingers along her hairline and behind her ear before dropping his hand.

She stepped even closer until there were scant inches between them. "We're partners," she breathed, and then her mouth was on his and they were kissing, and Dev had no more room for thoughts.

Jane's lips were sweet and plump and perfect. He could kiss her all night. He could kiss her forever.

She moaned, a tiny sound of pleasure that rumbled through him. His hands cradled her face, and he stroked along her cheeks, her neck, her hair. She was both gentle and strong, soft and tough as metal.

Her hands traveled over his shoulders and chest, leaving a trail of fire in their wake. Dev wanted to feel her touch on his bare skin, like it had been the night she'd cleaned his wound. It suddenly felt as if there were a thousand layers of clothing between them. He groaned in frustration, and Jane pulled back a step, panting.

"I want to touch you," she gasped.

Had she been reading his mind?

"…and I want you to touch me," she added.

Dev's blood turned molten hot. "Yes," he growled, and he stalked toward her.

He encircled her in his arms, and together they tumbled onto her bed. Dev's hands traveled up her arm, over her shoulder, and to the smooth skin of her upper chest.

All the while, he kissed her. Jane's mouth was wet and warm, and he wanted to feast on it, feast on her, until the ash tree outside the window had grown another twenty feet.

"Can I touch you here?" he asked, inching his fingers toward her breasts.

"Yes," she breathed. Her chest rose and fell with her rapid inhalations.

Dev's chest bellowed too. He was overwhelmed by feelings. This attraction, this connection between them, was unlike anything he'd ever felt before.

He wondered fleetingly if it was unlike anything he'd ever feel again.

And then his hand was on her breast, cupping her sweet curve through her gown.

"You are so beautiful," he whispered, the words feeling reverent somehow.

"Dev." She sighed, arching up into his touch.

He rubbed the gentle weight of her in his hand, and her nipple pebbled against the center of his palm. He touched her other breast, the soft curve also capped by a hard nipple. She wanted him. He knew it, but to feel the physical evidence in this way sent a surge of satisfaction through him.

"Can I kiss you here?" He held his breath and stilled his hand.

"Yes."

Jane rolled over, and he stared at the little row of buttons running down her back. He remembered undoing buttons just like this on her gown that day she'd needed to change into a maid's dress. The line of tiny buttons was somehow both staidly proper and also quite erotic, a row of locks that must be picked to enter into paradise.

Dev worked one button free and then the next. On and on it went, a never-ending collection of tiny, round circles until Jane's gown gaped open in the back. And then he tugged loose her undergarment, and there was the smooth, bare skin of her back.

Her ragged breathing was loud in the stillness of the night.

He was hard beneath his trousers. Hard as a stone from *buttons*, and it seemed she was affected as well. Perhaps being undressed felt as erotic as undressing.

Jane rolled over. She locked eyes with him, and in her brown-green depths, highlighted by the flickering candles, he saw her desire for him. He saw her intelligence. And he saw her strength.

Despite all the protection that her parents placed on her, all the fear they bundled her in, and the constant guarding, Jane was her own person. She did what she wanted.

And right now, she wanted to do this with him.

Jane dragged down the bodice of her gown. She wriggled her arms out of the dress and shoved it and her second layer—stays, Dev believed they were called—to her waist.

He watched in delight as her lovely breasts bounced with the movements under the thin layer of her nearly-transparent cotton chemise.

And then, as Dev held his breath, she plucked at a tiny bow between her breasts and loosened the final layer. With sure fingers, she parted the garment. She bared herself to him.

Dev knew what a gift this was. Not only the sharing of her body with him but the sharing of her trust.

"Jane," he whispered. "You are glorious."

And she smiled.

Not the faux-innocent smile she unleashed on the unsuspecting, the smile that hid her intelligence and knowing.

No, this smile was pure light. It was joyful and beautiful and all Jane. He saw *her*. The real Jane. She was here with him now, laying herself bare to him.

And he would worship her.

"My Jane," he murmured, before placing his hand on her bare breast.

She gasped.

Her skin was softer than the finest silk, and Dev groaned. He trailed his fingers over the plump swells, moving from one to the other. Her nipples were pink, the color of her lips. The thought brought a rush of heat over his skin. "I want to kiss you here," he rasped, circling her nipple with his fingertip.

"Yes," she gasped.

Dev lowered his head. She was hot and sweet in his mouth. He tried to go slowly, to not devour her, but her little mewls of pleasure tipped him over the edge. He was possessed. He could not get enough. He wanted to claim every inch of her skin, sear her, mark her as his with his kisses.

But no, that was the way of senseless animals. Jane belonged to herself.

For now, he was privileged to have her permission to share this pleasure with her.

"I am overcome by you," he whispered into her skin, into her very flesh. "You enchant me." He pulled back, forcing space between his lips and the perfect, wet tip of her breast. Glancing up, he met her hot stare, their gaze colliding and tangling. "But," he continued, "I will stop the instant you tell me to."

She answered by plowing her fingers into his hair and tugging his head back to her breast. "Don't stop," she panted. "I've never felt this way. Please, Dev…"

He continued to kiss and suck and nibble on her breasts, but now his free hand traveled down her side, along her hip, and to the juncture of her thighs.

"All right?" he asked as he pressed, the fabric of her gown— only lowered to her waist—between his fingers and her soft, secret place.

"Yes," she choked out, pressing herself against his hand. "Oh, Dev."

"Yes, my Jane," he whispered. "I'll take care of you."

And he pressed and rubbed where she needed him. He yearned to reach up under the clothing and feel her wet heat against his bare hand, but he didn't dare. It would be too much.

And so, while she opened her legs wider and strained against him, he gave her rhythmic pressure at her core.

"Dev," she panted.

He pressed harder.

"Dev!" she called, and then slapped a hand over her mouth to contain the sounds of her pleasure as she peaked.

Dev kissed and sucked and pressed and rubbed as she shook beneath him. It was glorious. *She* was glorious.

Dev had never seen such beauty as when Jane trembled in her pleasure.

With a final gasp, she slumped back on the bed, her body splayed as if boneless.

Dev moved up beside her and tugged her into his arms. They

panted together. Slowly, slowly, his pulse calmed from a gallop to a trot.

"Jane," he murmured, kissing the silky hair at the top of her head.

"Oh, Dev," she whispered, nestling her face into his neck. "That was…"

He squeezed her. "I know."

Her breathing evened out, and he knew she was falling asleep.

"Goodnight, my Jane." He kissed her head once more, then gently pulled away.

He tugged a blanket over her, and without a care for the delicacy of the branch or the weight of his heavy frame, he climbed out the window and onto the ash tree, shimmying to the thick trunk before dropping down to the ground.

And he was all the way back in his warm bed at Lady Rowling's house before he remembered that they hadn't examined the diary.

Chapter Fourteen

JANE ROLLED OVER in bed and grumbled before turning her face in the pillow to hide from the bright sun streaming in through her window.

Thank goodness she'd woken hours earlier when the first light of dawn had peeked in through her open curtains. She'd been able to put her night rail on before the maid came in to light the fire. It would not do to be discovered half-dressed on top of the covers with part of the counterpane folded over her.

She flipped her pillow over and pressed her hot cheeks against the cool cotton.

Oh, last night!

Jane wriggled, kicking her feet against the mattress. She had… and Dev…

She could hardly think of the things they'd done without feeling like she was going to burst into flames.

No wonder parents kept such a watchful eye on their daughters. If young ladies knew what pleasure could be had at the hand—ahem—of an attentive partner, no girl's virtue would remain intact.

Jane mulled that thought over for a moment.

The idea that it was virtuous—that it was *moral*—for a girl to remain untouched felt…wrong. Why was it sinful to kiss a person you cared for? Or to find pleasure in their touch?

What she and Dev had done last night hadn't felt wrong.

In fact, it had felt completely right.

Jane hopped out of bed, suddenly energized to start the day.

Her maid must have been listening for the sound of movement in her bedroom.

"Pardon me, miss, but are you ready to dress?" her maid asked.

"Can you bring me up a tray first? I'm quite famished," Jane replied. "Thank you so much." And she smiled at the girl, who blinked in a rather astonished way.

Jane really needed to be consistently appreciative to the servants.

Servants were people too. All people were people, obviously. But those with wealth didn't seem to hold much stock in the idea that regardless of whether someone worked for their living or inherited it from an ancient relative, all people deserved respect and kindness.

Speaking of inheritances…Jane glanced around her bedroom. There on the floor near the window was the diary she'd discovered in the Skevington's house.

She was surprised Dev hadn't taken it with him last night. He'd been so keen to examine it, but then they'd gotten distracted.

Jane's cheeks heated again, and she picked up the diary.

When she'd gone into the sitting room last night, she hadn't expected to find anything. Who would leave a secret clue to an undercover plot to steal a marquessate laying around in their front room where they received visitors?

The room had been full of the usual items: embroidered pillows, ugly paintings on the walls, a vase of flowers just starting to wilt. On a side table next to a well-worn armchair was a scattered stack of newspapers. Jane had nearly passed it by.

But at the last minute, she'd rifled through them.

And there, underneath articles about trade and farming and the Prince Regent and the House of Commons and the price of tea and all the other stories that made up the news, there had sat a small, worn leather book.

A handwritten book, she'd discovered upon picking it up.

There hadn't been enough light to make out anything, but perhaps there would be a clue in it that could point them in the right direction for this investigation.

Because so far they had a red-haired, broad-shouldered footman who may or may not have been at the scene of the burglary over a month ago, a baronet who stood to inherit the Rowling title but who likely didn't have the smarts to pull off the heist, and a mysterious alley attacker whose sharp knife had thankfully been overpowered by Jane's still-unidentified herb.

She layered her robe over her night rail before lowering herself into a comfy chair near the fireplace. Cracking open the diary, she found a random page near the middle of the book.

Il mio uomo inglese è più bello di un dipinto. Mi corteggia con parole dolci e piccoli regali ogni giorno che siamo in mare...

This was...Italian? Jane wasn't sure, as the only language she'd ever studied had been a bit of French. Actually, there had been a lot of Latin in her life since she'd begun her study of botany. It turned out that scientists liked Latin. A lot.

She worried her lip for a moment.

This was odd. Why did Lord Skevington—or his weaselly son Nigel—have an Italian journal? It could belong to the wife as well, but she was so...bland. Jane couldn't even picture her face—she'd been staring down at the ground in demure silence nearly the entire time Jane had spoken to the family at the musicale—let alone imagine her studying a romance language.

"Oh, thank you," she said as her maid entered with a tray. "Set it here, if you please. And before you go, can you help me get dressed for the day? I need to visit Lydia."

"I'm glad you get to see your friends, miss," her maid said after carefully placing the tray on the table beside the armchair.

"Me too." Jane smiled. "And it's extra lovely when one of

them is quite adept at languages."

LYDIA THUMBED THROUGH the pages of the diary in her office, frowning. "I can definitely translate this, but it will take me a while. My Italian isn't as good as my German. And let's not even talk about how behind I am with my Irish."

Jane just blinked at her friend.

How could one person be so smart?

Lydia was an exceptional writer with a keen political mind. Her newspaper articles, written under the pen name *Democratiam Liberum*, which meant *free democracy* in Latin, had taken London by storm with her razor-sharp arguments against corruption in the House of Commons.

And she spoke several languages.

And she usually hit her target more times than Jane when they practiced their knife throwing under Pippa's guidance.

Plus, she was beautiful and kind, and generous.

It was a good thing Lydia was terrible at parlor games, otherwise, Jane might have to hate her a little bit.

Once when they'd been playing charades, Lydia had guessed *women's suffrage* when her brother Jack had clearly been acting out milking a cow.

One of the members of her charades team had actually wept when they'd lost the point.

"Can you tell who wrote it?" Jane asked, leaning forward to peer over Lydia's shoulder at the foreign words.

"Well," Lydia said, scanning a page, "it was written twenty-five years ago." She pointed at the date at the beginning of an entry. "And it seems to be written by a woman. She's talking about a dress here."

Lydia read a bit more. Jane shifted on the wooden chair beside Lydia's desk. Unlike most ladies, instead of spending her day in a sitting room, Lydia spent hers in an office that her brother Jack had set up for her once the LCA had closed. Lydia now had her own place to write, to research, and—perhaps most importantly to the rest of the household—to contain her countless papers where she scribbled ideas and notes. Her desk was cluttered with stacks of paper, but Lydia always seemed to know where everything was.

A minute of silent reading stretched into five, and Jane realized her friend had forgotten about her.

Jane cleared her throat, and Lydia jumped.

"Why don't I visit my laboratory upstairs for an hour, and then I'll check on you?" Jane asked.

Lydia nodded, her blue eyes sheepish. "Sorry. I got lost in it. She's talking about traveling on a boat. I think the owner of this diary was a lady's maid."

Jane's pulse quickened. This was so unexpected. Who was the mystery woman, and why had her diary been in the Skevington's sitting room?

It didn't appear to connect with her and Dev's mission to prove the rightful heir to Rowling's title, but something in Jane's gut told her this mattered.

And Jane, despite her reliance on the scientific method and factual proof, did not make a habit of ignoring her gut.

Shortly, Jane was back in her laboratory. She examined the jar of the herb that had worked so well in deterring the attacker from the alley. She really did need to make time to visit her friend in the market to learn what plant this was from. For now, Jane refilled a little vial from the bigger jar and popped it into her bodice again. That gave her one vial at home and another on her person.

A lady never knew when she might need to defend herself.

After an hour of watering, measuring, recording, and planning for her next cross-pollination experiment, Jane returned to Lydia's office.

Lydia remained in the exact pose she'd been in when Jane had left her, hunched over her desk, her eyes tracking back and forth over the diary's pages.

"Anything?" Jane asked, plunking down into the wooden chair.

Lydia blinked at her owlishly for a moment before leaning back in a long stretch. Her eyebrows pulled together, and she nibbled on her bottom lip as if thinking of what to say.

Jane's stomach tightened.

"Your friend, Dev," Jane finally said. "What's his last name?"

Jane started. "It's…" She trailed off.

How did she still not know Dev's last name? He was her friend. Her partner in both solving crime *and* committing crimes since they'd now broken into someone's home. He'd seen her half-naked. And she didn't know his full name!

"I'm not sure," she finally admitted, heat radiating off her cheeks.

"Hm." Lydia frowned down at the diary.

"What is it?"

After drawing a full breath, Lydia turned intense eyes to Jane. "I only skimmed the diary."

Jane nodded.

"I might have gotten the gist of it wrong."

Jane nodded again.

"But what this woman seems to say is…"

Jane leaned forward.

Lydia nibbled on her lip again.

"What does it say?"

Lydia jumped at the volume of Jane's voice.

"Sorry." Jane wrung her hands together. "Please. Just tell me."

"This woman, she was a lady's maid to an Italian contessa. She traveled with the contessa on a ship." Lydia paused. "To India."

Jane frowned.

"On the ship, a *bell'uomo*, a handsome man, took a liking to our lady's maid. He told her she was the most beautiful woman he'd ever seen, gave her little trinkets, and took her for strolls along the deck of the ship. It seems he swept her off her feet. She couldn't believe her good fortune. She was a maid and was being courted by a great man. A rich man. An Englishman."

Jane leaned back in her chair. Her stomach felt queasy.

"After only a week at sea, the man asked for her hand and the ship's captain married them that very day. Then they arrived in India. In Calcutta."

The hairs on the back of Jane's neck prickled.

"It seemed things went sour once they settled into the new home that the East India Company had provided for them. She didn't speak much English and her new husband didn't speak any Italian. She knew no Bengali, so she was quite isolated. She only felt comfortable in the kitchen with the other servants. They taught her a few words and let her help with meals. They were her only friends." Lydia paused. "Soon she became pregnant."

"What…" Jane licked her lips. Her mouth was as dry as a succulent plant's soil. "What happened next?"

She didn't know how this story would end…and yet somehow, she knew. She *thought* she knew. Perhaps she was wrong.

Let me be wrong.

"Her baby was born. Her son. His name was Devin."

Devin.

Jane's head spun.

"The boy's father, her husband, was Henry Stokes"—Lydia paused to clear her throat—"the second son of Marquess Rowling. He was a loyal member of the East India Company. And he was quite content to ignore his wife, of whom he'd been so enamored with while at sea but soon became quite embarrassed by once they were in Calcutta with the other Company men and their allegedly proper English wives."

Jane struggled for breath.

Lydia continued on. "It seems she and her young son spent all their time with the servants, even though she was the lady of the household, and her son was their young master. The servants were kind to her and kind to her son, who didn't fit in anywhere else. His father completely ignored him. Jane…this is truly the saddest diary I've ever read."

Despite the buzzing in her ears, Jane idly wondered how Lydia had come to read multiple peoples' diaries.

"Toward the end of the diary, the entries become quite infrequent. It seems the woman was feeling ill. She did add that they'd received news that her husband's older brother had died, and that her husband was the new lord. By then, she was quite unwell and wrote very little. I believe her son was only four when she…when I assume she died." Lydia's voice had gone quiet at the end.

They sat in silence.

Jane didn't know where to look or what to say. She didn't know how to *feel*.

Dev, *her* Dev, a kind servant in Lady Rowling's household who had become her friend and partner and who'd made her fall apart in his arms last night, was actually Devin Stokes, son of an Italian lady's maid and the late Lord Rowling?

That meant Dev was…

Jane drew a shuddering breath.

Dev was the missing heir whose legitimacy they were trying to prove.

Sir Albert Skevington was his father's cousin, and either Sir Albert or his son was trying to steal the title away from Dev.

Dev had served champagne to the man while dressed in servant's livery. And all the while, *he* had been the true heir.

A marquess.

And he…he'd *lied* to her.

From the very first moment, she'd met him, he'd been lying. Every minute of his life was a lie, pretending to be a servant. Pretending there was some other son, some other heir, hiding away in India. The son of Lady Rowling, who was, it seemed, Lord Rowling's second wife. Did she even have a child? Was the story of the son encountering mysterious accidents even true?

Jane stood abruptly, her chair toppling over. She was faintly aware of a stack of books tumbling to the floor behind her.

"I have to go," she announced, already moving to the door.

"Jane," Lydia called. "The diary?"

"Keep it," Jane said over her shoulder. "Keep translating."

There might be something in that diary that they needed.

But right now, what Jane needed was to see a man about a lie.

Chapter Fifteen

DEV HUMMED UNDER his breath as he sorted documents into stacks on top of the desk.

"What's that tune?" Parth called from the other side of the study.

"And can you make it stop?" Meera asked from the sofa where she was thumbing through an old estate ledger. Her bright sari was spread out on the cushions around her like a queen's robe.

"Sorry," Dev said, sheepish. He hadn't realized they could hear him. He hadn't consciously been humming, come to think of it. It was the old Italian song he remembered his mother singing to him when he'd been a little boy. He barely knew the words, but the tune was as familiar to him as his own face.

"You do seem extra cheerful today." Parth shot him a look over the sheaf of papers in his hands. "Did you spend more time with a certain pretty lady?"

Parth batted his eyelashes.

Dev contemplated throwing a book at his head.

His skin tingled at the memory of last night. Of how they'd kissed. How she'd bared herself, giving instead of allowing him to take. He'd stayed up for hours last night, pondering the inherent power of her actions. The bravery of it. The strength.

Jane *was* powerful, brave, and strong.

And he couldn't wait to see her again.

"Ah," Meera said, interrupting his thoughts. She closed the ledger, her finger marking the page. "Is this Miss Jane you speak of? Parth mentioned she's been helping you search for clues. I like that lady, but her office always smelled."

"It was the fertilizer for her plants," Dev said, "and it didn't *always* smell."

Meera wrinkled her nose. "If you say so." She looked to the side and then asked, "Does she know?"

Dev inhaled sharply. "Know about the robbery? Yes."

Meera raised one dark eyebrow. "You know that I know that it's perfectly clear that's not what I'm asking if she knows."

Parth made a choking sound from the corner of the room where he sat next to a side table covered in documents. "Meera, *you* know the first rule of the LCA is that we don't talk about the LCA."

She huffed. "I'm *not* talking about the LCA. You boys, always thinking you're so funny and clever. I'm talking about Dev's real identity, of course."

Dev cleared his throat. "Meera," he said, his voice a warning.

She held up one hand, palm out. "Fine, fine. I won't ask if the pretty aristocratic lady knows that you're not a simple servant like the rest of us."

"Meera," he gritted out.

She made a show of covering her mouth with her free hand before flicking open the ledger and returning to her perusal.

Dev tried to sort the stacks of documents on the desk, but his mind was in a whirl. Thoughts of what he and Jane had done together last night mixed with feelings of guilt. But he couldn't tell her who he really was. No one outside their retinue from India could know the truth. It was too dangerous. Lady Rowling had been most clear on that.

"Your life is in danger," she had said, her pale eyes flashing sternly. "Someone wants Rowling's real heir dead and gone. The fewer people who know about your existence, the better."

And so, he'd hidden in plain sight.

And he would continue to do so until this mystery was solved and it was safe to come forward, to share who he truly was with the world.

With Jane.

A loud pounding jolted him from his thoughts.

Parth shrieked, scrambling out of his chair and backing away from the window.

"It seems that someone is outside," Meera drawled, turning a page in the ledger with a flick.

Dev approached the window. The afternoon light was hitting the glass at just the right angle to create a glare, making it impossible to see what or who was out there.

But he knew.

He reached to open the window.

"What are you doing?" Parth exclaimed. "It could be the burglars."

Dev ignored him and tugged the window open.

The sun glinted off her red-gold hair, creating a halo around her head. She was backlit so he couldn't read her expression, but her fisted hands and heaving chest suggested she was upset. Had something happened? Was she hurt?

"Jane," he croaked, fear clogging his throat.

"Dev," she growled.

Ah. Not hurt then.

He turned to Parth and Meera. "I think you should probably step out for a bit."

"Maybe the lovely plant lady needs you to till her fields," Meera whispered, her face all innocence as she stood.

Dev stifled a groan.

Parth grabbed Meera by the arm. "We're here if you need us," he murmured, eyes serious, before leading her out of the study and shutting the door behind them.

Dev took a deep breath and turned back to the open window. "Would you like to come in?"

Jane gave a sharp nod and took his outstretched hands. Just like before, Dev had to steady her once she was mostly inside while she scrambled to get her feet beneath her. If there was a graceful way to be tugged through a window, Dev would like to see it.

"Is anything wrong?" he asked once she righted herself.

Jane narrowed her eyes. She opened her mouth to speak but then snapped it shut and began to stalk back and forth around the study.

Dev watched, his heart sinking with each pass she made. She wasn't hurt—not physically hurt at least.

And she wasn't sad.

As far as he could tell, she was *furious*.

"Jane—"

"Don't." She sliced her hand through the air, cutting him off.

He waited another minute while she paced, her cheeks red and her eyes flashing.

"Are you—"

She cut her hand through the air again to stop his words, then came to a stop a few feet in front of him.

Her eyes glittered. "What's your name?"

"I…what?" His heart thudded loudly in his chest.

"What's. Your. Name." She enunciated each word carefully.

He swallowed. "Dev."

She inhaled sharply. "Isn't it actually Devin?"

Dev's legs wobbled.

He nodded.

"Devin Stokes, yes?"

He wanted to fall over in a heap. He wanted to sink through the floor. He wanted to be anywhere but here.

He wanted to be home.

But the truth was, he had no home.

I don't belong anywhere.

Although last night, for a little while, it had felt like maybe he belonged with her.

He forced himself to nod.

"Are you the son of an Italian woman who served as a maid for a contessa?" Jane inhaled and then cleared her throat. "I apologize for referring to her in such terms, but she never revealed her own name in her diary."

Dev's legs did betray him then, and he fumbled for the desk behind him, leaning against its edge.

His mother. She had written a diary.

And Jane…Jane had found it? Last night, at the Skevington's, that must have been what she'd found in the sitting room. He covered his face with his hand, needing a moment of privacy in the midst of his world flying into pieces and swirling around him.

"I…I do apologize for not breaking that more gently." Jane's voice had lost its hard, furious edge.

He wanted to laugh. He wanted to cry. He'd lied to her. He'd lied from the beginning. Incessantly. And now she was apologizing to *him*, comforting *him*?

The world did not deserve Miss Jane Brickley.

He did not deserve her.

He swallowed, praying for composure. "Yes." His voice only cracked a little. "Yes, my mother was an Italian woman. Her name was Lucretia Russo. She was a servant to a fine Italian lady before she married…before she married my father."

Jane was quiet.

But the room was not quiet. It wasn't still. There was no peace here in this study full of books and mahogany wood and documents, documents everywhere.

The very air vibrated with this…this thing between him and Jane. This lie.

He had not been truthful with her.

And she was furious.

He did not blame her.

He finally pulled his hand away from his face. He opened his eyes and looked at her.

"My…my father is…was"—he corrected, hating the tremble

in his voice—"Henry Stokes, Marquess Rowling."

"Ah, but you see"—Jane spoke quietly and ever so gently. So gently in fact, that it tore and ripped at his very bones—"*you* are Lord Rowling now."

⟫⟪

JANE'S RESOLVE SLIPPED another degree as she saw Dev's hand tremble. As his throat worked and worked again as if he attempted to swallow a lump that wouldn't go away. As his eyes, usually so bright and cheery, grew darker and darker with despair.

But he deserved to suffer.

To suffer as she had, learning that the man she…the man she'd grown to care for had *lied* to her for the entirety of their acquaintance.

How it tore at her, imagining him laughing at her. Perhaps pitying her even, knowing he was successful in his ruse and that she had foolishly believed his lies. He'd fooled the silly lady who lived with her silly family in her silly, pampered life. She snuck away from her armed guards, pretending to be so brave and strong when the truth was that she was terrified.

She was terrified of what she felt today, of what it meant.

But fear was a weak emotion. Fury was more powerful. It burned strong and hot and pure in her belly and had fueled her race here to this house. It had fired her fist pounding on the window and fired her accusation.

"You are Lord Rowling now," she repeated, even though she knew the words made him tremble.

"I am." His voice was hoarse.

"Why?" Her question emerged, raw and battered.

He stared at her.

"*Why* did you lie? Why did you lie to everyone?" She exhaled a shaky breath. "To me?"

"Jane, I'm so sorry—"

"Just tell me."

He held up a hand of appeasement. Was she some wild creature to calm?

Perhaps.

She felt like she could rip out someone's throat with the fury that churned inside her.

"When we learned that Lord Rowling...my father," he corrected with a little flinch, "had died, Roberta—that's Lady Rowling, my stepmother—was worried about me inheriting."

He drew a few slow breaths before continuing.

"My father had stopped acknowledging me, you see. I was an embarrassing reminder of a grand mistake he'd once made, marrying some lowly servant from a country that wasn't even civilized enough to speak English. She'd trapped him with her feminine wiles and sultry Italian eyes on that ship all those years ago, he would tell me, back when he used to speak to me."

Dev's lip curled in disgust at his father's cruelty as he spoke, and Jane briefly wondered what the words cost him. Some perverse part of her wanted to reach out to him, to wind her arms around him and stroke his dark hair. She wanted to comfort him almost as much as she wanted to make him bleed.

Almost.

"And since he didn't take me to Company dinner parties, no one seemed to know of my existence. I didn't go to school, although he did hire me a discreet tutor at least. I didn't play with the other English children in Calcutta. And no one back in England knew about me. At least, that's what Roberta said, and her family had looked into him before they'd married her off. They needed to know if he was wealthy enough to make it worthwhile."

Jane listened in silence.

"Roberta went ahead to London first with some of the household once we'd learned he'd died during his trip to England. She let the members of the household decide if they wanted to stay in India with a generous portion or move with her to

England. Some stayed, but most went. Rowling's young bride paid well and treated everyone fairly."

He ran his hand over his face.

"I initially stayed behind with a few others, including my friend Parth. My only friends were the servants, you see. They were the only ones who'd been kind to my mother. The kitchen was the only place she'd felt comfortable. So that was where I grew up. And when she died..."

He drew a shuddering breath, and Jane balled her hands in her skirt to keep herself from reaching for him.

"Well, I was still a small child, so the servants continued as they had before, entertaining me in the kitchen, giving me little chores to keep me out of trouble. And that's how it continued through the years. I was more one of them than the son and heir of an English marquess."

Jane wished for one wild moment that Dev's father was alive and standing in front of her right now so that she might poison someone for real.

"So, I was in Calcutta with Parth and a few others, trying to get my father's affairs with the Company in order, at least as well as we could. His secretary had chosen to remain in India, and he did most of the work to close out my father's role in the Company." Dev paused, his expression growing tense. "After a couple of months had passed, things started happening. Accidents. Or things that *seemed* like accidents."

Dev's shoulders tensed up.

"A poisonous snake," she murmured. "Some stones that almost tumbled onto you."

His eyes widened in surprise.

"You'd mentioned it once, the suspicious accidents that had befallen *Rowling's heir*."

He flinched at the tone she'd put on the last two words, but then he continued. "We chalked it up to coincidence at first, but after a few incidents became a pattern, it seemed...well, it seemed that someone wished me dead."

Jane's chest squeezed.

"I wrote Roberta and hid in Parth's parents' home to await her reply. Her letter said I was in danger. I should close up the house and come to London. And to…to travel as Dev, a humble servant." He laughed, but the sound held no mirth. "It required no acting skills whatsoever."

Jane could tell there was more to the story.

"Parth played the role of a wealthy Indian man with me as his trusty servant. At one of the ship's ports, someone shot at Parth."

Jane gasped.

Dev nodded, his expression grave. "It was a near thing." His jaw clenched and unclenched for a moment. "We assumed they thought that Parth was Rowling's son. So we got off the ship, laid low in that city awhile, and boarded another ship weeks later under false names. We finally made it to London, and I've remained as you've known me ever since."

Jane moved across the room to stare out the window. Her mind swirled. She'd known or guessed at parts of his story once Lydia had shared what she'd learned from skimming through the diary, but the new parts of Dev's history that he'd just shared had left her shaken.

Jane thought about the servants in this household. She'd known them since she'd joined the LCA, two years ago. The East India Company had been operating for hundreds of years, and thousands of English people lived in India, many of them there for generations. And so, the household that had traveled here with Lady Rowling was a mix of those who were ethnically Indian and those who were ethnically English. Some wore Indian clothes, like Meera, whose colorful saris were more beautiful than a handful of sparkling jewels. And like Dev, who wore what Jane had learned was called a kurta, a long-sleeved tunic that went nearly to his knees with slits up the sides, worn over a pair of loose-fitting trousers. And other members of the household wore English garb. Lady Rowling's household spoke English and Bengali. And, Jane had learned, some were Hindu, some were

Muslim, and some were Church of England.

Given all of this, it had been quite easy for Devin Stokes, Marquess of Rowling, to hide in plain sight.

How desperate Sir Albert, or perhaps his son Nigel, must be, knowing that the true heir to the title was out there somewhere and that all their plans and scheming had been unsuccessful. How they must fear the mysterious Devin Stokes showing up before the court tribunal which would determine the estate's rightful successor, proclaiming himself the true marquess with evidence in hand.

Only they hadn't found any evidence.

And as far as Sir Albert and Nigel knew, Dev and Jane were just a pesky servant and some strange woman following him about, likely sent by Lady Rowling to blunder about in their fruitless search for Lord Rowling's marriage certificate, or some other proof that Dev was his legitimate heir.

"Jane," Dev said from across the room, "for what it's worth, I despised lying to you. Especially once we..."

Jane stiffened. His casual reference to the intimacy they'd shared last night—intimacy between them when she hadn't even known his real identity—made her want to scream.

"Jane." He sighed her name.

She shook her head.

"I can't forgive you." She looked away from him to stare out the window. The usually calming sight of green, growing things in the garden did not soothe her, however. "I will see this through with you. It's the right thing to do, despite..." She waved her hand about, assuming he'd understand she was encompassing this whole mess between them.

"Plus," she continued, "it's the only way to get Lady Rowling to reopen the LCA." She licked her lips. "And that's the only reason I'm doing this."

Dev was silent behind her.

What was going through his mind?

After a lengthy pause, he replied, "I understand."

Later that night when she was finally alone, she congratulated herself that she hadn't cried there in Lady Rowling's study.

Chapter Sixteen

JANE MARCHED THROUGH the market, two armed footmen trailing behind her. She'd chosen not to sneak out of the house. After all, it was the middle of the day, and she was on a most proper outing for a lady of her stature—shopping.

Of course, her parents didn't need to know that her shopping mostly consisted of seeds, starters, and plants. Really, why buy a new pair of gloves when you could buy foxgloves instead?

Usually, Jane would tread carefully through the crowd at the market. She would make sure she wasn't in anyone's way, weaving to and fro to be as accommodating as possible.

But today she stormed forward in a straight line.

She collided with a man and didn't even apologize.

It was glorious. Perhaps she should become enraged more often. It felt quite liberating to not care a fig what anyone else thought of her.

Ever since her confrontation with Dev yesterday, Jane had been in a constant state of simmering anger. After a prolonged and awkward silence once all Dev's secrets had been exposed, Jane had simply walked out.

She hadn't even considered climbing through the window.

Instead, she'd marched right through the middle of Lady Rowling's home, where Jane most certainly was not meant to be. Lady Rowling's bruiser of a butler, a former boxer if Jane remembered correctly, had run to get the door open for her in time.

"Good day, miss," he'd said in his gravelly voice, and his gold-capped tooth had winked in the sunlight when he'd smiled his farewell.

The smile hadn't mattered. The sunshine hadn't mattered. And Dev's explanation and apology certainly hadn't mattered.

Jane had been *livid*.

Even her father, usually so mild and distracted, had commented on it at dinner last night, saying that Jane had looked "rather spiky-eyed."

Well, Jane wished she could drive a spike through *Dev's* eye, but here she was instead, trying to distract herself by finally sorting out what her new defensive weapon was made from.

And it was good to have something else to ponder as it felt like she'd been thinking of Dev nonstop for days now. Weeks, really. All right, *months* if she was being honest. It wasn't her fault that the man was handsome and kind and twinkled at her like the stars in the sky…

Dang it. She was furious at him.

She wasn't supposed to get distracted by thoughts of his shining, blue eyes.

"Hello, love," greeted Jane's favorite vendor at the market. Amos's wide face split into a cheery grin as Jane approached his stall. "Haven't seen hide nor hair of ye in a while."

Jane inhaled deeply, filling her lungs with the fresh, green scent of Amos's plant stand. Every day, rain or shine, he was here, selling beautiful cut flowers that many fine households filled their crystal vases with. But he also sold unusual plants, starters for gardens, and seeds. His seed collection was vast and spanned the globe, and Jane loved nothing so much as poking through his little wooden cabinet, pulling out drawers, and looking for new treasures.

"Come to see what's new?" he asked, giving her his full attention once he'd finished wrapping a bouquet for another customer.

"I've just got some seeds in from a bloke what went on a trading vessel to China. There's this one what's called ginseng, some sort of medicinal herb, that I think you'd find most in'tresting."

Jane shook her head. "I'll have to talk to you about ginseng next time. Right now, I have a question about the seeds you sold me from South America a while back."

Amos blanched.

"Ah, love, I'm so sorry." He squeezed his thick hands together. "I found out from me wife's uncle that the man what sold me those seeds was a bit of a rascal. Turned out he got 'em seeds off another bloke what stole 'em from some smugglers. T'is a right mess."

Jane leaned forward over his plant-covered stall table. "So, you don't know what sort of seeds they were?"

Amos grimaced "I don't know at all, love. I'm so terrible sorry."

Jane blew out a breath. "And you don't even know if they actually *were* from South America?"

Amos shook his head.

Jane pulled out the vial containing her mystery herb. "I planted the seeds and dried the plant once it grew. I thought it would be a fun little experiment even though I didn't know anything about the seeds other than their alleged continent of origin."

She passed the vial to Amos. He held the glass up to the sunlight, inspecting the dried flakes that shifted as he rotated the vial.

"I had to pack up my plants rather abruptly, and things got mixed up," Jane continued. "Long story short, I made a tea out of that by accident, thinking it was my new strain of mint. It caused a severe reaction in the person who drank it—respiratory distress, swollen eyes, and red face."

Amos's hand jerked as if the vial could bite him.

Jane gingerly took the herb back. "And I…ah…accidentally blew it in someone's face, and it caused a similar reaction. It was immediate and very extreme." She paused, remembering the way the attacker had scrambled away from her and Dev, coughing and swiping at his face. She'd felt so powerful, fighting off a man larger and stronger than her. A man who was armed and intent on doing harm. Ah, that had been a most satisfying moment.

Except for the part where Dev was sliced open, of course.

"Sounds like you've got yourself quite a lethal weapon, love." Amos eyed the vial in her hand with respect.

Jane sighed. "I just wish I knew what it was. It would be incredible to study the plant more, to understand all of its properties. And," she lowered her voice, "to dry it on a large scale, so I could give this as a powder to other women. For protection."

Amos leaned in, matching her hushed tone. "That sounds like a right good idea, love. I'd be quite happy if my Beth had something like that when she went out on her own. I do worry 'bout her, being on her own with the way the world is."

Jane wanted to cry. *The way the world is* was very different for women than for men, and it just wasn't right.

And…she wanted to hug Amos. The fact that he believed in her idea—impossible though it was—and that his first thought was to give the means of self-defense to his sweet wife who often helped him out at his stall in the market warmed Jane's heart.

Amos scratched his full beard. "Tell you what, love. I'll ask my wife's uncle to reach out to that scoundrel and see iffen he can't learn anything more 'bout where the rest of the smugglers' goods were from. That might be a starting place, iffen he can sort it out."

"Thank you so much, Amos. I'll come by soon to see if you've learned anything." Jane lay down a generous handful of coins. The way to thank him for his assistance was clear. "And I think I'll take a bit of that ginseng after all."

DEV STARED DOWN at the note that had just been delivered to him in the study.

"What's she say?" Parth asked, leaning over the desk.

They were at it again—sorting through the boxes and piles and stacks of documents that had comprised Dev's father's life.

Dev swatted his friend away. "Give me a minute."

Swallowing, Dev broke the seal and scanned the few lines written in Jane's messy scrawl. Apparently, the conscientious and careful methods of her science did not extend to her penmanship.

"She plans to pay a call on Lady Rowling this afternoon, and she wishes for me to be there."

Parth whistled. "She's going over your head and directly to the source. A bold move, Miss Brickley." Parth tipped an imaginary hat to the note.

Dev tapped his fingers against the desk. "What is she planning to say to Roberta?" This couldn't be good. Was she going to declare herself finished with their investigation? Was she angry enough to take his story public? It would put not only him but also everyone who lived under this roof in danger.

No.

No matter how furious Jane was at him—and she had every right to be—he knew with a bone-deep certainty that she wouldn't do anything that would hurt others.

She was too caring.

Unlike him.

He'd hurt her, and he'd *chosen* to do so. It didn't matter that it had been for a good reason. He'd hurt her, nonetheless. He'd kissed her and touched her when he was pretending to be someone else, and that was unconscionable.

For a moment, he allowed his thoughts to wander to two nights ago, when he had kissed her and taken her apart with his hand. The heat that had exploded between them. The soft hum of her sighs against his ears. The silk of her skin beneath his fingertips. The way she'd rubbed against his fingers, seeking her pleasure.

He inhaled sharply and forced himself to take in the massive stack of documents piled on the desk. It would not do to lose himself in the sweet memory of Jane's kisses with all these papers to read.

Dev shifted in his chair, making sure the desk hid the bulge in his pants from Parth's view.

"I hate to be the voice of pessimism," Parth said, flopping onto the sofa, "but if we haven't found any proof of your claim to the title yet, I don't know that we ever will."

Dev grimaced. He hadn't wanted to admit it, but similar thoughts had been plaguing him for a while now. There was only a week left until the courts met to hear testimony on who should inherit the Rowling title. And at this point, he had nothing.

He thought of his life without Jane in it.

He *really* had nothing.

A knock sounded at the study door, and Meera poked her head in. "Miss Brickley has arrived and is waiting for you and Lady Rowling in the front parlor."

Dev pushed back from the desk. "Already?" Her note had just arrived.

Meera shrugged. "I would recommend getting there quickly instead of pondering the meaning of time."

Dev rolled his eyes at Meera as he rushed past. The sound of her muffled laughter followed him down the hall.

Truly, with friends like these, who needed Dagger Dans or conniving Sir Alberts to make a person wish for an early grave?

Dev trotted down the hall and only slid a little bit on the polished marble floor when he rounded a corner. He paused in front of the closed double doors to the sitting room. Was his kurta wrinkled? Was his hair mussed?

He ran a hand over his shirt and through his hair. He drew a deep breath.

It would have to do.

After rapping on the door, he entered the sitting room. The two women swiveled toward him.

Dev cleared his throat. "Good afternoon," he said, hoping his voice didn't betray his nervousness.

"Dev, come sit." Roberta flicked her hand to the velvet settee where Jane perched. His stepmother's eyes—his *friend's* eyes— betrayed nothing.

He walked across the thick Aubusson carpet toward Jane. He wished he knew the words that could fully express his awareness of the wrong he'd done her, that would tell her how truly sorry he was.

He settled onto the settee, sticking to the far side so he wasn't crowding her.

Jane's hands were folded in her lap. Her posture was stiff. She was contained, closed off.

He'd done this to her. Closing his eyes for a moment, the shame of his actions abraded the very center of his soul.

"Dev," Roberta said, "Miss Brickley has filled me in a bit on your recent progress. I must say, I was most surprised to learn that you'd allowed one of the LCA members to assist with your investigation."

Roberta's tone was frosty.

Dev frowned. Perhaps Jane *hadn't* revealed all. Roberta was keeping up the formal mistress-servant routine they enacted whenever an outsider was present.

So, Jane hadn't told Roberta what she'd learned from the diary.

What did this all mean?

His stepmother raised her pale eyebrows. Ah, this was the part where he was supposed to answer.

"Er, yes"—Dev managed to scramble together an answer that hopefully sounded somewhat plausible—"Miss Brickley expressed an interest in finding justice for the LCA by uncovering the burglars and handing them over to the authorities."

One of Roberta's eyebrows rose even higher.

"And so, knowing how highly you regard the intelligence and abilities of your academy's members, I naturally worked with her to hunt for clues."

He felt Jane tense on the other side of the settee.

"And, uh"—Dev felt his cheeks grow warm—"I didn't wish to bother you with the details or have you worrying, so I didn't share that she and I had partnered together."

Partnered together.

His chest clenched.

Roberta leaned back in her ornate, gold-filigreed chair, a rather casual pose for the icy Lady Rowling when someone outside her household was present.

Alert the presses—the marchioness's back had touched the furniture!

"Well," Roberta said, "I can't say I approve of this…partnering."

Jane made a choking sound. Dev attempted to glare daggers with his eyes at his alleged friend, but Roberta pretended not to notice their reactions to the provocative slant she'd given that last word.

"However, since you are in rather too deep to call a halt to things, I say we proceed." Roberta placed her hands serenely in her lap. "It seems the only way we shall make progress in solving this mystery"—Dev noticed she did not specify which mystery, a very tidy way for her to believe she kept Jane in the dark about his identity—"is if we all work together."

"All?" Jane spoke for the first time since Dev had entered the room.

He looked over at her. She must have felt his stare even though her gaze was steady on Roberta, because she tilted her chin up in defiance and the corners of her mouth tightened.

"All." Roberta swept away an imaginary speck of dust off her gown with a lazy flick of her hand, looking at neither of them.

"What do you mean?" Dev asked through clenched teeth.

"Well," Roberta said, offering an icy smile, "Miss Brickley here was just sharing her suggestions for how we might catch our thief."

Dev's stomach flipped over.

"It seems that our number one and number two suspects are both in the same place." Roberta's expression turned into more of a baring of teeth than anything resembling a smile. "So that is where we shall go."

Dread slithered down Dev's back. "Where?"

"It seems Sir Albert Skevington and his greasy son Nigel, along with the mousy Lady Skevington, are at a very merry little house party hosted by Lord and Lady Brambleton in Surrey. And," Lady Rowling said narrowing her eyes fractionally at Dev, "it just so happens that *I* have an estate in Surrey as well."

Chapter Seventeen

T HAT EVENING AFTER dinner, Jane listlessly added another row to her knitting, a project she'd started too long ago to remember. Beside her on the sitting room settee, her mother worked on her needlepoint with her usual diligence while her father read in the armchair nearby.

Another peaceful, quiet, *boring* evening at home.

This was all that her parents wished for her—to be safely ensconced within the bosom of her family where no harm could befall her. If they could wrap her up in cotton wool and keep her from leaving home indefinitely, they would.

Jane sighed.

Waiting for her parents to approve an adventure would never work. Thankfully, she'd arranged for adventure to come to her.

There was a knock at the front door.

Jane's mother looked up from her embroidery hoop. "I wonder who that could be at this time of night."

Turning the page of his book, Jane's father mumbled, "Graves will take care of it."

Instead of taking care of it, thankfully Graves the butler announced himself at the sitting room door with a polite clearing of his throat. "Two callers, my lord. My lady."

"Send them away, Graves." Jane's mother frowned. "Whyever would someone pay a call at *night*?"

Jane bit back a smile. Her mother acted as if paying a call outside of the usual morning hours was equivalent to a person traipsing down Rotten Row without a stitch of clothing.

"My lady, it is your niece, Lady Hartwick, and her friend, Lady Lydia."

Jane's mother tossed her needlepoint onto the table in front of her. "Oh, for heaven's sake, Graves, show them in."

Beleaguered Graves merely bowed his head before backing out of the doorway. A moment later, Pippa and Lydia swept into the sitting room.

While Pippa greeted her aunt and uncle with warm words and kisses on their cheeks, Lydia shot Jane a surreptitious wink. Jane faked a cough to hide her smile.

"Sit down, girls, do sit down," Jane's father said, gesturing to the pair of chairs closest to the fireplace. "What a nice surprise to see you."

"Thank you, Uncle," Pippa said, taking a seat.

Pippa's late father and Jane's mother had been siblings, and the families had always been very close. Pippa stopping by unannounced wasn't that unusual, and the fact that she'd brought her new sister-in-law along wasn't surprising either.

But Jane imagined her parents *would* be surprised once Pippa explained her purpose.

After a bit of chatter about Pippa's new life married to Jack— "I've never seen my brother smile so much in my life," Lydia had exclaimed—and how Pippa's young brother got along at Eton— "like a fish to water with all that learning," Pippa had said with a laugh—it was finally time to get to the heart of the matter.

"Well, Aunt," Pippa said, beaming at Jane's mother, "I have just the loveliest news."

Jane tilted her head in feigned interest.

"Oh?" her mother said, not having to feign interest at all.

"Why, yes. Lady Rowling just invited some of the members of the Ladies Charitable Association to spend a week with her out at her country estate in Surrey."

"It will be a chance for us to rededicate ourselves to our charity work," Lydia chimed in, lowering her eyes in what she likely imagined was the look of a proper and modest woman.

Jane had to look away or risk snickering. For some reason, there was a permanent air of quiet subversion about Lydia that meant she never looked fully proper and modest. Perhaps it was the obvious intelligence in her blue eyes—a proper woman shouldn't be *proud* of her intelligence according to polite society—or the stubborn tilt of her chin.

Or perhaps it was simply her worldview. A person who held such strong political beliefs that it resulted in them being kidnapped would never be described as proper.

Thankfully, Jane's mother seemed focused entirely on Pippa. "I thought the charity group had shut down?" Then she turned to Jane. "Isn't that what you said last month, dear? That Lady Rowling had become too busy socially to act as benefactress anymore?"

"Well, that's just it, Aunt," Pippa said, rescuing Jane from having to perjure herself to her parents any more than she already had. "Lady Rowling missed us all so very much, and realized that the good we did as a group for those less fortunate in our community far outweighed the personal cost to her social schedule."

"Altruism before Almacks," Lydia said, nodding as if this was some common expression and not a phrase she'd just invented.

"Well." Jane's mother seemed at a loss. Perhaps she couldn't decide between commending Lady Rowling on her generous spirit or worrying about the possibility of her daughter leaving her sight for a week in the country.

She turned to her husband. "Thomas?"

"Yes, darling?" He'd been staring at his book, shut and on the side table, with a look of longing and perhaps had not tracked the entire conversation.

"Lady Rowling has invited Jane and the other ladies to her house in the country for a week." She wrung her hands. "To restart their charity club."

"An entire week?" His bushy eyebrows shot up. "All the way in the countryside? Nonsense. It's much too long. And too far. And too dangerous."

"Uncle," Pippa said smoothly, "Jack will be accompanying us, and he's already arranged for six armed riders to escort our carriages."

"Six armed riders, you say?" Jane's father ran his hand over his mouth before looking at Jane's mother.

The two of them exchanged a long glance which Jane knew would contain an entire silent conversation.

"Pippa dear, it's not that we don't trust Lord Hartwick or his guards, it's just that, well, ever since…" Jane's mother trailed off, and her eyes grew glassy.

Jane rolled her lips inside her teeth and bit down.

She knew how this would go. She'd witnessed it a hundred times. Her mother remained heartbroken despite the many years since her brother's murder.

And Jane sympathized.

Part of her longed to wrap an arm around her mother's shoulders while she wept. She loved her mother, and she wanted to give her comfort. Losing a sibling was a pain that would likely never go away, especially when the loss was so violent and senseless.

But another part of Jane—a part that seemed to grow louder with each passing day—had grown weary with all of it. Weary with her parents choosing sorrow over hope. Weary with the focus on fear instead of possibility. And oh-so weary of their view that the world was filled with danger lurking around every corner.

"Aunt," Pippa began, her voice gentle as she leaned forward in her chair. "I know my father's death is still a wound in your heart. I carry that same wound with me every day."

The sitting room grew silent.

Jane's father had ceased fidgeting in his chair. Jane's mother stopped sniffling. And Lydia held herself perfectly still.

"And for many years," Pippa continued, "I was too frightened of what I'd seen that day to even leave my house."

Jane's mother nodded. Pippa's inability to leave her home as a child after witnessing her father's murder had been very alarming to the whole family.

"But…I missed out on so many things because of how frightened I'd become." Pippa squeezed her hands together. "And my father wouldn't have wanted that for me. He wouldn't have wanted me to limit myself because of my fear. And he wouldn't want that for you either."

She stared at her aunt for a beat before swinging her gaze to Jane. "And," she added, "he definitely wouldn't want that for your daughter."

Jane trembled.

Her cousin was so very brave. She'd witnessed her father's murder, and now she fought back against her fear with her proficiency with her blade. The least Jane could do was fight back against her parents' fear with her voice.

Jane stood. "Mother, Father."

They both stared at her.

It was rather shocking, her literally standing up to them.

"It's fine if you want to send armed footmen with me," Jane said. "I can tolerate them following me everywhere I go. But…I *have* to go."

Her mother's mouth dropped open. Her father's bushy eyebrows shot up almost to his hairline.

"I can't stay here all the time. I can't not go where I wish simply out of fear of upsetting you. It's not how I want to live anymore. I've reined myself in so much, for so long, and I'm tired of it." She spread her hands out. Could she make them see? Would they hear the desperation, the pain, the finality in her voice?

"I want to live freely. I want to go places and do things. I want to go away to Lady Rowling's estate for a week with my friends. Can you understand how I feel?"

Jane's heart pounded loud in her ears, and it felt as if a nest of baby birds had taken up residency in her stomach, poking away with their little beaks.

But...I also feel free.

She'd been sneaking about for a while now. Lying to her parents. Ditching her guards. Pretending to be sedately sipping tea at Pippa's house when she was actually out conducting her investigation with Dev and occasionally fighting off armed murderers in alleyways.

All right, perhaps that last bit backed up her parents' point of view, but she still stood behind her argument.

Jane was no longer going to lie to make others feel safe. She wasn't going to placidly agree with her parents when they declared the world a dangerous place. She wasn't going to pretend that their restrictions didn't chafe at her very soul.

She was done.

It was time for her to be brave, like Pippa. Like Lydia.

And like she hoped Dev would be, when it was time for him to stop hiding.

Jane's mother sputtered. Her father sat unusually still.

Jane waited.

"Well, I...I certainly don't wish to keep you from your friends, Jane." Her mother's voice was wounded. "And your father and I never wish for you to feel as if you aren't *free*. But, Jane dear, it's simply not sa—"

"Elinor." Her father's quiet voice stopped his wife mid-word.

Jane's mother looked at him. Again, they had a silent conversation with their eyes. Jane wondered how they did that. Would she ever have someone who could speak to her with simply a look? She pictured Dev, his eyes dancing with mirth...but no. She would not think of him. He'd betrayed her, and that was all there was to that.

Jane's mother sighed, and her shoulders dropped. Whether it was due to her tension easing or simply in resignation, Jane couldn't tell.

Her father cleared his throat. "Your mother and I have perhaps been a bit overly zealous in our desire to keep you safe."

Jane nodded.

"We never meant for you to feel…restricted or smothered." He ran a hand over his mouth. "Or as if you had to appease us. It seems in our efforts to keep you safe, we actually did you harm. And we're sorry."

Jane's eyes burned, and she sank back onto the settee. Her mother took her hand and gave it a squeeze. Jane could only nod, afraid that if she tried to speak, she would end up weeping.

After a few calming breaths, she risked a glance across the table at her friends. Pippa's eyes were shining. Lydia nodded, her expression both proud and fierce.

When her mother spoke, her voice had lost its tremulous quality from before. "If you wish to go to Lady Rowling's country estate for the week, you may."

"As long," her father added, "as Hartwick doesn't mind us adding a few more guards to your trip."

⟫⟫⟫⟩⟨⟪⟪⟪

DEV GRUNTED AS he hoisted another trunk into the carriage. It felt like they'd been preparing for the trip to Roberta's country home in Surrey all morning.

Well, since it was part of his father's estate, technically the trip was to *Dev's* country home in Surrey.

He shook his head. That thought didn't feel correct either.

"Here's another one." Parth heaved a black leather trunk into the carriage.

Frowning, Dev circled the newest addition. He hadn't seen that particular trunk in the foyer earlier.

"When I was calculating what would fit where, this trunk wasn't part of the equation," he grumbled, eyeing the dwindling space remaining in the carriage.

Parth shrugged. "Lady Rowling told me to bring it out. May-be she needed back-up gowns for her back-up gowns."

It had become something of a joke between him and Parth, how many dresses fine ladies packed for a week-long trip to the countryside. Dev only needed a few kurtas, a few pairs of trousers, and a handful of other items. Parth, a dandy in the making if Dev ever saw one, had packed twice as much as him, but it had been nothing compared to the amount of luggage generated by Roberta.

Apparently, there were morning gowns, walking gowns, riding gowns, and evening gowns, all to be worn in the course of one day. Dev had never been so glad not to be a fine lady in his life.

If—*when*, he corrected—he took over his father's title and became a fine gentleman, would he have to purchase a new wardrobe and change clothing for no apparent reason, multiple times a day?

His sartorial musings were interrupted by the rumble of carriages and the clopping of horses' hooves. Beside him, Parth openly gawked as three gleaming carriages, one large wagon, and ten outriders, all heavily armed, pulled in behind Lady Rowling's measly two carriages.

Parth stepped back to admire the line of carriages and riders with his hands on his hips. "What a parade we'll create, driving down the road all in a line."

Dev scanned the new arrivals, waiting, wondering…

And then, the door to the second carriage opened and out stepped Jane.

Even though he'd seen her just yesterday afternoon when she'd paid her call on Roberta, his heart still leaped as if it had been a lengthy separation.

He supposed in some ways, it had been. She was so furious with him, and the pain caused by his deception had created a wide chasm between them.

He *missed* her. He knew it was strange, as she'd confronted him only yesterday morning, but somehow, every minute between then and now had echoed with a vast hollowness that could only be explained by her withdrawal.

Before, even when she'd return to her home after their work, he'd still felt her. He predicted what she might say to something funny that happened with Parth, or how her hazel eyes would comically widen in pretend-innocence when something just a touch scandalous was hinted at, or how she might move around the room while she was deep in thought, her body both graceful and energetic at the same time.

He'd felt all those things as a part of his very existence, but now they were gone.

Dev wanted to howl. This gulf between them, so clear now that she stood near him but at the same time so far away, was unbearable.

While everyone was busy with greetings and comparing the planned route to the estate or—in the case of the guards— keeping an eye out for suspicious activity on this clear, sunny morning in Mayfair, Dev hurried over to Jane.

Once he was beside her, she sniffed and looked away.

"Jane."

She ignored him.

"Jane, please. I must speak to you."

Her friend, Lydia, nudged Jane with her elbow. "Jane. He *must* speak to you."

Jane shot Lydia a dirty look.

"Please." He didn't mind begging. If this was a portion of his penance, then so be it. "We don't have to talk about what happened. But there are things I'll need to know, as we head into this…"

He trailed off, realizing he shouldn't have approached and spoken to her openly with Lydia present. Although, since Jane's cousin Pippa already knew about their partnership, the odds were high that Lydia knew as well.

"Fine," Jane bit out.

Dev's jaw unclenched. He glanced around. "Let's talk over there." He led the way behind the last carriage in the lineup.

Once they were out of sight of the others, Jane turned to him, arms folded across her chest. "Yes?"

Dev drew a deep breath. "I thought it would be helpful if I knew the plan. What you are thinking for approaching the Skevingtons, or finding the evidence we need, or..."

He trailed off as Jane's eyes grew narrower and narrower still.

"Just so I'm clear," she hissed, "you want *me* to tell *you*"—she poked Dev in the chest with a stiff finger—"*all* the information?"

Dev forced himself not to step back.

Her lips curled in disgust. "You told me *nothing* about who you really are. All you gave me was lies, yet you expect me to just give you my full honesty? How in the world is that bloody fair?"

Jane's curse showed just how furious she was. Dev decided it would be wise to step back.

Her eyes glinted, her hands were balled into fists, and he was certain that if she had a weapon at her disposal, he'd be dead.

Or at least severely maimed.

And...he couldn't fault her.

Everything she'd said was true. He *had* lied to her about who he was. And now he *was* asking her to open up to him. It was extremely unfair.

Even knowing this, even understanding that she was rightfully furious with him and that he could never undo the damage of his deceit, a part of him yearned to pull her close. He wanted to bury his face in her hair. He wanted to run his hands along the gentle slope of her back. He wanted to feel her chest rise against his as they breathed in time.

He wanted her.

He wanted all of her.

And he wanted to give all of himself to her in return.

The enormity of what he'd lost—what he'd never truly had but had seen just a hint of in their time together—swamped him with sorrow. Dev was now hollow. He was empty and alone and…lost.

He had no home.

He'd wanted a home, ever since his mother had died when he'd been so very small. A place where he belonged and was wanted and loved. And he knew now that he could have had that with her. But it was too late. Perhaps he would never have a home of his own.

Dev blinked rapidly, mortified at the tears that pooled in his eyes.

"I…" He swallowed, trying to speak past the lump in his throat. "Jane, I am so very sorry. I do not deserve your forgiveness."

She was silent.

"I know I've hurt you. I've hurt you deeply, by keeping the secret of who I really am and yet sharing something…something special with you when we…when we kissed. When we touched. That was not right, to be with you in deceit, and I know that now."

Jane did not reply.

Dev closed his eyes for a moment. What should he do? Should he call this whole thing off? It hardly seemed worth it anymore, trying to prove he was the heir.

Not at this cost.

But then he thought of India. He thought of Parth's parents, who had given him shelter for all those weeks while he hid from whoever was trying to stage his accidental death and waited for Roberta's reply. His friends who'd chosen to stay behind in Calcutta. Their families and friends. And *their* families and friends.

So many people, harmed every single day by the East India Company's exploitation of their land. By the taxes and dismantling of local rulers and forcing people to plant crops that would be useful in England instead of crops that would feed people in India.

The East India Company was evil.

And if Dev was officially granted the title of Lord Rowling, he would have some power, some sway, to create change. If he took a seat in the House of Lords, he could help craft policies to curtail the power of the bloated, greedy company that cared for its own power and profits over the humanity of the people of India.

He must do this.

He had to proceed with his mission—their mission, really—to prove his legitimacy and claim his birthright. And in order to do that, he needed to know what Jane was planning. It did no one any good for him to go into this trip ignorant.

He drew a deep breath and met her angry eyes.

"Jane, this investigation we've undertaken together matters to me. Not for my own sake. As you've seen the last two years, I do not mind the simple life of a servant."

Her face eased a bit as if his words had removed some of the hardness from her.

"But for the sake of the people I might help as a marquess, I need this mission to work. For it to work, I need to know what plan you've put in motion. So, although I do not deserve your honesty, I ask for it nonetheless."

He longed to take her hand in his, but he held himself still before her. "Jane, please, what are you planning?"

She looked away out into the square. The sky was gray, and the bare branches of the trees swayed in the wind. Finally, she replied.

"Lady Rowling sent a letter ahead to Lady Brambleton, who is hosting a house party at her country estate in Surrey. It's one of the largest house parties of the year, as they are quite wealthy and have a massive house. As we know, among the many guests in attendance are the Skevingtons. Lady Rowling wrote in her letter that she'd shortly be arriving at her own estate, which is just a few miles away from the Brambleton's, and she hopes she may pay a call upon Lady Brambleton at her leisure. Lady Rowling is certain this overture will result in an invitation to join some of the house party festivities, or at the very least, the grand ball which will be held at the party's culmination. At the ball, we will confront Sir Albert and his son Nigel. We will tell them what we know—that they sent someone to stage an accident to murder you in Calcutta once your father had died, that they sent an assassin to shoot you partway through your journey to England, that they hired Johnny the footman to assist with the burglary of Lady Rowling's home to steal evidence of your right to inherit, and that they arranged for the attack on us in the alley."

Dev rocked back on his heels. When compiled together like that, it was quite a comprehensive list of crimes.

"We don't have proof that they did any of those things though," he said.

Jane shrugged. "They don't know that. Plus," she added, scratching her nose, "I may have something in mind that will convince them to confess and to give up the evidence they stole."

Dev frowned. "What do you have planned?"

Jane wouldn't meet his gaze. "I can't tell you."

"What?"

She shook her head.

Dev studied her, the way her hands fidgeted at her side and her cheeks had turned pink.

He pursed his lips in thought. "Your poisonous herb."

Her head shot up. "How did you know?"

He pointed at her, not even trying to hide his smirk.

Jane slapped her hand over her mouth before exclaiming, "You were just guessing!"

Dev shrugged. "It was the most logical assumption."

"Well, I admit nothing."

"I think you just admitted everything."

They stared at one another, and Dev felt the familiar pull between them. The connection. The longing. The feelings. All of it.

"This is going to be a long week," he said.

Before she could respond, a voice called that it was time for everyone to load into the carriages.

Jane walked away, but before turning the corner around the carriage, she said over her shoulder, "I'll see you in Surrey."

Chapter Eighteen

JANE WATCHED OUT the window as another pasture came into view. Once the mighty caravan of carriages had left London proper, the densely packed buildings had given way to more pastoral scenes.

Meadows.

Cows.

Sheep.

Fields of fallow crops. At least that's what she assumed she was looking at, as they were late into autumn, and she couldn't imagine anyone deliberately planting a crop of chopped-off sticks.

On the opposite carriage bench, Lydia dozed, her head resting against the velvet-lined siding. In another carriage, Pippa and Jack rode with Jack's best friend, Benedict, against whom Lydia had lodged the serious accusation that he'd once inquired about her health.

The scoundrel.

There was a third carriage for the accompanying servants, the wagon for all their assorted luggage, and then the two carriages for Lady Rowling and her so-called servants. Jane wasn't sure who among the lady's retinue were real servants and who were in hiding like Dev. Perhaps he was the only one, but she hadn't thought to inquire before. Perhaps there was some deep-rooted smuggling service where princesses and rajahs and doges and all sorts of nobility were smuggled about the globe, hiding in plain sight with feather dusters for disguises.

What a plot for a novel that would be.

Through the window, Jane spied a hog rolling in a mud hole in a farmer's field. Ah, an apt image for Dev, the swine who'd lied to her every single day of their acquaintance.

Except…after their talk behind the carriages today, that didn't feel true. He'd been so very remorseful. In fact, he'd tried to hide it, but she'd seen the sheen of tears in his eyes.

It ripped at her, feeling torn between her righteous fury and her more tender feelings for him. He seemed genuinely devastated at the pain his lie had caused.

Could she forgive him?

They would be in one another's pockets this upcoming week, living in the same house and working together again to resolve the case of the missing heir. Would he be present at any of the house party's social events? A servant could go almost anywhere. Perhaps Lady Rowling would offer the use of her own servants to the Brambletons to assist with the heavy load of hosting so many guests.

She remembered the look in his eyes when she'd mentioned the ball that would mark the end of the house party.

She let herself dream for a moment. She would be dressed in a fine gown, perhaps something gold to bring out her hair. And Dev would be in a formal black coat, a snowy cravat at his throat. His boots would gleam as he'd lead her around the dance floor. His hand would be cradling hers as they waltzed in time to the music. She'd stare up into his blue eyes, and they'd twinkle at her once more, the way they used to before things became so complicated between them.

It would be magical.

And there was no way for it to be real.

Jane sighed.

Lydia stirred on the bench beside her. After a stretch and a yawn, she asked in a sleep-roughened voice. "Are we there yet?"

"No, it's only been a couple of hours."

Lydia slouched back in the seat. "Pity. I was hoping I'd missed all the boring parts of England."

"Unlucky for you, there are still many, many miles of pigs and cows and fields to bore you."

Lydia groaned but did turn to stare out the window. After only a few minutes, she announced. "I'm officially bored. Entertain me. Why don't you tell me all about this secret plan to find the evidence that Dev is the true heir and then get the LCA reopened?"

Jane grimaced.

In the end, she had told Pippa and Lydia everything. She never would have been able to convince her parents to allow her to leave without her friends' support, because if they were coming, then Jack was coming, and Pippa made sure he brought plenty of armed riders to keep Jane's parents happy. And to keep Pippa calm as well. She was so comfortable going out in public now that she knew how to defend herself with her sword, but she still tensed up if someone came barreling toward her. It was completely understandable given the violence she'd witnessed as a child.

And so, Lydia knew everything that had happened and now wanted Jane to explain her grand plan.

The only problem was... "I don't have a grand plan."

Lydia's eyes grew wide. "What?"

Jane shook her head. "I have the *start* of a plan. Maybe the *inkling* of a plan. But I don't have a full, complete, total plan."

"That is less than ideal." Lydia rubbed her chin. "All right. I can help you. Tell me what you've come up with so far."

"Well," Jane said slowly, "I convince Lady Rowling to get us to Surrey where our top suspects, Sir Albert and his son Nigel, are staying at the Brambleton's house party."

Lydia huffed in exasperation. "But you've already done that part."

"I know." Jane tapped her fingers against the seat. "But I

thought you wanted to hear what I've come up with so far, so I thought I'd start at the beginning."

Lydia rolled her eyes and then circled her finger for Jane to keep going.

"So, we all get to Surrey and stay in Lady Rowling's country house. She pays a call to the Brambletons, whom she's already reached out to via post. They will then feel obligated to invite her to some of the social events of their house party. She'll mention she has a few guests staying with her and the Brambletons will invite her to bring them along. The more the merrier, that sort of thing."

"But what if the Brambletons *don't* invite her to bring her guests along?"

"They will." Jane spoke with certainty. "It's the polite and proper thing to do. And the Brambletons are very polite and proper. They have a reputation for throwing the largest and grandest house parties in the ton, and so even more guests will be welcome as it only adds to their perceived grandness. Plus, Lady Rowling, the icy and lovely widow, is a bit of a mystery still among the well-heeled, so it will be a great coup to get her to their party."

Lydia nodded, looking impressed. "You really put some thought into this."

"Of course. Getting the LCA reopened is very important to me, and this is the way we get it done."

"So, what happens next?"

Jane shifted on the carriage bench. This part was where the plan devolved into more of a *concept* than an actual orderly plotline.

"Well, you see, what I'm envisioning is…" Jane squinted at the carriage ceiling.

Lydia tapped her foot on the floorboards.

Jane cleared her throat. "All right, so what I have so far—and this is just a starting place, remember—is that while we're at the house party's social events, I'll befriend the Skevingtons. My mother introduced me to them the night of the musicale, so it won't be hard to better our acquaintance. And then, later in the house party…maybe during the ball on the last night…I'll invite them into some room. On some pretext."

"*Some* room? On *some* pretext?" Lydia pursed her lips. "I retract my earlier comment about you putting some real thought into this."

Jane gave a little kick to Lydia's foot. "Quiet you. It gets better."

"For Dev's sake, I hope so," Lydia muttered.

Jane outlined the rest of her plan to Lydia, whose eyes slowly grew wider and wider.

When she finished, Jane nodded and leaned back in her seat, feeling quite pleased with herself.

Lydia blinked slowly. "That's that?"

"Yes."

"Jane, my sweet innocent girl. Please don't take this the wrong way, but you are wretched at extortion."

Jane huffed. This felt like an insult that was perhaps actually a compliment, but it was hard to tell.

"Listen, I have some experience with this, as I myself was extorted." Lydia's expression turned grim. "When I was kidnapped, they threatened to kill me if I didn't write a retraction article for the newspaper and say that the House of Commons *wasn't* a festering sewer of corruption and greed. So, basically the opposite of everything I believed and every article I had ever written." She shook her head. "They actually held a loaded pistol to my head to get me to comply." She shuddered.

"Oh, Lydia." Jane reached across the carriage and took her hand. She'd heard about the kidnapping from Pippa, of course, but Jane and Lydia hadn't become close until afterward, and Lydia rarely went into the details of her ordeal.

Lydia squeezed her hand and exhaled slowly. "I'm fine now, but in that moment, I was terrified. I *wanted* to write the retraction article. I would have done anything they asked of me because I truly believed they would kill me otherwise."

Jane's stomach ached. What a terrifying nightmare Lydia had gone through.

"I tell you this because if you want Sir Albert or Nigel to confess, then they have to *want* to confess. They have to be so motivated, either by fear or greed or whatever will work on them, that they'll comply with all your demands. And dear, right now, your plan will not make them want to do anything other than laugh at you."

Jane pulled her hand out of Lydia's grasp. "Why would you say that?"

"Darling, you are far too sweet and kind—and even worse, you *look* too sweet and kind, as well as innocent—to actually poison anyone. Well, poison them enough to make them feel quite wretched."

"But I already have. Twice!" Ah, the cruel irony of it all. Here Jane was, practically a seasoned poisoner, once with the accidental tea to Lydia's own brother, and the other time with blowing the herb into the attacker's face in the alley to save Dev, and yet no one would believe her capable of such acts.

It just wasn't fair.

"Jane, your plan is an excellent one, except for that component. I'm not telling you to give up or to start from scratch. You just need to refine the part where you extort the Skevingtons. You just need to be better at extorting. And," Lydia offered a tentative smile, "perhaps include your partner in the planning? You're doing this for him, as well, so it makes sense he'd want to be involved."

Jane heaved a sigh. "I'm doing this for the LCA. Getting it reopened is important to me."

Lydia cocked an eyebrow. "And is that the *only* reason this mission is important to you?"

Jane scowled. "I know what you're implying, and I don't approve."

A sly smile appeared on her friend's face. "I'm not *implying* it.

I'm outright *saying* it. You are doing this because you care about Dev."

Jane crossed her arms over her chest. "He's a liar."

"You lie to your parents."

"That's different!"

Lydia took a moment to inspect her fingernails before asking, "How?"

"I lied to them because it was the only way to make sure the real heir inherits the Rowling title and the only way to get the LCA reopened."

Lydia stared at her, eyes unblinking.

Jane scowled.

Her friend merely arched an eyebrow. She was very talented at that particular maneuver. Did she exercise her forehead muscles?

"Hmm…the only way," Lydia finally said as she seemed to give her full and undivided attention to smoothing out her skirt. "Perhaps Dev felt that keeping his identity a secret was *the only way* he could keep himself safe?"

Jane exhaled. *Blast it.*

Why did Lydia have to go around being so logical and fair? Jane wanted to hang on to her fury. It was a simple emotion. It didn't make her question things about herself. And it was easy to keep Dev at arm's length when her anger stood between them.

"I suppose," Jane admitted reluctantly, "Dev *had* to lie since someone was actually trying to have him murdered." She sighed. "I suppose that's a reasonable motive, trying to avoid death."

Lydia merely hummed in response.

"And…and I suppose I *may* have overreacted."

Lydia didn't reply.

Jane closed her eyes and banged her head against the back of the carriage. "All right. I admit it. I *did* overreact! I was just so angry at him. He lied to me. I didn't know the actual identity of the man I kissed and got half-naked for! It was just so shocking to learn the truth."

This time, Lydia's lack of reply felt less deliberate. The silence in the carriage stretched on, and Jane pried one eye open to peek at her friend.

Lydia gaped at her. "Got half naked for?" she squeaked.

Jane covered her face with both hands. "Oh no," she groaned. She hadn't meant to let that slip.

And for all that Lydia seemed so worldly with her keen intelligence and knowledge of politics and the overall glamour of being kidnapped and experiencing extortion firsthand, she'd never had a suitor that Jane was aware of. Perhaps she had never been kissed, and Jane's ever-so-casual mention of partial nudity with a man had shocked her to her core.

"Ah, can we forget I said that part?" Jane asked, peering through a crack in her fingers.

Lydia leaned forward. "Absolutely not. I want to hear all the details. Which half was naked? The top half?" Her eyes widened. "The *bottom* half?" She clutched her hands together. "*The left half?*"

Jane was saved from having to answer that particular question when the carriage slowed to a halt.

Lydia peered out the window. "We're not at a coaching inn. I wonder what's going on?"

Footsteps sounded outside, and Jane's pulse quickened. The story told to her so many times of her uncle's murder at the hands of highwaymen flashed through her mind. Oh, merciful heavens, how was Pippa at this moment? Was she feeling the same panic as Jane?

The door handle rattled.

Lydia balled her hands into fists in front of her like a boxer.

And Jane plunged her hand into her bodice, grasping for her vial, as her heart thundered in her ears.

"Hello ladies," boomed a familiar voice as the door swung open, and then Benedict, Lord Lovell, was stepping up into their carriage, his wide, muscular frame nearly filling the doorway.

Jane slumped back in her seat, hoping he hadn't noticed the location of her hand just a second ago.

"What are you doing in here?" screeched Lydia, fists dropping to her lap. "You scared us half to death!"

Benedict froze for a moment, his face blanched before he resumed his typical lazy, affable expression. He settled into the seat beside Lydia. "My apologies for startling you. I was becoming a bit smothered by all the newlywed lovey-doveys in the other carriage, so I asked to switch."

Lydia promptly switched seats, so she was beside Jane.

A flash of disappointment crossed his face but was quickly replaced by his usual breezy expression. He stretched, displaying a certain leonine grace with his large, sprawling frame, golden hair, and light brown eyes.

He was certainly a handsome man, and Jane did not find it at all hard to believe that he was on many a marriage-minded mama's lists for their daughters, but only once he reformed his rakish ways, of course.

"That was rather presumptuous of you, expecting you'd be welcome in our carriage," Lydia sniped.

Benedict sighed in response, stretching his long legs out between Jane and Lydia's. "If you want me to go, I will, but I swear I'm liable to find a most indiscreet sight if I return to the carriage now that Jack and Pippa have been alone for three whole minutes."

Lydia wrinkled up her nose.

Jane supposed no one wanted to imagine what their brother got up to with his new wife in the privacy of a carriage.

"Well, you were only with them for a couple of hours," Lydia finally replied. "I have to live with them. They are so sweetly in love that I'll likely have a toothache by Christmas."

Jane watched in interest as Benedict sat up straighter in his seat. "Are you…considering leaving your brother's house?"

Well, *this* was quite intriguing. The only acceptable way for a woman of Lydia's age and stature to move out of her family home was if she was married. Was Benedict fishing to see if Lydia was turning her mind to marriage?

Lydia glared at him. "Most certainly not. I'm quite happy in my home, although I occasionally have to put a pillow over my head at night."

After a heavy pause, Benedict looked away from Lydia, Lydia looked away from Benedict, and then both of them turned a very rosy color.

How fun. Jane had just found something more interesting to observe than cows and fields for the remainder of their journey.

Chapter Nineteen

DEV CREPT THROUGH the house in his stockings, shoes tucked under his arm. They'd arrived at the country estate in Surrey late the previous night. Thankfully, Roberta had sent word ahead to the elderly couple who served as caretakers, and they'd prepared bedrooms for their entire party.

Dev and Parth shared a room in the servants' quarters. Roberta had argued that Dev should have the marquess's bedroom as this was technically his house, but Dev had refused. When he'd pointed out that it didn't make sense for him to keep his identity a secret these past two years only to ruin it all at the eleventh hour for a comfier bed, she'd relented.

The caretakers had admitted that they didn't have enough firewood or coal to heat all the extra rooms, and so when Dev had woken before the rest of the household, he'd decided to see what he could do.

The thought of Jane chilly in her room did not sit well with him.

And so here he was, in the dim light of dawn, tip-toeing his way through the gloomy country home that was to be his if all went according to plan. Not that he knew much of the plan. Jane hadn't seen fit to confide in him, and in the face of her completely justified anger, he hadn't pressed the issue further.

The rooms of this place were dark with paneled wood walls

and heavy curtains. Dim paintings with thick, ornate frames lined the walls. The whole place felt old and musty.

When he slid open the bolt and pulled the front door open, he felt lighter just by stepping outside into the fresh air.

The lawn out front had long grass surrounded by a border of leafless trees. Jane probably knew their scientific names and what their leaves looked like. She probably knew if the leaves or bark were good for anything, like medicine or dye or even poisoning people.

He smiled.

Just the thought of her made him smile. He was ridiculous, and he knew it. And he was also rather heartbroken. She despised him now that she knew of his deception, and it felt as if he'd lost something very, very precious.

Dev slipped into his shoes before heading out, turning to the right. Unless he wanted to chop down one of the bordering trees out front, the wood for their fires would not be found here.

After circumnavigating two-thirds of the house, he found an outbuilding with a stack of dry, round logs. Dev had chopped wood before at the London house, so he felt comfortable as he set a log on a massive, round trunk just outside the outbuilding. He found a pair of leather gloves and an axe with a decent blade inside the little shed and got to work.

The steady rhythm of setting up the log, getting into place, bringing the axe behind him, then swinging with all his might became almost meditative after a few strokes. The pile of cut wood slowly grew, and soon sweat was trickling down his temple and back.

Dev pulled off his kurta and draped it over a nearby tree branch. Then he was back to work. Stack, axe behind him, and swing. Over and over. The thwack of the axe biting into the wood sounded in counterpoint to the birdsong coming from the nearby woods. The sun eased up the horizon, brightening the morning around him.

He paused, hand resting on the axe handle as he gulped in the air. It was a gorgeous morning. And it was so quiet and still here. In both Calcutta and London, it was never quiet during the day. But in the countryside, there were just the happy songs of the birds to interrupt a person's thoughts.

And one pair of very large hazel eyes.

Dev jumped. "Jane?"

The familiar figure ducked back behind the same tree where he'd hung his kurta.

He waited, giving her a moment.

"Good morning, Jane." He tried to keep his voice casual.

"Ah, good morning to you as well, Dev," she replied from behind the tree.

"Out for an early stroll?"

She cleared her throat. "It seemed too lovely a morning to spend it abed. Besides, I needed to stretch my legs after so long cramped in the carriage yesterday."

"That makes sense."

Silence.

Dev scratched his nose. "Ah, would you want to come out from there perhaps?"

A pause. "Perhaps."

A bird trilled in the distance. The delicate breeze cooled the sweat on the Dev's body. At last, Jane emerged from hiding.

Her eyes were downcast and her cheeks were bright red. A simple braid hung over her shoulder. The early morning sunshine set her red-gold hair aglow. Dev drank in the sight of her. He longed to pull her into his arms, kiss her good morning, and ask about her dreams from last night, but all he could do was stare.

"I was chopping wood," he said, and immediately winced at his inanity. He was standing here with an axe in his hand. What did she think he was doing, painting a watercolor?

"I, uh, noticed." Jane looked up, but her eyes didn't make it to his face. Her gaze seemed to get caught midway up.

Was...was she looking at his bare chest? Dev was struck by the sudden urge to flex his muscles. But given the warm look in her eyes, he didn't need to puff up to impress her.

She continued to stare, and Dev let her. The memory was a bolt of lightning directly to his veins.

Jane licked her lips. Her hazel eyes were hungry. Hungry for him. He nearly went to her then, but he recalled her anger at him yesterday behind the coach. She was *so* angry. His lie was still between them. The heat in her gaze now wasn't really for him. It was just a physical reaction of one young, healthy person to another.

Dev stepped forward. Jane's eyes widened, but when he grabbed his kurta off the branch, she looked away. Turning his back to her, he pulled the shirt over his head. It was strange given how close they'd been only days before, but dressing in front of her felt strangely intimate.

He cleared his throat. "Shall I walk you back to the house?"

Jane frowned. "Are you finished here?"

They both eyed the large pile of split logs. He must have really been in the rhythm of chopping because he'd cut far more wood than he'd realized.

"I still need to cart this inside, but I'm done chopping." He'd seen a wheelbarrow in the outbuilding. He could stack the wood into the wheelbarrow, then haul it to the back door and per-haps—

"I can help you."

Dev glanced at her pretty gown, her ungloved hands, and her dainty shoes poking out below. "I don't think that's a good idea."

He turned and went into the little building for the wheelbar-row. He maneuvered it to face the door, but Jane blocked the exit.

"I need to talk to you."

His hands flexed on the wooden handles. What was she going to say? That she wanted out of their partnership? That she'd still help him but then never wanted to see him again? His stomach hollowed.

"Fine." He'd let her say her piece, but he wasn't going to fall to his knees and pound his fists into the ground with her here to witness him falling apart.

After Dev nodded toward the doorway, Jane moved aside so he could roll the wheelbarrow over to the log pile.

"So," Jane began, "I was thinking a lot yesterday—"

Bang. Dev dropped a piece of split wood into the wheelbarrow.

Jane frowned before continuing. "I realized that I may have—"

Bang.

She raised her voice. "As I was saying, I may have over—"

Bang.

"Dev," she said, stepping closer, "I'm trying to tell you—"

Bang.

"Will you stop that?" she shouted.

Dev threw the log in his hand to the ground. He peeled off his leather gloves and flung them into the wheelbarrow. "What? What's so important that you're interrupting my work? These are very important logs, Jane."

She stepped closer and lay a hand on his chest. "I don't care two figs about the logs, Dev. I don't think you do either. Can you just listen for a minute, you big oaf? I'm trying to apologize."

Dev's chest rose and fell under her hand.

Her eyes flashed with emotion, and her hand was hot against the center of his chest. Could she feel his heart pounding? He could feel it through every inch of his body. It felt like a giant clock, bonging away each second that they weren't partners. That they weren't together.

"Jane," he whispered. But he kept his hands at his side. He couldn't touch her.

"You kept a secret from me," she said, her voice quiet now.

He flinched.

Jane shook her head. "No, no. It's all right. I understand now. You weren't trying to trick me or hurt me. You *had* to do it. Your life was in danger. And"—she swallowed—"it still is."

Jane stepped even closer, placing her other hand on his chest as well. "I've been so self-centered, thinking about myself and how your deception affected my feelings. But I hadn't stopped to consider what it meant for you."

Dev's breath came shaky now. He stared down into her eyes. Jane's words had such power over him that she could flay him open or heal the battered parts of his heart with what she chose to say next.

"You lost your mother," she continued, "and then your father abandoned you. When he died, instead of grieving and being able to move forward, you had to contend with people trying to kill you. And the only thing you could do was hide. You had to protect yourself and those around you. I see it now." She blinked up at him, her eyes glistening with tears. "I see it so clearly, Dev. And…and I see *you* so clearly too."

Dev could scarcely breathe. His eyes burned as her words of understanding washed over him. Over his very soul.

She smoothed her hands up his chest and around his neck. "Dev, I'm so, so sorry. Will you forg—"

Before she could finish, he hauled her close and captured her mouth with his. The kiss was fire, searing away the hurt and loneliness that had been his companions since she'd come through the study window for the second time.

"Jane," he moaned between kissing her.

Her lips were a prayer on his mouth. The sweet slopes and curves of her back and hips and waist were a goblet of water in the desert. He'd been lost, but with her in his arms, he felt the peace of a home.

"Dev, I want to touch you," she gasped once he pulled away from her mouth and began to trail kisses down her neck.

"Yes, touch me," he managed to say between tastes of the soft, tender skin of her beautiful neck.

"Take your shirt off," she commanded.

Dev pulled back, tearing off his kurta before flinging it blindly toward the tree branch. He reached for her, his hands greedy for the feel of her, but she held up a hand.

He stopped. Of course, he stopped. He wouldn't touch her if she did not wish it.

"It's my turn," she said. Her cheeks turned a delightful shade of pink, but she still tilted her chin up and regarded him with a determined expression. "You touched me the other night, so it's only fair that now I get to touch you."

Dev thought he might combust on the spot.

Jane taking control and feeling her power was more erotic than anything else on the entire earth.

He drew a deep breath before nodding. "You can touch me however you wish."

Jane's fingers moved tentatively at first. She lightly brushed across his chest, feeling the rise and dip of his muscles. Dev forced himself to remain still as she explored. She grew bolder, stroking across his stomach. Her hands left a trail of fire in their wake. Dev's stomach muscles spasmed at the sensation.

"You are so handsome," she whispered.

And then she leaned in and put her mouth on his chest.

Dev sucked in a breath.

Her tongue darted out, tracing one nipple and then the other. She grazed his sides with her fingernails. Dev wanted to leap on her, tumble them to the ground, and throw her skirts up. He wanted to sink into her.

But instead, he stood absolutely still.

He let her kiss and lick along his chest and touch his stomach. He would stand here like a rock carving until she was ready for more. He could do this for her. He would do anything for her.

And he realized at that moment when it was so clear that her pleasure was paramount to his own, that he loved her.

He loved Jane Brickley.

She was everything to him.

"Jane," he moaned. He was on fire. She was both the flame and the only thing that could quench this blissful burning.

She panted his name in reply, and then she was lifting her face to his and they were kissing once more.

He grabbed her, pulling her flush against him. The soft curves of her breasts felt divine against his chest. His caresses roamed down her back and cupped her bottom. Her curves were so round and sweet. He wanted to press her hips tightly against him to ease the ache in his hard cock, but that felt like crossing a line.

He nearly choked when *she* pressed her pelvis against him and swiveled.

"Oh, Jane," he growled.

His hand reached down and began gathering up her skirt, pulling the endless fabric up higher and higher. He had to touch her. He had to feel her sweetness against his bare fingers. He had to—

A cheerful whistle sliced through the fog of desire.

Jane stiffened in his arms. Dev dropped her skirts and stepped back, although he might have left part of his soul with her.

The whistling sounded again, coming from around the corner of the house.

"Someone's approaching," she whispered.

Even as Dev grabbed his kurta from the ground—apparently the tree branch had not held up its end of the bargain—and drew it on, he noticed Jane's kiss-swollen lips, her trembling hands, and her flushed face.

He likely appeared just as disheveled, but he wasn't a proper young lady whose honor was viewed by a judgmental society as something that could be ruined.

"Go into the shed," he whispered, gesturing to the outbuilding.

Jane blinked.

"Hide," he urged. "I'll pretend I was out here alone and got all…" He gestured to his wrinkled kurta and doubtlessly flushed face. "…like this from chopping wood."

She nodded and bolted into the outbuilding just as two figures rounded the corner of the house.

Lord and Lady Hartwick, who Jane affectionately called Jack and Pippa, walked hand in hand. Jack would whistle a jaunty tune, and then they would both peer up at the birds, apparently waiting for them to reply.

Wealthy people were strange.

Dev rolled his eyes at himself. If all went according to plan, *he* would be a wealthy person. He supposed he'd technically been one until his father's death and his subsequent charade as a servant, but it hadn't felt that way. He had dressed simply. He'd socialized with the household servants. And he never went to parties or events with the other wealthy or aristocratic families in Calcutta.

How odd to think that very soon he might be waking up early for the simple purpose of strolling in the morning sunshine and trying to strike up a conversation with animals.

"Good morning, Dev," Lady Hartwick called once they were closer. "You've been hard at work already." She nodded toward the pile of wood and half-full wheelbarrow beside it.

Dev nodded in greeting. Was he supposed to bow his head as he had in the past? Most of his interactions with the LCA members had been when he was lowly Dev, Lady Rowling's helpful servant. And he'd always interacted with just ladies before. Somehow, Lord Hartwick being here made things feel more official.

"Jack, this is Devin Stokes, the secret Lord Rowling."

Dev's lungs seized.

Lord Hartwick merely smiled, sticking out his hand. Dev could only stare at it.

"It's all right," Lady Hartwick murmured. "We won't tell anyone who you really are."

Her expression was open and kind. Her husband's face was more inscrutable, but there was a steadiness in his gaze that set Dev at ease.

He finally reached out and shook Lord Hartwick's hand.

"It's a pleasure to meet you, Rowling. When you get yourself situated with the court tribunal and are ready to take your seat in the House of Lords, I'd be happy to take you around and make the introductions."

Dev blinked.

Rowling. That was his father's name. No one had ever called him that before. He'd always been Dev, a name that had worked in both India and here in England. *Rowling* felt like someone else.

"I…thank you," he finally replied.

"We'll do everything we can to assist you this week," Lady Hartwick said. "I know Jane has a plan for approaching the Skevingtons, but she hasn't shared the details with me yet."

Dev stopped himself from saying, *me neither.*

"But whatever you need, you can count on Jack and me. On all of us, really. We haven't told Benedict as he's a bit of a sieve when it comes to secrets." Lady Hartwick rolled her eyes. "But I'm sure he'd help out if asked. And Lydia too. Plus I'm certain your stepmother is ready to do whatever it takes."

Dev's tense muscles relaxed a degree.

Lady Hartwick was right. He did have a lot of people on his side, including his stepmother, whom he'd always regarded as more of a friend than a maternal figure.

Everyone imagined Roberta to be an ice queen, full of frosty disdain, but they didn't know her like he did. She had built quite a thick wall and deep moat around herself, but it was the only way she'd known how to protect herself in the strange life she'd been thrust into at seventeen. Dev knew the truth though, that she believed in justice and fairness with all her being.

It still boggled him that even the members of the Ladies Covert Academy couldn't see who Roberta really was, that they didn't realize that a woman who spent a fortune and years of her life setting up a secret academy to help young ladies would be a fierce believer in allowing women to choose their lives for themselves.

Because Roberta's choice had been taken from her when she had been but a girl.

"Yes," he finally answered. "I'm quite lucky to have Lady Rowling in my corner, and you all as well. Thank you."

Lord Hartwick gave a deep nod which Dev supposed was the gentleman-to-gentleman equivalent of a bow. Lady Hartwick smiled, and the two of them continued on their walk.

Dev busied himself stacking more logs into the wheelbarrow until the couple had disappeared around the other side of the house.

"You can come out now," he called to Jane.

She poked her head out. "Well, that was a near thing." She walked toward him, her fingers toying with the folds of her dress.

"I'm glad they didn't see you." Dev refrained from taking her hand. The interruption by Lord and Lady Hartwick was a good reminder that it wasn't safe to kiss out in the open. It likely wasn't safe for them to kiss at all, but once he was Lord Rowling…

He stared at her.

"What?" she asked, touching her cheek.

Dev couldn't speak. Once he was really Devin Stokes, Lord Rowling, he could openly court Jane. Lord Rowling, the marquess, and Miss Jane Brickley, daughter of a baron, were surely a proper match? He could take her for walks in the park and bring her flowers—well, living plants for her laboratory would likely be appreciated more—and maybe someday ask her to be his wife.

His gaze roved over her face, committing her to memory as if he didn't already have Jane imprinted on his very soul. Her wide hazel eyes, which blended together brown and gold and green. Her sweet pink lips. The shine of her hair, loose tendrils that had escaped her braid stroking her temple and jaw.

How he loved this face.

How he loved this woman.

But he would only be deserving of her if he found irrevocable proof that he was his father's legitimate heir.

Everything depended on it.

Chapter Twenty

JANE WANDERED THE first floor of the house, her stomach growling. They'd gotten in so late last night that there hadn't been time for a tour, and this morning she knew she'd woken up too early to expect breakfast to be ready.

But now her empty stomach demanded eggs, toast, and if she was lucky, some very crispy bacon.

If only she could find the confounded dining room.

The house was maze-like, with lots of small rooms connected by dark-paneled hallways that seemed to zig and zag in no sensical order. So, Jane realized she must follow her nose. Ah, the sweet scent of bacon in the morning. There was nothing like it.

Well, except perhaps for Dev. He'd smelled like fresh soap, good clean sweat, and freshly cut wood. It had been heady, devouring his mouth and inhaling his intoxicating scent in the crisp morning light.

"Good morning," Lydia greeted once Jane made it to the source of the bacon smell. "The scones are delicious."

Jane smiled and headed to the sideboard. "How'd you sleep?" she asked, filling her plate with food. The scones *did* look quite tasty. Perhaps what this country estate lacked in modern décor, it made up for in pastries.

"Fine," Lydia replied. "Actually, that's not true. I stayed up much too late once we got in last night. I was quite engrossed with reading a book."

Jane sat next to her at the table. "Oh? Are you reading Jane Austen's latest? I hear it's quite good."

"No." Lydia sipped her tea. "Dev's mother's diary."

Jane dropped her scone onto her plate. "I thought you'd already read through it?"

"I *skimmed* through it." Lydia stole a piece of bacon off Jane's plate. "Now I'm reading through it slowly and writing the translation. I thought Dev would want to read it himself."

Jane stared at her friend. "Lydia. That's…" She shook her head, struggling to find the words. "That's the kindest thing. I…thank you. Thank you so much."

Lydia lifted her teacup to her mouth, but Jane could still see her smile.

Jane's mind spun. Dev had been so young when his mother had died, only four years old. And it seemed from his description of her that aside from a general sense of her motherly love, his main memory was the Italian lullaby she'd sung.

If Jane could give him his mother's own words through Lydia's translation work, it would be like restoring her to him in a small way. He could know his mother's thoughts, her feelings, and what her life was like until the end. He could feel connected. He'd mentioned not feeling like he had a home. Perhaps this would be a small step in giving that to him.

Jane pressed her hand to the center of her chest. All these feelings, they were quite a lot of work on one's heart.

She thought of Dev's horrid father who'd ignored him so terribly that Dev hadn't felt at home in the house he'd lived for his entire life. What if the diary brought up difficult memories as well?

She set down her fork. "The diary entries, are they…appropriate?"

Lydia frowned. "What do you mean? There's no…you know, naughty bits or anything."

Jane rolled her eyes. *Naughty bits.* "No, I mean, will it upset him? Does she write about Dev's father hurting her, his cruelty to Dev, or anything like that?"

Lydia cocked her head to the side in consideration. "She described falling in love with her husband on the boat, and then her unhappiness when they arrived in Calcutta and he began to ignore her. Perhaps those things would upset Dev. But from what you've told me, he already knows about that."

Jane nodded. It was true. Dev had no misconceptions about the type of man Lord Rowling had been.

Lydia watched her, eyes assessing. "Jane, I know you want to protect him. And that's so caring. But don't you think he deserves the truth? And besides, what she wrote about the most was Dev. I don't think reading his mother's diary will upset him, at least not in a bad way."

So…upset in a *good* way. Jane sighed.

"Once you finish eating," Lydia said, "we can fetch the diary and transcription from my bedroom."

Jane thought of Dev holding her with both care and passion earlier at the woodshed. She wanted to do something kind for him. Of course, they were partners in this investigation, but she had her selfish motives for that. She'd said from the beginning that she was only doing this to reopen the LCA.

Although Jane wondered if that was strictly true anymore.

Well, giving him this diary would be something special she could do apart from trying to prove he was the legitimate heir to the Rowling title.

Jane shoved a forkful of eggs into her mouth, downed the remains of her tea, and stood up from the table. "Let's go."

DEV STACKED WOOD into a tidy pile in the kitchen under the watchful eye of the gray-haired woman who, along with her husband, served as the caretakers of this property.

He noticed how her hands shook as she kneaded the bread that would likely be served with their supper that evening. She'd told him when he'd first come to the backdoor with the wheelbarrow of wood that she'd worked at this estate for forty years.

Dev had decided then and there that when—or perhaps *if*, depending on how the next few days went—he became Lord Rowling, he'd offer this couple a pension and lifelong home in one of the cottages on the corner of the estate. They were far too old to be burdened with this much labor. His father should have seen to their well-being when he'd been alive. However, it seemed his father had thought of little beyond his beloved East India Company. Even inheriting the title when his older brother had died had not been enough to entice the man to leave his post in Calcutta.

And nothing, it seemed, had been enough to make him care about his son.

If Dev slammed a log or two down with more force than was necessary, who was to know? It was just harder than he'd anticipated, being here in his family's house, a house that had never been a home to him or his mother.

No, instead of giving them a home, his father had given them his indifference.

"Dev?"

He looked up to find Parth staring at him, his mouth pulled down at the corners in a look of concern.

Parth gestured at the wood stack. "It looks as if you've gotten that in as tight as it will go."

Dev followed his friend's gesture and realized he'd been leaning all his weight onto the last log, trying to force it into the already full wood bin.

"Ah." Dev dusted his hands together awkwardly. "It seems that this last one won't fit in."

Parth nodded.

Dev pretended not to notice the look of pity in his friend's gaze.

"If you're done here, Lady Rowling needs you upstairs."

Dev glanced over to the caretaker. "I'll be back for the wheelbarrow later."

She nodded, and Dev followed Parth out of the kitchen and through the dim hallways of the house.

"Don't the English believe in ghosts?" Parth asked as they passed a particularly gloomy portion of the house where a portrait of a bewigged man seemed to stare down at them with disdain. "Perhaps your house is haunted."

"It's not my house," Dev mumbled as he tried to discern if the eyes in the portrait were following him. It *felt* like they were following him. Perhaps he'd best not look too closely if he wanted to sleep tonight. "At least not yet."

"But soon," Parth replied, leading him up the narrow set of stairs.

Dev shrugged. It all felt so foreign and overwhelming here. It was hard to even imagine that this strange country house could be his someday. What did one do with a dark, moldering, possibly haunted estate?

"In here." Parth directed Dev through an ornately carved door. Dev blinked as he entered a large bedroom. The heavy velvet curtains had been pulled back, revealing the largest window he'd seen in the house so far and allowing the late morning sunshine to stream in. The massive four-poster bed was elevated so high that there was a set of steps along the side of it, presumably so one could crawl into bed without the need for a running start.

Up on the ceiling, Greek gods and goddesses were painted gathering around a temple. The furniture in the room was as loud and ugly as could be, the dark wood carved with such ostentatious designs that surely the tree it had been hewn from would cringe in embarrassment.

As Dev took it all in, the back of his neck began to prickle.

He turned to face his friend who remained in the open doorway. "Parth, what room is this?"

"This is the marquess's bedroom." Lady Rowling stepped out from an adjoining door, perhaps the dressing room. "Would you send him in now?" she said to Parth.

Dev's friend nodded before disappearing.

"What are you doing?" Dev asked Lady Rowling, working to keep his voice low.

"It's time, Dev." She circled the room, running a hand over the full-length oval mirror, along the dresser with its gaudy curlicues and swirls, and across a large black trunk sitting in the corner.

Dev narrowed his eyes. He recognized that trunk. Hadn't Parth said it had extra dresses for Roberta? But if it was in the marquess's room …

His gaze shot to hers. "No."

"Dev, you can't stay hiding forever. This thing is almost at an end. Are you going to make your entrance into polite society looking like a servant?"

He buried his fists in the loose fabric of his kurta. "I'm not ready."

Roberta merely sighed before opening the trunk. "I ordered you riding clothes, formal wear, breeches and jackets, cravats, boots—"

"I don't want them."

She carried on as if he hadn't spoken, digging through the trunk. "…night shirts—"

Dev interjected. "I don't want to wear nightshirts." He pictured an old man with a long flannel gown and nightcap askew over his grizzled hair. No. He wouldn't do it. He couldn't do it.

She glanced over her shoulder. "Proper Englishmen wear nightshirts."

"I'm *not* a proper Englishman."

Whatever sharp, clever retort Roberta doubtlessly had planned for him was interrupted by a voice clearing from the doorway. "My lady," Parth said, "I've brought the valet."

Roberta straightened from the trunk. "Wonderful. Thank

you, Parth."

Parth smiled at her before he departed. *Traitor.*

Left behind was one rather confused-looking valet—Lord Hartwick's valet if Dev wasn't mistaken. Although the servants hadn't partaken of their usual communal meal in the kitchen here yet, he'd seen the man about as they'd been unloading the carriages last night.

"My lady." The valet bowed to Lady Rowling. "Sir." He bowed to Dev, although his eyebrows were rather high on his forehead as he did so.

"Ah, no." Dev raised his hands up. "There's been a misunderstanding."

"No misunderstanding at all." Lady Rowling hurried over to Dev as if she might need to tackle him to the ground to keep him in the room. "Thank you for your assistance, Franklin. Dev will be needing a haircut and shave, assistance with dressing, and whatever other grooming you deem necessary for him to look the part of a gentleman. And," she added, narrowing her already icy eyes into slits of glacier blue, "this is a most discreet matter."

"I understand, my lady." Franklin, apparently in cahoots with today's traitors, bowed once more.

Lady Rowling gave Dev a final glare before sweeping out of the room, shutting the door behind her with an ominous thud.

Franklin stared at Dev.

Dev stared at Franklin.

The valet was short and thin with a full head of luxurious black waves. He held a case in one hand, Dev noticed. Doubtlessly it contained torture devices.

"Shall we begin, sir...er, Dev?" Franklin looked as at sea as Dev felt.

Dev sighed. There was no way he could outmaneuver Roberta, not once she'd made up her mind. He'd once witnessed her eat an entire bowl of mashed potatoes because Meera had suggested it was far too much food for one person to consume.

Stubborn, stubborn woman.

With a recently acquired aversion to potatoes.

"I suppose I have no choice," Dev replied.

After a bit of exploration, frequent tugs of the bell followed by deliveries of steaming jugs of water, and the occasional whispered curse, Franklin had established what he deemed "a proper dressing room" behind the side door Roberta had used earlier. He arranged a comfortable chair, copious lighting, a steaming ewer of water, flannel cloths, and other items and gadgets that Dev had no knowledge of.

He decided to put himself at Franklin's mercy.

Dev was washed. He was given the closest shave of his life. His hair was cut and styled, which included Franklin snipping here, staring at him with one eye half-closed for a full minute, and then snipping there followed by another round of assessment. His nails were filed and buffed. Franklin tutted mightily over the state of Dev's hands.

Dev decided not to mention he'd been chopping and hauling wood only hours earlier.

His callouses were exfoliated.

The clothing from the trunk was examined and pressed.

And finally, Dev was dressed.

He felt like a ripe mango, ready to burst against its confining peel.

"Well," Franklin said, mopping his forehead with a handkerchief, "if my best is not up to snuff, then I do not know what else can be done. Tell me what you think."

Dev took a bracing inhalation before moving in front of the floor-length mirror.

He blinked.

"Franklin," he croaked after taking himself in, "I think you should ask for a raise."

Gone was Dev, the humble servant in his comfortable kurta with the messy, overlong hair. Dev with rough hands. Dev with a relaxed posture. Dev with an easy smile.

Instead, staring back at him through the mirror was…

He shook his head.

He didn't even know who that was.

It certainly wasn't Lord Rowling as he'd known him. His father, hair silver, skin perpetually red from the Indian sun, mouth turned down in a cold, disappointed frown.

This was some other Lord Rowling, one who didn't really exist yet.

This man wore a perfectly tailored jacket of dark green wool with a complicated froth of bright white cravat knotted at his throat. His buff-colored breeches hugged his legs before disappearing into gleaming boots. Hoby, Franklin had proclaimed, as if that meant something. This man's hands were soft, betraying no trace of a life of labor. His hair was styled in a swooping wave across his forehead.

This man wasn't Dev…and yet, he was.

Dev was so confused.

He wished Jane were here with him. She'd know what to say, to help ease this strange unease in his chest.

If she were here, perhaps he'd feel like himself again. Like Dev, who helped mix her fertilizer and posed as her fellow herb-seller at Boodle's and whose knife wound she so carefully cleaned.

That was the Dev he wanted to be.

Not this pretend version, this fancy Englishman who didn't know a thing about what was happening in India right now, how the people there were being exploited by greedy men in the East India Company.

Men like his father.

Men he most certainly didn't want to emulate.

And yet here he was, in their clothes. Wearing their hairstyle. With their soft, grasping hands.

He hated it. He hated this. All of it. He just wanted to be home.

Home with Jane.

"Thank you, Franklin." He nodded to the valet, hoping the

man would know he was grateful for his labor even though he was unsettled by the results.

Franklin gathered up his things, and then the marquess's bedroom was empty except for one not-quite-a-marquess.

Chapter Twenty-One

A KNOCK AT the door pulled Dev out of his reverie. How long had been staring out the bedroom window? It felt like he'd been standing here in these boots that pinched a bit on his left foot for hours, but a glance at the clock showed it had only been thirty minutes since Franklin had left.

Dev crossed the room and opened the door.

"Jane."

She'd changed since he'd seen her that morning by the wood stack. Her hair was pinned up and her simple dress—was that a morning dress?—had been swapped out for something a bit fancier, with bits of embroidery along the edges.

She didn't say anything but merely stood in the hall, staring.

Oh. His new look.

His hand went reflexively to his neck where the full folds of the cravat felt like someone had attached a billowing ship sail.

Her gaze wandered up and down, lingering on his carefully styled hair, the trim fit of his jacket, and the top of his breeches, which—Dev had noticed when Franklin had helped him dress— were quite a bit tighter than the flowing pants Dev wore under his loose kurta.

Her cheeks turned pink, and she bit her lip as her gaze darted away. "Ah, you changed."

Dev nodded. "Roberta thought I should…" He shrugged

before tugging on his fitted sleeve.

He didn't really know what Roberta had intended. Was this a trial run? A dress rehearsal before the big reveal?

"Well, you look very handsome." She didn't make eye contact.

Something cold slid along the back of Dev's neck. "Do you think so?"

She nodded. "Very. Like a proper gentleman."

Dev swallowed and swallowed again. She…she preferred him looking like this. Looking like all the other fine Englishmen. Looking like someone else.

That was who she wanted. She wanted Lord Rowling.

Not Dev.

"Well," he said, forcing a calm he did not feel into his voice, "I suppose this was bound to happen sooner or later."

Jane looked at him then, really looked at him. She must have seen some of his unhappiness, because she straightened up, her eyes flashing.

"No," she announced.

He froze.

"This wasn't *bound* to happen," Jane continued. "You don't need to change. You looked handsome before. You looked like…yourself."

Dev's breath stalled in his lungs.

She nodded as if she'd come to a decision. "Dev, you should dress how you want, not how Lady Rowling thinks you should dress or how proper society thinks you should dress." She marched into the room and slammed the door shut behind her.

"Proper society doesn't think I should study botany." She took a step toward him, then another. "It thinks Pippa shouldn't fence and Lydia shouldn't write about politics and Lucy shouldn't run a shipping company and…and all the other ladies shouldn't do the things they want to do that don't include needlepoint and watercolors and marrying the first man who smiles at them and spending their entire lives raising babies and fussing over menus and gossip and ribbons."

Her chin was up and her expression fierce. She stood right in front of him now, and Jane pressed her hands to his chest.

He noticed for the first time that she was carrying a leather-bound book. His mother's diary. But he was too entranced by her words and her power to wonder about it.

"Dev, you need to be yourself." She flexed her hands against him for emphasis. "That's the most important thing. Don't you see?"

He wanted to wrap his arms around her. He wanted to press her to the door and then press himself against her and make her moan and make her cry out his name.

But instead, he reached up and crushed the folds of the cravat. "I hate this thing."

She smiled.

"Would you…would you help me?" Dev wasn't even sure what he was asking, but he knew he couldn't wait another minute to be close to her.

Jane set the diary on the dresser, then returned to him. She reached up and began to work on the cravat. He stared down at her. Her eyes were intent, her lips slightly pursed in concentration. Her hands felt like butterfly wings at his throat. When she brushed his skin as she smoothed the excess fabric of the cravat down into the top of his shirt, he jerked.

"Sorry," she murmured. "Almost done." And then she stepped back, looked him over, and nodded. "Much better."

Dev turned to look in the mirror. Instead of the poofy froths of white, she'd adjusted the cravat into a simple knot, cutting the volume down tremendously.

"Thank you."

She moved next to him, and together, they regarded their reflection in the mirror. Side by side, they looked like a proper couple, like how Lord and Lady Hartwick had looked this morning, walking hand in hand through the early sunshine as they'd whistled at birds and smiled into one another's eyes.

Dev wanted that. He wanted it with Jane. Slowly, he reached toward her hand. He watched in the mirror, breath held, as her fingers twitched, and then she reached for him in return. Their hands met in the middle, and he wove his fingers through hers. Something shifted in his chest at the rightness of her hand in his, of the picture they made, standing together like this.

"It would look just as nice if you were in your kurta," Jane murmured.

Dev squeezed her hand, unable to form a reply around the lump in his throat.

"I brought your mother's diary." Jane watched him carefully in the mirror as if she worried about his reaction.

"I can't read Italian," Dev replied.

"Then it's a good thing Lydia wrote out a translation for us."

Dev's muscles tightened. "Truly?"

Jane nodded before releasing his hand to collect the diary. "Would you like to read it in private or—"

"Stay." Dev spoke without thinking. He didn't need to mull it over. There was no one else he'd rather share this with than Jane. "Please."

Her sweet mouth tipped up in a smile, and she nodded toward the hideous yellow velvet chairs in the corner of the room beside a window. Once they were seated, she handed him the diary which bulged open with a folded sheaf of paper at the back.

He pulled out the pages where entries in English were written in a sure hand. He fanned through the paper. "I'll have to thank Lydia. This must have taken her a very long time."

Jane smiled. "She likes projects where she gets to stretch that big brain of hers. I'm sure she'd say that you were doing her a favor."

Dev continued to sift through all the pages. There were so many entries. Where should he start?

"We have time," Jane said, voice gentle. "Maybe we can read the whole thing?"

Dev swallowed and tugged at the already-loosened cravat. He

cleared his throat, then began with the first passage.

The contessa is impatient to leave Florence and the rumors of another affair, and this time she says she wants to see tigers and ride an elephant and taste a mango. So, in a week, we board a ship for India. I am sad to leave behind Andrea and Flavio, but adventure beckons.

Life at sea is tedium, and it has only been three days. The contessa cannot abide the rocking ship, and although I tell her that her stomach will calm down if she goes on deck for fresh air, she does not listen to me. The rocking of the ship does not bother me, but I wish to be above board, seeing the ocean and meeting other travelers instead of cleaning her sick bowl.

The contessa is too miserable for my company any longer, or so she says, and so today I was free to wander the ship. And I met a very handsome English man. His name is Henry, and he is moving to India to work on trade. He escorted me around the ship and was most attentive to me. And he even said I had eyes the color of the sea. He asked me to meet him again tomorrow.

The contessa asked me to read to her, but I told her the captain is in need of my assistance which was not too much of a lie as Henry has arranged for me to join him in dining with the captain and the other rich guests. I am to sit beside him, and perhaps the other fine ladies will think I am one of them as I have borrowed a silk shawl from the contessa. Henry knows I am a ladies' maid, but he says he does not care because my ocean eyes have enchanted him.

Henry kissed me under the stars last night and asked me to marry him! I am the happiest woman this ocean has ever seen. He asked me to sneak into his room, but I said we must first find a priest. He laughed and said the captain could marry us as he could not wait for a priest, so tomorrow Captain Lambert will marry us before the other guests. I have to tell the contessa when she awakes.

My new home in Calcutta is almost as large as the contessa's. She wept when I bid her farewell at the dock. The house is new to Henry as well, and we explored each floor, running down the halls and laughing like children. He said he must kiss me in every room. I am so very happy to be here with my handsome Henry. He loves me so, and he said that very soon he would take me out to meet the other ladies.

My stomach is quite upset today, and I felt ill yesterday morning as well. Henry says that perhaps when I am well, he shall finally take me along to one of the parties he attends with the other English who live in Calcutta. He did not say anything sweet to me about my ocean eyes today. I visited Diya in the kitchen and she taught me how to make biryani, a very tasty dish with rice and meat.

Diya and Noor told me that my stomach trouble and tiredness are because I am with child! These women never went to school, but they are so smart. I told Henry, but he was quite busy with his important work. Perhaps tomorrow we will celebrate, and he might take me to meet his friends. I am so happy to have a child. I will give this baby all the love in my heart.

My sweet baby is here. Henry named him Devin, but he did not kiss me or hold my hand. I am so happy to have a sweet son, but I only wish my Henry still loved me. I see the disappointment in his eyes when he looks at me. I think he wishes he'd married a proper English lady. But it doesn't matter, because now I have my Devin. Diya, Noor, and the others told me they'd help me take care of him. My baby will be surrounded by love.

Today Devin took his first steps. We were in the kitchen and Noor held out a nibble of naan and Devin walked right to it! I went to tell Henry, but he said I should not interrupt him when he is in his study. It doesn't matter, because my son is so strong and quick. When he smiles at me, my heart melts.

We visited the market today, and Dev even picked out the mangos. He was so proud to hand the coins to the seller. I have a strange ache in my belly that hasn't gone away all week. Perhaps I will ask Diya to fetch a doctor if it is still there tomorrow.

The doctor cannot find the cause of my pain, and it has on-

ly grown worse. I try to smile for my sweet Devin, but I can see the worry in his eyes even though he is so young. I fear what will become of him if I worsen. His father pays us no mind. But my friends in the kitchen love Devin, and I know they will look out for him no matter what.

My sweet Dev brought a cup of lassi to me in bed this morning as I cannot get up again today. I miss playing with him in the kitchen, but it just hurts too much. Henry has not visited me in a week. All I have strength for is singing to my sweet boy. I love him so very much. I cannot regret marrying Henry for otherwise I would not have my Devin.

Dev turned over the final page of his mother's diary.

"There's nothing more?" Jane whispered.

Dev shook his head. A drip fell onto the last piece of paper, and he realized with a start that it was a tear. He wiped at his eyes and cheeks. Jane hopped up and returned with a handkerchief, likely found in the trunk of clothes.

Dev ran his fingers over the last page of the diary itself, the actual Italian words penned by his mother. She had loved him. He'd had a place while she'd been alive, and although she hadn't possessed much power, she made sure there were people to watch after him and care for him when she was gone. He remembered Diya and Noor. Diya had grown old and gone to live with her daughter a few years before Dev's father had died. Noor was one of the servants who'd chosen to remain in India and received a pension from Roberta after remaining in the house up until the end.

Dev was glad. He was glad that they were taken care of, and that they'd cared for his mother and then him in turn. They'd created a place where he'd felt welcome despite the barriers between them.

And his mother…she'd been so very strong. She survived despite her husband's neglect and casual cruelty. He was in awe of her.

"I can picture her." His voice broke through the comfortable silence that had descended upon the room after he'd finished reading. "It's been so long, and I'd forgotten, but now..." He shook his head.

"There wasn't a portrait done of her?"

"My father wanted to forget he'd married her, so he never brought anyone in to paint her likeness." Dev traced the loops and swirls of his mother's writing. "But that doesn't matter anymore because after reading this, I can picture her so clearly."

Jane's eyes were like her laboratory, soft brown and fresh green swirled together. The way she looked at him right now made this ache bearable somehow.

"What did she look like?"

Dev closed his eyes. "Her hair was dark with a bit of curl. She was tall and strong and laughed often. She had kind eyes. They were blue, but as she wrote in her diary, they were a particular shade...dark blue."

"Ocean eyes," Jane murmured. "Like yours."

Dev had his mother's eyes. He'd never noticed before, never realized. He carried this piece of her with him everywhere he went.

Dev looked at Jane, stunned. She nodded, ever so gently, as if knowing the effect her words would have on him. How they would tug at his very center.

"From the diary, it's clear she loved you very much." Jane leaned forward in her chair. "She would want you to be happy."

"But would she want me to be a marquess?" Dev was surprised by how bitter his words sounded.

Jane spread her hands wide. "I don't know. But she sounded like she saw the bright light inside you that I see. Your kindness. Your goodness. How caring you are. And I think that's what would matter to her, not whether or not you inherit your father's title. And besides," Jane added, "he seemed like a terrible person even before he inherited, so you can't blame the marquessate for that."

A huff of laughter escaped him. He looked down at the pages

laying in his lap. "Thank you."

"For what?"

"For asking your friend to make this translation. For reading it with me. For…seeing me for who I really am."

"I see you, Dev," she whispered. And then Jane rose and held her hand out to him.

JANE WAITED WHILE Dev stared at her hand, blinking slowly. Would he come to her?

Gently, carefully, he gathered up the translated pages and tucked them into the diary once more, then set it all on a nearby table. He rose.

His mouth worked a moment before he said, "What are you doing?"

"Let me comfort you," Jane replied, hand still outstretched.

She hadn't planned on this. She didn't have intentions. But she knew, without doubt, or uncertainty, that she had to return the sparkle to Dev's eyes.

His ocean eyes.

It was so fitting. The way Dev's voice had hitched over those passages made Jane's chest ache. And toward the end of the diary entries, when his mother had been ill and knowing that her son would be without a loving parent, when the tears had fallen down his face, she'd realized a most astonishing thing.

She loved him.

She was in love with Dev.

He felt so much. It was all right there, in his ocean eyes, on his face, in the words he shared so freely. He had kept his identity hidden from her, but in truth, he'd always shown her who he really was.

The sort of person who would mix recipe after recipe of fertilizer for her until the proportions were just right.

A person who asked before shutting the door when they were alone in a room together.

A person who would fight off an armed assailant so that she could run to safety.

Dev had always been exactly himself, even when he was hiding.

And now it was Jane who couldn't hide anymore. She couldn't hide her feelings from herself. And so, she stretched out a hand to him.

And he took it.

"Dev," she murmured, and then she pulled him close and tipped up her mouth to meet his.

She lay a hand against his face as their lips met and pressed and opened. She ran her hand along his firm jaw, down the strong column of his neck, and onto his shoulders. Her other hand still clasped his, pressed between their bodies. She never wanted to let go.

She wanted to give him comfort and joy and, above all, herself.

"Dev, I want you."

He pulled back, studying her expression. "Do you know what that means?"

Heat crept up her cheeks, but she held his gaze and nodded.

"I want you too," he replied. "But we can stop at any time. Any time. Do you understand?"

Jane nodded again, then grabbed the back of his neck and pulled his lips to hers once more. She moaned into his mouth as fire licked at her skin and raced through her veins. She pressed her breasts against the firm planes of his chest. How incredible it had felt, when she'd opened her gown to him in her room several nights ago, and he'd touched her there. Pressed his mouth to her there. Made her feel the pounding of her desire there.

She wanted that again.

"Dev," she sighed, and he must have sensed the request in the sound because he pulled away from their kiss.

"Jane?"

"I want you to take off my gown."

Dev's neck moved behind his cravat, crushed quite flat now, as he swallowed. "Turn around," he ordered.

She shivered at the command in his voice. She knew he would not actually command her to do anything, but the feeling of him taking charge made her knees weak and caused the pulse between her legs to throb.

Jane turned her back to him.

Just like that first day of their partnership when she'd changed into a borrowed maid's gown, he plucked at her buttons. But this time he did not take care to leave distance between his fingers and the tender skin of her back. This time, he caressed. He smoothed. He pressed hot, open-mouthed kisses into her skin as he bared more and more of her with each button he loosened.

Jane's head lolled forward, the pleasure of his illicit touch melting her very spine. Anticipation thrummed through her, turning her into a petal that would only unfurl with his touch.

She wanted him so much.

At last, her gown was loosened, and she shimmied, sending it swooshing to the floor. She turned in the pool of fabric.

Eying his jacket, his waistcoat, his cravat, and his shirt, she said, "You are wearing more articles of clothing than me for the first time." She set her hands on the lapels of his jacket. "We should do something about that."

And his eyes went dark and hot. He watched, breath growing increasingly loud as she peeled off his layers.

Conscious of his pressed garments, she draped them over a chair. It would not do to announce to the world through careless wrinkles that Dev had engaged in a liaison.

At last, his upper body was bare. Jane recalled this morning when she'd left the house for an early morning walk only to find him chopping wood, his muscles bunching and straining as he brought the axe down with tremendous power onto the logs. How his skin had glowed in the early morning sunshine. How he'd pulled her against him, and she'd felt those hard muscles, so warm under her hands.

She wanted to touch him again. But she wanted to see all of him this time. She surveyed his lower half and frowned.

"Your boots."

He looked down, puzzled. "Franklin spent a good deal of time putting these on me, but he failed to explain how I was to take them off."

Jane gestured to the chair that wasn't covered in clothing. "I'll help."

Dev sat, and Jane pulled. Then she tugged. Then she swore—just a little bit—and yanked.

"I remember," she panted, "hearing something about doing it from the back."

Dev gave a throaty, wicked laugh, and Jane tilted her head at him.

"I'm sorry," he said, eyes dancing. "That just sounded a bit…naughty."

"I have no clue what that means, but perhaps"—Jane slowly raised one eyebrow, determined not to let him be the only wicked one—"you can show me."

Dev suddenly coughed, apparently choking on a bit of saliva.

Jane turned away so he wouldn't see her secret smile, and once he caught his breath, she grabbed one of his heels and threw a leg over his so that she was straddling his shin backward. Before working on the boot, she peered over her shoulder. Dev's hot gaze roamed over her back and bottom, covered only by her chemise, stays, and drawers, and then up to her face.

"Like what you see?" she asked, keeping her eyes wide in mock innocence.

"You know I do." His voice was gravelly.

Jane's pulse leaped. Turning her attention back to the task at hand, she tugged forward and up and the boot finally slid off.

"You are a woman of many talents," he murmured, reaching for her.

Jane swatted away his hand from her backside. "Perhaps once I have the other one off, we might resume our earlier activity, but I do beg your patience as I've no wish to kiss a man balancing on one boot."

Dev laughed, and Jane smiled as she removed his other boot.

She'd never have imagined that laughter and passion could pair so well, but it felt natural, teasing and laughing with Dev in the middle of their intimacy.

It was an intimacy all its own.

And she loved it.

Chapter Twenty-Two

THE INSTANT HIS second boot hit the ground, Dev grabbed Jane around her waist and pulled her back onto his lap. She was sitting facing away from him in the chair.

"You," he whispered into her ear, "are a very"—he paused to kiss her neck—"naughty girl."

She arched her head back, giving him full access to her graceful neck, her delicate ear, and the sweet curve of her jaw.

"You *make* me naughty." Her voice was throaty.

She pressed her bottom against the hard ache in his lap, and Dev groaned. He wanted her. He wanted her fiercely, but he had to be sure.

"Is this what you want?" he asked, forcing his roaming hands to still.

"Yes," she breathed, catching one of his hands and pressing it to her breast.

Dev gave a gentle squeeze, the delicious weight of her breast through her stays and chemise fitting perfectly in his hand. His other hand gathered up what felt like endless gossamer-thin fabric, pulling her chemise up and up until he felt the silk of her thigh with his hand.

"Can I touch you here?" He trailed his fingers up her leg.

After a little gasp, Jane said, "You can touch me anywhere." Then she parted her thighs, both her words and her movements an invitation.

Dev did not hesitate.

He ran his hand up her soft leg and over the delicate cotton of her drawers until he reached the slit in her undergarment. He parted the fabric, holding his breath until his fingers brushed her curls. He gently parted her, and she moaned as his fingers slid through her slick folds.

"Oh, Jane," he breathed.

She was molten against his fingers. He traced her seam, exploring and discovering what made her sigh and what made her squirm. He found her tight bundle of nerves and circled it with two fingers.

Jane gasped and threw her head back against his shoulder. His other hand roamed her breasts, gently plucking at her nipples.

"Dev," she moaned, rocking against him.

"Jane, you are so lovely," he whispered. "You feel like a dream."

He increased the pressure of his fingers, and she squirmed beneath him.

"Dev, oh Dev," she called. Her hands fisted against his arms.

He moved faster. She was so wet, so responsive to his touch. His cock ached where he pressed against her bottom. With a shudder, she arched and cried out. Dev whispered in her ear as she came. *You are beautiful. You are such a good girl. Oh, my heart. Yes, yes, keep going.*

He kept his fingers moving with increasingly light pressure until her movements slowed. He pressed kisses to her neck and jaw.

"My Jane," he whispered.

She slumped back against him, her head lolling onto his shoulder.

"Dev." Her voice was thick, as if she'd drunk too much champagne.

He stared down at her and marveled at the beauty of her spread out on his lap, form supine, legs splayed open, chest rising and falling with deep gulps of air. He had never seen a more sensual sight.

"Dev," she whispered.

"Yes, my heart."

"I want to make you feel good."

His pulse leaped. Dev exhaled before kissing her neck. "You have."

She wriggled her bottom against his erection. "I want to make *this* feel good."

Dev closed his eyes for a moment and prayed for strength. He could not simply toss her on the bed, rip his pants down, and ease this ache. He would not.

He rose, easily shifting her into his arms. "The bed?"

She nodded. "The bed."

He eyed the behemoth as he carried her over. It wasn't only the widest bed he'd ever seen, but it was also elevated much higher off the ground than a normal bed.

"You'll have to stand for a bit."

She held onto his shoulders for balance as he eased her to her feet. He moved forward and tugged down the coverlet.

Please, let there be fresh sheets.

Ah, he would be sure the caretakers received a raise. They'd changed the linens on this bed as well as the others.

He went back for Jane, and hand in hand, they climbed the steps to the bed.

At the last step, she flung herself onto the mattress, bouncing with a little laugh that did strange things to his chest.

She rolled to face him. "You still have pants on. And I'm still in my underthings." Jane tugged at her stays and made a face.

"Roll over," Dev ordered. He'd noticed earlier when he'd put a bit of command into his voice that Jane's eyes had gone all hot and sultry.

She turned, and Dev crawled across the massive bed to work at her laces. Then he pulled down her stays, drawers, and chemise.

Jane was naked.

He stared, scarcely daring to believe that he was here with her like this. That this was real. She stretched, arching her back and thrusting her breasts, the tips a rosy pink, up at him.

"Shouldn't you join me?" she purred.

A slow, wolfish smile spread across Dev's face. His sweet Jane, so clever and brave and kind, was a minx in bed. What a delightful surprise.

Dev had the rest of his clothes off in the blink of an eye, and now it was her turn to look. Her eyes widened and her cheeks turned red when she stared at his cock, jutting out toward her.

"Is…" She licked her lips. "Is that how it usually is?"

Dev eased himself onto the bed beside her, careful to keep a few inches separating them. He didn't want her to feel rushed or crowded.

"In a normal state, it does not look like this. It's not as large or as hard. But when a man's mind turns to kisses and touches, this happens."

She reached out, then paused, her hand a few inches from his cock, and asked, "Can I touch you?"

He wanted to pounce on her. He wanted to groan. Instead, he echoed her words from earlier, trying to keep his voice calm. "You can touch me anywhere."

Jane ran one finger along the side of his erection, seeming to watch in fascination when he jerked at her touch. Dev closed his eyes.

"Was that all right?" she whispered.

"It was perfect," he said, forcing himself to look at her. "It's just so intense, you touching me."

She bit her lip, then said, "It's the same for me."

Dev groaned and rolled to her, claiming her mouth with his. She tasted so sweet, and as their tongues stroked, he felt the tentative stroke of her hand on him as well. His Jane. His beautiful, generous lady.

Dev cupped her breast, and she arched into his touch. Then

he grabbed her soft bottom and pulled her against him. She gasped, and he pressed some more. Soon, they were rocking together.

"Dev," she gasped. "Please."

"Yes?" he asked, wanting to be sure.

"I need you."

Dev eased her thighs apart. Then he touched her, circling her sensitive nub again until she was panting. And then, carefully and slowly, he eased a finger into her.

She gasped, and he slowed.

"All right?"

She rocked against him in answer. Dev moved his finger, curling forward as he pumped to hit a woman's special spot. When he circled her sensitive nub with his thumb, she gasped.

"Oh, Dev," she breathed. "More."

Dev kissed her and added a second finger. She was so tight and slick. He flicked his thumb across her nub, and she cried out, arching against him. He felt her tender muscles pulsing around his fingers as she peaked.

Dev couldn't tear his eyes away from her face. Her soft lips were parted, her head thrown back, and her red-gold hair haloed her head, the silken strands gleaming in the light of day.

How perfect, that they came together like this for the first time in the daylight, to feast on one another with all their senses as the sunshine illuminated their bodies.

"Dev," she murmured.

"My Jane." He kissed her, then eased himself between her legs. "Are you ready?"

"I want this."

She tensed a bit when he first nudged at her softness with his cock. Dev rubbed against her most sensitive place until she relaxed, then he eased in a bit.

He would not hurt her if he could avoid it.

He wouldn't hurt her for anything. And so, he would go slow although the hungry, desperate, growling part of him wanted nothing more than to plunge into her sweet warmth.

"You feel so good," he whispered, kissing along her neck as he eased in a bit more.

"You feel so big." Her voice was shaky, but when he tried to ease back, she clamped her arms around him. "Don't stop."

Slowly, carefully, he moved inside her. When he was fully seated, they both exhaled.

"Jane," he said, meeting her eyes. "You are mine."

Her eyes were the earth, green and brown and alive with emotion.

"And I am yours."

"Yes," she replied.

He sealed their words with a kiss and began to move.

Jane tightened her thighs around him, her hands caressing his chest and shoulders. They kissed, the wet heat of their mouths a mirror of their bodies—joining, stroking, undulating. Dev's skin felt scorched where her hands traveled. The tight clamp of her around his cock was so good, so right, that he felt each sensation through his entire body. The musky smell of sex engulfed him. Jane's breathy gasps were a counterpoint to his quiet grunts as they moved together. This was everything. It was a feast for all the senses, and he never wanted it to end.

"Jane," he moaned, and circled her sensitive spot with his thumb.

"Dev, oh Dev," she called out, and then she was shaking beneath him, her fingernails pricking his back as she tightened and tightened around him.

Dev's balls tingled, and he pumped into her, giving himself just a few more strokes before he pulled out and thrust against her belly. He groaned as he spilled himself onto her skin, stars lighting up behind his closed eyelids.

"Jane," he whispered, his heart thundering.

Her fingers sifted through his hair, her chest rising and falling beneath him. He must be so heavy. He began to roll off, but she murmured a denial and tightened her arms around him.

"Just another minute," she murmured.

Dev trailed kisses across her cheek, her jaw, and her neck. "You are so lovely."

"You aren't too bad to look at either." She managed a half-hearted waggle of her eyebrows.

Dev smiled, then eased himself to her side before sliding off the bed. He found another handkerchief in the trunk and wet it from the ewer.

He brought the damp cloth to her. "Do you want me to help, or would you rather…?"

Jane blushed once more and reached for the cloth. He turned to give her a bit of privacy, and once she was done, he climbed back up the mountain of a bed, pulled her into his arms, and tugged a sheet over them both before they drifted into slumber.

⇢⇢⇢✳⇠⇠⇠

JANE SNUGGLED INTO the cozy warmth, savoring the soft, dreamy in-betweenness that happened when one awoke slowly from a good nap.

Her body felt sated, like she'd practiced extra hard at her fencing lesson and then taken a long bath. She wiggled a bit and felt a twinge between her legs.

Oh.

Oh my.

She opened her eyes and found herself cocooned by Dev. They lay on their sides, with him at her back, his arm around her, hand cupping her breast, and his legs tucked up behind hers. She inhaled, the scent of soap, clean linens, and the heady musk of their afternoon activity filling her senses.

She smiled.

Was this how a seedling felt the first time it poked a sprouting tendril above the soil and felt the warmth of the sun? There was nothing bad about living in the soil. The earth was rich and safe and nurturing. But to be in the full light of day, to feel the energy of the sun seep inside…it was like nothing else.

It was like being with Dev.

Jane eased away and slowly turned until she was facing him. Dev continued to sleep, his thick lashes like a dark fan upon his cheeks. His face was softer, and younger, although he was neither hard nor old when he was awake. But it was like some painted version of him now, a little bit blurred and soft and dreamy.

Perhaps he felt her regard in his slumber because his eyelids twitched and he stretched, the muscles of his arms and shoulders shifting. Jane felt a lightness in her chest when he reached out a hand as if searching for her.

He frowned, so she scooted closer. His hand found her, and the frown eased.

Again, she felt that spread of lightness through her chest.

"Dev," she whispered.

They'd been away from the household for a couple of hours. Although lounging in bed with him the rest of the day and into the night sounded better than a lifetime of free potting soil, there was the risk that their prolonged absence would be noticed.

She leaned forward, pressing her lips to his. "Dev," she said against his mouth.

He inhaled, and then his lips moved against hers.

"It wasn't a dream," he murmured between kisses.

"It's real," she whispered back, then kissed him once more before pulling away.

His eyelids lifted, and he smiled at her. He smiled *into* her, like that first sunshine hitting the seedling, filling it with energy and life.

"Jane," he whispered, stroking a finger along her bare arm, "this is very special. You know that, right?"

Her heart thudded. What was he saying?

"It's not…" His mouth twisted as if he struggled to find the right words. "I've not done this much"—he gestured between them—"but it's never been like this before. It's never felt like …like it was *everything*."

Jane slid her hand into his and laced their fingers together. "Are we very lucky?"

His eyes twinkled. "I'm a marquess posing as a servant. You're a botanist in a secret academy. I think we've moved way past luck."

Jane laughed and couldn't remember a time when she'd been happier.

Chapter Twenty-Three

JANE DESCENDED THE cramped staircase to the dining room. Earlier, after a few more kisses with Dev, she'd returned to her own room and ordered a bath. Although the hip tub was small and the amount of warm water was scant, Jane had still thanked the servants profusely. They were quite understaffed here at the country estate, and she imagined a last-minute request for bathing water was not the easiest to accommodate as they were also preparing supper.

Jane never would have considered something like that before. But since she'd come to know Dev, she saw everything with new eyes. She saw the people behind the labor. She thought about what it took on their end to make life comfortable on her end. And it was rather… uncomfortable.

It was definitely something for her to think about more when she wasn't trying to work through the complex details of her strategy to uncover a devious plot of title theft and attempted murder.

Jane turned out of the dim hallway into the dining room.

"Good evening," she greeted the others.

Lady Rowling sat at the head of the table. On one side were Jack, Pippa, and an empty seat next to the unoccupied foot of the table. On the other side sat Benedict, looking cheerful, and Lydia, who was glowering.

Jane moved to sit beside her cousin.

"I apologize for keeping you waiting," Jane said, directing her words to Lady Rowling.

The lady glanced at the empty chair at the foot of the table, her expression inscrutable as usual.

Jane recalled seeing Lady Rowling hugging Dev through the window. She'd seemed emotional then. Why did she keep that side of herself so carefully locked away from those who knew her secrets? It wasn't like the LCA members were strangers off the street.

"Lucky for you," Lady Rowling said, "you aren't tonight's tardiest dinner guest."

Jane frowned.

Rapid footsteps echoed from the hallway, and Dev burst into the dining room. He was in his English finery once again, although it appeared he'd been on his own with his cravat this time as it rather resembled a hot air balloon Jane had once seen at an exhibition after the burner had been turned off and the balloon had deflated, laying crumpled on the grass.

"Apologies." Dev nodded to Lady Rowling before moving to take a seat.

At the foot of the table.

Beside Jane, Pippa gaped. Across the table, Lydia eyed Dev with a glint in her eye that Jane did not care for.

"I say," Benedict exclaimed. "Aren't you the servant who helped with the luggage?"

Jane wished the table was narrower so she could reach Benedict with a swift kick. A moment later, he grimaced. Lydia's expression turned to one of satisfaction, so it seemed the deed had been done after all. *Good.*

"Er, my pardons," Benedict mumbled. At least he looked Dev in the face when he said it.

"It's quite all right," Dev replied, but his posture was so stiff that it was clear he was uncomfortable. "I *am* the servant who helped with the luggage."

Benedict took a sip from his wine.

Dev inhaled deeply before adding, "And I'm also the rightful owner of this estate."

Benedict coughed and sputtered. Lydia rolled her eyes before pounding him on the back with what appeared to be more force than necessary.

"Er, *my* pardons," Dev said, echoing Benedict's mumbled apology, but he did it without a trace of mumbling and one eyebrow proudly arched.

Jane wanted to applaud.

"Dev, although I acquiesced to your request regarding to-night's dinner seating," Lady Rowling said, her voice an icicle, "I thought the plan was to keep things quiet until the matter was resolved?"

Jane watched several expressions travel across Dev's face in rapid fire. Frustration. Anger. Determination.

"I've thought about it a bit more, and while we're here at the house, it would be good practice for me to be Lord Rowling."

"Lord Rowling?" Benedict sputtered.

"Dev is the dead marquess's secret heir from his first mar-riage," Lydia snapped. "Keep up, man."

Jane coughed into her fist to hide her snicker.

Poor Benedict raised his hands up as if Lydia had him at gun-point. "I didn't know. No one told me the nice servant was actually a nice lord. Deuced business, keeping secrets from me."

And then Benedict turned to Dev and stretched out his hand. "A pleasure to make your acquaintance, Rowling."

Dev shot Jane a glance, and when she smiled in approval, he gave his hand to Benedict for what appeared to be a hearty handshake.

Jane wanted to cheer. Dev was doing it. He was dropping the pretense and claiming his birthright. She wanted to give all her friends a bright, cheery bouquet of flowers to thank them for supporting Dev. Well, Benedict wasn't really a friend, but given the way he stared longingly at Lydia whenever she wasn't looking, Jane guessed that might change in the near future.

"What about gossip?" Lady Rowling asked once the men were done with their formal introduction.

"Everyone from our household in town already knows who I am," Dev replied. "And now that Lord Lovell here is in on the secret, the only people at the estate who don't know are the caretakers. And as they're elderly and we've worked them more today than they've probably worked in the last decade, they're already in bed. Therefore, there's no one to spread any gossip about the servant-turned-lord." Dev shot his stepmother a pleased smile before taking a sip of wine.

"Who wants mutton?" sang Dev's friend, Parth, sailing into the room with a tray held aloft.

Jane's stomach growled. It seemed that her afternoon activities with Dev had worked up an appetite.

"It would be my most humble privilege to serve you, my liege." Parth bowed dramatically at Dev's side while managing to keep the tray steady, an impressive feat.

Dev's cheekbones turned ruddy. "What is this?"

Parth grinned. "I thought I'd have a bit of fun now that you are a fancy man. But don't worry," he added, throwing a wink Jane's way, "I know that you have a fair skill for beating carpets, so I won't let your improved circumstances go to your head."

Jane grinned at the merry delight on Parth's face. It could have been awkward for Parth to serve his friend, but he'd addressed it head-on with humor and diffused any tension. Dev's shoulders had dropped an inch or two as he relaxed, and Parth chatted with all of them about the challenges the cook had faced with the limited food supplies here at the house and the glories of this mutton dish.

Once they all settled into eating, Jane felt a tap against her foot. She glanced up to find Dev watching her as he slid his fork between his lips. His foot shifted against hers. She looked down at her plate, then moved her foot along his.

It was a small thing, touching feet under the table, but she felt rooted because of it, connected to him somehow. This proved helpful a moment later when Lady Roberta set down her fork and studied Jane with cool, appraising eyes.

"So, tell us your plan, Miss Brickley."

Jane lowered her fork. "Ah, yes. My plan." She swallowed. "First, can you tell me where we stand with the Brambletons?"

"I paid Lady Brambleton a call today. She seemed most pleased to make my acquaintance as we are nearly neighbors out here in the countryside." Lady Rowling nodded at Dev, and everyone understood she meant that Dev was the Brambleton's neighbor.

"She invited me to join in several of the house party's social events over the next few days, including a picnic tomorrow midday. I mentioned that I had a handful of guests staying here, and she graciously extended the invitation to all of you." Lady Rowling turned her gimlet eye back to Jane. "Just as you'd predicted, Miss Brickley. Now," she steepled her fingers together under her chin, "what is the next move in this plan of yours?"

Jane dabbed at her mouth with her napkin. The next move. Her plan. Right.

"Well," she began, "we know the Skevingtons are behind everything that's happened—"

Lady Rowling's eyebrows shot up. "Do we?"

Jane clenched her hands together under the table. "We strongly suspect it, and aside from a lead on a footman, no other suspicious persons have cropped up in our investigation."

Lady Rowling frowned. "And so, what are you planning for tomorrow?"

Jane glanced around at the others. Aside from Lydia who already knew the broad strokes of her strategy, the others all watched her with expressions ranging from curious to concerned.

"She has it all mapped out," Lydia piped up, nodding at Jane in solidarity.

And yet…did she? Would her plan work at all? So much rested on them getting this next part right. Jane's hands were beginning to tingle from lack of blood circulation, she was gripping them so tightly. It was hard to draw a full breath.

Oh, merciful heavens. She was going to fail. Right here, right now, it would all unravel. Dev would lose his title. The LCA would never reopen. Her vision began to narrow as her lungs burned for breath.

Dev's foot pressed against hers in silent support and suddenly her lungs began to work once more.

She drew a deep breath before pressing back against his foot in thanks. She wasn't alone in this.

"Tomorrow is a reconnaissance day." Jane returned Lady Rowling's steely stare. "We shall watch the Skevingtons like hawks. Every word they say, every person they speak to, every glance they exchange, we shall monitor. And once we have more intelligence, I will complete the final pieces of my plan."

"What?" Lady Rowling threw her napkin onto the table. "That is no plan at all." She turned from icy to fire in the blink of an eye. "We've put our faith in you, Miss Brickly. Dev and I were counting on you to bring this mess to a close, but it seems you are not to be trusted." Her breathing was loud in the dining room.

Jane turned completely motionless in her chair, unable to move, to breathe, to say a single word in her defense.

"I trust her."

Everyone turned to Dev.

He repeated his words. "I trust her, and I know she's going to come up with the perfect plan. You don't need to worry, Roberta. Jane is the smartest, cleverest person I know, and she can do this."

Tension crackled through the room as Lady Rowling and Dev stared at one another in an apparent unblinking contest of wills.

"Well." Lady Rowling rose from her seat. "I shall excuse myself." And she stomped out, her usual gliding movements nowhere in sight.

Once her angry footsteps could no longer be heard, the dining room was still as a tomb for several moments.

"Well," Pippa said, finally breaking the terrible, awkward

silence. "This mutton *is* delicious."

Jane snickered before slapping a hand over her mouth. This was not a time to laugh. This was a crisis. Dev's entire future was on the line, and she had been found lacking.

Lydia snorted, then Benedict let out a laugh. Soon all six of them were laughing.

"Oh my, she was most cross." Pippa dabbed at her eyes with her napkin.

"Remind me never to get on that woman's bad side," Jack said, the corners of his mouth twitching. "I fear she'd poison me on purpose."

Jane snorted a laugh. She caught Dev's eye, and they smiled at one another. Oh, that had been a very grim, terrifying encounter, but somehow knowing that Dev was with her and that all her friends supported her had completely changed her outlook.

She couldn't do it without them.

They would be a team.

Jane stilled as an idea took shape. If they all… and then…

She clapped her hands together once all the pieces clicked into place. Dev and the others turned to her.

"Listen up, everyone," Jane said. "I *do* have a plan for tomorrow, and I'm going to need each of you to help."

JANE PACED IN her bedroom, wishing the chamber was larger to accommodate her need to walk as she mulled things over.

From somewhere in the house, a grandfather clock chimed, announcing to all who remained awake that it was midnight.

Jane pushed her hair behind her ear. She'd decided to leave it down when she'd gotten into her night clothes earlier. When they'd left the dining room hours earlier, after Jane had shared the details of her plan for the picnic with everyone, Dev had brushed by her and whispered, "I'll come at midnight."

And now she waited, her skin tingling in anticipation of more kisses and more touches and more of that incredible sensation he gave her. She knew what it was called. *An orgasm. The little death,* the French called it.

And it was like dying in a way. It had felt as if her soul was leaving her body for those intense, pulsing moments. As if she *was* only body, only sensation. And then the two halves of her rushed back together and she was reborn.

What a miraculous thing.

She wished to do it again, as soon as possible. With Dev, of course. Only with Dev.

There was a faint knock at her door, and she rushed to open it.

And then Dev was in her room and the door was shut and locked and she was in his arms, and everything was right once more.

"Jane," he whispered between kisses, "I missed you."

She smiled against his mouth. "It's only been three hours."

"Three hours too long," he murmured before engulfing her in hot, wet kisses.

Jane moaned, squeezing his arms, his shoulder, and once she was feeling steady, his tight bottom. Oh heavens, the man had a posterior of firm, juicy muscle. She wanted to dig her fingers into the taut firmness of his behind. She wanted to bite him there. Perhaps he would let her, later.

"Jane," he murmured, pulling back a few inches, "I can practically hear you thinking naughty thoughts."

"Perhaps," she purred.

She *purred!* Who was this wanton creature, with wild thoughts of biting and purring words to her lover? Jane liked this new leaf she'd turned. She liked being bold and brave and taking charge.

Speaking of...

"Take off your clothes," she commanded.

Dev's eyes flared hot at her words. "Yes, Miss Brickley," he said before pulling off his clothing and tossing them onto the floor.

Jane had the fleeting thought that they should take better care of his new wardrobe, but then his chest was bare, and her mouth went dry, and wrinkled garments were the furthest thing from her mind.

Shortly, he was completely naked while Jane remained fully dressed. She liked it. She felt powerful and in control.

"Lay on the bed," she commanded.

Dev's eyes were dark and hot as he complied.

She crawled onto the mattress next to him and trailed her hands across his chest. Down his stomach. And to his erection, which jumped at the slide of her fingers.

"You are so hard for me," she murmured.

"Yes," Dev groaned, his jaw clenched.

Jane ran her hand up and down his length. She gently touched the sac hanging below. Dev jumped at the contact.

She jerked her hand away.

"It's all right," he gritted out. "It feels good."

Jane resumed her exploration. Dev's hips pumped in subtle movement, pushing into her hand as she stroked up and down his length and smoothed her fingers across his sac.

"Oh, Jane," he moaned. His eyes glittered through narrowed slits. "You feel so good."

Jane leaned down and kissed him. Their tongues tangled as she continued to touch him. Her blood sizzled in her veins. *She* was making him move like this, making him moan and buck. She was the one creating his pleasure. It became a pleasure of its own, creating his pleasure. Her body sang with it. Her core pulsed with its own need.

"Jane," he groaned out. "Stop or I'll come."

Jane gave him one more slow slide of her hand, and he made a wanting noise as she pulled away. He grabbed her, rolling until he was on top of her.

"Jane, my Jane," he murmured between long, hot kisses. "Let me undress you."

She nodded, and soon they were skin to skin. She had the fleeting thought that she ought to feel embarrassed at the noises she made as he sucked on her breasts and slid his fingers through her folds. But she wasn't embarrassed. She was free of any shameful emotion when she was with him. Together, they were free to be themselves, to feel their feelings, and to want and to love with their bodies.

His beautiful body.

Jane wanted him so very much.

"Dev, please," she gasped.

He trailed hungry kisses down from her breasts to her stomach and then to the crease of her thigh.

"What..." She trailed off, uncertain of her question and also quite distracted by the delicious things he was doing to her.

"Let me make you feel good," he murmured, licking and nibbling along the edge of her curls.

Jane relaxed back onto the bed, but she watched, propping her head up on a pillow, as his head moved between her legs. She bucked at the explosion of pleasure when he licked along her seam.

"Dev," she cried.

He licked and licked again, and then his mouth was *there* and Jane was pure sensation. The pleasure was all-encompassing, a tidal wave of sensation drawing her under its power. He slid a finger inside her, and Jane gasped. She was tender there, likely from earlier, but it felt so right, to have that pressure inside her even as he licked and sucked at her most sensitive place.

"Oh, oh Dev," she moaned as the little death was upon her, and her soul shattered as her body was nothing but pleasure, nothing but sensation, nothing but pulsing energy radiating from her center.

He slowed his movements as she came down from the pinnacle. She lay panting, her skin tingling, as he crawled up the bed to lay beside her.

"Jane," he murmured, pressing kisses to her breasts, her cheeks, her mouth.

She tasted herself there, a sweet tang, and it felt so very wicked that her face grew hotter still.

"Dev, that was..." She exhaled, without enough energy to search for adequate words to describe what had just happened.

He looked at her, his ocean eyes so full of passion and hope and...yes, love.

Jane had no words.

But she could show him.

She pressed a weak hand against his chest, and he complied with her unspoken command, laying down beside her. Jane kissed his shoulder. His neck. His collarbone. The flat circles of his nipples. She trailed down his stomach, his muscles leaping under her mouth. Yes, she was doing this to him, giving him this pleasure. It was a heady sort of power, to make another person come undone with your touch.

She neared his erection.

"Jane, you don't need to..."

She looked up at him, knowing her smile was coy and womanly and mysterious. Reveling in it. "But I want to," she murmured, and then she took him in her mouth.

He moaned, his body tightening. Jane swirled her tongue around the tip, a taste of salt on her tongue. He smelled of soap and musk. Jane brought her hand around his base, and she moved her mouth and her hand in time, slowly pumping him.

Dev groaned, and his fingers threaded through her hair. He didn't push or move her but kept his hands light. Jane's heart surged with love for him, for his gentleness with her. He could have taken her as he had earlier, but he'd used his mouth instead, knowing she would be sore. He could force her head down, making her take him deeper into her mouth, but he didn't. He cared for her. He respected her. And she knew, even without the words being spoken, that he loved her.

She moved quicker, her mouth sliding up and down while her tongue swirled. Her hand pumped at his base, and she brought her other hand to his sac to lightly stroke along the sensitive skin there.

Dev tightened and groaned. "I'm going to come." It felt like a warning.

Jane wasn't sure what to do, so she kept licking and stroking, and he moaned loud and long while he spurted into her mouth. Jane kept moving until he collapsed back on the bed. She grabbed a handkerchief from the nightstand and spit into it, balling up the cloth before settling beside him.

"Jane," he whispered, pulling her close.

She lay her head on his chest, hearing the pounding of his heart.

His heart, which beat for her.

Chapter Twenty-Four

DEV TUGGED AT the neck of his borrowed livery as he waited for his assignment from the Brambleton's housekeeper. The kitchen was a hive of activity with all the Brambleton's servants rushing about, plus the additional servants, here with their own lords and ladies, who'd been conscripted into assisting with the house party.

"No rest for the weary, eh?" a footman said, nudging Dev with his elbow.

Dev nodded. Weary was an understatement.

He and Jane had been up last night until the wee hours, talking and kissing and touching and coming undone over and over again. He'd never had a night like it in his life.

He felt satisfied all the way to his marrow. Although so much of his life was still undetermined, this thing with Jane felt right, and that made everything else feel right.

"You," called the harried-looking housekeeper, "take this crate of champagne to the picnic site around the side lawn of the house. Put the bottles into the tubs of ice there, then report back to the kitchen."

Dev nodded and took up the crate.

He exited the kitchen, glad to get some fresh air outside where there wasn't such a crush of working bodies. Despite the crispness of autumn, the sun was bright, lending warmth wherever it landed. Dev strolled across the grass. The Brambletons had a grand estate, the creamy stone of the three-story building glowing in the sunshine and the sprawling grounds dotted with gardens, benches, and several shady copses of trees.

Dev paused under a bit of shade and set down the crate of champagne. They'd really loaded it with bottles back in the kitchen. He shook out his hands and gave his arms a moment to rest.

From around the other side of the house came the sound of laughter, the murmurs of conversation, and the occasional whacking sound. Perhaps they played a game of some sort.

And around the corner was Jane. His brilliant, beautiful Jane.

Dev pressed his hand to his sternum, as if he could contain the pressure that emerged whenever he thought of her. When this was all over, he'd ask her if she would make him the happiest of men by being his wife. He knew he didn't have the correct qualifications to be a proper husband. He wasn't born in England. He didn't know how to be a lord, not in any real way that mattered. He wasn't comfortable in fine English clothing. He preferred curry over many traditional English dishes. All it had taken was one look at kippers for him to make up his mind on that issue. And his best friend was a servant. Actually, all his friends were servants. And he didn't intend to change that. What sort of person would he be if he no longer claimed the friendship of those who'd been at his side all his life, just because the aristocracy looked down on them?

With all this, would she have him?

If he was a lord, it would definitely increase his chances.

And if this didn't work, and he wasn't able to prove he was his father's legitimate heir, then what?

Dev imagined most barons and baronesses would not relish the idea of their daughter marrying a servant.

He sighed before hoisting up the crate once more.

Along strode another footman in livery, carrying a tray of sandwiches.

The footman had bright red hair.

And very broad shoulders.

The back of Dev's neck tingled. Without thinking, Dev called, "Johnny."

The footman turned around and scowled when he saw Dev. "I'm not going to trade just because your load is too heavy for you."

Dev shook his head. "I don't want to trade. I was wondering if you've heard from…" What was the name of the maid who'd told them about Johnny? The one who said he owed her money? "…from Franny lately?"

The footman's eyes narrowed. "What's that Franny been saying now?"

Ah, his hunch was right! Dev's crate suddenly felt much lighter. "Oh, she just wanted me to remind you that you owe her two quid and to sod off."

Johnny huffed and moved the sandwich tray up and down as if he couldn't decide whether to move along or set it on the grass and come after Dev. While the footman sorted himself out, Dev strode off and around the corner to the picnic, whistling as he went.

Jane sipped lemonade, hoping the look of pleasant interest she'd plastered on her face when she'd joined a cluster of young ladies appeared genuine. Personally, she didn't care two figs about what hemlines were doing this season, but that wasn't an indictment of this crowd's interest in fashion.

It was just that she had a most urgent matter to attend to.

Her whole group did.

When she'd divvied up the assignments for her plan last night at dinner, her friends had agreed without question. How had she come to be the leader in this operation? What qualifications did she have to lead a clandestine mission to uncover a nefarious plot of attempted murder and title theft?

None. She was as qualified as a ham-handed blockhead attempting to re-pot a fragile orchid.

And yet, here she was, somehow the mastermind of this whole thing and all she could think of was Dev's tongue driving her to madness last night again and again.

And again.

She blushed.

Jane took a gulp of lemonade to cool herself.

"…and my modiste said that trim at the sleeves would no longer be *au courante* by next season, but I'm not sure I believe her…" one of the ladies was saying.

"Pardon me," Jane murmured, stepping away from the group. No one seemed to take any notice. Well, she hadn't exactly been a sparkling example of wit up to this point, so she would try not to take offense.

Jane wound her way through the picnic. Many of the house guests sat on blankets spread out across the lawn, munching on cold chicken and finger sandwiches. Others stood in groups, drinks in hand as they flirted and laughed. To the side, some played badminton and pall mall. It was indeed a large house party.

Jane spied Benedict talking with Nigel, glasses of something that appeared to be stronger than lemonade in their hands. The two men laughed, and Jane felt a surge of satisfaction at her decision to put Benedict on Nigel-duty. Benedict's rakish reputation and natural bonhomie were perfect for charming a weasel-like Nigel into dropping his guard.

Pippa ambled by, a plate in her hand. "I'm off to see if I can get a stone to bleed," she whispered to Jane before heading to the picnic blanket where mousy Lady Skevington sat alone. That she was by herself was no surprise. The woman was not likely to endear herself to anyone with her thick silence and downcast eyes.

Jane nodded to an acquaintance and continued her circulation. She neared the tables where food and beverages had been placed. Her heart skipped a beat when she spied Dev.

He was dressed once more in borrowed livery, this time a regal red. His dark hair gleamed in the sunshine like a raven's wing. He bent to load champagne bottles into a bucket with ice, and Jane watched as his trousers pulled tight over his muscular bottom.

She'd stroked that rear last night. She'd felt the flex and release of his taut muscles there. No one else at this party had any idea what naughtiness she and the man with the champagne had gotten up to in the wee hours.

Perhaps he felt the weight of her stare because he looked up. Even from ten yards away, she could see the way the corners of his eyes crinkled with his smile. Her heart leaped in her chest, and she wanted to run to him and wrap her arms around him right here, right now. What did it matter if everyone saw her kissing a man they believed to be a servant?

But…it would matter.

They had a plan, *her* plan, and she would not sabotage it despite her heart's wishes.

And so, she gave him a smile in return, one she hoped expressed all that was in her heart, before tearing herself away to continue her quest for information.

Past the food tables, three women were clustered, their heads all bent in. *Ah, gossip.* Jane dropped down to one knee when she was a few yards away, pretending to have a pebble in her shoe. Hopefully, she was far enough that they wouldn't pay her any mind but close enough to hear what they were saying.

"…conduct all my dalliances at house parties," one of them said. Jane recognized her as a baroness who'd been widowed a few years ago. "It's so very easy to invite a gentleman into one's chamber after the rest of the party has retired for the night."

Another of the women giggled. "Why wait for the night? I had a rather titillating tupping in the woods the other day when we went on that boring walk that Lady Brambleton insisted on." She touched her hand to the back of her head. "My only piece of advice, ladies—check for tree sap before you begin."

The women all laughed.

Jane continued to adjust her shoe even as her cheeks burned. She'd never realized that house parties provided cover for so much dalliance. Although, come to think of it, hadn't that been exactly what she and Dev had done?

She stilled.

What if that was all he saw this as—a dalliance? That couldn't be…could it?

They hadn't spoken of the future. He had made no promises. But he'd told her it had never been like this for him before. That it was special. She was special. And his words had rung true. Dev was the most honest person she knew.

She frowned.

Well…that wasn't exactly accurate.

How long had he lied about his identity? Even when he'd come into her bedroom late at night after their break-in at the Skevington's and he'd brought her such pleasure, even then he hadn't told her the truth of who he was. If not for her discovery of the diary, she still might not know that *he* was the heir they were working to find evidence for, not some mystery child hidden away in India.

Jane frowned down at the grass. She should not let these women's tales of casual bed sport affect how she viewed Dev. Just because others used house parties as a means to casually dally, that didn't mean there was anything casual between her and Dev.

"…and I never would have guessed it," one of the women was saying now, "but the noises coming from the room next to mine last night had me in quite a state. I was jealous of whatever woman was getting plowed in that bedroom. She was crying out in pleasure for nigh upon an hour."

The other women made appreciative noises.

"Who has the room next to you?" one asked, fanning herself

with gusto.

"I'm not sure."

The other woman chimed in. "I know. It's Sir Albert and Lady Skevington. I saw her leaving the chamber beside yours when I came by the other day to borrow your shawl."

The first woman tutted. "Well, who knew they had it in them? Maybe that's why she never speaks a word. She's too hoarse from her husband making her scream all night."

Jane must have made some sound in reaction because she suddenly felt them all looking at her. Jane peered up from her shoe which she'd been pretending to adjust for some time now.

"Ah, hello," she said.

The three women peered down at her in suspicion.

"Ah, there it is." Jane pretended to find a little pebble and tossed it over her shoulder before rising. "All better."

The women continued to stare. One's eyes were narrowed. Another had her arms folded across her chest. And the third slapped her folded fan across her open palm.

Jane gulped.

"Um, did I hear you say that someone was hoarse?" She widened her eyes and blinked, channeling innocence and naiveté and youth as if her life depended on it. "I hope there isn't a cold making the rounds. I have a deathly fear of the ague." Jane put her hand to her throat and shivered.

The women exchanged glances with one another. One rolled her eyes, the other attempted to hide her expression of disdain behind her fan, and the third did little to quiet a snicker.

"Yes, there's a cold going around," the one with the fan answered. "But I'm sure no one is worried about *you* catching it."

They all pealed with laughter as they walked away.

Jane sighed. That had been a close call.

It would not do to bring attention to herself or have members of the house party—especially those who were fond of gossip— telling others that she'd been listening in on conversations.

Frowning as she continued her circumnavigation of the picnic, Jane tried to make sense of what she'd overheard. Sir Albert and his nearly mute wife had a passionate love life. The news was surprising, to be sure, but did not seem to have any bearing on the mystery. And yet Jane could not quiet the niggling at the back of her mind that insisted this clue fit into a larger puzzle.

Near the pall mall players who smashed their balls through wickets with varying degrees of success, Jane spied Jack speaking to Sir Albert. The baronet appeared to be in the middle of a long speech, his hands gesticulating as he opined. Jack's yawn, quickly covered by his hand, was visible even from afar. *Oh, dear.* Perhaps assigning Jack to Sir Albert had been a mistake. Jack did not suffer fools gladly, and Sir Albert was clearly a fool.

Unless it was an act.

Jane still wasn't entirely convinced he was innocent in this scheme.

Jack had a keen head for figures since he'd had to take over the family coffers at a young age. Pippa had told her how his parents had been quite flighty, always surrounding themselves with artists, philosophers, and actors at the expense of the estate, their coffers, and, most distressingly, their children.

Jane had thought Jack would be the perfect candidate for bringing up a conversation about business with Sir Albert in an attempt to learn the state of the family's finances. Hopefully, Sir Albert wasn't rambling on about why the Renaissance was most famed for the state of its cuisine again.

Jane rounded the picnic area and found herself in the eyeline of Lady Rowling, who stood with a group of rather intimidating matrons.

Lady Rowling lifted her lemonade to her mouth and took a sip, all while maintaining eye contact with Jane. It felt menacing somehow.

Dev had assured her that Lady Rowling—or *Roberta* as he called his stepmother—was actually quite lovely and only hid behind an icy exterior due to the circumstances of her life. Jane could understand a person being prickly to others after being basically sold in marriage by their parents at a young age to pay off the family's debts. But why did Lady Rowling continue to be so cold with those who were trying to help her and her stepson fight for his rightful inheritance of the title? What else had shaped the woman to make her so mistrusting?

Jane nodded at Lady Rowling, then carried on with her circling.

There was much to do today if her plan had any hope of success.

Chapter Twenty-Five

AFTER THE PICNIC, their party returned to the dim rooms of the Rowling country home to debrief on what everyone had learned during their assignments. Dev was glad to be out of the borrowed livery and back in his familiar kurta. He stoked the fire in the sitting room while everyone got comfortable in the various mismatched chairs and divans spread about.

"I say," Benedict drawled, stretching his legs out across the worn carpet. "That Nigel bloke is not a gentleman in the least. You should have heard the things the rotter bragged about getting into during his Cambridge days."

Jane circled the room, as was her habit when she was thinking.

"What did you learn about him that might pertain to the affairs at hand?" she asked.

Benedict scratched the back of his head. "Well, he invited me out to a gambling hell with him and his friends when we're back in town. Sounds like he goes out quite a bit, but he's limited in which hells he can visit now as he's run out of credit at some of the establishments. He bragged about how you have to lose before you can win and it's just a matter of waiting for his luck to change." Benedict stretched. "I almost feel sorry for the bloke. Well, if it wasn't for what he did up at Cambridge. And the whole trying-to-steal-your-title thing."

He shot Dev an apologetic look.

Dev nodded. For all that Benedict seemed full of bluster, he wasn't without merit.

Jane hummed and continued her march around the room. "All right, so Nigel is in debt and loves to lose money at the hells. What else did people learn?"

"I learned absolutely nothing," Pippa complained, folding her arms across her chest. "Talking to Lady Skevington is like trying to have a conversation with a wall. Are we sure the woman isn't some sort of automaton?"

Jane paused by her cousin's side. "You didn't learn *anything*?"

Pippa shook her head. "Aside from an intimate knowledge of the sound she makes when chewing her food, I've got nothing."

Dev wrinkled his nose. Everyone chewed their food. Why was contemplating the sound of it in particular so unpleasant?

"Jack, what did you learn?" Jane asked, perching on the sofa arm beside her cousin, Pippa.

Dev hoped the old, worn furniture was up for a bit of arm sitting. Truly, this country home was in need of some serious refurbishment.

Jack ran his hand over his face. "I'm quite certain I spoke to the dimmest person in all of England today."

Dev moved from the fire to an open seat. This was going to be good.

"First of all, the man believes that Italy is part of Asia and not Europe," Jack said. "Then he shared his thoughts on beekeeping with me, which was most mystifying as he mentioned several times that he keeps no bees and in fact, has never spoken to anyone with a relationship to bees beyond consuming honey."

Pippa patted her husband's leg. "And you were patient enough to continue speaking to the man without giving him the cut direct? Why Jack, I'm so impressed."

Dev caught Jane's eye, and they shared a smile.

Was she perhaps thinking as he was, that someday it would be lovely to have a marriage like Pippa and Jack's, filled with gentle teasing and obvious affection?

Jack snorted. "Eventually, I was able to steer him into talk of business and finance, but it was the most peculiar thing. He declared that he had no head for numbers—no hard thing to believe, actually—and that his wife, who you all claim has only wind blowing between her ears, was in charge of the finances."

Jane frowned. "The *household* finances?"

Jack shook his head. "All of it. The bank accounts, the estate finances… everything. He even told me he wouldn't know where to start with investments because he has no idea how much money they have."

Dev watched as Jane stared up at the ceiling. He could tell she was frustrated that all these separate pieces of intelligence hadn't snapped together into a coherent whole yet by the way she tapped her fingers on her leg.

"Well, I learned something from the Brambleton's house-keeper," Lydia announced. "I'm not sure if this pertains or not, but I asked if there would be room for any of us to stay in the house the night of the ball. She said that because several of the married couples had asked for separate chambers from their spouse once they'd arrived, she was unsure if they had any rooms available. And then when she looked at her map to see where everyone was roomed, I snuck a peek and saw that Sir Albert and Lady Skevington were in separate chambers."

Jane gasped and jumped to her feet. "When I was on gossip patrol, I overheard some ladies talking about all the, um, nocturnal activities that were occurring at the house party."

Dev enjoyed the way Jane's cheeks turned pink.

"One of the women was roomed next door to Lady Skeving-ton and shared that she'd heard her, ah, enjoying herself most thoroughly the night before."

Lydia frowned. "But if she and her husband chose to sleep apart—"

"Then who is she sleeping with?" Benedict interjected, slap-ping his hand on his leg.

Dev cleared his throat. "I might have the answer to that."

Everyone turned to look at him. Dev shifted in his seat. It was still strange, sitting amongst English aristocrats and not pouring their drinks or clearing their plates. They looked at him as an equal. If this all worked out, he would need to get used to it.

"When I was working with the other servants at the picnic, I ran into a broad-shouldered, red-haired footman—"

"Johnny," Jane gasped.

Dev nodded. "One and the same. He even confirmed that he knew our helpful housemaid Franny who initially alerted us to his likely presence the night of the robbery."

"Wait, who's Johnny?" Pippa asked.

Dev and Jane brought the rest of them up to speed.

Jane paced back and forth across the sitting room, muttering to herself for a minute.

"So, Nigel loves to gamble and has rung up untold debt in the hells," she said to the group once it seemed she sorted everything out for herself. "Sir Albert doesn't pay any attention to the household coffers, and instead his wife runs the ship. We all discounted her as having any involvement because she appears to be the meekest of creatures in public. We know she doesn't sleep with her husband but was enjoying some very vigorous pursuits in her bed chambers. And the same footman who was fingered as being at the burglary is in attendance at the house party."

She paused in front of the fire and turned to face the group. Her face was alight, her eyes sparkling, and her cheeks rosy.

She looked, in a word, glorious.

Dev knew with full certainty that Jane had clicked all the pieces together and had a specific plan for how they should proceed to unmask the villain and allow Dev to claim his title. And to re-open the Ladies Covert Academy, of course. That was never far from his mind.

"So…" Benedict leaned forward.

Jane waited.

"What's it all mean?" he finally asked.

It was clear he was unhappy with not connecting the dots himself. Dev didn't blame him. He hadn't fully followed Jane's list of facts to a conclusion either.

"The villain of this story isn't doltish Sir Albert," Jane said.

"So it's Nigel?" Pippa asked.

Jane shook her head.

"It isn't either of our initial suspects." Jane paused, allowing the tension to build. "Our villain is Lady Skevington."

THE EVENING OF the Brambleton's ball was clear, the stars twinkling in the night sky like diamonds.

Dev waited downstairs with the other gentlemen, each in their evening finery. Dev tugged at his cravat.

"You'll ruin it," Jack warned.

"It's too tight." Dev attempted to loosen the knot without destroying the whole thing.

"I'd get a running start if I were you," Benedict drawled, leaning back against the wall, all leonine grace. "If Jack's valet catches you messing with his creation, he'll come at you with a pair of hair shears and that will be the end of you."

Dev smiled and slid his hands into his pockets to avoid the temptation of cravat-tugging. He did not wish to die at the well-manicured hands of Franklin the valet.

It had been two days since the picnic and Jane's realization that it was Lady Skevington, she of the downcast eyes and zero words to say, who had orchestrated the plot to steal the Rowling title.

Whether her motivation was simply power and prestige for her family or filling their coffers dwindled by her son's gambling habit was unclear. What *did* seem clear was that she'd taken broad-shouldered Johnny as her lover and had recruited him to help carry out her plans.

Had it been him in the alley behind Boodle's that day? Dev shivered. It had been a near thing, and the reminder that Jane's life had been in danger made him feel rather feral.

"We are ready to be admired," called Pippa from the top of the stairway.

All three men looked up.

Although this house was dim and worn, it was still a sight to behold seeing three lovely women descend the stairs one after the other. Jack made a sound of appreciation deep in his throat at the sight of his wife Pippa in her blue silk gown. Dev noted the way Benedict straightened up from the wall when Lydia came into sight, her pastel pink dress allowing her golden hair to shine. And then came Jane.

Dev's mouth went dry.

Her gown was emerald-green, turning her red-gold hair into a lustrous halo. Her pink lips were upturned in a soft, secret smile. The gown's neckline, lower than her usual dresses, framed her sweet breasts.

Jane's eyes held his as she descended the steps, and Dev resisted blinking so that he might look upon her even longer.

When she stood in front of him at last, he could only say, "You are beautiful."

Perhaps it was enough. Or perhaps it was the look of admiration that was surely written across his face, because she beamed in response, and it took his breath away.

"And you look quite handsome." She reached up and tweaked his cravat. "Although I think you look quite fine in your kurta as well," she whispered.

This woman. Once the issues of the title and re-opening the LCA were behind them, he would ask for her hand and they could be together in public. They could claim one another. But oh, how he wished he could claim her right now.

A throat cleared from the top of the stairs, and they all turned to find Lady Rowling perched on the upper landing, her pale blue gown the color of her eyes.

"Are the carriages ready?" she asked as she made her descent.

Jack looked out the front window. "They're ready and waiting."

"You look quite regal, Roberta," Dev said once she reached the floor.

Roberta sniffed. "Only a monarch can be regal. I am merely a marchioness. Well, a dowager marchioness, in fact."

Dev glanced at Jane. Had she thought at all about their future, that if she agreed to marry him then she'd be the new Lady Rowling?

"Time and titles wait for no man," Benedict announced, opening the front door. "Shall we?"

They filtered out into the night, the stars above dancing in the black sky in an imitation of the dancers moving across the Brambleton's ballroom.

"Good evening, gov," Parth called, tipping an imaginary hat from his position next to the first carriage.

Dev narrowed his eyes at his friend. "If you ever call me *gov* again, I'll tell everyone about that time with the ghee in the kitchen when you—"

"Ah, no need for that, my good chap," Parth quickly interrupted. "No need at all. In you go, miss."

Jane stifled a laugh as Parth handed her into the carriage.

"Good luck tonight," Parth whispered as Dev entered the carriage. "I'll be outside the ball if you need me."

Soon they rolled up to the Brambleton's grand home once more, but this time instead of merely the house guests being present, every fine family in the county seemed to have been invited.

Dev fidgeted with his gloves as they stood in the receiving line.

"It will be all right," Jane murmured. "You look as if you belong here, and Lady Rowling's explanation will do. There are simply too many people here tonight for anyone to care about your identity."

Dev nodded.

He knew all of that. It made perfect, logical sense. And yet, the way he felt didn't seem to be affected by logic to any degree. Dressing up in his aristocratic, lordly garb and attending a ball right under the noses of some of the very people who would be deciding his fate at the tribunal in a few days in London felt like a risk.

But Jane had insisted that his attendance—as a real guest, not in livery—was crucial to her plan, and so here he was.

"Ah, Lady Rowling," greeted Lady Brambleton once they reached the front of the receiving line. "How good of you to join us this evening with your guests."

Roberta introduced the others to the duchess, a handsome matron with a streak of white through her otherwise dark hair. Dev's pulse picked up speed the closer he came to her in the line.

"And this is Mr. Devin Smith, a distant relative of my late husband, come to visit me in the country for the week."

Dev accepted Lady Brambleton's outstretched hand and bent over it as he'd seen the other men do. "My pleasure, your grace."

Lady Brambleton stared at him in open curiosity, and Dev's shoulders tightened. Was she going to question him? How could he answer without sputtering over a huge lie or blowing his cover too early?

A throat cleared behind him, and the duchess looked past Dev to the long line stretching after his party.

"Thank you for attending our ball," she said, giving a smile of dismissal.

Lady Rowling led them further into the house, and Dev sagged in relief.

"Well done," Jane murmured.

She wove her hand through his arm and gently guided them through the throng.

"A bit of champagne will do nicely." She handed him a glass before taking one for herself from a circling footman.

Dev sipped, the tiny bubbles fizzing in his mouth. He sipped again. It was delicious. The bubbles rising to the top of the champagne reminded him of the stars out that night, tiny specks of light dancing across the sky.

Every day should be an occasion for champagne.

He glanced at Jane, with her wide, verdant eyes, her sweet mouth curved in a conspiratorial smile, and her hair glowing like the dawn sunrise atop her head. Every day with her felt like champagne.

His throat grew tight with emotion. From across the ballroom, the musicians began to play.

"Do you know how to dance?" Jane asked, leaning her head close.

Dev recalled the silly afternoons he'd spent with Roberta back in Calcutta where she would teach him the steps she'd learned as a girl back home.

"A bit." His voice was hoarse.

Jane's eyes glowed up at him like jewels. "Will you waltz with me? Just this once?"

Dev drew a deep breath. Could he do this? Could he publicly take to the center of the ballroom in front of all these aristocrats? What if they noticed him and asked questions about his identity? What if he embarrassed her by not knowing the steps well enough?

What if he couldn't be who he was supposed to become?

But the way Jane looked at him, the longing to dance clear on her face, was far too compelling. He stretched out a gloved hand, and they walked out onto the dance floor together.

Dev started out hesitantly, counting *one, two, three* as they moved around the room with the other dancers. But after a turn around the dance floor, the music filled him, and his feet knew what to do. Instead of counting or worrying about stepping on her toes, he twirled Jane. Her skirt swishing around his legs, she smiled up into his face. Into his heart.

And Dev just danced.

"You're quite a natural, you know," she murmured.

Dev hummed and pulled her a few inches closer.

"Careful," she warned, her eyes dancing with mirth, "or Lady Rowling will give me a scold for corrupting you."

Dev leaned in close to whisper in her ear. "I think we corrupted each other."

Jane raised one sleek eyebrow. "I was rather fond of how you corrupted me last night."

He missed a step, and she laughed, low and quiet, just for him.

His minx.

She could knock him off his feet, but he didn't mind.

"Have you seen the Skevingtons yet?" she asked.

Dev kept the disappointment off his face. Yes, they were here to end this attempted title theft, but he'd hoped they could steal a bit of time for just the two of them. Before, he'd never imagined such a moment, dancing across the shining floor of a ballroom with the woman he loved above all else in his arms. He wanted to savor it. He wanted it never to end.

He glanced over her head and around the room as they spun.

"I see Nigel," he murmured, "but it looks like he's leaving the ballroom."

Jane's nose wrinkled. "He's likely headed for the gaming room. Events like these usually have them for the men who prefer wilder pursuits than quadrilles." She was silent for a moment, scanning the crowd before straightening in his arms. "I see our favorite broad-shouldered footman carrying a tray of champagne."

Dev found him along the side of the room. And not too far away was mousy, quiet, oh-so-devious Lady Skevington, sneaking the occasional peek at Johnny. If Jane's deductions were correct, the man was her footman, lover, *and* co-conspirator. Or perhaps less conspirator and more minion. Hopefully, that too would be revealed tonight.

"And there's Sir Albert." Dev pointed with his chin to the corner where his father's cousin appeared to be putting several matrons to sleep with his doubtlessly inane chatter.

Jane's eyebrows shot up when they turned. "Two of the women just *yawned.*"

"The Skevingtons are the oddest couple I've ever seen," Dev mused. "One has no thoughts to say but speaks incessantly. The other has so many thoughts she plots an entire crime but says not a peep to anyone."

Jane was quiet for a moment. "Are they odder than we are?"

She stared up at him, a little wrinkle between her eyebrows.

Dev's heart lurched, and his hand convulsed around hers.

He looked away, trying to regain his composure.

Did she see them as being so very different then? Did she believe they didn't have a future together?

But all his plans, all his dreams…

His one true wish, to find a place that could be his home—he thought he'd found it with Jane. Was this just…just a tryst for her?

Perhaps she saw him as tainted. He'd been living as a servant for too long. His mother had been a servant. He hadn't thought that mattered to Jane, but perhaps he'd been wrong.

Everything was spinning away from him in the blink of an eye.

All that he thought he knew was like the notes of music, fleeting in the air and then vanishing in a moment.

The musicians interrupted his frenzied thoughts, bringing the waltz to a close with a flourish. Dev somehow managed to bow to Jane while she curtsied. Even as his heart raced in a panic, he spared a moment's thought of gratitude for Roberta who'd shown him this nicety all those years ago. At least he wouldn't make a fool of himself or Jane as he tried to grasp hold of these doomsday thoughts.

But it seemed that panic or no, the plan must go on because Jane turned toward the hallway leading out of the ballroom, her expression determined.

"It's time."

Chapter Twenty-Six

JANE MARCHED DOWN a long, empty hallway with Dev trailing silently behind her. Thanks to Lydia's chat with the Brambleton's housekeeper on the day of the picnic, they'd learned that this wing of the house would be closed to guests during the ball, making it the perfect place for the next step in her plan.

She opened one door and then another, peeking into various rooms and finding them all lacking. For her plan to work, she needed atmosphere. She needed adequate seating. And she needed an appropriate environment to serve tea.

"How about this room?" she asked Dev, peering through yet another doorway. It was a sitting room with heavy drapes, a stack of unlit logs in the fireplace, and a cozy seating arrangement.

He glanced in but didn't say anything.

He hadn't said a word since they'd left the dance floor, come to think of it. But there was no time to check in now. The clock was ticking.

She tugged a ribbon from her hair and looped it around the doorknob, signaling their location to the others. Jane asked Dev to start a fire while she hurried to light all the candles. A handful of minutes later, Lydia rushed in pushing a serving cart.

"You don't want to know," she gasped, out of breath, "what I had to do to obtain this during a ball."

Jane looked over the cart. Hot kettle. Teapot. Cups and saucers. A carafe of water. Even sugar and tea. It was perfect.

"As long as you didn't resort to murder," Jane said while conducting her inventory, "I don't really care."

Lydia snorted.

Footsteps sounded in the hallway, and they all stilled. Jane sought out Dev's gaze from across the room, but he was staring into the fire.

She frowned.

But there wasn't time to see if he was harboring any last-minute doubts about what came next. The plan was in motion and they couldn't stop until it was complete.

"…quite a fascination with all things dental," droned Sir Albert's voice from outside the door. "Why, did you know that in the Andes mountains, the residents sharpen their teeth with stones?"

"I'm sure that's patently untrue," Jack responded, sounding annoyed, before opening the door. "Right this way, Sir Albert."

"Oh, are we to have a tea party?" Sir Albert's limpid eyes lit up once he stepped inside and took in the tea service. He clasped his hands together. "How refreshing to have a bit of, er, refreshment in the middle of a ball."

"Won't you come in and take a seat, Sir Albert?" Jane gestured to one of the settees near the fire.

"So good of you, Miss Brickley." Sir Albert sat, not looking the least perturbed about being lured into a remote room under dubious pretenses in the middle of a ball. "And how is your mother? Still doing well after taking the waters in Bath?"

Jane bit her lips together and made the mistake of looking at Jack. He rolled his eyes, and she almost snickered thinking of the inanity he must have suffered as he chatted up Sir Albert and convinced him to join him for a stroll down a deserted hallway.

"My mother remains quite well after her trip to Bath." Jane couldn't resist adding, "All those months ago."

"Splendid, splendid." Sir Albert looked around. "I say, is there cake?"

They were saved from having to answer by the sound of approaching footsteps.

"Are you sure there's a card game in this part of the house?" Nigel was saying, his voice growing louder as they approached. "None of the other chaps said anything about it."

"They didn't know because they aren't true gamblers like you and I," Benedict replied smoothly.

Benedict was really coming through for them. Although he wasn't Lydia's favorite person, he'd certainly risen to the occasion once they'd included him in their plans.

"Right through here," Benedict said, then the door swung open.

Unlike his father, Nigel immediately grew suspicious, his eyes narrowing as he surveyed the tableau before him.

"What's this?" he asked.

"Ah, my boy, come and sit with your old pater," Sir Nigel cried, patting the space beside him on the settee. "There's a rumor of cake!"

Nigel crept into the room. "Father, what's going on? Why aren't you at the ball?"

"Come." Jack's voice was cold and brooked no argument. "Take a seat beside your father."

Nigel blanched but followed orders.

Jane drew a deep breath. Truly, she could not do this without her friends. Without their dedication to her plan, Dev would lose his title and the LCA would remain permanently closed. This felt like a debt that could never be repaid.

Although perhaps when it came to friends, there were no debts.

She glanced at Dev, hoping for an encouraging smile, but his eyes were downcast.

The sound of running footsteps echoed from the hallway. "Matilda?" cried a voice. "Matilda, where are you?"

"I say." Sir Albert sat forward and looked at his son with alarm. "Is your mother all right?"

Nigel jumped to his feet, his face hard. "What's the meaning of this?"

Jane nodded to Benedict, and he cracked the door open so their next visitor would know where to go. A man in livery burst into the room, chest heaving. A broad-shouldered man with red hair, in fact.

"Matilda!" he cried, looking about wildly.

Sir Albert cocked his head. "Ah, one of our servants has come. Perhaps he knows what's what. Looking for Lady Skevington, are you?" he said loudly to his footman.

"Hello, Johnny," Jane said, folding her hands in front of her. How beneficial that this pose not only gave her the look of command but also hid her trembling.

The footman attempted to regain his composure, smoothing his livery and pulling himself up straight.

"Ah, my pardons, Sir Albert," he said, only stammering a little bit. "I was under the impression that Mat—er, Lady Skevington had a most urgent need of me."

"And why is that?" Nigel demanded, taking a step toward the footman.

Jack shifted forward, checking Nigel's progress, and the young man flinched back. Jack, although broody, was not implicitly a frightening person, so Jane imagined the look he'd shot the Skevingtons' son must be rather terrifying to elicit such a response from the churlish Nigel.

"Ah, you received our note." Jane nodded to the crumpled piece of paper in Johnny's hand. "How splendid. Won't you take a seat?" She gestured to the second settee, across a low table from where Sir Albert and Nigel sat.

"*Your* note?" Johnny's chest puffed up. "Now see here—"

"I rather think you ought to *sit* here." Benedict placed a heavy hand on the footman's shoulder and gave him a friendly shove toward the divan.

Johnny seemed to finally take in the fact that he was in a room full of not only aristocrats who outranked him by an enormous factor on the social scale, but also several strapping men who did not look pleased with his existence. He slunk across the room and took a seat.

Of the strapping men in the room, Jane realized, only one seemed…unprepared to strap. Dev continued his apparent task of propping up the fireplace mantle with his arm since he hadn't moved since lighting the fire. And he continued to avoid meeting her eyes. What was going on? Jane's stomach tightened with worry.

"Miss Brickley," Nigel said, drawing her attention as he attempted to look down his nose at her, a rather bold move considering she stood across the room. "I demand an explanation at once."

"An explanation shall be forthcoming," Jane replied. "We only wait for our last guest to join our little party."

Footsteps sounded in the hall once more, and they all waited in quiet.

"Johnny," a voice whispered. "Johnny, where are you?"

The footman opened his mouth to reply, but at Jack's glower, he clamped his lips together.

Again, Benedict opened the door just enough that neither he nor any of the room's occupants were visible from the hallway.

"I got your note," whispered the person. "What an insatiable rascal you are…"

After fully entering the room, Lady Skevington's amorous words trailed off. Her mouth dropped open and her eyes grew so wide, Jane pondered the likelihood of them popping right out of her face.

Benedict pushed on the door so that it was only open a crack before moving to stand guard in front of it.

"Matilda?" Sir Albert was visibly confused.

Their son, however, appeared to connect the dots much quicker. "Mother, have you been *fornicating* with the *footman*?"

Jane wasn't sure if Nigel was more appalled that his mother was cheating on his father, or that she'd done so with a servant.

Matilda Skevington, she of the few words and mousy demeanor, quickly took in the scene. Jane understood why the woman always kept her gaze so modestly lowered. If she'd allowed others to see the sharp cunning in her eyes, they would have realized she was the mastermind behind this wicked scheme.

And the way her face tightened when she caught sight of Dev was certainly interesting.

Jane guessed that Lady Skevington was used to being underestimated and turning it into an advantage. How clever. Jane knew a thing or two about that as well, but she reserved her innocent expressions for far less devious purposes.

"It seems I have been outmaneuvered," Lady Skevington said, her sharp chin raised up in stark contrast to the soft, youthful ringlets framing her face.

Jane gestured to the seat beside Johnny on the settee. "Won't you join the party, Lady Skevington?"

"Oh, I prefer to stand, Miss Brickley."

Jane moved to the service cart and poured hot water from the kettle into the teapot. "We don't need this to be unpleasant. We've just gathered this group of friendly acquaintances to sort out a few items."

Jane measured out loose-leaf tea and added it to the pot before arranging the cups and saucers to her liking.

"What do you want?" Lady Skevington asked, voice shrewd.

"Matilda, what's going on?" Sir Albert wrung his hands, and Jane felt a moment's pity for the foolish man. How strange it must be to realize one's partner had kept secrets.

Jane shot a look at Dev. He'd kept quite a powerful secret from her for a very long time. But they had patched things up between them. Hadn't they? But why was he so stony-faced? Perhaps facing the architect of his planned destruction was proving harder than he'd anticipated?

Or perhaps, so close to the finish line, he was having second thoughts about Jane?

She tried to swallow past the sudden lump in her throat.

"Let me handle this, Albert." Matilda's voice was like metal.

She turned narrowed eyes to Jane. "I'm certain the audience is not required, Miss Brickley. Surely you and I can work this out between the two of us."

Jane adjusted the tea pot's placement on the tray. "As you've tried to have Lord Rowling's heir murdered, I rather imagine he'd wish to be here for this conversation."

Sputters and shouts emerged from the settee where Sir Albert and Nigel sat.

"But I'm Lord Rowling's heir!" Sir Albert cried, his face turning sallow.

Johnny's broad shoulders grew so tense they almost touched his ears.

Jane looked at Dev. This was the part where he was supposed to enter the conversation. Instead, he remained by the fireplace, his mouth pulled into a tense line. He didn't look at her. Jane's stomach knotted even tighter.

She took a steadying breath before taking over. "Actually," she said, gesturing toward Dev, "*he* is Lord Rowling's son from his first marriage. Devin Stokes is the heir to the Rowling title."

Sir Albert gaped. Nigel scowled.

"That's where I know you from," Johnny exclaimed, pointing at Dev. "You were in the alley."

"Shut up, Johnny," Lady Skevington spat.

Jane bit the inside of her cheek. So, it *had* been Johnny in the alley with the knife and not Nigel. She'd suspected, but since Dev hadn't been recognized by the footman at the picnic, she hadn't been certain.

Lucky for them, Johnny was not the sharpest tool in the shed.

"H-him?" Sir Albert looked from Jane to Dev and back again, his mouth opening and closing like a fish. "But I thought those old tales of a child were merely rumors…or that there was some illegitimate bastard floating around somewhere."

Jane's vision went red for a moment. This man had suspected

his cousin had a child—a child *floating around somewhere*—and hadn't bothered to look into his wellbeing?

Her cousin must have taken note of Jane's current state.

"Oh, he's quite legitimate." Pippa stepped forward with a dagger in her hand. She flipped it in the air and caught it by the handle a few times. She even did it once without looking. The whole room watched in stunned silence.

"There's just one little catch." Lydia strolled between the two settees, stroking her chin. "The mystery of the missing marriage certificate. Our sources tell us that a break-in, planned by this woman"—she gestured at Lady Skevington—"and carried out by her loyal servant and lover"—she pointed at Johnny—"resulted in many important documents being stolen from Lady Rowling's home."

Jane nodded her thanks to Pippa and Lydia. She'd needed that minute to regain her composure.

"Matilda?" Sir Albert turned damp, pleading eyes to his wife.

She flicked the merest look of disdain his way before returning her attention to Jane.

"This is a most unfortunate tale," Lady Skevington said, "but do you have any *proof* to back it up? I'd hate for the authorities to have their time wasted with such an obviously false claim made by some grasping chit with an overactive imagination."

And then she faked a yawn.

Jane clenched her teeth. The gall of this woman, pretending to be bored as they revealed her evil plan. She had tried to kill Dev, and it was time for her to pay.

Jane gritted her teeth and then poured the first cup of tea.

"Proof is a tricky thing." Jane kept her tone light even though she clenched the teapot so tightly that her knuckles shone white. "For example, we have an eyewitness who can place your footman at the break-in."

Lady Skevington inhaled sharply.

"Ah, didn't know that one, did you?" Jane smiled at her, being sure to throw in a few wide-eyed blinks of innocence for good measure. Lady Skevington wasn't the only one who'd hidden her true capabilities.

"And," Jane continued, pouring more tea, "we found a most interesting book inside your sitting room, didn't we Dev?"

Jane's heart skipped a beat as Dev remained motionless, but he finally reached into his pocket and pulled out his mother's diary.

Lady Skevington gasped.

"Oh, does that look familiar?" Lydia asked, grabbing the diary from Dev. "Had a bit of trouble reading it yourself though, I imagine. I bet your governess taught you French like most young ladies." Lydia marched through the two settees again and waved the diary at Lady Skevington. "Lucky for us, I know Italian."

Lady Skevington's glare was sharp enough to rival Pippa's dagger. "That doesn't belong to you."

"Doesn't belong to you either, does it?" Lydia poked her in the chest with the book.

"It belongs to me." Dev spoke for the first time, and everyone swiveled to stare at him.

Jane wanted to go to him, to offer her hand in support, but she somehow knew the gesture would not be welcomed.

"You stole my mother's diary." He glared at Lady Skevington, all his fury and sorrow there in his eyes. "And you tried to steal the title for yourself."

"I had to!" Lady Skevington's cool scorn had vanished, and she screeched in fury. "My idiot son Nigel is the world's worst gambler, and the bank's going to seize everything in a matter of weeks." Her chest heaved as she turned to face her husband. "And I couldn't stand another moment in that ghastly little house with England's stupidest man." She shot a look of such venom at Sir Nigel that he recoiled in his seat. She shook her head. "My only respite in this hell has been getting railed by Johnny whose only possession larger than his sniveling wish to please me is his cock."

Lady Skevington's words seemed to echo through the room

as everyone sat in stunned silence. Even unflappable Jack's mouth hung open a bit.

Johnny the footman's face had turned red, and he looked as if he couldn't decide between crying or trying to jump out the window.

"Thankfully," Lady Skevington continued, turning to Dev, "your father came to town for a visit. It was a simple matter to place a pillow over his face while he slept. No one would have been any the wiser when my husband inherited if it hadn't been for you two mucking things up where you didn't belong."

Jane couldn't breathe. She looked at Dev and he was frozen, his face a mask of shock.

Lady Skevington hadn't just tried to kill Dev. She'd also killed his father.

A murder confession certainly had not been a part of Jane's plan.

She didn't know what to do, what to say. Dev hadn't liked his father, but still, to learn that Lord Rowling had been murdered over a title was beyond shocking. She yearned to toss the teapot to the side and go to Dev, to wrap her arms around him and cover his face in healing kisses.

But she couldn't.

The plan was not complete, and they only had this one shot.

Dev stomped across the room until he stood only a foot away from Lady Skevington. "You..." His chest rose and fell in loud, heavy breaths. "You will pay for what you've done."

She threw back her head and laughed. The sound was high and piercing. Demented. Perhaps Lady Skevington was insane.

"I most certainly will not," she crowed. "You can't prove any of this. You can't even prove you're the legitimate heir." Her sneer was barbed and wicked.

Jane glanced at Jack who nodded, indicating he had an eye on things. Jane quickly finished her work with the teacups. And it was perfectly clear what to do with them.

"Where's. The. Marriage. Certificate?" Dev spat each word

through clenched teeth.

Lady Skevington folded her arms over her chest. "I'll never tell."

Dev's hands fisted at his side.

Jane caught Jack's eye before holding up a teacup. He moved to Dev's side and laid a gentle hand on his shoulder. "Let's just take a moment to catch our breath."

"A good idea," Jane agreed, moving around the cart with two teacups on saucers in her hands. "We need to sort this out with level heads. Here, everyone, have a bit of tea to help calm your nerves."

Pippa hurried over and helped Jane distribute the cups. Everyone got a cup. Dev sipped, although his hand shook. Sir Albert drank in a daze. Lydia eschewed the saucer as her other hand still clasped the diary. Johnny gaped at his cup. He'd likely never been served tea by a countess before.

Once the silence settled in the room with only the soft noises of sipping, even Lady Skevington lifted the teacup to her mouth.

Jane watched her sip. She watched the woman's eyebrows pucker in confusion. And then understanding dawned in Lady Skevington's eyes, and she dropped her cup.

"What…" Lady Skevington coughed. "What did you give me?" She clutched at her neck as she sputtered and coughed.

"Oh," Jane replied after sipping her own tea, "just a bit of poison."

"Poison?" Lady Skevington managed to choke out. She looked around the room wildly.

Nigel had jumped to his feet and was shouting. Sir Albert's mouth hung open, and he rocked forward and back on the settee as if he couldn't decide whether or not to go to his wife. Johnny looked from Dev to Jack to Benedict and wisely kept his seat.

"You see, I wasn't certain who to give the poison to at first," Jane said, pitching her voice above the chaos. "None of us had any inkling how you felt about anyone, so I didn't know if your husband, your son, or your lover and co-conspirator would make the best target to get you to comply. But then you made your disdain for all of them quite clear. There's only one person you care about."

After her carriage ride to Surrey with Lydia, Jane had pondered Lydia's theory about extortion. It was crucial to make the person *want* to tell you what you needed to know. And so, threatening to poison everyone here would have been ineffective. The only way her plan would work would be to poison whomever the criminal mastermind loved the most.

Lady Skevington sank to her knees, her face red and her eyes streaming. "Please," she wheezed.

Jane moved to stand beside her. "Since you care so much for yourself, I'll give you one chance to save your own life—a truthful answer in exchange for the antidote." Jane held up a vial of clear liquid. "Understand?"

Lady Skevington nodded, her choked wheezes filling the room.

Jane stared down into her red, swollen, evil face. "Where," she whispered, "is the marriage certificate?"

The whole room held its breath.

Lady Skevington lifted a trembling finger and pointed at Lydia. Her eyes focused on the diary.

"Where?" Jane demanded, her voice sharp.

"In the…back," Lady Skevington said between coughs. "P-peel…the binding."

Lydia tossed her teacup over her shoulder, flung open the diary, and scrabbled at the thick paper attached to the inside of the back cover.

Jane's blood whooshed in her ears. She looked at Dev. Every muscle in his body strained. She could not help him in this terrible moment that stretched out while Lydia tugged, everyone watched, and Jane held her breath.

Lydia cried out as the thick binding tore away. She yanked a piece of paper from the back of the book and held it up. Even from a distance, the official-looking script and seal were visible.

It was the marriage certificate.

It proved that Lord Rowling had indeed married an Italian maid. The court would have to accept that Dev was the legitimate heir.

Oh, thank heavens.

Dev gave a little choking sound. Jane slumped against the service cart. Lydia relaxed her arm. And Lady Skevington jumped to her feet with a screech.

Before anyone could move, she snatched the diary and certificate out of Lydia's hand and threw them into the fire. The flames blazed as they consumed the fresh fuel.

Jane screamed. Dev leaped toward the fire, but the low table between the settees was in his way and he went down. Jack and Benedict both rushed to the fireplace. Pippa seized Lady Skevington by the arm, dagger pointed threateningly.

"The antidote," Lady Skevington choked out, her voice hoarse from coughing before someone reassured her that she just needed to drink some water and that she was in no danger of dying.

The door burst open, and Lady Rowling and a man rushed in.

"We heard everything," Lady Rowling gasped.

Through the haze of her panic, Jane realized that she'd never seen her looking so discomposed.

"Dev," Lady Rowling choked, and she dropped to her knees.

Jane turned and gasped. Dev lay still on the ground. Blood streamed from a gash on his forehead. He must have hit the table's edge when he went down.

Her stomach plummeted, and Jane flung herself onto the ground at his other side.

"Dev," she cried, reaching out with hands that trembled. She stopped short of touching him though. What if he was injured somewhere else? She didn't wish to hurt him.

With feather-light movements, she touched his cheek, careful to stay away from the wound. His second wound. The cut on his arm was still healing. How many times would this man have to bleed to get what he was owed? To fight for both himself and for the LCA?

He didn't stir.

"Dev, wake up," she cried, tears streaming down her cheeks.

"I'll get a doctor." Benedict ran out of the room.

All around her was noise and confusion and movement. But here, it was just her and Dev. She took his hand in hers. It felt so still and lifeless. This hand had held hers just a bit ago as they'd spun around the dance floor. As she'd dreamed and hoped that perhaps there could be a future for them. This hand had given her pleasure, given her comfort, and given her everything she needed from the very first time she'd seen him in her laboratory with a water jug in his arms.

"Dev, please," she whispered, leaning over him. "I need you. I...I love you."

She faintly heard the voice of the man who'd accompanied Lady Rowling, the magistrate she'd been tasked with inviting to the ball and bringing to the hallway outside the door cracked just enough for him to hear every word of the villain's confession.

She faintly heard Lady Skevington's shrieks as she was led away by the lawman.

And she faintly heard her friends telling her it was all right, that Dev would recover, that it was over.

But it didn't matter.

Without Dev, nothing mattered at all.

Chapter Twenty-Seven

JANE PACED BACK and forth along the hallway outside Dev's room. Well, it was really Sir Albert's room at the house party, but he'd offered it for their use as soon as he'd stopped weeping. Benedict had returned with the doctor in tow in record time. Luckily, the man had been a guest at the ball.

Faint strains of music filtered their way up from the ballroom a floor below. How odd to think that the dancing and merriment continued while Dev lay unconscious in the bed of the husband of the woman who'd killed his father.

Jane paced past Lydia who was gently prodding the charred remains of the diary, resting on a tea tray in the hallway. She turned a crispy page with the handle of a teaspoon and grimaced.

"I'm so sorry, Jane, but I think it's burned beyond recognition. And Jack said he couldn't find any remains of the marriage certificate in the fire."

Jane turned to pace in the other direction and wiped away a stray tear.

Tears were useless. They were idiotic. This whole thing was idiotic.

She'd had a plan, and it had worked…right up to the point where it hadn't.

And really, what did any of it matter when Dev was unconscious? He'd suffered a head wound, and the doctor had looked rather grim as Benedict had filled him in.

Why was it taking so long?

She dashed away another tear and fought against the urge to howl. She wanted to scream. She wanted to yank out her hair. She wanted to burn the whole world to the ground. What did any of it matter if Dev was… if he…

She shook her head. No.

She wouldn't think that way.

The door opened, and Jane whirled around. Lady Rowling came out, her lips pressed tightly together.

Jane rushed to her. "How is he?" she asked, clasping her hands together.

"The doctor stitched the gash in his head," Lady Rowling said. "He didn't think there would be any long-term damage, but it may take a while for Dev to regain consciousness."

Jane grabbed Lady Rowling's hand. "So he'll be all right?"

Please let him be all right.

Fear was a block of ice surrounding her heart.

Lady Rowling squeezed her hand. "He should be all right."

Jane's knees crumpled. Lady Rowling grabbed her arm and hoisted her up.

"Oh," Jane whispered. "Oh my."

Lydia rushed over, and together she and Lady Rowling lowered Jane to the floor, so she was sitting with her back to the wall.

"I'll fetch some tea," Lady Rowling announced, casting a worried glance over her shoulder before hurrying down the hall.

Lydia wrapped an arm around Jane's shoulders. "She said he'd be all right."

Jane let out a shaky breath. "I know. I just…"

"You love him," Lydia said, her voice matter of fact. "And worrying that someone you love is in danger is most vexing. Jack has told me all about it. Repeatedly."

Jane managed a weak laugh. Lydia's brother had feared for his sister's life when she'd been kidnapped, and indeed, it had been a close thing. But here she was, right as rain.

And Dev would be right as rain as well. The doctor had said so.

So why did her bones feel as if they were made of jelly?

"It's the after-effects of your plan," Lydia explained, guessing at her thoughts. "You carried it out to perfection, which takes nerves of metal. Then Lady Skevington did the unexpected, throwing the whole operation into chaos. And then Dev was hurt, and it took so much of your energy just to keep going in those moments that now you have no energy left."

Jane nodded. It all made sense. Lydia was so practical, so logical, and also so very much herself. One thing to come of all of this—aside from the wretched magic of falling in love—was a new appreciation for her friends.

"I just wish that we had that marriage certificate." Jane sighed. "All this work and the only proof out there in the world is now ash in the bottom of a fireplace."

Lydia frowned.

They sat in silence for a minute. Jane rested her head against the wall and closed her eyes, but something niggled at the back of her mind.

The only proof out there in the world...

Was that true?

Lucretia Russo, an Italian lady's maid accompanied a contessa on a sea voyage to India. She met Henry Stokes, second son of a marquess on his way to his new post with the East India Company. They met at sea. On a boat.

They were married...

On a boat...

By a sea captain.

Jane's eyes flew open. "Oh my word, there might be another record of the marriage!"

"What?" Lydia's arm jerked against her shoulders. "Where, Jane?"

Scrabbling to her feet, Jane's mind worked through the steps. Parth getting the carriage. The translation pages of the diary in her room at Lady Rowling's country estate. Only a handful of hours to London. Lucy Moreton, her fellow LCA member, who worked as an apprentice at a shipping company.

"I have to go." Jane rushed down the hall.

"But Jane," Lydia called, "where are you going? What shall I tell the others?"

"I'm off to London," she called over her shoulder. "I'll meet you there, at the court hearing."

And with a wave, Jane ran around the corner and left them all behind.

⇛⇚

DEV BLINKED AGAINST the bright light. His head throbbed. Something wasn't right. Something was terribly, terribly wrong.

"Dev?"

He fought against the weight of his eyelids, finally managing to open them. Roberta peered down at him, her face tight.

"Oh, thank God you're awake." She squeezed his hand.

He licked his dry lips before croaking out, "Where—"

"We're still at the Brambleton's home," she interrupted. "The house party has ended, but they've graciously allowed us to stay until you're well."

He shook his head, although that made the throbbing pound like two rocks smashing into one another. "Where's—"

"I'm afraid we don't have the marriage certificate." She shook her head, and her eyes glistened. "It burned to a crisp when that wretched woman threw it into the fire. Oh Dev, I'm so very sorry."

He tried to speak, but only managed a grunt.

Roberta turned away to discreetly brush at her cheeks. "Thankfully, the magistrate was able to hear Lady Skevington's whole confession from the hallway. She was taken to Newgate and will stand trial for Henry's murder."

A beat of silence passed. They both felt it—a shared sorrow over the distressing manner of his death as well as the complicated feelings about his life as he'd never been kind to either of them.

Dev drew a deep breath. Right now, there was something else he needed to know.

He shook his head once more, bracing himself for the accompanying pain. "Roberta, where is Jane?"

Roberta's hand tightened around his. "I was afraid you would ask that."

Dev struggled to rise from the bed. He had to get up. He had to get out of here and find Jane. *Where was she?*

"Lay down," Roberta commanded, pressing her hand to his shoulder.

Dev was shocked that her gentle pressure sent him back against the mattress. He must be quite weak.

"You've been unconscious for three days," she said, "so you need to go slowly. The doctor said you rattled your brain quite thoroughly when you decided to acquaint your forehead with the sharp corner of a table."

Three days? That meant—

"The court hearing on the title is tomorrow," Lady Rowling said.

He gritted his teeth. She somehow answered every question he had except for the most important one.

"Where," he growled, "is Jane?"

Roberta sat back, her eyebrows pinching together. "She's not here, Dev. She left after the doctor examined you. I'm so sorry."

He shut his eyes against a pain far worse than the pounding in his head. She was not here. She'd left.

She'd left him, when he was hurt and unconscious.

"Why?" he croaked out.

"I was told she rushed back to London. That's all I know. Dev, I'm so sorry." She paused.

Even with his eyes closed, he could imagine the expression on her face. The hesitation as she searched for the right words to say next.

"I know you had tender feelings for the girl—"

"Stop," he whispered.

Mercifully, she didn't finish her sentence.

After a moment, she said, "I'll send for the doctor. He'll want to examine you once more now that you're awake."

Dev listened, eyes still shut, to the sound of Roberta's footsteps and then the soft click of the door closing.

She'd left. Jane. His Jane. She was gone.

He could barely believe such a thing of her, but with proof of his legitimacy burned to nothing, he would not become a marquess. He would never be Devin Stokes, Lord Rowling. He wouldn't inherit the land, the houses, the fortune. He'd never be a member of polite society, the society that she belonged to. She was a lady, a daughter of a baron, and she was meant to be with someone from her world. Someone of her station. Someone like her.

And now that would never be him.

He would simply be Dev, son of a servant. Friend of servants. A servant himself, when all the facts were examined.

And apparently, that wasn't enough for Jane.

She'd fled home to London at the first opportunity. She hadn't even waited for him to awaken, to say goodbye, to break things off gently.

He recalled her words from before, sharing how all the ladies had spoken of the great fun to be had enjoying secret trysts while at a house party. How she'd said that the two of them were as unalike as Sir Albert and his murderous wife.

Everything he'd hoped for once—the title, the houses, the wealth, the position in society, it turned out that none of that mattered. Those things wouldn't give his life meaning, bring him joy, or fill his heart with love.

It was ironic that in this quest to claim his title, he'd discovered that he didn't care very much about the title.

This quest had brought him Jane. They'd been partners, then friends, and finally lovers. And he'd hoped she'd be his partner for life. His wife. His true love.

His home.

A title was just a house.

The only thing he wanted was to be *home*, in the arms of the woman he loved.

And now that was gone forever.

Dev stared up at the ceiling and wept.

Chapter Twenty-Eight

D EV CLOSED HIS eyes against the pounding in his head. Perhaps traveling for hours in a carriage the day after waking from a coma had not been the wisest of choices.

"We're almost there," Roberta murmured, casting him a worried glance.

She'd argued that Dev should stay in Surrey and fully recover before returning to London. The doctor had warned against too much movement when his head was still recovering from the blow.

But Dev had decided to make his case before the tribunal. If the panel of House of Lords members had the final say in who would inherit the Rowling title, then he had to be here. He would tell them the truth about his parents. He didn't have the marriage certificate, and knew there was no way they would rule in his favor without it, but he didn't care.

After waking yesterday and learning that Jane had left, he'd mourned. He'd cried. He'd pounded his hands against the mattress. And then, he'd forced his heart into numbness. He was hollow, a gaping hole of emptiness where nothing could hurt him.

Well…aside from sharp table corners.

He winced at the pain in his head.

The carriage rolled to a stop, and Roberta pulled out her

watch for the hundredth time since they'd left early that morning.

"It starts in five minutes," she said. "Hurry."

Dev jumped down, leaving the carriage door open since she would be right behind him. He ran across the cobblestones and burst through the doors of Westminster Palace.

"Where's the House of Lords tribunal?" he gasped out to a guard.

The man looked Dev up and down with a frown before eventually pointing in the direction and saying a room number.

Dev knew he looked a sight. He'd thrown on one of the tailored jackets from the trunk of new clothes over his kurta. He had a large white bandage on his head. He wore the shiny Hoby boots but had no cravat. Thank goodness the guard hadn't barred his entrance to the building where both the House of Commons and House of Lords met and conducted their business given his ungentlemanly appearance.

Dev ran down a hall and up a set of stairs. His head throbbed with each step. His stomach roiled. Perhaps skipping lunch had not been the wisest of choices.

But it didn't matter.

He knew the outcome already, but he still had to be there.

He had to speak up for himself and let them all know that he existed. That he was here. That he fought for what belonged to him.

He had to fight for this one thing at least, because the thing he really wanted, the *person* he really wanted, couldn't be his.

He turned a corner and skidded to a halt.

A young woman in a light blue dress was striding along the hallway, her back to him. Her movements were energetic. She tapped her fingers against the leather book in her hand. And her hair, even in the dim light of the corridor, shone red-gold.

Even as his eyes cataloged each clue, his heart already knew.
Jane.

His heart would always know. She was imprinted on it after all.

She turned around, and he realized she was pacing. Pacing right in front of the room where the trial on the Rowling title was to take place. Why was she here?

She saw him and stumbled to a halt. Her mouth formed his name, but no sound emerged.

He wanted to run to her. And he wanted to run away. His stomach churned and for a moment he feared he'd be sick right there on the hideous rug lining the hallway.

And so, he stood absolutely still, breathing through his mouth as she ran down the corridor to him.

She threw her arms around his neck. "Dev," she breathed.

She was warm and soft against him. Her hair smelled like soap and flowers and sunshine. Dev refused to mold his form against hers. He refused to run his hand along the gentle curve of her back. He refused to nuzzle against her temple and feel the silken wisps of hair. But some traitorous part of his body had him closing his eyes and breathing deeply. Imprinting her scent in his lungs. Memorizing the soft press of her breasts against his chest. Savoring the brush of her fingers against the nape of his neck.

"Dev, are you in pain?" She pulled back, her face growing tight as she took in the bandage on his head. "I wasn't sure if you'd make it in time, so I sent the others in to talk to—"

"Don't."

It took all his strength to interrupt her, to deny the sound of her voice.

She took a step back. Juggling the large leather-bound book in her hands, she bit her lip as if uncertain of what to say.

Good.

She *should* feel uncertain. She'd left him, and the only thing he had now was the uncertainty of a bleak future stretching out before him.

Dev shook his head. There was nothing for him here. Why was he lingering even a minute in this hallway with her? He stepped toward the door for the tribunal.

She grabbed hold of his sleeve. "Dev, don't you know? I left to find—"

He rounded on her, his numb heart suddenly a ball of raging fire in his chest. "How *could* you?"

Her eyes widened.

"I woke up after three days to learn you'd left. You'd *left* me." The words were ripped from his throat. They were raw and painful and true. "Jane, I…I loved you. *And you left me.*"

Her chin trembled. "Dev—"

"You didn't want me anymore after the certificate was destroyed." He blinked against the stinging pain. "Once it was clear I wouldn't be a marquess, you left. I thought…" He swallowed. "I thought you cared for *me*. Not for the title. Not because I could become a proper English gentleman, your equal in rank. But for who I was on my own. Even if I was just Dev, the servant, and never Lord Rowling, the marquess."

Her face was agony. "I *do* want you for you—"

"Don't say a word." He held up a hand to stop her, his breath heaving. "Don't say a damned thing. I can't be gracious. Not in this, Jane. Not about you. There is nothing gracious or accommodating about how it feels to lose you."

"Dev—"

"No." He stormed away even as he crumbled inside.

"You haven't lost me!" she yelled. "Just listen, you stubborn man!"

Dev put a hand against the wall. It felt as if the earth was tilting on its axis and he didn't have the strength to keep himself upright any longer.

"I left to find the evidence you needed." Her voice behind him was ragged. "I waited outside your room until the doctor announced you would be all right. And then…"—she paused to breathe, the sound harsh and desperate—"And then I had Parth drive me to town all through the night. I showed up at the crack of dawn at an LCA member's house, pounding on the door. Her butler tried to send me away. I must have looked like a madwoman, but I didn't care what anyone thought of me, Dev. I didn't care."

The last part came out in a whisper.

Dev leaned harder against the wall, his back still to her. Her words were pummeling him. They beat against the hard ice barrier he'd erected around his heart.

"This woman, she works as an apprentice at a shipping company," Jane continued. Her voice was desolate, the voice of the desert. "She had told me once that she met all these old seafaring captains through her work. And so, I asked her if she knew Captain Lambert."

Dev inhaled sharply.

"You recognize that name, don't you?" Jane had moved closer now, her voice like a caress against his skin despite its sorrow. "It was in your mother's diary. I have the translation that Lydia made. You still have her words, Dev. Those didn't burn. And I found the name of the ship, the date your parents were married, and the name of the captain. We found him, Dev. My friend Lucy and I, we tracked him down after two days of searching and countless dead ends, and more pints bought for grizzled old seamen in dingy bars by the docks than you'd care to know. And do you know what old Captain Lambert still had?"

Dev turned. He kept his hand on the wall, for he knew he'd fall without it. But he had to see her. He had to see her face as she told him what a fool he'd been.

She licked her lips before delivering the final blow. "He had all his old ship logs."

The room tilted, and Dev leaned more heavily against the wall. "Jane—"

She shook her head. "Let me tell you, Dev. Let me tell you about it." She flipped open the book to a marked page. "Do you see? Right here, the captain recorded the marriage of your parents. Lucretia Russo to Henry Stokes. It even lists the witnesses, which included an Italian contessa. It's hard to discredit such a record and so many witnesses. This is it, Dev. This is the proof to get your title."

He stared unseeing at the page.

There it was. The proof he needed. Lady Skevington hadn't won. He could claim the title and stop hiding who he really was.

But…he still felt hollow.

Jane studied him, and her verdant eyes glistened with tears. "It doesn't matter, does it?" She took a step back and closed the ship's log with trembling hands. "You still don't believe me. You think I'll only be yours if you have a title."

A tear trickled down her cheek.

This hallway in Westminster Palace was a knife, and Dev balanced on the edge of the blade, teetering first one way and then the other. He wanted to believe her. But the notion that a lady could love a servant was just too ludicrous.

Wasn't it?

She turned away, but not before he saw her face crumple.

Oh, what was he doing? He *did* believe her. The truth had been right there, written on her face. Written in her eyes.

Jane's eyes had glowed when she looked at him. The green and the brown and the gold all mixed together like a garden, they had glowed at him. With determination. With ferocity.

And with love.

He'd seen it there. It was undeniable. He didn't need to hear anymore. He only needed her. She was air and water and the sun. She was all he needed.

"Jane…" His voice was rough.

Rough like him. But it seemed, despite everything, that she didn't mind.

She turned toward him, but at that moment, the door to the tribunal burst open.

"There you are," Lydia exclaimed. "We've been so worried."

Benedict, Pippa, and Jack poured out behind her. And from the other direction of the corridor hurried Roberta. They all gathered around him and Jane, their expressions ranging from curiosity to concern.

Lydia gave the others a sharp look before stepping forward to grab Dev's arm. "We spoke to the judges on the tribunal and explained what happened. We told them that we have the ship's log with the marriage recorded, but that we don't actually have the marriage certificate." Lydia's gaze flicked between Dev and Jane. "I'm so sorry, but they said…they said it would not be admissible evidence."

The corridor was silent.

Benedict stared at Lydia. The others all looked away.

Dev exhaled before running a hand over his face.

The outcome wasn't any different than what he'd expected coming here today, and yet Jane's news of the ship's log had filled him with hopeful notions. He'd been able to picture all he could do with his title, how he could fight in the House of Lords to end the East India Company's reign of terror. How he could use the full power of the marquessate and its vast wealth to help the people of his birthland.

But it was not to be.

Dev breathed through the pain. He looked at it, acknowledged it…and then he set it aside.

If he had Jane, if he had her heart and her smiles and her love, then he could live without the title.

But did *he have her love?*

He thought so. He hoped so.

No, he didn't need hope. He knew she loved him. He *knew.*

He looked at Jane who was staring down at the ship's log in her hands, her face stricken. "Oh Dev, I'm so, so sorry." She looked up, tears pooling in her eyes. "I know you wanted this so very much."

She dropped the book to the ground and ran to him, wrapping him in her arms. "We can still fight against the East India Company," she choked out. "You and I, we can still be partners if you want, and…and someday I'll have an inheritance of my own, and we can use it…we can use that money to help…if…if you still want me." She drew a shuddering breath. "If you can love me again…"

He tightened his arms around her, each tremble as she wept landing like a punch.

It was wrong. It was all wrong.

She should never have thought such a thing, that it was the *proof* he needed, or the title or respectability or money. That wasn't what he'd needed.

He'd only needed her.

But she'd doubted him, and it was his fault. He hadn't told her what she meant to him, that she was everything.

And so the doubt had crept into him as well. It had wormed its way inside his own heart and taken root like a stubborn weed.

But love was stronger. It bloomed and filled the world with its beautiful color, its delicious scent, soft petals, and sometimes even thorns.

He pulled back, gazing into her tear-filled eyes. He swallowed before whispering, "My Jane. My heart. I'm so sorry. I doubted you and I doubted myself, and I am sorrier than you can know."

Her mouth trembled. "Dev, I was so scared I'd lost you."

"You haven't lost me." He ran a finger along her cheek. "I love you, Jane. With all my heart. Please forgive me."

She pressed herself close to him. "If you'll love me forever, then there's nothing to forgive."

"Oh, my sweet, sweet darling." His voice cracked, and he took a steadying breath before continuing. "I do promise to love you forever if you'll promise the same to me."

Jane pulled her head back and looked up at him. Her smile was wide and complete. "I promise. I do love you, Dev. So very much."

And he kissed her, their lips merging even as their hearts did. Dev held her tightly against him, never wanting to let go. Never wanting to leave her side. Never wanting to be separated from Jane's light.

The sound of an aggressive throat clearing interrupted them.

Dev pulled away reluctantly.

"Well, thank goodness that worked out," Lydia declared.

Dev blinked at her.

She continued, "I wasn't sure if Benedict could hold it in a second longer." She was grinning, her expression mischievous.

Benedict rolled his eyes but there was a hint of a smile on his face. The others finally looked at them, and everyone was smiling aside from Roberta who looked as confused as Dev felt.

"What?" Jane asked, looking from Lydia to Benedict and then back to Dev. "What's going on?"

Lydia scooped up the ship's log from the floor and then gave Dev a look.

His hand tightened around Jane's as a suspicion formed in his mind. *Would Lydia do something so extreme?* She was a member of the Ladies Covert Academy, which meant she was brave, clever, and daring, so... of course, she would.

Lydia ran her hand over the book's cover. "We had entered the tribunal early to explain everything to the judges while we waited for Dev to arrive. I was standing in the back of the room, and I *might* have overheard a bit of your conversation through the door."

She didn't even have the grace to appear remorseful.

Shameless.

Dev glanced down to find Jane staring at her friend with wide eyes. Given what he assumed was coming next, her lovely eyes were likely to get even wider.

Lydia continued. "I thought a little lie—a *temporary* lie, please note—might be helpful, so I was dishonest about the ship's log." She held up the logbook. "According to legal precedent, a ship's official record *is* considered admissible evidence and the members of the tribunal assured us it will be enough to secure your title."

Dev's head swam.

Jane made a squeaking sound, her hand a vise around his. She turned to him, her face wreathed in wonder. "We did it."

Dev shook his head. "*You* did it. None of this would have happened without you, my clever lady. Your determination, your brilliant plan, and your daring." He inhaled deeply, his heartbeat steadying. "This is all because of your faith in me. Your faith in us."

He leaned down and pressed his forehead to hers. They simply breathed together for a few moments, two weary sailors who'd survived a storm only to see a glorious sunrise on the horizon, promising a new day.

"Will you be my wife, Miss Jane Brickley?" he whispered, his heart in his throat.

"Yes, Dev." Her smile was the most radiant thing he'd ever seen.

After another glorious kiss, Dev looked around at the people in the hallway, people he now called friends. He'd come to this country fearing for his life, hiding his true identity, and without a place to call home.

And now…

His chest swelled.

And now he no longer needed to live in fear.

He knew who he was, regardless of the title, and he would never hide himself again.

And, he knew with bone-deep certainty as he gazed into Jane's sweet, loving face, that as long as they were together, he would always have a home.

Epilogue

Three months later

"I THINK YOU'VE killed my nose," Pippa groaned, waving her gloved hand in front of her face.

"The fertilizer won't kill your nose," Jane replied, "but it will make these herbs grow big and strong and *extra* poisonous."

Jane stood back to admire the rows of seedlings she and her cousin had planted into larger pots before adding fertilizer and water. Eventually, these seedlings would be harvested, dried, ground up, and placed into little glass vials.

And then Jane would distribute the vials to every single woman she knew. And lots of women she didn't. Because although the world could be a scary place, women shouldn't have to live in fear. They should be able to go where they wanted and do what they pleased, just as Jane had told her parents months ago when she'd finally stood up to them. A woman's safety should not depend on her parents' worldview, the family's ability to pay for armed guards or fencing lessons, or owning a fancy home in a quiet neighborhood.

Everyone deserved to feel safe.

"Your laboratory is so organized." Pippa ran her fingers along a tidy shelf of clearly labeled jars.

The shelf next to it contained Jane's scientific notebooks,

sitting in chronological order. There was also a shelf with a well-organized seed box, which just so happened to contain the latest shipment from Amos, the plant vendor, who *had* managed to track down the information about the plant's origin from his wife's uncle's acquaintance's acquaintance who knew a smuggler who knew a grower who…

Well, suffice it to say, Jane had finally gotten her hands on more seeds, and she planned to put her growing knowledge of the wonderfully inflammatory South American *capsicum* to good use.

"Well, it's easy to be organized now that we're back in the LCA," Jane said, looking fondly around her large corner office in the Rowling house.

Which was now also *her* house.

A voice came from the doorway. "And it helps to have a very handsome assistant."

She turned to find her husband leaning against the door frame, a full jug of water at his feet. He must have grown hot lugging the water up the stairs because the sleeves of Dev's kurta were rolled up, exposing his muscular forearms. Jane's stomach went fluttery. Even after months of waking up to her husband's handsome face on the pillow beside her each morning, the sight of him still gave her butterflies.

And she knew it would always be that way.

After peeling off her work apron and gloves, Jane hurried over to Dev. "I have the *handsomest* assistant," she whispered before giving him a kiss. "And the cleverest, kindest, and most charming one too."

He wrapped his arms around her waist and grinned. "It doesn't hurt if your lab assistant is also a marquess."

Jane shook her head. "Marquess or servant, either would be fine with me."

His ocean eyes shined with love, and Jane couldn't resist a few more kisses even though the house was filled with people.

All the Ladies Covert Academy ladies had returned with Roberta's blessing after Dev was ruled the new Lord Rowling and both Lady Skevington and Johnny the footman were locked away where they couldn't harm anyone. There was no longer any threat to either Dev's safety or the LCA and its secrets. The house hummed with activity as the members sculpted, composed music, fenced, wrote, discussed, and continued to grow in this amazing, supportive community.

"Any word from Roberta?" Jane asked once she'd pulled away, breathless from Dev's kisses.

Dev tugged a letter out of his pocket. "She assures us that with the latest renovations, the Surrey estate no longer feels like a haunted house from a gothic novel."

Her new stepmother-in-law had decided to relocate to Surrey, turning the repair and redecorating of the Rowling country home into her own special project. And she'd left the running of the Ladies Covert Academy in the hands of Jane, Pippa, and Lydia.

Jane frowned. Come to think of it, she hadn't seen Lydia for a few days. The last time they'd spoken, Lydia had been even more vexed with Benedict than usual, and that was saying something. Perhaps her absence was due to their head-butting?

Normally, when all three women were together, they decided on the LCA's course as a team along with input gathered from the members.

And one of the benefits of working where she lived was that now Jane could retire to her bedroom at any time.

"Oh Dev," she whispered, running the tip of her nose along the edge of his ear, causing him to shiver. "After our late hours last night, I do feel rather sleepy." She stretched, pressing her breasts against his chest.

Dev's breath caught.

"Care to join me for a nap?"

And with the sound of Pippa's snickers following them out of the room, Jane and her husband dashed for their bedroom. It was an adventurous life indeed.

THE END

I played loose with the history of pepper spray in this story, but Jane was on to something when she realized the potential for self-defense uses with certain plants. Pepper spray wasn't available for purchase until the 1960s, but it *was* derived from a South American plant: the capsicum, or pepper. Pepper spray causes inflammation of the eyes, nose, throat, and lungs, and is carried by many people today as a way to ensure their safety, whether from bears when they're hiking in the woods or, like Jane and Dev, from a scary figure lurking in an alley. Stay safe out there, friends, and remember—you should be able to go where you want to go and do as you please!

Jenny Hartwell has a confession–she loves People magazine as much as Pride and Prejudice. Her fun, pop culture adoring side shines in her contemporary rom-com set in a gourmet chocolate factory while Jenny's Regency romances feature strong damsels and swoony lords. Her writing has won or finaled in numerous contests including the Golden Heart, The Emily, Four Seasons, Fool for Love, and The Catherine. Jenny lives with her family in the verdant Pacific Northwest. She loves movies, travel, and staying up late with a good book. And, of course, chocolate. Jenny is represented by Lesley Sabga of The Seymour Agency.